Dynevor Terrace
Or The Clue Of Life
Vol. I

by

Charlotte M. Yonge

Dynevor Terrace
Or The Clue Of Life
Vol. I
by Charlotte M. Yonge

Copyright © 2024

All Rights reserved.

No part of this publication may be reproduced, stored in a retrieval system, or transmitted in any form or by any means, electronic, mechanical, photocopying or Otherwise, without the written permission of the publisher.
The author/editor asserts the moral right to be identified as the author/editor of this work.

ISBN: 978-93-63050-46-4

Published by

DOUBLE 9 BOOKS

2/13-B, Ansari Road
Daryaganj, New Delhi – 110002
info@double9books.com
www.double9books.com
Tel. 011-40042856

This book is under public domain

ABOUT THE AUTHOR

Charlotte M. Yonge was an English novelist and historian, born on August 11, 1823, in Otterbourne, Hampshire, England. She is best known for her prolific writing career, which spanned over 60 years and produced more than 160 works, including novels, children's books, and historical studies. Yonge's writing was strongly influenced by her deep religious beliefs and her interest in history and education. Many of her novels, such as "The Heir of Redclyffe" and "Heartsease," explore moral and religious themes and are known for their wholesome and uplifting tone. She also wrote numerous works for children, including the popular "Book of Golden Deeds," which features stories of heroism and selflessness. In addition to her writing, Yonge was a prominent figure in the Church of England and was involved in various philanthropic and educational endeavours. She founded a school for girls in her hometown and was a supporter of the National Society for Promoting Religious Education. Yonge died on May 24, 1901, in Otterbourne, Hampshire, England. Her legacy as a writer and educator continues to be celebrated, and her works remain popular with readers today.

CONTENTS

CHAPTER I
CHARLOTTE 7

CHAPTER II
AN OLD SCHOOLMISTRESS 12

CHAPTER III
LOUIS LE DEBONNAIRE 23

CHAPTER IV
THISTLE-DOWN 37

CHAPTER V
THE TWO MINISTERS 53

CHAPTER VI
FAREWELLS 65

CHAPTER VII
GOSSAMER 79

CHAPTER VIII
A TRUANT DISPOSITION 91

CHAPTER IX
THE FAMILY COMPACT 107

CHAPTER X
THE BETTER PART OF VALOUR 121

CHAPTER XI
A HALTING PROPOSAL 127

CHAPTER XII
CHILDE ROLAND 143

CHAPTER XIII
FROSTY, BUT KINDLY 163

CHAPTER XIV
NEW INHABITANTS 172

CHAPTER XV
MOTLEY THE ONLY WEAR.. 186

CHAPTER XVI
THE FRUIT OF THE CHRISTMAS-TREE 207

CHAPTER XVII
THE RIVALS.. 217

CHAPTER XVIII
REST FOR THE WEARY 229

CHAPTER XIX
MOONSHINE 241

CHAPTER XX
THE FANTASTIC VISCOUNT 253

CHAPTER XXI
THE HERO OF THE BARRICADES... 268

CHAPTER XXII
BURGOMASTERS AND GREAT ONE-EYERS 283

Who wisdom's sacred prize would win,
Must with the fear of God begin;
Immortal praise and heavenly skill
Have they who know and do His will.
   New Version.

CHAPTER I
CHARLOTTE

Farewell rewards and fairies,
Good housewives now may say,
For now foul sluts in dairies
May fare as well as they.
   BP. CORBET.

An ancient leafless stump of a horse-chesnut stood in the middle of a dusty field, bordered on the south side by a row of houses of some pretension. Against this stump, a pretty delicate fair girl of seventeen, whose short lilac sleeves revealed slender white arms, and her tight, plain cap tresses of flaxen hair that many a beauty might have envied, was banging a cocoa-nut mat, chanting by way of accompaniment in a sort of cadence—

'I have found out a gift for my fur,
I have found where the wood-pigeons breed;
But let me the plunder forbear,
   She will say—'

'Hollo, I'll give you a shilling for 'em!' was the unlooked-for conclusion, causing her to start aside with a slight scream, as there stood beside her a stout, black-eyed, round-faced lad, his ruddy cheeks and loutish air showing more rusticity than agreed with his keen, saucy expression, and mechanic's dress.

'So that's what you call beating a mat,' said he, catching it from her hands, and mimicking the tender clasp of her little fingers. 'D'ye think it's alive, that you use it so gingerly? Look here! Give it him well!' as he made it resound against the tree, and emit a whirlwind of dust. 'Lay it into him with some jolly good song fit to fetch a stroke home with! Why, I heard my young Lord say, when Shakspeare was a butcher, he used to make speeches at the calves, as if they was for a sacrifice, or ever he could lift a knife to 'em.'

'Shakspeare! He as wrote Romeo and Juliet, and all that! He a butcher! Why, he was a poet!' cried the girl, indignantly.

'If you know better than Lord Fitzjocelyn, you may!' said the boy.

'I couldn't have thought it!' sighed the maiden.

'It's the best of it!' cried the lad, eagerly. 'Why, Charlotte, don't ye see, he rose hisself. Anybody may rise hisself as has a mind to it!'

'Yes, I've read that in books said Charlotte. 'You can, men can, Tom, if you would but educate yourself like Edmund! in the *Old English Baron*. But then, you know whose son you are. There can't be no catastrophe—'

'I don't want none,' said Tom. 'We are all equal by birth, so the orator proves without a doubt, and we'll show it one of these days. A rare lady I'll make of you yet, Charlotte Arnold.'

'O hush, Tom, I can never be a lady—and I can't stand dawdling here—nor you neither. 'Tisn't right to want to be out of our station, though I do wish I lived in an old castle, where the maidens worked tapestry, and heard minstrels, never had no stairs to scour. Come, give me my mats, and thank you kindly!'

'I'll take 'em in,' said Tom, shouldering them. ''Tis breakfast-hour, so I thought I'd just run up and ax you when my young Lord goes up to Oxford.

'He is gone,' said Charlotte; 'he was here yesterday to take leave of missus. Mr. James goes later—'

'Gone!' cried Tom. 'If he didn't say he'd come and see me at Mr. Smith's!'

'Did you want to speak to him?'

'I wanted to see him particular. There's a thing lays heavy on my mind. You see that place down in Ferny dell—there's a steep bank down to the water. Well, my young Lord was very keen about building a kind of steps there in the summer, and he and I settled the stones, and I was to cement 'em. By comes Mr. Frost, and finds faults, what I thought he'd no call to; so I flings down my trowel, and wouldn't go on for he! I was so mortal angry, I would not go back to the work; and I believe my Lord forgot it—and then he went back to college; and Frampton and Gervas, they put on me, and you know how 'twas I come away from Ormersfield. I was not going to say a word to one of that lot! but if I could see Lord Fitzjocelyn, I'd tell him they stones arn't fixed; and if the frost gets into 'em, there'll be a pretty go next time there's a tolerablish weight! But there—it is his own look-out! If he never thought it worth his while to keep his promise, and come and see me—'

'O Tom! that isn't right! He only forgot—I hear Mrs. Beckett telling him he'd forget his own head if it wasn't fixed on, and Mr. James is always at him.'

'Forget! Aye, there's nothing gentlefolks forget like poor folks. But I've done with he! Let him look out—I kept my promises to him long enough, but if he don't keep his'n—'

'For shame, for shame, Tom! You don't mean it!' cried Charlotte. 'But, oh!' with a different tone, 'give me the mat! There's the old Lord and Mr. Poynings riding down the terrace!'

'I ain't ashamed of nothing!' said the lad, proudly; and as Charlotte snatched away the mats, and vanished like a frightened hare, he stalked along like a village Hampden, muttering, 'The old tyrant shall see whether I'm to be trampled on!' and with both hands in his pockets, he gazed straight up into the face of the grave elderly gentleman, who never even perceived him. He could merely bandy glances with Poynings, the groom, and he was so far from indifferent that he significantly lifted up the end of his whip. Nothing could more have gratified Tom, who retorted with a grimace and murmur, 'Don't you wish you may catch me? You jealous syc—what is the word, sick of uncles or aunts, was it, that the orator called 'em? He'd say I'd a good miss of being one of that sort, and that my young Lord there opened my eyes in time. No better than the rest of 'em—'

And the clock striking eight, he quickened his pace to return to his work. He had for the two or three previous years been nominally under the gardener at Ormersfield, but really a sort of follower and favourite to the young heir, Lord Fitzjocelyn—a position which had brought on him dislike from the superior servants, who were not propitiated by his independent and insubordinate temper. Faults on every side had led to his dismissal; but Lord Fitzjocelyn had placed him at an ironmonger's shop in the town of Northwold, where he had been just long enough to become accessible to the various temptations of a lad in such a situation.

Charlotte sped hastily round the end of the block of buildings, hurried down the little back garden, and flew breathlessly into her own kitchen, as a haven of refuge, but she found a tall, stiff starched, elderly woman standing just within the door, and heard her last words.

'Well! as I said, 'tis no concern of mine; only I thought it the part of a friend to give you a warning, when I seen it with my own eyes!— Ah! here she is!' as Charlotte dropped into a chair. 'Yes, yes, Miss, you need not think to deceive me; I saw you from Miss Mercy's window—'

'Saw what?' faintly exclaimed Charlotte.

'You know well enough,' was the return. 'You may think to blind Mrs. Beckett here, but I know what over good-nature to young girls comes to. Pretty use to make of your fine scholarship, to be encouraging followers and sweethearts, at that time in the morning too!'

'Speak up, Charlotte,' said the other occupant of the room, a pleasant little brisk woman, with soft brown, eyes, a clear pale skin, and a face smooth, in spite of nearly sixty years; 'speak up, and tell Mrs. Martha the truth, that you never encouraged no one.'

The girl's face was all one flame, but she rose up, and clasping her hands together, exclaimed—'Me encourage! I never thought of what Mrs. Martha says! I don't know what it is all about!'

'Here, Jane Beckett,' cried Mrs. Martha; 'd'ye see what 'tis to vindicate her! Will you take her word against mine, that she's been gossiping this half hour with that young rogue as was turned off at Ormersfield?'

'Tom Madison! cried the girl, in utter amaze. 'Oh! Mrs. Martha!'

'Well! I can't stop!' said Martha. 'I must get Miss Faithfull's breakfast! but if you was under me, Miss Charlotte, I can tell you it would be better for you! You'll sup sorrow yet, and you'll both recollect my advice, both of you.'

Wherewith the Cassandra departed, and Charlotte, throwing her apron over her face, began to cry and sob piteously.

'My dear! what is it now? exclaimed her kind companion, pulling down her apron, and trying to draw down first one, then the other of the arms which persisted in veiling the crimson face. 'Surely you don't think missus or I would mistrust you, or think you'd take up with the likes of him!'

'How could she be so cruel—so spiteful,' sobbed Charlotte, 'when he only came to ask one question, and did a good turn for me with the mats. I never thought of such a thing. Sweetheart, indeed! So cruel of her!'

'Bless me!' said Jane, 'girls used to think it only civility to say they had a sweetheart!'

'Don't, Mrs. Beckett! I hate the word! I don't want no such thing! I won't never speak to Tom Madison again, if such constructions is to be put on it!'

'Well, after all, Charlotte dear, that will be the safest way. You are young yet, and best not to think of settling, special if you aren't sure of one that is steady and religious, and you'd better keep yourself up, and not get a name for gossiping—though there's no harm done yet, so don't make such a work. Bless me, if I don't hear his lordship's voice! He ain't never come so early!'

'Yes, he is,' said Charlotte, recovering from her sobs; 'he rode up as I came in.'

'Well, to be sure, he is come to breakfast! I hope nothin's amiss with my young Lord! I must run up with a cup and plate, and you, make the place tidy, in case Mr. Poynings comes in. You'd better run into the scullery and wash your face; 'tis all tears! You're a terrible one to cry, Charlotte!' with a kind, cheering smile and caress.

Mrs. Beckett bustled off, leaving Charlotte to restore herself to the little handy piece of household mechanism which kind, patient, motherly training had rendered her.

Charlotte Arnold had been fairly educated at a village school, and tenderly brought up at home till left an orphan, when she had been taken into her present place. She had much native refinement and imagination, which, half cultivated, produced a curious mixture of romance and simplicity. Her insatiable taste for reading was meritorious in the eyes of Mrs. Beckett, who, unlearned herself, thought any book better than 'gadding about,' and, after hearing her daily portion of the Bible, listened to the most adventurous romances, with a sense of pleasure and duty in keeping the girl to her book. She loved the little fragile orphan, taught her, and had patience with her, and trusted the true high sound principle which she recognised in Charlotte, amid much that she could not fathom, and set down alternately to the score of scholarship and youth.

Taste, modesty, and timidity were guards to Charlotte. A broad stare was terror to her, and she had many a fictitious horror, as well as better-founded ones. Truly she said, she hated the broad words Martha had used. One who craved a true knight to be twitted with a sweetheart! Martha and Tom Madison were almost equally distasteful, as connected with such a reproach; and the little maiden drew into herself, promenaded her fancy in castles and tournaments, kept under Jane's wing, and was upheld by her as a sensible, prudent girl.

CHAPTER II
AN OLD SCHOOLMISTRESS

> I praise thee, matron, and thy due
> Is praise, heroic praise and true;
> With admiration I behold
> Thy gladness unsubdued and bold.
> Thy looks and gestures all present
> The picture of a life well spent;
> Our human nature throws away
> Its second twilight and looks gay.
> WORDSWORTH.

Unconscious of Charlotte's flight and Tom's affront, the Earl of Ormersfield rode along Dynevor Terrace—a row of houses with handsome cemented fronts, tragic and comic masks alternating over the downstairs windows, and the centre of the block adorned with a pediment and colonnade; but there was an air as if something ailed the place: the gardens were weedy, the glass doors hazy, the cement stained and scarred, and many of the windows closed and dark, like eyes wanting speculation, or with merely the dreary words 'To be let' enlivening their blank gloom. At the house where Charlotte had vanished, he drew his rein, and opened the gate—not one of the rusty ones—he entered the garden, where all was trim and fresh, the shadow of the house lying across the sward, and preserving the hoar-frost, which, in the sunshine, was melting into diamond drops on the lingering China roses.

Without ring or knock, he passed into a narrow, carpetless vestibule, unadorned except by a beautiful blue Wedgewood vase, and laying down hat and whip, mounted the bare staircase, long since divested of all paint or polish. Avoiding the door of the principal room, he opened another at the side, and stood in a flood of sunshine, pouring in from the window, which looked over all the roofs of the town, to the coppices and moorlands of Ormersfield. On the bright fire sung a kettle, a white cat purred on the hearth, a canary twittered merrily in the window, and the light smiled on a languishing Dresden shepherdess and her lover on the mantelpiece, and danced on the ceiling, reflected from a beautifully chased silver cream-jug—an inconsistent companion for the homely black teapot and willow-patterned plates, though the two cups of rare Indian porcelain were not unworthy of it. The furniture was the same mixture of the ordinary and the choice, either worn and shabby, or such as would suit a virtuoso, but the whole arranged with taste and care that made the effect bright, pleasant, and comfortable. Lord Ormersfield stood on the hearth-rug waiting. His face was that of one who had learnt to wait, more considerate than acute, and bearing the stamp both of toil and suffering, as if grief had taken away all mobility of expression, and left a stern, thoughtful steadfastness.

Presently a lady entered the room. Her hair was white as snow, and she could not have seen less than seventy-seven years; but beauty was not gone from her features—smiles were still on her lips, brightness in her clear hazel eyes, buoyancy in her tread, and alertness and dignity in her tall, slender, unbent figure. There was nothing so remarkable about her as the elasticity as well as sweetness of her whole look and bearing, as if, while she had something to love, nothing could be capable of crushing her.

'You here!' she exclaimed, holding out her hand to her guest. 'You are come to breakfast.'

'Thank you; I wished to see you without interrupting your day's work. Have you many scholars at present?'

'Only seven, and three go into school at Easter. Jem and Clara, wish me to undertake no more, but I should sorely miss the little fellows. I wish they may do me as much credit as Sydney Calcott. He wrote himself to tell me of his success.'

'I am glad to hear it. He is a very promising young man.'

'I tell him I shall come to honour, as the old dame who taught him to spell. My scholars may make a Dr. Busby of me in history.'

'I am afraid your preferment will depend chiefly on James and young Calcott.'

'Nay, Louis tells me that he is going to read wonderfully hard; and if he chooses, he can do more than even Sydney Calcott.'

'If!' said the Earl.

Jane here entered with another cup and plate, and Lord Ormersfield sat down to the breakfast-table. After some minutes' pause he said, 'Have you heard from Peru?'

'Not by this mail. Have you?'

'Yes, I have. Mary is coming home.'

'Mary!' she cried, almost springing up—'Mary Ponsonby? This is good news—unless,' as she watched his grave face, 'it is her health that brings her.'

'It is. She has consulted the surgeon of the Libra, a very able man, who tells her that there is absolute need of good advice and a colder climate; and Ponsonby has consented to let her and her daughter come home in the Libra. I expect them in February.'

'My poor Mary! But she will get better away from him. I trust he is not coming!'

'Not he,' said Lord Ormersfield.

'Dear, dear Mary! I had scarcely dared to hope to see her again,' cried the old lady, with tears in her eyes. 'I hope she will be allowed to be with us, not kept in London with his sister. London does her no good.'

'The very purport of my visit,' said Lord Ormersfield, 'was to ask whether you could do me the favour to set aside your scholars, and enable me to receive Mrs. Ponsonby at home.'

'Thank you—oh, thank you. There is nothing I should like better, but I must consider—'

'Clara would find a companion in the younger Mary in the holidays, and if James would make Fitzjocelyn his charge, it would complete the obligation. It would be by far the best arrangement for Mary's comfort, and it would be the greatest satisfaction to me to see her with you at Ormersfield.'

'I believe it would indeed,' said the old lady, more touched than the outward manner of the Earl seemed to warrant. 'I would—you know I would do my very best that you and Mary should be comfortable together'—and her voice trembled—'but you see I cannot promise all at once. I must see about these little boys. I must talk to Jem. In short, you must not be disappointed'—and she put her hands before her face, trying to laugh, but almost overcome.

'Nay, I did not mean to press you,' said Lord Ormersfield, gently; 'but I thought, since James has had the fellowship and Clara has been at school, that you wished to give up your pupils.'

'So I do,' said the lady, but still not yielding absolutely.

'For the rest, I am very anxious that James should accept Fitzjocelyn as his pupil. I have always considered their friendship as the best hope, and other plans have had so little success, that—'

'I'm not going to hear Louis abused!' she exclaimed, gaily.

'Yes,' said Lord Ormersfield, with a look nearly approaching a smile, 'you are the last person I ought to invite, if I wish to keep your nephew unspoiled.'

'I wish there were any one else to spoil him!'

'For his sake, then, come and make Ormersfield cheerful. It will be far better for him.'

'And for you, to see more of Jem,' she added. 'If he were yours, what would you say to such hours?'

The last words were aimed at a young man who came briskly into the room, and as he kissed her, and shook hands with the Earl, answered in a quick, bright tone, 'Shocking, aye. All owing to sitting up till one!'

'Reading?' said the Earl.

'Reading,' he answered, with a sort of laughing satisfaction in dashing aside the approval expressed in the query, 'but not quite as you suppose. See here,' as he held up maliciously a railway novel.

'I am afraid I know where it came from,' said Lord Ormersfield.

'Exactly so,' said James. 'It was Fitzjocelyn's desertion of it that excited my curiosity.'

'Indeed. I should have thought his desertions far too common to excite any curiosity.'

'By no means. He always has a reason.'

'A plausible one.'

'More than plausible,' cried James, excitement sparkling in his vivid black eyes. 'It happens that this is the very book that you would most rejoice to see distasteful to him—low morality, false principles, morbid excitement, not a line that ought to please a healthy mind.'—

'Yet it has interest enough for you.'

'I am not Fitzjocelyn.'

'You know how to plead for him.'

'I speak simple truth,' bluntly answered James, running his hand through his black hair, to the ruin of the morning smoothness, so that it, as well as the whole of his quick, dark countenance seemed to have undergone a change from sunny south to stormy north in the few moments since his first appearance.

After a short silence, Lord Ormersfield turned to him, saying 'I have been begging a favour of my aunt, and I have another to ask of you,' and repeating his explanation, begged him to undertake the tutorship of his son.

'I shall not be at liberty at Easter,' said James, 'I have all but undertaken some men at Oxford.'

'Oh, my dear Jem!' exclaimed the old lady, 'is that settled beyond alteration?'

'I'm not going to throw them over.'

'Then I shall hope for you at Midsummer,' said the Earl.

'We shall see how things stand,' he returned, ungraciously.

'I shall write to you,' said Lord Ormersfield, still undaunted, and soon after taking his leave.

'Cool!' cried James, as soon as he was gone. 'To expect you to give up your school at his beck, to come and keep house for him as long as it may suit him!'

'Nay, Jem, he knew how few boys I have, and that I intended to give them up. You don't mean to refuse Louis?' she said, imploringly.

'I shall certainly not take him at Easter. It would be a mere farce intended to compensate to us for giving up the school, and I'll not lend myself to it while I can have real work.'

'At Midsummer, then. You know he will never let Louis spend a long vacation without a tutor.'

'I hate to be at Ormersfield,' proceeded James, vehemently, 'to see Fitzjocelyn browbeaten and contradicted every moment, and myself set up for a model. I may steal a horse, while he may not look over the wall! Did you observe the inconsistency?—angry with the poor fellow first for having the book, and then for not reading the whole, while it became amiable and praiseworthy in me to burn out a candle over it!'

'Ah! that was my concern. I tell him he would sing another note if you were his son.'

'I'd soon make him! I would not stand what Louis does. The more he is set down and sneered at, the more debonnaire he looks, till I could rave at him for taking it so easily.'

'I hoped you might have hindered them from fretting each other, as they do so often.'

'I should only be a fresh element of discord, while his lordship will persist in making me his pattern young man. It makes me hate myself, especially as Louis is such an unaccountable fellow that he won't.'

'I am sorry you dislike the plan so much.'

'Do you mean that you wish for it, grandmamma? cried he, turning full round on her with an air of extreme amazement. 'If you do, there's an end of it; but I thought you valued nothing more than an independent home.'

'Nor would I give it up on any account,' said she. 'I do not imagine this could possibly last for more than a few months, or a year at the utmost. But you know, dear Jem, I would do nothing you did not like.'

'That's nothing to the purpose,' replied James. 'Though it is to be considered whether Ormersfield is likely to be the best preparation for Clara's future life. However, I see you wish it—'

'I confess that I do, for a few months at least, which need interfere neither with Clara nor with you. I have not seen Lord Ormersfield so eager for many years, and I should be very sorry to prevent those two from being comfortably together in the old home—'

'And can't that be without a chaperon?' exclaimed James, laughing. 'Why, his lordship is fifty-five, and she can't be much less. That is a good joke.'

'It is not punctilio,' said his grandmother, looking distressed. 'It is needful to be on the safe side with such a man as Mr. Ponsonby. My fear is that he may send her home with orders not to come near us.'

'She used to be always at Ormersfield in the old times.'

'Yes, when my sister was alive. Ah! you were too young to know about those matters then. The fact was, that things had come to such a pass from Mr. Ponsonby's neglect and unkindness, that Lord Ormersfield, standing in the place of her brother, thought it right to interfere. His mother went to London with him, to bring poor Mary and her little girl back to Ormersfield, and there they were till my sister's death, when of course they could not remain. Mr. Ponsonby had just got his appointment as British envoy in Peru, and wished her to go with him. It was much against Lord Ormersfield's advice, but she thought it her duty, poor dear. I believe he positively hates Lord Ormersfield; and as if for a parting unkindness, he left his little girl at school with orders to spend her holidays with his sister, and never to be with us.'

'That accounts for it!' said James. 'I never knew all this! nor why we were so entirely cut off from Mary Ponsonby. I wonder what she is now! She was a droll sturdy child in those days! We used to call her Downright Dunstable! She was almost of the same age as Louis, and a great deal stouter, and used to fight for him and herself too. Has not she been out in Peru?'

'Yes, she went out at seventeen. I believe she is an infinite comfort to her mother.'

'Poor Mary! Well, we children lived in the middle of a tragedy, and little suspected it! By the bye, what relation are the Ponsonbys to us?'

'Mrs. Ponsonby is my niece. My dear sister, Mary—'

'Married Mr. Raymond—yes, I know! I'll make the whole lucid; I'll draw up a pedigree, and Louis shall learn it.' And with elaborate neatness he wrote as follows, filling in the dates from the first leaf of an old Bible, after his grandmother had left the room. The task, lightly undertaken, became a mournful one, and as he read over his performance, his countenance varied from the gentleness of regret to a look of sarcastic pride, as though he felt that the world had dealt hardly by him, and yet disdained to complain.

```
                              KING ARTHUR
                    Pendragons and Dynevors innumerable
                         Roland Dynevor, d. 1793
        1.                          2.                             3.
------------------------------------------------------------------------------
Catharine, m. James Frost Dynevor, Esq.   Elizabeth, m. Jocelyn, 3rd Earl of Ormersfield   Mary, m. Ch. Raymond, Esq.
b. 1770         b. 1765                   b. 1772        b. 1760                          b. 1774        d. 1802
                d. 1816                   d. 1835        d. 1833                          d. 1800
    1.                  2.
-------------------------------------     Jocelyn, m. Louisa Villars,                     Mary, m. Robert Ponsonby Esq.,
Henry Roland m. Frances Preston   Oliver J. Frost   4th Earl of   b. 1805                 b. 1796        British Envoy
Frost Dynevor   b. 1802           Dynevor           Ormersfield   d. 1826                                in Peru.
b. 1794         d. 1832           b. 1797           b. 1792
d. 1832
  1.          2.         3.          4.         5.
-----------------------------------------------------
James Roland  Frances    Catharine  Oliver     Clara          Louis Fitzjocelyn           Mary Ponsonby
Frost Dynevor b. 1826    b. 1827    b. 1829    b. 1831        Viscount Fitzjocelyn        b. 1826
b. 1824       d. 1832    d. 1832    d. 1832                   b. 1826.
Fellow of St.
F. College,
Oxford.
```

'Since 1816,' muttered James, as he finished. 'Thirty years of drudgery! When shall I be able to relieve her? Ha! O. J. F. Dynevor, Esquire, if it were you who were coming from Peru, you would find a score to settle!'

He ran down stairs to assist his grandmother in the Latin lessons of her little school, the usual employment of his vacations.

Catharine Dynevor had begun life with little prospect of spending nearly half of it as mistress of a school.

Her father was the last male of the Dynevors of Cheveleigh—a family mounting up to the days of the Pendragons—and she had been made to take the place of an eldest son, inheriting the extensive landed property on condition that her name and arms should be assumed in case of her marriage. Her choice was one of the instances in which her affections had the mastery over her next strongest characteristic, family pride. She married a highly-educated and wealthy gentleman, of good family, but of mercantile connexions, such as her father, if living, would have disdained. Her married life was, however, perfectly unclouded, her ample means gave her the power of dispensing joy, and her temperament was so blithe and unselfish that no pleasure ever palled upon her. Cheveleigh was a proverb for hospitality, affording unfailing fetes for all ages, full of a graceful ease and freedom that inspired enjoyment.

Mr. Frost Dynevor was a man of refined taste, open-handed even to extravagance, liberal in all his appointments, and gratifying to the utmost his love of art and decoration, while his charities and generous actions were hearty and lavish enough to satisfy even his warm-hearted wife.

Joined with all this was a strong turn for speculations. When the mind has once become absorbed in earthly visions of wealth and prosperity, the excitement exercises such a fascination over the senses that the judgment loses balance. Bold assumptions are taken as certainties, and made the foundation of fresh fabrics—the very power of discerning between fact and possibility departs, and, in mere good-will, men, honest and honourable at heart, risk their own and their neighbours' property, and ruin their character and good name, by the very actions most foreign to to their nature, ere it had fallen under the strong delusion.

Mr. Frost Dynevor had the misfortune to live in a country rich in mineral wealth, and to have a brother-in-law easily guided, and with more love of figures than power of investigating estimates on a large scale. Mines were set on foot, companies established, and buildings commenced, and the results were only to be paralleled by those of the chalybeate springs discovered by Mr. Dynevor at the little town of Northwold, which were pronounced by his favourite hanger-on to be destined 'literally to cut the throat of Bath and Cheltenham.'

Some towns are said to have required the life of a child ere their foundations could be laid. Many a speculation has swallowed a life and fortune before its time for thriving has come. Mr. Frost Dynevor and Lord Ormersfield were the foremost victims to the Cheveleigh iron foundries and the Northwold baths. The close of the war brought a commercial crisis that their companies could not stand; and Mr. Dynevor's death spared him from the sight of the crash, which his talent and sagacity might possibly have averted. He had shown no misgivings, but, no sooner was he removed from the helm, than the vessel was found on the brink of destruction. Enormous sums had been sunk without tangible return, and the liabilities of the companies far surpassed anything that they had realized.

Lord Ormersfield was stunned and helpless. Mrs. Dynevor had but one idea—namely, to sacrifice everything to clear her husband's name. Her sons were mere boys, and the only person who proved himself able to act or judge was the heir of Ormersfield, then about four-and-twenty, who came forward with sound judgment and upright dispassionate sense of justice to cope with the difficulties and clear away the involvements.

He joined his father in mortgaging land, sacrificing timber, and reducing the establishment, so as to set the estate in the way of finally becoming free, though at the expense of rigid economy and self-denial.

Cheveleigh could not have been saved, even had the heiress not been willing to yield everything to satisfy the just claims of the creditors. She was happy when she heard that it would suffice, and that no one would be able to accuse her husband of having wronged him. But for this, she would hardly have submitted to retain what her nephew succeeded in securing for her—namely, an income of about 150 pounds per annum, and the row of houses called Dynevor Terrace, one of the building ventures at Northwold. This was the sole dependence with which she and her sons quitted the home of their forefathers. 'Never mind, mother,' said Henry, kissing her, to prevent the tears from springing, 'home is wherever we are together!' 'Never fear, mother,' echoed Oliver, with knitted brow and clenched hands, 'I will win it back.'

Oliver was a quiet lad, of diligent, methodical habits, and willingly accepted a clerkship in a mercantile house, which owed some obligations to his father. At the end of a couple of years he was sent to reside in South America; and his parting words to his mother were—'When you see me again, Cheveleigh shall be yours.'

'Oh, my boy, take care. Remember, 'They that haste to be rich shall not be innocent.''

That was the last time she had seen Oliver.

Her great object was to maintain herself independently and to complete Henry's education as a gentleman. With this view she took up her abode in the least eligible of her houses at Northwold, and, dropping the aristocratic name which alone remained of her heiress-ship, opened a school for little boys, declaring that she was rejoiced to recall the days when Henry and Oliver wore frocks and learnt to spell. If any human being could sweeten the Latin Grammar, it was Mrs. Frost, with the motherliness of a dame, and the refinement of a lady, unfailing sympathy and buoyant spirits, she loved each urchin, and each urchin loved her, till she had become a sort of adopted grandmamma to all Northwold and the neighbourhood.

Henry went to Oxford. He gained no scholarship, took no honours, but he fell neither into debt nor disgrace; he led a goodnatured easy life, and made a vast number of friends; and when he was not staying with them, he and his mother were supremely happy together. He walked with her, read to her, sang to her, and played with her pupils. He had always been brought up as the heir—petted, humoured, and waited on—a post which he filled with goodhumoured easy grace, and which he continued to fill in the same manner, though he had no one to wait on him but his mother, and her faithful servant Jane Beckett. Years passed on, and they seemed perfectly satisfied with their division of labour,—Mrs. Frost kept school, and Henry played the flute, or shot over the Ormersfield property.

If any one remonstrated, Henry was always said to be waiting for a government appointment, which was to be procured by the Ormersfield interest. More for the sake of his mother than of himself, the Ormersfield interest was at length exerted, and the appointment was conferred on him. The immediate consequence was his marriage with the first pretty girl he met, poorer than himself, and all the Ormersfield interest failed to make his mother angry with him.

The cholera of 1832 put an end to poor Henry's desultory life. His house, in a crowded part of London, was especially doomed by the deadly sickness; and out of the whole family the sole survivors were a little girl of ten months old, and a boy of seven years, the latter of whom was with his grandmother at Northwold.

Mrs. Frost was one of the women of whom affection makes unconscious heroines. She could never sink, as long as there was aught to need her love and care; and though Henry had been her darling, the very knowledge that his orphans had no one but herself to depend on, seemed to brace her energies with fresh life. They were left entirely on her hands, her son Oliver made no offers of assistance. He had risen, so as to be a prosperous merchant at Lima, and he wrote with regularity and dutifulness, but he had never proposed coming to England, and did not proffer any aid in the charge of his brother's children. If she had expected anything from him, she did not say so; she seldom spoke of him, but never without tenderness, and usually as her 'poor Oliver,' and she abstained from teaching her grandchildren either to look to their rich uncle or to mourn over their lost inheritance. Cheveleigh was a winter evening's romance with no one but Jane Beckett; and the grandmother always answered the children's inquiries by bidding them prove their ancient blood by resolute independence, and by that true dignity which wealth could neither give nor take away.

Of that dignity, Mrs. Frost was a perfect model. A singular compound of the gentle and the lofty, of tenderness and independence, she had never ceased to be the Northwold standard of the 'real lady,' too mild and gracious to be regarded as proud and poor, and yet too dignified for any liberty to be attempted, her only fault, that touch of pride, so ladylike and refined that it was kept out of sight, and never offended, and everything else so sweet and winning that there was scarcely a being who did not love, as well as honour her, for the cheerfulness and resignation that had borne her through her many trials. Her trustful spirit and warm heart had been an elixir of youth, and had preserved her freshness and elasticity long after her sister and brother-in-law at Ormersfield had grown aged and sunk into the grave, and even her nephew was fast verging upon more than middle age.

CHAPTER III
LOUIS LE DEBONNAIRE

> I walked by his garden and saw the wild brier,
> The thorn and the thistle grow broader and higher.
> ISC WATTS.

Ormersfield Park was extensive, ranging into fine broken ground, rocky and overgrown with brushwood; but it bore the marks of retrenchment; there was hardly a large timber tree on the estate, enclosures had been begun and deserted, and the deer had been sold off to make room for farmers' cattle, which grazed up to the very front door.

The house was of the stately era of Anne, with a heavy portico and clumsy pediment on the garden side, all the windows of the suite of rooms opening on a broad stone terrace, whence steps descended to the lawn, neatly kept, but sombre, for want of openings in the surrounding evergreens.

It was early March, and a lady wrapped in a shawl was seated on the terrace, enjoying the mild gleam of spring, and the freshness of the sun-warmed air, which awoke a smile of welcome as it breathed on her faded cheek, and her eyes gazed on the scene, in fond recognition.

It had been the home of Mrs. Ponsonby's childhood; and the slopes of turf and belts of dark ilex were fraught with many a recollection of girlish musings, youthful visions, and later, intervals of tranquillity and repose. After fourteen years spent in South America, how many threads she had to take up again! She had been as a sister to her cousin, Lord Ormersfield, and had shared more of his confidence than any other person during their earlier years, but afterwards their intercourse had necessarily been confined to brief and guarded letters. She had found him unchanged in his kindness to herself, and she was the more led to ponder on the grave, stern impassiveness of his manner to others, and to try to understand the tone of mind that it indicated.

She recalled him as he had been in his first youth—reserved, sensible, thoughtful, but with the fire of ambition burning strongly within, and ever and anon flashing forth vividly, repressed at once as too demonstrative, but filling her with enthusiastic admiration. She remembered him calmly and manfully meeting the shock of the failure, that would, he knew, fetter and encumber him through life—how resolutely he had faced the difficulties, how unselfishly he had put himself out of the question, how uprightly he had dealt by the creditors, how considerately by his father and aunt, how wise and moderate his proceedings had been throughout. She recollected how she had shared his aspirations, and gloried in his consistent and prudent course, without perceiving what sorrow had since taught her-that ambition was to him what pleasure was to other young men. What had it not been to her when that ambition began to be gratified! when he had become a leading man in Parliament, and by-and-by held office.

There, a change came over the spirit of her dream; and though she sighed, she could not but smile at the fair picture that rose before her, of a young girl of radiant loveliness, her golden curls drooping over her neck, and her eyes blue as the starry veronica by the hedge side, smiling in the sunshine. She thought of the glances of proud delight that her cousin had stolen at her, to read in her face, that his Louisa was more than all he had told her. Little was needed to make her love the sweet, caressing young creature who had thrown her arms round her, and told her that she saw it was all nonsense to tell her she was such a good, grave, dreadful cousin Mary! Yet there had been some few misgivings! So short an acquaintance! Her cousin too busy for more than being bewitched by the lovely face! The Villiers family, so gay and fashionable! Might not all have been foreseen? And yet, of what use would foresight have been? The gentleman was deeply attached, and the lady's family courted the match, the distinction he had won, atoning for his encumbered fortune.

Other scenes arose on her memory—Louisa, a triumphant beauty, living on the homage she received, all brilliance, grace, and enjoyment. But there was a darkening background which grew more prominent. Poor Louisa had little wisdom by nature, and her education had been solely directed to enable her to shine in the world, not to render her fit for the companionship of a man of domestic tastes, accustomed to the society of superior women. There was nothing to fall back upon, nothing to make a home, she was listless and weary whenever gaiety failed her—and he, disappointed and baffled, too unbending to draw her out, too much occupied to watch over her, yielded to her tastes, and let her pursue her favourite enjoyments unchecked.

A time had come when childish vanity and frivolity were verging on levity and imprudence. Expostulations fell powerless on her shallowness. Painful was the remembrance of the deprecating roguish glance of the beautiful eyes, and the coaxing caresses with which she kissed away the lecture, and made promises, only to forget them. She was like the soulless Undine, with her reckless gaiety and sweetness, so loving and childish that there was no being displeased with her, so innocent and devoid of all art or guile in her wilfulness, that her faults could hardly bear a harsher name than follies.

Again, Mrs. Ponsonby thought of the days when she herself had been left to stay with her old uncle and aunt. In this very house while her husband was absent abroad, when she had assisted them to receive the poor young wife, sent home in failing health. She thought of the sad weeks, so melancholy in the impossibility of making an impression, or of leading poor Louisa from her frivolities, she recalled the sorrow of hearing her build on future schemes of pleasure, the dead blank when her prattle on them failed, the tedium of deeper subjects, and yet the bewitching sweetness overpowering all vexation at her exceeding silliness. Though full one-and-twenty years had passed, still the tears thrilled warm into Mrs. Ponsonby's eyes at the thought of Louisa's fond clinging to her, in spite of many an admonition and even exertion of authority, for she alone dared to control the spoilt child's self-will; and had far more power than the husband, who seemed to act as a check and restraint, and whose presence rendered her no longer easy and natural. One confidence had explained the whole.

'You know, Mary dear, I always was so much afraid of him! If I had had my own way, I know who it would have been; but there were mamma and Anna Maria always saying how fortunate I was, and that he would be Prime Minister, and all the rest. Oh! I was far too young and foolish for him. He should have married a sober body, such as you, Mary! Why did he not? She wished she had never teased him by going out so much, and letting people talk nonsense; he had been very kind, and she was not half good enough for him. That confession, made to him, would have been balm for ever; but she had not resolution for the effort, and the days slid away till the worst fears were fulfilled. Nay, were they the worst fears? Was there not an unavowed sense that it was safer that she should die, while innocent of all but wayward folly, than be left to perils which she was so little able to resist?

The iron expression of grief on her husband's face had forbidden all sympathy, all attempt at consolation. He had returned at once to his business in London, there to find that poor Louisa's extravagance had equalled her folly, and that he, whose pride it had been to redeem his paternal property, was thrown back by heavy debts on his own account. This had been known to Mrs. Ponsonby, but by no word from him; he had never permitted the most distant reference to his wife, and yet, with inconsistency betraying his passionate love, he had ordered one of the most beautiful and costly monuments that art could execute, for her grave at Ormersfield, and had sent brief but explicit orders that, contrary to all family precedent, his infant should bear no name but Louis.

On this boy Mrs. Ponsonby had founded all her hopes of a renewal of happiness for her cousin; but when she had left England there had been little amalgamation between the volatile animated boy, and his grave unbending father. She could not conjure up any more comfortable picture of them than the child uneasily perched on his papa's knee, looking wistfully for a way of escape, and his father with an air of having lifted him up as a duty, without knowing what to do with him or to say to him.

At her earnest advice, the little fellow had been placed as a boarder with his great aunt, Mrs. Frost, when his grandmother's death had deprived him of all that was homelike at Ormersfield, He had been with her till he was old enough for a public school, and she spoke of him as if he were no less dear to her than her own grandchildren; but she was one who saw no fault in those whom she loved, and Mrs. Ponsonby had been rendered a little anxious by a certain tone of dissatisfaction in Lord Ormersfield's curt mention of his son, and above all by his cold manner of announcing that this was the day when he would return from Oxford for the Easter vacation.

Could it be that the son was unworthy, or had the father's feelings been too much chilled ever to warm again, and all home affections lost in the strife of politics? These had ever since engaged him, whether in or out of office, leaving little time for society or for any domestic pursuit.

Her reflections were interrupted by a call of 'Mamma!' and her daughter came running up the steps. Mary Ponsonby had too wide a face for beauty, and not slightness enough for symmetry, but nothing could be more pleasing and trustworthy than the open countenance, the steady, clear, greenish-brown eyes, the kind, sensible mouth, the firm chin, broad though rather short forehead, and healthy though not highly-coloured cheek; and the voice—full, soft, and cheerful—well agreed with the expression, and always brought gladness and promise of sympathy.

'See, mamma, what we have found for you.'

'Violets! The very purple ones that used to grow on the orchard bank!'

'So they did. Mary knew exactly where to look for them,' said Mrs. Frost, who had followed her up the steps.

'And there is Gervas,' continued Mary; 'so charmed to hear of you, that we had almost brought him to see you.'

Mrs. Ponsonby declared herself so much invigorated by Ormersfield air, that she would go to see her old friend the gardener. Mary hurried to fetch her bonnet, and returned while a panegyric was going on upon her abilities as maid-of-all-work, in her mother's difficulties with male housemaids—black and brown—and washerwomen who rode on horseback in white satin shoes. She looked as if it were hardly natural that any one but herself should support her mother, when Mrs. Frost tenderly drew Mrs. Ponsonby's arm into her own; and it was indeed strange to see the younger lady so frail and broken, and the elder so strong, vigorous, and active; as they moved along in the sunshine, pausing to note each spring blossom that bordered the gravel, and entered the walled kitchen-garden, where espaliers ran parallel with the walks, dividing the vegetables from the narrow flower-beds, illuminated by crocuses opening the depths of their golden hearts to the sunbeams and the revelling bees. Old Gervas, in a patriarchal red waistcoat, welcomed Mrs. Ponsonby with more warmth than flattery. Bless me, ma'am, I'm right glad to see you; but how old you be!'

'I must come home to learn how to grow young, Gervas,' said she, smiling; 'I hear Betty is as youthful as my aunt here.'

'Ay, ma'am, Betty do fight it out tolerablish,' was the reply to this compliment.

'Why, Gervas, what's all that wilderness? Surely those used to be strawberry beds.'

'Yes, ma'am, the earliest hautboys; don't ye mind? My young Lord came and begged it of me, and, bless the lad, I can't refuse him nothing.'

'He seems to be no gardener!'

'He said he wanted to make a Botany Bay sort of garden,' said the old man; 'and sure enough 'tis a garden of weeds he's made of it, and mine into the bargain! He has a great big thistle here, and the down blows right over my beds, thick as snow, so that it is three women's work to be a match for the weeds; but speak to him of pulling it up, ye'd think 'twas the heart out of him.'

'Does he ever work here?'

'At first it was nought else; he and that young chap, Madison, always bringing docks and darnel out of the hedges, and plants from the nursery gardens, and bringing rockwork, and letting water in to make a swamp. There's no saying what's in the lad's head! But, of late, he's not done much but by times lying on the bank, reading or speaking verses out loud to himself, or getting young Madison off his work to listen to him. Once he got me to hear; but, ma'am, 'twas all about fairies and such like, putting an ass's head on an honest body as had lost his way. I told him 'twas no good for him or the boy to read such stuff, and I'd ha' none of it; but, if he chose to read me some good book, he'd be welcome—for the candles baint so good as they used, and I can't get no spectacles to suit me.'

'And did he read to you?'

'A bit or two, ma'am, if the humour took him. But he's young, you see, ma'am. I'm right glad he'll find you here. My old woman says he do want a lady about the place to make him comfortable like.'

'And who is this young Madison?' asked Mrs. Ponsonby, when they had turned from the old gardener.

'To hear Jem, you would believe that he is the most promising plant rearing for Botany Bay!' said Mrs. Frost. 'He is a boy from that wild place Marksedge, whom Louis took interest in, and made more familiar than Jem liked, or than, perhaps, was good for him. It did not answer; the servants did not like it, and it ended in his being sent to work with Smith, the ironmonger. Poor Louis! he took it sadly to heart, for he had taken great pains with the boy.'

'I like to hear the old name, Louis!'

'I can't help it,' said Mrs. Frost. 'He must be his old aunt Kitty's Louis le Debonnaire! Don't you, remember your calling him so when he was a baby?'

'Oh yes, it has exactly recalled to me the sort of gracious look that he used to have—half sly, half sweet-and so very pretty!'

'It suits him as well now. He is the kind of being who must have a pet name;' and Mrs. Frost, hoping he might be already arrived, could hardly slacken her eager step so as to keep pace with her niece's feeble movements. She was disappointed; the carriage had returned without Lord Fitzjocelyn. His hat and luggage were come, but he himself was missing. Mrs. Frost was very uneasy, but his father silenced conjectures by saying, that it was his usual way, and he would make his appearance before the evening. He would not send to meet another train, saying, that the penalty of irregularity must be borne, and the horses should not suffer for such freaks; and he would fain have been utterly indifferent, but he was evidently listening to every sound, and betrayed his anxiety by the decision with which he checked all expression of his aunt's fears.

There was no arrival all that evening, no explanation in the morning; and Betty Gervas, whom Mary went to visit in the course of the day, began to wonder whether the young Lord could be gone for a soldier—the usual fate of all missing village lads.

Mary was on her way home, through the park, along a path skirting the top of a wooded ravine, a dashing rivulet making a pleasant murmur among the rocks below, and glancing here and there through the brushwood that clothed the precipitous banks, when, with a sudden rustling and crackling, a man leaped upon the path with a stone in each hand.

Mary started, but she did not lose her presence of mind, and her next glance showed her that the apparition was not alarming, and was nearly as much amazed as herself. It was a tall slight young man, in a suit of shepherd's plaid, with a fair face and graceful agile form, recalling the word debonnaire as she had yesterday heard it applied. In instant conviction that this was the truant, she put out her hand by the same impulse that lighted his features with a smile of welcome, and the years of separation seemed annihilated as he exclaimed, 'My cousin Mary!' and grasped her hand, adding, 'I hope I did not frighten you—'

'Oh no; but where did you come from?'

'Up a hill perpendicular, like Hotspur,' he replied, in soft low quiet tones, which were a strange contrast to the words. 'No, see here,' and parting the bushes he showed some rude steps, half nature, half art, leading between the ferns and mountain-ash, and looking very inviting.

'How delightful!' cried Mary.

'I am glad you appreciate it,' he exclaimed; 'I will finish it off now, and put a rail. I did not care to go on when I had lost the poor fellow who helped me, but it saves a world of distance.'

'It must be very pretty amongst those beautiful ferns!'

'You can't conceive anything more charming,' he continued, with the same low distinct utterance, but an earnestness that almost took away her breath. 'There are nine ferns on this bank—that is, if we have the Scolopendrium Loevigatum, as I am persuaded. Do you know anything of ferns? Ah! you come from the land of tree ferns.'

'Oh! I am so glad to exchange them for our home flowers. Primroses look so friendly and natural.'

'These rocks are perfect nests for them, and they even overhang the river. This is the best bit of the stream, so rapid and foaming that I must throw a bridge across for Aunt Catharine. Which would be most appropriate? I was weighing it as I came up—a simple stone, or a rustic performance in wood?'

'I should like stone,' said Mary, amused by his eagerness.

'A rough Druidical stone! That's it! The idea of rude negligent strength accords with such places, and this is a stone country. I know the very stone! Do come down and see!'

'To-morrow, if you please,' said Mary. 'Mamma must want me, and—but I suppose they know of your return at home.'

'No, they don't. They have learnt by experience that the right time is the one never to expect me.'

Mary's eyes were all astonishment, as she said, between wonder and reproof, 'Is that on purpose?'

'Adventures are thrust on some people,' was the nonchalant reply, with shoulders depressed, and a twinkle of the eye, as if he purposed amazing his auditor.'

'I hope you have had an adventure, for nothing else could justify you,' said Mary, with some humour, but more gravity.

'Only a stray infant-errant, cast on my mercy at the junction station. Nurse, between eating and gossiping left behind—bell rings—engine squeaks—train starts—Fitzjocelyn and infant vis-a-vis.'

'You don't mean a baby?'

'A child of five years old, who soon ceased howling, and confided his history to me. He had been visiting grandmamma in London, and was going home to Illershall; so I found the best plan would be to leave the train at the next station, and take him home.'

'Oh, that was quite another thing!' exclaimed Mary, gratified at being able to like him. 'Could you find his home?'

'Yes; he knew his name and address too well to be lost or mislaid. I would have come home as soon as I had seen him in at the door; but the whole family rushed out on me, and conjured me first to dine and then to sleep. They are capital people. Dobbs is superintendent of the copper and tin works—a thoroughly right-minded man, with a nice, ladylike wife, the right sort of sound stuff that old England's heart is made of. It was worth anything to have seen it! They do incalculable good with their work-people. I saw the whole concern.'

He launched into an explanation of the process, producing from his pocket, papers of the ore, in every stage of manufacture, and twisting them up so carelessly, that they would have become a mass of confusion, had not Mary undertaken the repacking.

As they approached the house, the library window was thrown up, and Mrs. Frost came hurrying down with outstretched arms. She was met by her young nephew with an overflow of fond affection, before he looked up and beheld his father standing upright and motionless on the highest step. His excuses were made more lightly and easily than seemed to suit such rigid looks; but Lord Ormersfield bent his head as if resigning himself perforce to the explanation, and, with the softened voice in which he always spoke to Mrs. Ponsonby, said, 'Here he is—Louis, you remember your cousin.'

She was positively startled; for it was as if his mother's deep blue eyes were raised to hers, and there were the same regular delicate features, fair, transparent complexion, and glossy light-brown hair tinted with gold—the same careless yet deprecating glance, the same engaging smile that warmed her heart to him at once, in spite of an air which was not that of wisdom.

'How little altered you are!' she exclaimed. 'If you were not taller than your father, I should say you were the same Louis that I left fourteen years ago.'

'I fear that is the chief change,' said Lord Ormersfield.

'A boy that would be a boy all his life, like Sir Thomas More's son!' said Louis, coolly and simply, but with a twinkle in the corner of his eye, as if he said it on purpose to be provoking; and Mrs. Frost interposed by asking where the cousins had met, and whether they had known each other.

'I knew him by what you said yesterday,' said Mary.

'Louis le Debonnaire? asked Mrs. Frost, smiling.

'No, Mary; not that name!' he exclaimed. 'It is what Jem calls me, when he has nothing more cutting to say—'

'Aye, because it is exactly what you look when you know you deserve a scolding—with your shoulders pulled down, and your face made up!' said his aunt, patting him.

When Mrs. Ponsonby and Mary had left the room to dress, Louis exclaimed, 'And that is Mrs. Ponsonby! How ill she does look! Her very voice has broken down, though it still has the sweet sound that I could never forget! Has she had advice?'

'Dr. Hastings saw her in London,' said his father. 'He sent her into the country at once, and thinks that there is fair hope that complete rest of spirits may check the disease.'

'Will she stay here?' said Louis, eagerly. 'That would be like old times, and we could make her very comfortable. I would train those two ponies for her drives—'

'I wish she would remain here,' said his father; 'but she is bent on becoming my aunt's tenant.'

'Ha! That is next best! They could do nothing more commendable. Will they be a windfall for the House Beautiful?'

'No,' said Mrs. Frost. 'They wish to have a house of their own, in case Mr. Ponsonby should come home, or Miss Ponsonby to stay with them.'

'The respected aunt who brought Mary up! How long has she been at Lima?'

'Four years.'

'Four years! She has not made use of her opportunities! Alas for the illusion dispelled! The Spanish walk and mantilla melt away; and behold! the primitive wide-mouthed body of fourteen years since!'

Mrs. Frost laughed, but it seemed to be a serious matter with Lord Ormersfield. 'If you could appreciate sterling worth,' he said, 'you would be ashamed to speak of your cousin with such conceited disrespect.'

All the effect was to make Louis walk quietly out of the room; but his shoulder and eyebrow made a secret telegraph of amazement to Mrs. Frost.

The new arrival seemed to have put the Earl into a state of constant restless anxiety, subdued and concealed with a high hand, but still visible to one who knew him so intimately as did Mrs. Ponsonby. She saw that he watched each word and gesture, and studied her looks to judge of the opinion they might create in her. Now the process was much like weighing and balancing the down of Fitzjocelyn's own favourite thistle; the profusion, the unsubstantiality, and the volatility being far too similar; and there was something positively sad in the solicitous heed taken of such utter heedlessness.

The reigning idea was the expedition to Illershall, and the excellent condition of the work-people under his new friend the superintendent. Forgetful that mines were a tender subject, the eager speaker became certain that copper must exist in the neighbourhood, and what an employment it would afford to all the country round. 'Marksedge must be the very place, the soil promises metallic veins, the discovery would be the utmost boon to the people. It would lead to industry and civilization, and counteract all the evils we have brought on them. Mary, do you remember Marksedge, the place of exile?'

'Not that I know of.'

'No; we were too young to understand the iniquity. In the last generation, it was not the plan to stone Naboth, but to remove him. Great people could not endure little people; so, by way of kindness, our whole population of

Ormersfield, except a few necessary retainers, were transported bodily from betwixt the wind and our nobility, located on a moor beyond our confines, a generous gift to the poor-rates of Bletchynden, away from church, away from work, away from superintendence, away from all amenities of the poor man's life!'

This was one of the improvements to which Mr. Dynevor had prompted the last Earl; but Louis did not know whom he was cutting, as he uttered this tirade, with a glow on his cheek and eye, but with his usual soft, modulated intonation and polished language, the distinctness and deliberation taking off all air of rattle, and rendering his words more impressive.

'Indeed! is there much distress at Marksedge?' said Mrs. Ponsonby.

'They have gifts with our own poor at Christmas,' said Lord Ormersfield, 'but they are a defiant, ungrateful set, always in distress by their own fault.'

'What cause have they for gratitude?' exclaimed his son. 'For being turned out of house and home? for the three miles' walk to their daily work! Yes, it is the fact. The dozen families left here, with edicts against lodgers, cannot suffice for the farmer's work; and all Norris's and Beecher's men have to walk six miles every day of their lives, besides the hard day's work. They are still farther from their parish, they are no one's charge, they have neither church nor school, and whom should we blame for their being lawless?'

'It used to be thought a very good thing for the parish,' said Mrs. Frost, looking at her niece. 'I remember being sorry for the poor people, but we did not see things in the light in which Louis puts it.'

'Young men like to find fault with the doings of their elders,' said Lord Ormersfield.

'Nothing can make me regard it otherwise than as a wicked sin!' said Louis.

'Nay, my dear,' mildly said Aunt Catharine, 'if it were mistaken, I am sure it was not intentionally cruel.'

'What I call wicked is to sacrifice the welfare of dependents to our own selfish convenience! And you would call it cruel too, Aunt Catharine, if you could hear the poor creatures beg as a favour of Mr. Holdsworth to be buried among their kin, and know how it has preyed on the minds of the dying that they might not lie here among their own people.'

'Change the subject, Fitzjocelyn,' said his father: 'the thing is done, and cannot be undone.'

'The undoing is my daily thought,' said Louis. 'If I could have tried my plan of weaving cordage out of cotton-grass and thistle-down, I think I could have contrived for them.'

Mary looked up, and met his merry blue eye. Was he saying it so gravely to try whether he could take her in? 'If you could—' she said, and he went off into a hearty laugh, and finished by saying, so that no one could guess whether it was sport or earnest, 'Even taking into account the depredations of the goldfinches, it would be an admirable speculation, and would confer immeasurable benefits on the owners of waste lands. I mean to take out a patent when I have succeeded in the spinning.'

'A patent for a donkey,' whispered Aunt Catharine. He responded with a deferential bow, and the conversation was changed by the Earl; but copper was still the subject uppermost with Louis, and no sooner was dinner over than he followed the ladies to the library, and began searching every book on metals and minerals, till he had heaped up a pile of volumes, whence be rang the changes on oxide, pyrites, and carbonate, and octohedron crystals—names which poor Mrs. Frost had heard but too often. At last it came to certainty that he had seen the very masses containing ore; he would send one to-morrow to Illershall to be analysed, and bring his friend Dobbs down to view the spot.

'Not in my time,' interposed Lord Ormersfield. 'I would not wish for a greater misfortune than the discovery of a mine on my property.'

'No wonder,' thought Mrs. Ponsonby, as she recollected Wheal Salamanca and Wheal Catharine, and Wheal Dynevor, and all the other wheals that had wheeled away all Cheveleigh and half Ormersfield, till the last unfortunate wheal failed when the rope broke, and there were no funds to buy a new one. No wonder Lord Ormersfield trembled when he heard his son launch out into those easily-ascending conjectural calculations, freely working sums in his head, so exactly like the old Earl, his grandfather, that she could have laughed, but for sympathy with the father, and anxiety to see how the son would take the damp so vexatiously cast on his projects.

He made the gesture that Mrs. Frost called debonnaire—read on for five minutes in silence, insisted on teaching his aunt the cause of the colours in peacock ores, compared them to a pigeon's neck, and talked of old Betty Gervas's tame pigeons; whence he proceeded to memories of the days that he and Mary had spent together, and asked which of their old haunts she had revisited. Had she been into the nursery?

'Oh yes! but I wondered you had sent the old walnut press into that lumber-room.'

'Is that satire?' said Louis, starting and looking in her face.

'I don't know what you mean.'

'I have a better right to ask what you mean by stigmatizing my apartment as a lumber-room?'

'It was only what I saw from the door,' said Mary, a little confused, but rallying and answering with spirit; 'and I must maintain that, if you mean the room over the garden entrance, it is very like a lumber-room.'

'Ah, Mary! you have not outgrown the delusions of your sex. Is an Englishman's house his castle while housemaids maraud over it, ransacking his possessions, irritating poor peaceful dust that only wants to be let alone, sweeping away cherished cobwebs?'

'Oh, if you cherish cobwebs!' said Mary.

'Did not the fortunes of Scotland hang on a spider's thread? Did not a cobweb save the life of Mahomet, or Ali, or a mediaeval saint—no matter which? Was not a spider the solace of the Bastille? Have not I lain for hours on a summer morning watching the tremulous lines of the beautiful geometrical composition?'

'More shame for you!' said Mary, with a sort of dry humorous bluntness.

'The very answer you would have made in old times,' cried Louis, delighted. 'O Mary, you bring me back the days of my youth! You never would see the giant who used to live in that press!'

'I remember our great fall from the top of it.'

'Oh yes!' cried Louis; 'Jem Frost had set us up there bolt upright for sentries, and I saw the enemies too soon, when you would not allow that they were there. I was going to fire my musket at them; but you used violence to keep me steady to my duty—pulled my hair, did not you?'

'I know you scratched me, and we both rolled off together! I wonder we were not both killed!'

'That did not trouble Jem! He picked us up, and ordered us into arrest under the bed for breach of discipline.'

'I fear Jem was a martinet,' said Mrs. Frost.

'That he was! A general formed on the model of him who, not contented with assaulting a demi-lune, had taken une lune toute entiere. We had a siege of the Fort Bombadero, inaccessible, and with mortars firing double-hand grenades. They were dandelion clocks, and there were nettles to act the part of poisoned spikes on the breach.'

'I remember the nettles,' said Mary, 'and Jem's driving you to gather them; you standing with your bare legs in the nettle-bed, when he would make me dig, and I could not come to help you!'

'On duty in the trenches. Your sense of duty was exemplary. I remember your digging on, like a very Casablanca, all alone, in the midst of a thunderstorm, because Jem had forgotten to call you in, crying all the time with fear of the lightning!'

'You came to help me,' said Mary. 'You came rushing out from the nursery to my rescue!'

'I could not make you stir. We were taken prisoners by a sally from the nursery. For once in your life, you were in disgrace!'

'I quite thought I ought to mind Jem,' said Mary, 'and never knew whether it was play or earnest.'

'Only so could you transgress,' said Louis,—'you who never cried, except as my amateur Mungo Malagrowther. Poor Mary! what an amazement it was to me to find you breaking your heart over the utmost penalties of the nursery law, when to me they only afforded agreeable occasions of showing that I did not care! I must have been intolerable till you and Mrs. Ponsonby took me in hand!'

'I am glad you own your obligations,' said Lord Ormersfield.

'I own myself as much obliged to Mary for making me wise, as to Jem for making me foolish.'

'It is not the cause of gratitude I should have expected,' said his father.

'Alas! if he and Clara were but here!' sighed Louis. 'I entreated him in terms that might have moved a pyramid from its base, but the Frost was arctic. An iceberg will move, but he is past all melting!'

'I respect his steadiness of purpose,' said the Earl; 'I know no young man whom I honour more than James.'

His aunt and his son were looking towards each other with glistening eyes of triumph and congratulation, and Mrs. Frost cleared her voice to say that he was making far too much of her Jemmy; a very good boy, to be sure, but if he said so much of him, the Marys would be disappointed to see nothing but a little fiery Welshman.

CHAPTER IV
THISTLE-DOWN

> Lightly soars the thistle-down,
>   Lightly does it float—,
> Lightly seeds of care are sown,
>   Little do we note.
> Watch life's thistles bud and blow,
>   Oh, 'tis pleasant folly;
> But when all life's paths they strew,
>   Then comes melancholy.
>   Poetry Past and Present.

Mary Ponsonby had led a life of change and wandering that had given her few strong local attachments. The period she had spent at Ormersfield, when she was from five to seven years old, had been the most joyous part of her life, and had given her a strong feeling for the place where she had lived with her mother, and in an atmosphere of affection, free from the shadow of that skeleton in the house, which had darkened her childhood more than she understood.

The great weakness of Mrs. Ponsonby's life had been her over-hasty acceptance of a man, whom she did not thoroughly know, because her delicacy had taken alarm at foolish gossip about herself and her cousin. It was a folly that had been severely visited. Irreligious himself, Mr. Ponsonby disliked his wife's strictness; he resented her affection for her own family, gave way to dissipated habits, and made her miserable both by violence and neglect. Born late of this unhappy marriage, little Mary was his only substantial link to his wife, and he had never been wanting in tenderness to her: but many a storm had raged over the poor child's head; and, though she did not know why the kind old Countess had come to remove her and her mother, and 'papa' was still a loved and honoured title, she was fully sensible of the calm security at Ormersfield.

When Mr. Ponsonby had recalled his wife on his appointment at Lima, Mary had been left in England for education, under the charge of his sister in London. Miss Ponsonby was good and kind, but of narrow views, thinking all titled people fashionable, and all fashionable people reprobate, jealous of her sister-in-law's love for her own family, and, though unable to believe her brother blameless, holding it as an axiom that married people could not fall out without faults on both sides, and charging a large share of their unhappiness on the house of Fitzjocelyn. Principle had prevented her from endeavouring to weaken the little girl's affection to her mother; but it had been her great object to train her up in habits of sober judgment, and freedom from all the romance, poetry, and enthusiasm which she fancied had been injurious to Mrs. Ponsonby. The soil was of the very kind that she would have chosen. Mary was intelligent, but with more sense than fancy, more practical than intellectual, and preferring the homely to the tasteful. At school, study and accomplishments were mere tasks, her recreation was found in acts of kindness to her companions, and her hopes were all fixed on the going out to Peru, to be useful to her father and mother. At seventeen she went; full of active, housewifely habits, with a clear head, sound heart, and cramped mind, her spirits even and cheerful, but not high nor mirthful, after ten years of evenings spent in needlework beside a dry maiden aunt.

Nor was the home she found at Lima likely to foster the joyousness of early girlhood. Mr. Ponsonby was excessively fond of her; but his affection to her only marked, by contrast, the gulf between him and her mother. There was no longer any open misconduct on his part, and Mrs. Ponsonby was almost tremblingly attentive to his wishes; but he was chill and sarcastic in his manner towards her, and her nervous attacks often betrayed that she had been made to suffer in private for differences of opinion. Health and spirits were breaking down; and, though she never uttered a word of complaint, the sight of her sufferings was trying for a warm-hearted young girl.

Mary's refuge was hearty affection to both parents. She would not reason nor notice where filial tact taught her that it was best to be ignorant; she charged all tracasseries on the Peruvian republic, and set herself simply to ameliorate each vexation as it arose, and divert attention from it without generalizing, even to herself, on the state of the family. The English comfort which she brought into the Limenian household was one element of peace; and her brisk, energetic habits produced an air of ease and pleasantness that did much to make home agreeable to her father, and removed many cares which oppressed her mother. To her, Mary was all the world—daughter, comforter, friend, and nurse, unfailing in deeds of love or words of cheer, and removing all sense of dreariness and solitude. And Mary had found her mother all, and more than all she remembered, and admired and loved her with a deep, quiet glow of intense affection. There was so much call for

Mary's actual exertion of various kinds, that there was little opportunity for cultivating or enlarging her mind by books, though the scenes and circumstances around her could not but take some effect. Still, at twenty-one she was so much what she had been at seventeen—so staid, sensible, and practical, that Miss Ponsonby gladly pronounced her not in the least spoilt.

Fain would her aunt have kept both her and her mother as her guests; but Mrs. Ponsonby had permission to choose whatever residence best suited her, and felt that Bryanston-square and Miss Ponsonby would be fatal to her harassed spirits. She yearned after the home and companions of her youth, and Miss Ponsonby could only look severe, talk of London doctors, and take Mary aside to warn her against temptations from fashionable people.

Mary had been looking for the fashionable people ever since, and the first sign of them she had seen, was the air and figure of her cousin Fitzjocelyn. Probably good Aunt Melicent would distrust him; and yet his odd startling talk, and the arch look of mischief in the corners of his mouth and eyes, had so much likeness to the little Louis of old times, that she could not look on him as a stranger nor as a formidable being; but was always recurring to the almost monitorial sense of protection, with which she formerly used to regard him, when she shared his nursery.

Her mother had cultivated her love for Ormersfield, and she was charmed by her visits to old haunts, well remembering everything. She gladly recognised the little low-browed church, the dumpy tower, and grave-yard rising so high that it seemed to intend to bury the church itself, and permitted many a view, through the lattices, of the seats, and the Fitzjocelyn hatchments and monuments.

She lingered after church on Sunday afternoon with Mrs. Frost to look at Lady Fitzjocelyn's monument. It was in the chancel, a recumbent figure in white marble, as if newly fallen asleep, and with the lovely features chiselled from a cast taken after death had fixed and ennobled their beauty.

'It is just like Louis's profile!' said Mrs. Frost, as they came out.

'Well,' said Louis, who was nearer than she was aware, 'I hope at least no one will make me the occasion of a lion when I am dead.'

'It is very beautiful,' said Mary.

'May be so; but the sentiment is destroyed by its having been six months in the Royal Academy, number 16,136, and by seeing it down among the excursions in the Northwold Guide.'

'Louis, my dear, you should not be satirical on this,' said Mrs. Frost.

'I never meant it,' said Louis, 'but I never could love that monument. It used to oppress me with a sense of having a white marble mother! And, seriously, it fills up the chancel as if it were its show-room, according to our family tradition that the church is dedicated to the Fitzjocelyns. Living or dead, we have taken it all to ourselves.'

'It was a very fair, respectable congregation,' said his aunt.

'Exactly so. That is my complaint. Everything belonging to his lordship is respectable—except his son.'

'Take care, Louis; here is Mary looking as if she would take you at your word.'

'Pray, Mary, do they let no one who is not respectable go to church in Peru?'

'I do not think you would change your congregation for the wretched crowds of brown beggars,' said Mary.

'Would I not?' cried Louis. 'Oh! if the analogous class here in England could but feel that the church was for them!—not driven out and thrust aside, by our respectability.'

'Marksedge to wit!' said a good-humoured voice, as Mr. Holdsworth, the young Vicar, appeared at his own wicket, with a hearty greeting. 'I never hear those words without knowing where you are, Fitzjocelyn.'

'I hope to be there literally some day this week,' said Louis. 'Will you walk with me? I want to ask old Madison how his grandson goes on. I missed going to see after the boy last time I was at home.'

'I fear he has not been going on well, and have been sorry for it ever since,' said the Vicar. 'His master told me that he found him very idle and saucy.'

'People of that sort never know how to speak to a lad,' said Louis. 'It is their own rating that they ought to blame.'

'Not Tom Madison, I know,' said Mr. Holdsworth, laughing. 'But I did not come out to combat that point, but to inquire after the commissions you kindly undertook.'

'I have brought you such a set of prizes! Red rubrics, red margins; and for the apparatus, I have brought a globe with all the mountains in high relief;—yes, and an admirable physical atlas, and a box of instruments and models for applying mathematics to mechanics. We might give evening lectures, and interest the young farmers.'

'Pray,' said the Vicar, with a sound of dismay, 'where may the bill be? I thought the limits were two pounds eighteen.'

'Oh! I take all that on myself.'

'We shall see,' said Mr. Holdsworth, not gratefully. 'Was Origen sent home in time for you to bring?'

'There!' cried Louis, starting, 'Origen is lying on the very chair where I put him last January. I will write to Jem Frost to-morrow to send him to the binder.'

'Is it of any use to ask for the music?'

'I assure you, Mr. Holdsworth, I am very sorry. I'll write at once to Frost.'

'Then I am afraid the parish will not be reformed as you promised last Christmas,' said the Vicar, turning, with a smile, to Mrs. Frost. 'We were to be civilized by weekly concerts in the school.'

'What were you to play, Louis?' said Mrs. Frost, laughing.

'I was to imitate all the birds in the air at once,' said Louis, beginning to chirp like a melee of sparrows, turning it into the croak of a raven, and breaking off suddenly with, 'I beg your pardon—I forgot it was Sunday! Indeed, Mr. Holdsworth, I can say no more than that I was a wretch not to remember. Next time I'll write it all down in the top of my hat, with a pathetic entreaty that if my hat be stolen, the thief shall fulfil the commissions, and punctually send in the bill to the Rev. W. B. Holdsworth!'

'I shall hardly run the risk,' said Mr. Holdsworth, smiling, as he parted with them, and disappeared within his clipped yew hedges.

'Poor, ill-used Mr. Holdsworth!' cried Aunt Catharine.

'Yes, it was base to forget the binding of that book,' said Louis, gravely. 'I wish I knew what amends to make.'

'You owe amends far more for making a present of a commission. I used to do the like, to save myself trouble, till I came down in the world, and then I found it had been a mere air de grand seigneur.'

'I should not dare to serve you or Jem so; but I thought the school was impersonal, and could receive a favour.'

'It is no favour, unless you clearly define where the commission ended and the gift began. Careless benefits oblige no one.'

Fitzjocelyn received his aunt's scoldings very prettily. His manner to her was a becoming mixture of the chivalrous, the filial, and the playful. Mary watched it as a new and pretty picture. All his confidence, too, seemed to be hers; but who could help pouring out his heart to the ever-indulgent, sympathizing Aunt Catharine? It was evidently the greatest treat to him to have her for his guest, and his attention to her extended even to the reading a sermon to her in the evening, to spare her eyes; a measure so entirely after Aunt Melicent's heart, that Mary decided that even she would not think her cousin so hopelessly fashionable.

Goodnatured he was, without doubt; for as the three ladies were sitting down to a sociable morning of work and reading aloud, he came in to say he was going to see after Tom Madison, and to ask if there were any commands for Northwold, with his checked shooting-jacket pockets so puffed out that his aunt began patting and inquiring. 'Provisions for the House Beautiful,' he said, as forth came on the one side a long rough brown yam. 'I saw it at a shop in London,' he said, 'and thought the Faithfull sisters would like to be reminded of their West Indian feasts.' And, 'to make the balance true,' he had in the other pocket a lambswool shawl of gorgeous dyes, with wools to make the like, and the receipt, in what he called 'female algebra,' the long knitting-pins under his arm like a riding-whip. He explained that he thought it would be a winter's work for Miss Salome to imitate it, and that she would succour half-a-dozen families with the proceeds; and Mrs. Ponsonby was pleased to hear him speak so affectionately of the two old maiden sisters. They were the nieces of an old gentleman to whom the central and handsomest house of Dynevor Terrace had been let. He had an annuity which had died with him, and they inherited very little but the furniture with which they had lived on in the same house, in hopes of lodgers, and paying rent to Mrs. Frost when they had any. There was a close friendship and perfect understanding between her and them, and, as she truly assured them, full and constant rent could hardly have done her as much good as their neighbourhood. Miss Mercy was the Sister of Charity of all Northwold; Miss Salome, who was confined to her chair by a complaint in her knee, knitted and made fancy-works, the sale of which furnished funds for her charities. She was highly educated, and had a great knowledge of natural history. Fitzjocelyn had given their abode the name of the House Beautiful, as being redolent of the essence of the Pilgrim's Progress; and the title was so fully accepted by their friends, that the very postman would soon know it. He lingered, discoursing on this topic, while Mary repacked his parcels, and his aunt gave him a message to Jane Beckett, to send the carpenter to No. 5 before Mary's visit of inspection; but she prophesied that he would forget; and, in fact, it was no good augury that he left the knitting-pins behind him on the table, and Mary was only just in time to catch him with them at the front door.

'Thank you, Mary—you are the universal memory,' he said. 'What rest you must give my father's methodical spirit! I saw you pile up all those Blackwoods of mine this morning, just as he was going to fall upon them.'

'If you saw it, I should have expected you to do it yourself,' said Mary, in her quaint downright manner.

'Never expect me to do what is expected,' answered he.

'Do you do that because it is not expected?' said Mary, feeling almost as if he were beyond the pale of reason, as she saw him adjusting a plant of groundsel in his cap.

'It is for the dicky-bird at my aunt's. There's no lack of it at the Terrace; but it is an old habit, and there always was an illusion that Ormersfield groundsel is a superior article.'

'I suppose that is why you grow go much.'

'Are you a gardener? Some day we will go to work, clear the place, and separate the botanical from the intrusive!'

'I should like it, of all things!'

'I'll send the horse round to the stable, and begin at once!' exclaimed Louis, all eagerness; but Mary demurred, as she had promised to read to her mother and aunt some of their old favourites, Madame de Sevigne's letters, and his attention flew off to his restless steed, which he wanted her to admire.

'My Yeomanry charger,' he said. 'We turn out five troopers. I hope you will be here when we go out, for going round to Northwold brought me into a direful scrape when I went to exhibit myself to the dear old Terrace world. My father said it was an unworthy ambition. What would he have thought, if he had seen Jane stroking me down with the brush on the plea of dust, but really on the principle of stroking a dog! Good old Jane! Have you seen her yet? Has she talked to you about Master Oliver?'

The horse became so impatient, that Mary had no time for more than a monosyllable, before Louis was obliged to mount and ride off; and he was seen no more till just before dinner, when, with a shade of French malice, Mrs. Frost inquired about Jane and the carpenter: she had seen the cap, still decorated with groundsel, lying in the hall, and had a shrewd suspicion, but the answer went beyond her expectations—'Ah!' he said, 'it is all the effect of the Norman mania!'

'What have you been doing? What is the matter?' she cried, alarmed.

'The matter is not with me, but with the magistrates.'

'My dear Louis, don't look so very wise and capable, or I shall think it a very bad scrape indeed! Pray tell me what you have been about.'

'You know Sir Gilbert Brewster and Mr. Shoreland are rabid about the little brook between their estates, of which each wishes to arrogate to himself the exclusive fishing. Their keepers watch like the Austrian guard on the Danube, in a life of perpetual assault and battery. Last Saturday, March 3rd, 1847, one Benjamin Hodgekin, aged fifteen, had the misfortune to wash his feet in the debateable water; the belligerent powers made common cause, and haled the wretch before the Petty Sessions. His mother met me. She lived in service here till she married a man at Marksedge, now dead. This poor boy is an admirable son, the main stay of the family, who must starve if he were imprisoned, and she declared, with tears in her eyes, that she could not bear for a child of hers to be sent to gaol, and begged me to speak to the gentlemen.' He started up with kindling eyes and vehement manner. 'I went to the Justice-room!'

'My dear! with the groundsel?'

'And the knitting-needles!'

On rushed the narration, unheeding trifles. 'There was the array: Mr. Calcott in the chair, and old Freeman, and Captain Shaw, and fat Sir Gilbert, and all the rest, met to condemn this wretched widow's son for washing his feet in a gutter!'

'Pray what said the indictment?' asked Mrs. Ponsonby.

'Oh, that he had killed an infant trout of the value of three farthings! Three giant keepers made oath to it, but I had his own mother's word that he was washing his feet!'

No one could help laughing, but Fitzjocelyn was far past perceiving any such thing. 'Urge what I would, they fined him. I talked to old Brewster! I appealed to his generosity, if there be room for generosity about a trout no bigger than a gudgeon! I talked to Mr. Calcott, who, I thought, had more sense, but Justice Shallow would have been more practicable! No one took a rational view but Ramsbotham of the factory, a very sensible man, with excellent feeling. When it is recorded in history, who will believe that seven moral, well-meaning men agreed in condemning a poor lad of fifteen to a fine of five shillings, costs three-and-sixpence—a sum he could no more pay than I the National Debt, and with the alternative of three months' imprisonment, branding and contaminating for life, and destroying all self-respect? I paid the fine, so there is one act of destruction the less on the heads of the English squirearchy.'

'Act of destruction!'

'The worst destruction is to blast a man's character because the love of adventure is strong within him—!'

He was at this point when Lord Ormersfield entered, and after his daily civil ceremonious inquiries of the ladies whether they had walked or driven out, he turned to his son, saying, 'I met Mr. Calcott just now, and heard from him that he had been sorry to convict a person in whom you took interest, a lad from Marksedge. What did you know of him?'

'I was prompted by common justice and humanity,' said Louis. 'My protection was claimed for the poor boy, as the son of an old servant of ours.'

'Indeed! I think you must have been imposed on. Mr. Calcott spoke of the family as notorious poachers.'

'Find a poor fellow on the wrong side of a hedge, and not a squire but will swear that he is a hardened ruffian!'

'Usually with reason,' said the Earl. 'Pray when did this person's parents allege that they had been in my service?'

'It was his mother. Her name was Blackett, and she left us on her marriage with one of the Hodgekins.'

Lord Ormersfield rang the bell, and Frampton, the butler and confidential servant, formed on his own model, made his appearance.

'Do you know whether a woman of the name of Blackett ever lived in service here?'

'Not that I am aware of, my Lord. I will ascertain the fact.'

In a few moments Frampton returned. 'Yes, my Lord, a girl named Blackett was once engaged to help in the scullery, but was discharged for dishonesty at the end of a month.'

'Did not Frampton know that that related to me?' said Louis, sotto voce, to his aunt. 'Did he not trust that he was reducing me from a sea anemone to a lump of quaking jelly?'

So far from this consummation, Lord Fitzjocelyn looked as triumphant as Don Quixote liberating Gines de Pasamonte. He and his father might have sat for illustrations of

'Youth is full of pleasance,
Age is full of care,'

as they occupied the two ends of the dinner-table; the Earl concealing anxiety and vexation, under more than ordinary punctilious politeness;

the Viscount doing his share of the honours with easy, winning grace and attention, and rattling on in an under-tone of lively conversation with Aunt Catharine. Mary was silently amazed at her encouraging him; but perhaps she could not help spoiling him the more, because there was a storm impending. At least, as soon as she was in the drawing-room, she became restless and nervous, and said that she wished his father could see that speaking sternly to him never did any good; besides, it was mere inconsiderateness, the excess of chivalrous compassion.

Mrs. Ponsonby said she thought young men's ardour more apt to be against than for the poacher.

'I must confess,' said Aunt Catherine, with all the reluctance of a high-spirited Dynevor,—'I must confess that Louis is no sportsman! He was eager about it once, till he had become a good shot; and then it lost all zest for him, and he prefers his own vagaries. He never takes a gun unless James drives him out; and, oddly enough, his father is quite vexed at his indifference, as if it were not manly. If his father would only understand him!'

The specimen of that day had almost made Mrs. Ponsonby fear that there was nothing to understand, and that only dear Aunt Kitty's affection could perceive anything but amiable folly, and it was not much better when the young gentleman reappeared, looking very debonnaire, and, sitting down beside Mrs. Frost, said, in a voice meant for her alone—'Henry IV; Part II., the insult to Chief Justice Gascoigne. My father will presently enter and address you:

'O that it could be proved
That some night-tripping fairy had exchanged
In cradle-cloths our children as they lay,—
Call'd yours Fitzjocelyn—mine, Frost Dynevor!'

'For shame, Louis! I shall have to call you Fitzjocelyn! You are behaving very ill.'

'Insulting the English constitution in the person of seven squires.'

'Don't, my dear! It was the very thing to vex your father that you should have put yourself in such a position.'

'Bearding the Northwold bench with a groundsel plume and a knitting-needle:

'With a needle for a sword, and a thimble for a hat,
Wilt thou fight a traverse with the Castle cat?'

The proper champion in such a cause, since 'What cat's averse to fish?''

'No, Louis dear,' said his aunt, struggling like a girl to keep her countenance; 'this is no time for nonsense. One would think you had no feeling for your father.'

'My dear aunt, I can't go to gaol like Prince Hal. I do assure you, I did not assault the bench with the knitting-pins. What am I to do?'

'Not set at nought your father's displeasure.'

'I can't help it,' said he, almost sadly, though half smiling. 'What would become of me if I tried to support the full weight? Interfering with institutions, ruining reputation, blasting bulwarks, patronizing poachers, vituperating venerated—'

'Quite true,' cried Aunt Catherine, with spirit. 'You know you had no business there, lecturing a set of men old enough to be your grandfathers, and talking them all to death, no doubt.'

'Well, Aunt Kitty, if oppression maddens the wise, what must it do to the foolish?'

'If you only allow that it was foolish—'

'No; I had rather know whether it was wrong. I believe I was too eager, and not respectful enough to the old squire: and, on reflection, it might have been a matter of obedience to my father, not to interfere with the prejudices of true-born English magistrates. Yes, I was wrong: I would have owned it sooner, but for the shell he fired over my head. And for the rest, I don't know how to repent of having protested against tyranny.'

There was something redeeming in the conclusion, and it was a comfort, for it was impossible to retain anger with one so gently, good-humouredly polite and attentive.

A practical answer to the champion was not long in coming. He volunteered the next day to walk to Northwold with Mrs. Frost and Mary, who wanted to spend the morning in selecting a house in Dynevor Terrace, and to be fetched home by-and-by, when Mrs. Ponsonby took her airing. Two miles seemed nothing to Aunt Catharine, who accepted her nephew's arm for love, and not for need, as he discoursed of all the animals that might be naturalized in England, obtained from Mary an account of the llamas of the Andes, and rode off upon a scheme of an importation to make the fortune of Marksedge by a manufacture of Alpaca umbrellas.

Meantime, he must show the beautiful American ducks which he hoped to naturalize on the pond near the keeper's lodge: but, whistle and call as he would, nothing showed itself but screaming Canada geese. He ran round, pulled out a boat half full of water, and, with a foot on each side, paddled across to a bushy island in the centre,—but in vain. The keeper's wife, who had the charge over them, came out: 'Oh, my Lord, I am so sorry! They pretty ducks!'

'Ha! the foxes?'

'I wish it was, my Lord; but it is they poachers out at Marksedge that are so daring, they would come anywheres—and you see the ducks would roost up in the trees, and you said I was not to shut 'em up at night. My master was out up by Beech hollow; I heerd a gun, and looked out; I seen a man and a boy—I'd take my oath it was young Hodgekin. They do say Nanny Hodgekin, she as was one of the Blacketts, whose husband was transported, took in two ducks next morning to Northwold. Warren couldn't make nothing of it; but if ever he meets that Hodgekin again, he says he *shall* catch it!'

'Well, Mrs. Warren, it can't be helped—thank you for the good care you took of the poor ducks,' said Louis, kindly; and as he walked on through the gate, he gave a long sigh, and said, 'My dainty ducks! So there's an end of them, and all their tameness!' But the smile could not but return. 'It is lucky the case does not come before the bench! but really that woman deserves a medal for coolness!'

'I suppose,' said Mary, 'she could have paid the fine with the price of the ducks.'

'Ah! the beauties! I wish Mr. Hodgekin had fallen on the pheasants instead! However, I am thankful he and Warren did not come to a collision about them. I am always expecting that, having made those Marksedge people thieves, murder will be the next consequence.'

A few seconds sufficed to bring the ludicrous back. 'How pat it comes! Mary, did you prime Mrs. Warren, or did Frampton?'

'I believe you had rather laugh at yourself than at any one else,' exclaimed his aunt, who felt baffled at having thrown away her compassion.

'Of course. One knows how much can be borne. Why, Mary, has that set you studying,—do you dissent?'

'I was thinking whether it is the best thing to be always ready to laugh at oneself,' said Mary. 'Does it always help in mending?'

'"Don't care" came to a bad end,' said Louis; 'but on the other hand, care killed a cat—so there are two sides to the question.'

While Mary was feeling disappointed at his light tone, he changed it to one that was almost mournful. 'The worst of it is, that 'don't care' is my refuge. Whatever I do care about is always thwarted by Frampton or somebody, and being for ever thrown over, I have only to fall as softly as I can.'

'You know, my dear,' said Mrs. Frost, 'that your father has no command of means to gratify you.'

'There are means enough for ourselves,' said Louis; 'that is the needful duty. What merely personal indulgence did I ever ask for that was refused me?'

'If that is all you have to complain of, I can't pity you,' said Mary.

'Listen, Mary. Let me wish for a horse, there it is! Let me wish for a painted window, we can't afford it, though, after all, it would not eat; but horses are an adjunct of state and propriety. So again, the parish feasted last 18th of January, because I came of age, and it was *proper*; while if I ask that our people may be released from work on Good Friday or Ascension Day, it is thought outrageous.'

'If I remember right, my dear,' interposed his aunt, 'you wanted no work to be done on any saint's-day. Was there not a scheme that Mr. Holdsworth called the cricket cure!'

'That may yet be. No one knows the good a few free days would do the poor. But I developed my plan too rapidly! I'll try again for their church-going on Good Friday.'

'I think you ought to succeed there.'

'I know how it will be. My father will ring, propound the matter to Frampton; the answer will be, 'Quite impracticable, my Lord,' and there will be an end of it.'

'Perhaps not. At least it will have been considered,' said Mary.

'True,' said Louis; 'but you little know what it is to have a Frampton! If he be a fair sample of prime ministers, no wonder Princes of Wales go into the opposition!'

'I thought Frampton was a very valuable superior servant.'

'Exactly so. That is the worst of it. He is supreme authority, and well deserves it. When la Grande Mademoiselle stood before the gates of Orleans calling to the sentinel to open them, he never stirred a step, but replied merely with profound bows. That is my case. I make a request, am answered, 'Yes, my Lord;' find no results, repeat the process, and at the fourth time am silenced with, 'Quite impracticable my Lord.''

'Surely Frampton is respectful?'

'It is his very essence. He is a thorough aristocrat, respecting himself, and therefore respecting all others as they deserve. He respects a Viscount Fitzjocelyn as an appendage nearly as needful as the wyverns on each side of the shield; but as to the individual holding that office, he regards him much as he would one of the wyverns with a fool's-cap on.'

And with those words, Fitzjocelyn had sprung into the hedge to gather the earliest willow-catkins, and came down dilating on their silvery, downy buds and golden blossoms, and on the pleasure they would give Miss Faithfull, till Mary, who had been beginning to compassionate him, was almost vexed to think her pity wasted on grievances of mere random talk.

Warm and kindly was his greeting of his aunt's good old servant, Jane Beckett, whom Mary was well pleased to meet as one of the kind friends of her childhood. The refinement that was like an atmosphere around Mrs. Frost, seemed to have extended even to her servants; for Jane, though she could hardly read, and carried her accounts in her head, had manners of a gentle warmth and propriety that had a grace of their own, even in her racy, bad grammar; and there was no withstanding the merry smile that twitched up one side of her mouth, while her eyes twinkled in the varied moods prompted by an inexhaustible fund of good temper, sympathy, and affection, but the fulness of her love was for the distant 'Master Oliver,' whose young nursery-maid she had been. Her eyes winked between tears and smiles when she heard that Miss Mary had seen him but five months ago, and she inquired after him, gloried in his prosperity, and talked of his coming home, with far less reserve than his mother had done.

Mary was struck, also, with the pretty, modest looks of the little underling, and remarked on them as they proceeded to the inspection of the next house.

'Yes,' said Louis, 'Charlotte is something between a wood sorrel and a five-plume moth. Tom Madison, as usual, shows exquisite taste. She is a perfect Lady of Eschalott.'

'Now, Louis!' said his aunt, standing still, and really looking annoyed, 'you know I cannot encourage any such thing. Poor little Charlotte is an orphan, and I am all the more responsible for her.'

'There's a chivalry in poor Tom—'

'Nonsense!' said his aunt, as if resolved not to hear him out, because afraid of herself. 'Don't say any more about it. I wish I had never allowed of his bringing your messages.'

'Who set him down in the kitchen to drink a cup of beer?' said Louis, mischievously.

'Ah! well! one comfort is, that girls never care for boys of the same age,' replied Aunt Catharine, as she turned the key, and admitted them into No. 7; when Fitzjocelyn confused Mary's judgment with his recommendations, till Aunt Catharine pointing out the broken shutter, and asking if he would not have been better employed in fetching the carpenter, than in hectoring the magistrates, he promised to make up for it, fetched a piece of wood and James's tools, and was quickly at work, his Aunt only warning him, that if he lost Jem's tools she would not say it was her fault.

By the time Mary's imagination had portrayed what paper, paint, furniture, and habitation might make the house, and had discerned how to arrange a pretty little study in case of her father's return; he had completed the repair in a workmanlike manner, and putting two fingers to his cap, asked, 'Any other little job for me, ma'am?'

Of course, he forgot the tools, till shamed by Mary's turning back for them, and after a merry luncheon, served up in haste by Jane, they betook themselves to Number 8, where the Miss Faithfulls were seated at a dessert of hard biscuits and water, of neither of which they ever partook: they only adhered to the hereditary institution of sitting for twenty minutes after dinner with their red and purple doileys before them.

Mary seemed to herself carried back fourteen years, and to understand why her childish fancy had always believed Christiana's Mercy a living character, when she found herself in the calm, happy little household. The chief change was that she must now bend down, instead of reaching up, to receive the kind embraces. Even the garments seemed unchanged, the dark merino gowns, black silk aprons, white cap-ribbons, the soft little Indian shawl worn by the elder sister, the ribbon bow by the younger, distinctions that used to puzzle her infant speculation, not aware that the coloured bow was Miss Mercy's ensign of youth, and that its absence would have made Miss Salome feel aged indeed. The two sisters were much alike—but the younger was the more spare, shrivelled up into a cheery nonpareil, her bloom changed into something quite as fresh and healthful, and her blithe tripping step always active, except when her fingers were nimbly taking their turn. Miss Salome had become more plump, her cheek was smoother and paler, her eye more placid, her air that of a patient invalid, and her countenance more intellectual than her sister's. She said less about their extreme enjoyment of the yam, and while Mrs. Frost and Mary held counsel with Miss Mercy on servants and furniture, there was a talk on entomology going on between her and Fitzjocelyn.

It was very pretty to see him with the old ladies, so gently attentive, without patronizing, and they, though evidently doting on him, laughing at him, and treating him like a spoilt child. He insisted on Mary's seeing their ordinary sitting room, which nature had intended for a housekeeper's room, but which ladylike inhabitants had rendered what he called the very 'kernel of the House Beautiful.' There were the stands of flowers in the window; the bullfinch scolding in his cage, the rare old shells and china on the old-fashioned cabinets that Mary so well remembered; and the silk patchwork sofa-cover, the old piano, and Miss Faithfull's arm chair by the fire, her little table with her beautiful knitting, and often a flower or insect that she was copying; for she still drew nicely; and she smiled and consented, as Louis pulled out her portfolios, life-long collections of portraits of birds, flowers, or insects. Her knitting found a sale at the workshop, where the object was well known, and the proceeds were diffused by her sister, and whether she deserved her name might be guessed by the basket of poor people's stores beside her chair.

Miss Mercy was well known in every dusky Northwold lane or alley, where she always found or made a welcome for herself. The kindly counsel and ready hand were more potent than far larger means without them.

Such neighbours were in themselves a host, and Mary and her mother both felt as if they had attained a region of unwonted tranquillity and repose, when they had agreed to rent No. 5, Dynevor Terrace, from the ensuing Lady-day, and to take possession when carpenters and upholsterers should have worked their will.

Louis was half-way home when he exclaimed, 'There! I have missed Tom Madison a second time. When shall I ever remember him at the right time?'

Little did Louis guess the effect his neglect was taking! Charlotte Arnold might have told, for Mrs. Martha had brought in stories of his unsteadiness and idle habits that confirmed her in her obedience to Jane. She never went out alone in his leisure hours; never looked for him in returning from church—alas! that was not the place to look for him now. And yet she could not believe him such a very bad boy as she was told he had become.

CHAPTER V
THE TWO MINISTERS

'The creature's neither one nor t'other.
I caught the animal last night,
And viewed him o'er by candle-light;
I marked him well, 'twas black as jet.
You stare, but sirs, I've got him yet,
And can produce him.' 'Pray, sir, do;
I'll lay my life the thing is blue.'
'And I'll be sworn, that when you've seen
The reptile, you'll pronounce him green.'
'Well, then, at once to end the doubt,'
Replies the man, 'I'll turn him out;
And when before your eyes I've set him,
If you don't find him black, I'll eat him.'
He said—then, full before their sight
Produced the beast, and lo! 'twas white!
    MERRICK.

Mrs. Ponsonby had seen in the tropics birds of brilliant hues, that even, whilst the gazer pronounced them all one beaming tint of gorgeous purple, would give one flutter, and in another light would flash with golden green or fiery scarlet. No less startling and unexpected were the aspects of Lord Fitzjocelyn, 'Every thing by starts, and nothing long;' sometimes absorbed in study, sometimes equally ardent over a childish game; wild about philanthropic plans, and apparently forgetting them the instant a cold word had fallen on them; attempting everything, finishing nothing; dipping into every kind of book, and forsaking it after a cursory glance; ever busy, yet ever idle; full of desultory knowledge, ranging through all kinds of reading and natural history, and still more full of talk. This last was perhaps his most decided gift. To any one, of whatever degree, he would talk, he could hardly have been silent ten minutes with any human being, except Frampton or his father, and whether deep reflections or arrant nonsense came out of his mouth, seemed an even chance, though both alike were in the same soft low voice, and with the same air of quaint pensive simplicity.

He was exceedingly provoking, and yet there was no being provoked with him!

He was so sincere, affectionate, and obliging, that not to love him was impossible, yet that love only made his faults more annoying, and Mrs. Ponsonby could well understand his father's perpetual restless anxiety, for his foibles were exactly of the sort most likely to tease such a man as the Earl, and the most positively unsatisfactory part of his character was the insouciance that he displayed when his trifling or his wild projects had given umbrage. Yet, even here, she could not but feel a hope, such as it was, that the carelessness might be the effect of want of sympathy and visible affection from his father, whose very anxiety made him the more unbending; and that, what a worse temper might have resented, rendered a good one gaily reckless and unheeding.

She often wondered whether she should try to give a hint—but Lord Ormersfield seemed to dread leading to the subject, although on all else that interested him he came to her as in old times, and seemed greatly refreshed and softened by her companionship.

An old friend and former fellow-minister had proposed spending a night at Ormersfield. He was the person whom the Earl most highly esteemed, and, in his own dignified way, he was solicitous that the household should be in more than usually perfect order, holding a long conference with the man of whom he was sure, Frampton. Would that he could have been equally sure of his son! He looked at him almost wistfully several times during breakfast, and at last, as they rose, gave an exhortation 'that he would be punctual to dinner at half-past seven, which would give him ample time, and he hoped he would be—' He paused for a word, and his son supplied it. 'On my good behaviour, I understand.' With that he walked off, leaving Lord Ormersfield telling Mrs. Ponsonby that it was the first introduction, as he had 'for various reasons' thought it undesirable to bring Fitzjocelyn early to London, and betraying his own anxiety as to the impression he might produce on Sir Miles Oakstead. His own perplexity and despondency showed themselves in his desire to view his son with the eyes of others, and he also thought the tenor of Fitzjocelyn's future life might be coloured by his friend's opinion.

Evening brought the guest. Mrs. Ponsonby was not well enough to appear at dinner, but Mary and Mrs. Frost, pleased to see an historical character, were in the drawing-room, enjoying Sir Miles's agreeable conversation, until they caught certain misgivings reflected in each other's looks, as time wore on and nothing had been seen or heard of Louis. The half-hour struck; the Earl waited five minutes, then rang the bell. 'Is Lord Fitzjocelyn come in?'

'No, my Lord.'

'Bring in the dinner.'

Mary longed to fly in search of him, and spare further vexation. She had assumed all an elder sister's feelings, and suffered for him as she used to do, when he was in disgrace and would not heed it. She heard no more of the conversation, and was insensible to the honour of going in to dinner with the late Secretary of State, as she saw the empty place at the table.

The soup was over, when she was aware of a step in the hall, and beside her stood a grey figure, bespattered with mud, shading his eyes with his hand, as if dazzled by the lights. 'I beg your pardon,' were the words, 'but I was obliged to go to Northwold. I have shot a rose-coloured pastor!'

'Shot him!' cried Mary. 'Was he much hurt?'

'Killed! I took him to Miss Faithfull, to be sketched before he is stuffed—'

A clearer view of the company, a wave of the hand from the Earl, and the young gentleman was gone. Next he opened the library door, saying, 'Here's my pretty behaviour!'

'Louis! what is the matter?' cried Mrs. Ponsonby.

'I entirely forgot the right honourable, and marched into the dining-room to tell Aunt Catharine that I have killed a rose-coloured pastor.'

'Killed what?'

'A bird, hardly ever seen in England. I spied him in the fir-wood, went to Warren for a gun, brought him down, and walked on to the House Beautiful, where Miss Faithfull was enchanted. She will copy him, and send him to the bird-stuffer. I looked in to give directions, and old Jenyns was amazed; he never knew one shot here before, so early in the year too. He says we must send the account to the Ornithological—'

'Do you know how wet you are? exclaimed Mrs. Ponsonby, seeing rivulets dropping from his coat.

'I see. It rained all the way home, and was so dark, I could not see the footpath; and when I came in, my eyes were blinded by the light, and my head so full of the pastor, that the other minister never occurred to me, and remains under the impression that I have confessed a sacrilegious murder.'

'You really are incorrigible!' cried Mrs. Ponsonby. 'Why are you not dressing for dinner?'

'Because you are going to give me a cup of your tea.'

'Certainly not. I shall begin to think you purposely mortified your father, when you know he wanted you to be reasonable.'

'The lower species never show off well to strangers,' said Fitzjocelyn, coolly; but, as he lighted his candle, he added, with more candour, 'I beg your pardon—indeed I did not do this on purpose, but don't say anything about appearances—there's something in me that is sure to revolt.'

So noiselessly that the moment was unknown, the vacant chair was filled by a gentleman irreproachably attired, his face glowing with exercise, or with what made him very debonnaire and really silent, dining rapidly and unobtrusively, and never raising his eyes even to his aunt, probably intending thus to remain all the evening; but presently Sir Miles turned to him and said, 'Pray satisfy my curiosity. Who is the rose-coloured pastor?'

Louis raised his eyes, and meeting a pleasing, sensible face, out beamed his arch look of suppressed fun as he answered, 'He is not at all clerical. He is otherwise called the rose-coloured ouzel or starling.'

'Whence is that other startling name?'

'From his attending flocks of sheep, on the same mission as jackdaws fulfil here—which likewise have an ecclesiastical reputation—

'A great frequenter of the church.''

Fearing alike nonsense and ornithology, Lord Ormersfield changed the subject, and Louis subsided, but when the gentlemen came into the drawing-room, Mrs. Ponsonby was surprised to see him taking a fair share, and no more, of the conversation. Some information had been wanted about the terms of labour in the mining districts, and Louis's visit to Illershall enabled him to throw light on the subject, with much clearness and accuracy. Sir Miles had more literature than Lord Ormersfield, and was more used to young men; and he began to draw Fitzjocelyn out, with complete success. Louis fully responded to the touch, and without a notion that he was showing himself to the best advantage, he yielded to the pleasure, and for once proved of what he was capable—revealing unawares an unusual amount of intelligence and observation, and great power of expression. Not even his aunt had ever seen him appear so much like a superior man, and the only alloy was his father's, ill-repressed dread lest he should fall on dangerous ground, and commit himself either to his wildly philanthropical or extravagantly monarchical views, whichever might happen to be in the ascendant. However, such shoals were not approached, nor did Louis ever plunge out of his depth. The whole of his manner and demeanour were proofs that, in his case, much talk sprang from exuberance of ideas, not from self-conceit.

He was equally good in the morning: he had risen early to hunt up some information which Sir Miles wanted, and the clearness and readiness with which he had found it were wonderful. The guest was delighted with him; gave him a warm invitation to Oakstead, and on being left alone with Mrs. Ponsonby, whom he had formerly known, expressed his admiration of his friend's son—as a fine, promising young man, of great ability and originality, and, what was still more remarkable, of most simple, natural manners, perfectly free from conceit. He seemed the more amazed, when he found, what he would hardly believe, that Fitzjocelyn was twenty-one, and had nearly finished his university education.

The liking was mutual. No sooner had Sir Miles departed, than Louis came to the library in a rapture, declaring that here was the refreshing sight of a man unspoilt by political life, which usually ate out the hearts of people.

Mary smiled at this, and told him that he was talking 'like an old statesman weary of the world.'

'One may be weary of the world beforehand as well as after,' said he.

'That does not seem worth while,' said Mary.

'No,' he said, 'but one's own immediate look-out may not be flattering, whatever the next turn may bring;' and he took up the newspaper, and began to turn it over. ''As butler—as single-handed man—as clerk and accountant.' There, those are the lucky men, with downright work, and some one to work for. Or, just listen to this!' and he plunged into a story of some heroic conduct during a shipwreck. While he was reading it aloud, with kindling eyes and enthusiastic interest, his father opened the door. 'Louis,' he said, 'if you are doing nothing, I should be obliged if you would make two copies of this letter.'

Louis glanced at the end of what he was reading, laid the paper down, and opened a blotting-book.

'You had better come into the study, or you will not write correctly.'

'I can write, whatever goes on.'

'I particularly wish this to be legible and accurate. You have begun too low down.'

Louis took another sheet.

'That pen is not fit to write with.'

'The pens are delusions,' said Louis, trying them round, in an easy, idle way: 'I never could mend a quill! How is this steel one? Refuses to recognise the purpose of his existence. Aunt Catherine, do you still forbid steel pens in your school? If so, it must be the solitary instance. How geese must cackle blessings on the inventor! He should have a testimonial—a silver inkstand representing the goose that laid the golden eggs,—and all writing-masters should subscribe. Ha! where did this pen come from? Mary, were you the bounteous mender! A thousand thanks.'

If Louis fretted his father by loitering and nonsense, his father was no less trying by standing over him with advice and criticisms which would have driven most youths beyond patience, but which he bore with constant good-humour, till his father returned to the study, when he exclaimed, 'Now, Mary, if you like to finish the wreck, it will not interrupt me. This is mere machine-work.'

'Thank you,' said Mary; 'I should like it better afterwards. Do you think I might do one copy for you? Or would it not suit Lord Ormersfield?'

Louis made polite demurs, but she overruled them and began.

He stretched himself, took up his Times, and skimmed the remaining incidents of the shipwreck, till he was shamed by seeing Mary half-way down the first page, when he resumed his pen, overtook her, and then relapsed into talk, till Mrs. Frost fairly left the room, to silence him.

As the two copies were completed, Lord Ormersfield returned; and Mary, with many apologies, presented her copy, and received most gracious thanks and compliments on her firm, clear writing, a vexation to her rather than otherwise, since 'Fitzjocelyn' was called to account for dubious scrawls, errors, and erasures.

He meekly took another sheet, consoling himself, however, by saying, 'I warn you that pains will only make it Miss Fanny.'

'What do you mean?'

As if glad to be instigated, he replied, 'Did you never hear of my signature being mistaken by an ingenious person, who addressed his answer to 'Miss Fanny Jocelyn? Why, Fanny has been one of Jem's regular names for me ever since! I have the envelope somewhere as a curiosity. I'll show it to you, Mary.'

'You seem to be proud of it!' exclaimed his father, nearly out of patience. 'Pray tell me whether you intend to copy this creditably or not.'

'I will endeavour, but the Fates must decide. I can scrawl, or, with pains, I can imitate Miss Fanny; but the other alternative only comes in happy moments.'

'Do you mean that you cannot write well if you choose?'

'It is like other arts—an inspiration. Dogberry was deep when he said it came by nature.'

'Then make no more attempts. No. That schoolgirl's niggle is worse than the first.'

'Fanny, as I told you,' said Louis, looking vacantly up in resigned despair, yet not without the lurking expression of amusement, 'I will try again.'

'No, I thank you. I will have no more time wasted.'

Louis passively moved to the window, where he exclaimed that he saw Aunt Catharine sunning herself in the garden, and must go and help her.

'Did you ever see anything like that?' cried Lord Ormersfield, thoroughly moved to displeasure.

'There was at least good-humour,' said Mrs. Ponsonby. 'Pardon me, there was almost as much to try his temper as yours.'

'He is insensible!'

'I think not. A word from Aunt Catharine rules him.'

'Though you counselled it, Mary, I doubt whether her training has answered. Henry Frost should have been a warning.'

Mary found herself blundering in her new copy, and retreated with it to the study, while her mother made answer: 'I do not repent of my advice. The affection between him and Aunt Catherine is the greatest blessing to him.'

'Poor boy!' said his father, forgetting his letters as he stood pondering. Mrs. Ponsonby seized the moment for reporting Sir Miles's opinion, but the Earl did not betray his gratification. 'First sight!' he said. 'Last night and this afternoon he is as unlike as these are,' and he placed before her Louis's unlucky copies, together with a letter written in a bold, manly hand. 'Three different men might have written these! And he pretends he cannot write like this, if he please!'

'I have no doubt it is to a certain extent true. Yes, absolutely true. You do not conceive the influence that mood has on some characters before they have learnt to master themselves. I do not mean temper, but the mere frame of spirits. Even sense of restraint will often take away the actual power from a child, or where there is not a strong will.'

'You are right!' said he, becoming rigid as if with pain. 'He is a child! You have not yet told me what you think of him. You need not hesitate. No one sees the likeness more plainly than I do.'

'It is strong externally,' she said; 'but I think it is more external than real, more temperament than character.'

'You are too metaphysical for me, Mary;' and he would fain have smiled.

'I want you to be hopeful. Half the object would be attained if you were, and he really deserves that you should.'

'He will not let me. If I hope at one moment, I am disappointed the next.'

'And how? By nothing worse than boyishness. You confirm what my aunt tells me, that there has never been a serious complaint of him.'

'Never. His conduct has always been blameless; but every tutor has said the same—that he has no application, and allows himself to be surpassed by any one of moderate energy!'

'Blameless conduct! How many fathers would give worlds to be able to give such a character of a son!'

'There are faults that are the very indications of a manly spirit,' began the Earl, impatiently. 'Not that I mean that I wish—he has never given me any trouble—but just look at James Frost, and you would see what I mean! There's energy in him—fire—independence; you feel there is substance in him, and like him the better for having a will and way of his own.'

'So, I think, has Louis; but it is so often thwarted, that it sinks away under the sense of duty and submission.'

'If there were any consistency or reason in his fancies, they would not give way so easily; but it is all talk, all extravagant notions—here one day, gone the next. Not a spark of ambition!'

'Ambition is not so safe a spark that we should wish to see it lighted.'

'A man must wish to see his son hold his proper station, and aim high! No one can be satisfied to see him a trifler.'

'I have been trying to find out why he trifles. As far as I can see, he has no ambition, and I do not think his turn will be for a life like yours. His bent is towards what is to do good to others. He would make an admirable country gentleman.'

'A mere farmer, idling away his time in his fields.'

'No; doing infinite good by example and influence, and coming forward whenever duty required it. Depend upon it, the benefit to others is the impulse which can work on Louis, not personal ambition. Birth has already given him more than he values.'

'You may be right,' said Lord Ormersfield, 'but it is hard to see so many advantages thrown away, and what sometimes seems like so much ability wasted. But who can tell? he is never the same for an hour together.'

'May it not be for want of a sphere of wholesome action?'

'He is not fit for it, Mary. You know I resolved that the whole burthen of our losses should fall on me; I made it my object that he should not suffer, and should freely have whatever I had at the same age. Everything is cleared at last. I could give him the same income as I started in life with; but he is so reckless of money, that I cannot feel justified in putting it into his hands. Say what I will, not a vacation occurs but he comes to tell me of some paltry debt of ten or fifteen pounds.'

'He comes to tell you! Nay, never say he has no resolution! Such debts as those, what are they compared with other young men's, of which they do not tell their fathers?'

'If he were like other youths, I should know how to deal with him. But you agree with me, he is not fit to have a larger sum in his hands.'

'Perhaps not; he is too impulsive and inexperienced. If you were to ask me how to make it conduce to his happiness, I should say, lay out more on the estate, so as to employ more men, and make improvements in which he would take interest.'

'I cannot make him care for the estate. Last winter, when he came of age, I tried to explain the state of affairs; but he was utterly indifferent—would not trouble himself to understand the papers he was to sign, and made me quite ashamed of such an exhibition before Richardson.'

'I wish I could defend him! And yet—you will think me unreasonable, but I do believe that if he had thought the welfare of others was concerned, he would have attended more.'

'Umph!'

'I am not sure that it is not his good qualities that make him so hard to deal with. The want of selfishness and vanity seem to take away two common springs of action, but I do believe that patience will bring out something much higher when you have found the way to reach it.'

'That I certainly have not, if it be there!'

'To cultivate his sympathies with you,' said Mrs. Ponsonby, hesitating, and not venturing to look into his face.

'Enough, Mary,' he said, hastily. You said the like to me once before.'

'But,' said Mrs. Ponsonby, firmly, '*here* there is a foundation to work on. There are affections that only need to be drawn out to make you happy, and him—not, perhaps, what you now wish, but better than you wish.'

His face had become hard as he answered, 'Thank you, Mary; you have always meant the best. You have always been kind to me, and to all belonging to me.'

Her heart ached for the father and son, understanding each other so little, and paining each other so much, and she feared that the Earl's mind had been too much cramped, and his feelings too much chilled, for such softening on his part as could alone, as it seemed, prevent Louis from being estranged, and left to his naturally fickle and indolent disposition.

Mary had in the mean time completed her copies, and left them on the Earl's table; and wishing neither to be thanked nor contrasted with Louis, she put on her bonnet, to go in search of Aunt Catharine. Not finding her in the garden, she decided on visiting old Gervas and his wife, who had gladly caught at her offer of reading to them. The visit over, she returned by the favourite path above Ferny dell, gathering primroses, and meditating how to stir up Louis to finish off his rocky steps, and make one piece of work complete. She paused at the summit of them, and was much inclined to descend and examine what was wanting, when she started at hearing a rustling beneath, then a low moan and an attempt at a call. The bushes and a projecting rock cut off her view; but, in some trepidation, she called out, 'Is any one there?' Little did she expect the answer—

'It is I—Fitzjocelyn. Come!—I have had a fall.'

'I'm coming—are you hurt?' she cried, as with shaking limbs she prepared to begin the descent.

'Not that way,' he called; 'it gave way—go to the left.'

She was almost disobeying; but, recalling herself to thought, she hurried along the top till the bank became practicable, and tore her way through brake and brier, till she could return along the side of the stream.

Horror-struck, she perceived that a heavy stone had given way and rolled down, bearing Louis with it, to the bottom, where he lay, ghastly and helpless. She called to him; and he tried to raise himself, but sank back. 'Mary! is it you? I thought I should have died here,' he said; as she knelt by him, exclaiming, 'Oh, Louis! Louis! what a dreadful fall!'

'It is my fault,' he eagerly interrupted. 'I am glad it has happened to no one else.'

'And you are terribly hurt! I must go for help! but what can I do for you? Would you like some water?'

'Water! Oh! I have heard it all this time gurgling there!'

She filled his cap, and bathed his face, apparently to his great relief, and she ventured to ask if he had been long there.

'Very long!' he said. 'I must have fainted after I got the stone off my foot, so I missed Gervas going by. I thought no one else would come near. Thank God!'

Mary almost grew sick as she saw how dreadfully his left ankle had been crushed by a heavy stone; and her very turning towards it made him shudder, and say, 'Don't touch me! I am shattered all over.'

'I am afraid I should only hurt you,' she said, with difficulty controlling herself. 'I had better fetch some one.'

He did not know how to be left again; but the damp chilliness of his hands made her the more anxious to procure assistance, and, after spreading her shawl over him, she made the utmost speed out of the thicket. As she emerged, she saw Lord Ormersfield riding with his groom, and her scream and sign arrested him; but, by the time they met, she could utter nothing but 'Louis!'

'Another accident!' was the almost impatient answer.

'He is dreadfully hurt!' she said, sobbing and breathless. 'His foot is crushed! He has been there this hour!'

The alarm was indeed given. The Earl seemed about to rush away without knowing whither; and she had absolutely to withhold him, while, summoning her faculties, she gave directions to Poynings. Then she let him draw her on, too fast for speaking, until they reached the spot where Louis lay, so spent with pain and cold, that he barely opened his eyes at their voices, made no distinct answers as to his hurts, and shrank and moaned when his father would have raised him.

Mary contrived to place his head on her lap, bathed his forehead and chafed his hands, while Lord Ormersfield stood watching him with looks of misery, or paced about, anxiously looking for the servants.

They came at last, all too soon for poor Louis, who suffered terribly in the transport, and gave few tokens of consciousness, except a cry now and then extorted by a rougher movement.

None of the household, scarcely even Mrs. Frost, seemed at first to be able to believe that Lord Fitzjocelyn could really have hurt himself seriously. 'Again!' was the first word of every one, for his many slight accidents were treated like crying 'Wolf;' but Frampton himself looked perfectly pale and shocked when he perceived how the matter really stood; and neither he nor

Lord Ormersfield was half so helpful as Mrs. Frost. The shock only called out her energy in behalf of her darling, and, tender as her nature was, she shrank from nothing that could soothe and alleviate his suffering; and it did infinitely comfort him, as he held her hand and looked with affection into her face, even in the extremity of pain.

Fain would others have been the same support; but his father, though not leaving him, was completely unnerved, and unable to do anything; and Mrs. Ponsonby was suffering under one of the attacks that were brought on by any sudden agitation. Mary, though giddy and throbbing in every pulse, was forced to put a resolute check on herself—brace her limbs, steady her voice, and keep her face composed, while every faculty was absorbed in listening for sounds from her cousin's room, and her heart was quivering with an anguish of prayer and suspense. Could she but hide her burning cheeks for one moment, let out one of the sobs that seemed to be rending her breast, throw herself on her knees and burst into tears, what an infinite relief it would be! But Mary had learnt to spend her life in having no self.

CHAPTER VI
FAREWELLS

> What yet is there that I should do,
>   Lingering in this darksome vale?
> Proud and mighty, fair to view,
>   Are our schemes, and yet they fail,
> Like the sand before the wind,
>   That no power of man can bind.
>   ARNDT, Lyra Germanica.

Dynevor Terrace was said to have dark, damp kitchens, but by none who had ever been in No. 5, when the little compact fire was compressed to one glowing red crater of cinders, their smile laughing ruddily back from the bright array on the dresser, the drugget laid down, the round oaken table brought forward, and Jane Beckett, in afternoon trim, tending her geraniums, the offspring of the parting Cheveleigh nosegay, or gauffreing her mistress's caps. No wonder that on raw evenings, Master James, Miss Clara, or my young Lord, had often been found gossiping with Jane, toasting their own cheeks as well as the bread, or pinching their fingers in her gauffreing machine.

Yet, poor little Charlotte Arnold learnt that the kitchen could be dreary, when Mrs. Beckett had been summoned to nurse Lord Fitzjocelyn, and she remained in sole charge, under Mrs. Martha's occasional supervision. She found herself, her household cares over all too soon, on a cold light March afternoon, with the clock ticking loud enough for midnight, the smoke-jack indulging in supernatural groans, and the whole lonely house full of undefined terrors, with an unlimited space of the like solitude before her. She would even have been glad to be sure of an evening of Mrs. Martha's good advice, and of darning stockings! She sat down by the round table to Mr. James's wristbands; but every creak or crack of the furniture made her start, and think of death-watches. She might have learnt to contemn superstition, but that did not prevent it from affecting her nerves.

She spread her favourite study, The Old English Baron, on the table before her; but the hero had some connexion in her mind with Tom Madison, for whom she had always coveted a battle-field in France. What would he feel when he heard how he had filled up his course of evil, being well-nigh the death of his benefactor! If any one ought to be haunted, it would assuredly be no other than Tom!

Chills running over her at the thought, she turned to the fire as the thing nearest life, but at the moment started at a hollow call of her own name. A face was looking in at her through the geraniums! She shrieked aloud, and clasped her hands over her eyes.

'Don't make a row. Open the door!'

It was such a relief to hear something unghostly, that she sprang to the door; but as she undid it, all her scruples seized her, and she tried to hold it, saying, 'Don't come in! You unfortunate boy, do you know what you have done?'

But Tom Madison was in a mood to which her female nature cowered. He pushed the door open, saying authoritatively, 'Tell me how he is!'

'He is as ill as he can be to be alive,' said Charlotte, actuated at once by the importance of being the repository of such tidings, and by the excitement of communicating them to one so deeply concerned. 'Mr. Poynings came in to fetch Mrs. Beckett—he would have no one else to nurse him—and he says the old Lord and Missus have never had their clothes off these two nights.'

'Then, was it along of them stones?' asked the lad, hoarsely.

'Yourself should know best!' returned Charlotte. 'Mr. Poynings says 'twas a piece of rock as big as that warming-pan as crushed his ankle! and you know—'

'I know nothing,' said Tom. 'Master kept me in all day yesterday, and I only heard just now at Little Northwold, where I've been to take home some knives of Squire Calcott's. Master may blow me up if he likes, but I couldn't come till I'd heard the rights of it. Is he so very bad?'

'They've sent up to London for a doctor,' pursued Charlotte. 'Mr. Walby don't give but little hope of him. Poor young gentleman, I'm sure he had a good word from high and low!'

'Well! I'm gone!' cried Tom, vehemently. 'Goodbye to you, Charlotte Arnold! You'll never see me in these parts more!'

'Gone! Oh, Tom! what do you mean!'

'D'ye think I'll stay here to have this here cast in my face? Such a one as won't never walk the earth again!' and he burst out into passionate tears. 'I wish I was dead!'

'Oh, hush, Tom!—that is wicked!'

'May be so! I am all that's wicked, and you all turn against me!'

'I don't turn against you,' sobbed Charlotte, moved to the bottom of her gentle heart.

'You! you turned against me long ago. You've been too proud to cast one look at me these three months; and he forgot me; and that's what drew me on, when who cared what became of me—nor I neither now.'

'Don't speak that way! Don't say 'twas pride. Oh no! but I had to behave proper, and how should I keep up acquaintance when they said you went on—unsteady—'

'Aye, aye! I know how it is,' said poor Tom, with broken-down humility: 'I was not fit for you then, and I'm next thing to a murderer now; and you're like a white dove that the very fingers of me would grime. I'll take myself out of your way; but, let what will come of me, I'll never forget you, Charlotte.'

'Oh, wait, Tom! If I could but say it right!—Oh! I know there's something about biding patiently, and getting a blessing—if you'd only stop while I recollect it.'

'I thought I heard voices!' exclaimed Mrs. Martha, suddenly descending on them. 'I wonder you aren't ashamed of yourselves, and the family in such trouble! Downright owdacious!'

'Be this your house?' said Tom, stepping before Charlotte, his dejection giving way instantly to rude independence.

'Oh, very well,' said Martha, with dignity. 'I know what to expect from such sort of people. The house and young woman is in my charge, sir; and if you don't be off, I'll call the police.'

'Never trouble your old bones!' retorted Tom.

'Good-bye to you, Charlotte;' and, as in defiance of Martha, he took her passive hand. 'You'll remember one as loved you true and faithful, but was drove desperate! Good-bye! I'll not trouble no one no more!'

The three concluding negatives with which he dashed out of the house utterly overwhelmed Charlotte, and made her perfectly insensible to Mrs. Martha's objurgations. She believed in the most horrible and desperate intentions, and sobbed herself into such violent hysterics that Miss Mercy came in to assist—imagined that the rude boy had terrified her, misunderstood her shamefaced attempts at explanation, and left her lying on her bed, crying quietly over her secret terrors, and over that first, strangely-made declaration of love. The white dove! she did not deserve it, but it was so poetical! and poor Tom was so unhappy! She had not time even to think what was become of her own character for wisdom and prudence.

The next morning, between monition and triumph, Martha announced that the good-for-nothing chap was off with a valuable parcel of Mr. Calcott's, and the police were after him; with much more about his former idle habits,—frequenting of democratic oratory, public-houses, and fondness for bad company and strolling actors. Meek and easily cowed, Charlotte only opened her lips to say she knew that he had taken home Mr. Calcott's parcel. But this brought down a storm on her for being impertinent enough to defend him, and she sat trembling till it had subsided; and Martha retreating, left her to weep unrestrainedly over her wild fancies, and the world's cruelty and injustice towards one whom, as she was now ready to declare, she loved with her whole heart.

The bell rang sharply, knocks rattled at the front door! She was sure that Tom had been just taken out of the river! But instinct to answer the bell awoke at the second furious clattering and double pealing, which allowed no time for her to compose her tear-streaked, swollen face, especially as the hasty sounds suggested 'Mr. James.'

Mr. James it was, but the expected rebuke for keeping him waiting was not spoken. As he saw her sorrowful looks, he only said, low and softly, 'Is it so, Charlotte?' In his eyes, there could be but one cause for grief, and Charlotte's heart smote her for hypocrisy, when she could barely command her voice to reply, 'No, sir; my Lord has had a little better night.'

He spoke with unusual gentleness, as he made more inquiries than she could answer; and when, after a few minutes, he turned to walk on to Ormersfield, he said, kindly, 'Good-bye, Charlotte; I'll send you word if I find him better:' and the tears rose in his eyes at the thought how every one loved the patient.

He was not wrong. There was everywhere great affection and sympathy for the bright, fantastic being whom all laughed at and liked, and Northwold and the neighbourhood felt that they could have better spared something more valuable.

The danger was hardly exaggerated even by Charlotte. The chill of the long exposure had brought on high fever; and besides the crushed ankle, there had been severe contusions, which had resulted in an acute pain in the side, hitherto untouched by remedies, and beyond the comprehension of the old Northwold surgeon, Mr. Walby. As yet, however, the idea of peril had not presented itself to Louis, though he was perfectly sensible. Severe pain and illness were new to him; and though not fretful nor impatient, he had not the stoicism either of pride or of physical indifference, put little restraint on the expression of suffering, and was to an almost childish degree absorbed in the present. He was always considerate and grateful; and his fond affection for his Aunt Catharine, and for good old Jane, never failed to show itself whenever they did anything for his relief; and they were the best of nurses.

Poor Lord Ormersfield longed to be equally effective; but he was neither handy nor ready, and could only sit hour after hour beside his son, never moving except to help the nurses, or to try to catch the slightest accent of the sufferer. Look up when Louis would, he always saw the same bowed head, and earnest eyes, which, as Mrs. Ponsonby told her daughter, looked as they did when Louisa was dying.

The coming of the London surgeon was an era to which Louis evidently looked anxiously, with the iteration of sickness, often reckoning the hours till he could arrive; and when at last he came, there was an evident effort to command attention.

When the visit was over, and the surgeon was taking leave after the consultation, Fitzjocelyn calmly desired to know his opinion, and kept his eyes steadily fixed on his face, weighing the import of each word. All depended on the subduing the inflammatory action, in the side; and there was every reason to hope that he would have strength for the severe treatment necessary. There was no reason to despond.

'I understand—thank you,' said Louis.

He shut his eyes, and lay so still that Mrs. Frost trusted that he slept; but when his father came in, they were open, and Lord Ormersfield, bending over him, hoped he was in less pain.

'Thank you, there is not much difference.' But the plaintive sound was gone, the suffering was not the sole thought.

'Walby is coming with the leeches at two o'clock,' said Lord Ormersfield: 'I reckon much on them.'

'Thank you.' Silence again, but his face spoke a wish, and his aunt Catharine said, 'What, my dear?'

'I should like to see Mr. Holdsworth,' said Louis, with eyes appealing to his father.

'He has been here to inquire every day,' said the Earl, choosing neither to refuse nor understand. 'Whenever it is not too much for you—'

'It must be quickly, before I am weaker,' said Louis. 'Let it be before Walby returns, father.'

'Whatever you wish, my dear—' and Lord Ormersfield, turning towards the table, wrote a note, which Mrs. Frost offered to despatch, thinking that her presence oppressed her elder nephew, who looked bowed down by the intensity of grief, which, unexpressed, seemed to pervade the whole man and weigh him to the earth: and perhaps this also struck Louis for the first time, for, after having lain silent for some minutes, he softly said, 'Father!'

The Earl was instantly beside him, but, instead of speaking, Louis gazed in his face, and sighed, as he murmured, 'I was meant to have been a comfort to you.'

'My dear boy—' began Lord Ormersfield, but he could not trust his voice, as he saw Louis's eyes moist with tears.

'I wish I had!' he continued; 'but I have never been anything but a care and vexation, and I see it all too late.'

'Nay, Louis,' said his father, trying to assume his usual tone of authority, as if to prove his security, 'you must not give way to feelings of illness. It is weak to despond.'

'It is best to face it,' said the young man, with slow and feeble utterance, but with no quailing of eye or voice. 'But oh, father! I did not think you would feel it so much. I am not worth it.'

For the Earl could neither speak nor breathe, as if smothered by one mighty unuttered sob, and holding his son's hand between both his own, pressed it convulsively.

'I am glad Mrs. Ponsonby is here,' said Louis; 'and you will soon find what a nice fellow Edward Fitzjocelyn is, whom you may make just what—'

'Louis, my own boy, hush! I cannot bear this,' cried his father, in an accent wrung from him by excess of grief.

'I may recover,' said Louis, finding it his turn to comfort, 'and I should like to be longer with you, to try to make up—'

'You will. The leeches must relieve you. Only keep up your spirits: you have many years before you of happiness and success.'

The words brought a look of oppression over Louis's face, but it cleared as he said, 'I am more willing to be spared those years!'

His father positively started. 'Louis, my poor boy,' he said, 'is it really so? I know I have seemed a cold, severe father.'

'Oh, do not say so!' exclaimed Louis; 'I have deserved far less-idle, ungrateful, careless of your wishes. I did not know I could pain you so much, or I would not have done it. You have forgiven often, say you forgive now.'

'You have far more to forgive than I,' said the Earl.

'If I could tell you the half-waywardness, discontent, neglect, levity, wasted time—my treatment of you only three days back. Everything purposed—nothing done! Oh! what a life to bring before the Judge!' And he covered his face, but his father heard long-drawn sobs.

'Compose yourself, my dear boy,' he exclaimed, exceedingly grieved and perplexed. 'You know there is no cause to despond; and even—even if there were, you have no reason to distress yourself. I can say, from the bottom of my heart, that you have never given me cause for real anxiety, your conduct has been exemplary, and I never saw such attention to religion in any young man. These are mere trifles—'

'Oh, hush, father!' exclaimed Louis. 'You are only making it worse; you little know what I am! If Mr. Holdsworth would come!'

'He could only tell you the same,' said his father. 'You may take every comfort in thinking how blameless you have been, keeping so clear of all the faults of your age. I may not have esteemed you as you deserved, my poor Louis; but, be assured that very few can have so little to reproach themselves with as you have.'

Louis almost smiled. 'Poor comfort that,' he said, 'even if it were true; but oh, father!' and there was a light in his eye, 'I had thought of "He hath blotted out like a cloud thy transgressions."'

'That is right. One like you must find comfort in thinking.'

'There is comfort ineffable,' said Louis; 'but if I knew what I may dare to take home to myself! It is all so dim and confused. This pain will not let anything come connectedly. Would you give me that little manuscript book!'

It was given; and as the many loose leaves fell under Louis's weak hand, his father was amazed at the mass of copies of prayers, texts, and meditations that he had brought together; the earlier pages containing childish prayers written in Aunt Catharine's hand. Louis's cheeks coloured at the revelation of his hidden life, as his father put them together for him.

'It is of no use,' he said, sadly; 'I cannot read. Perhaps my aunt would come and read this to me.'

'Let me,' said his father; and Louis looked pleased.

Lord Ormersfield read what was pointed out. To him it was a glimpse of a very new world of contrition, faith, hope, and prayer; but he saw the uneasy expression on Louis's face give place to serenity, as one already at home in that sphere.

'Thank you,' he said. 'That was what I wanted. Mr. Holdsworth will soon come, and then I don't want to say much more. Only don't take this too much to heart—I am not worth it; and but for you and the dear Terrace home, I can be very glad. If I may hope, the hope is so bright! Here there are so many ways of going wrong, and all I do always fails; and yet I always tried to do Him service. Oh, to have all perfect!—no failure—no inconsistency—no self! Can it be?'

'I always tried to do Him service!' Sadly and dejectedly as the words were spoken—mournful as was the contrast between the will and the result, this was the true cause that there was peace with Louis. Unstable, negligent, impetuous, and weak as he had been, the one earnest purpose had been his, guarding the heart, though not yet controlling the judgment. His soul was awake to the unseen, and thus the sense of the reality of bliss ineffable, and power to take comfort in the one great Sacrifice, came with no novelty nor strangeness. It was a more solemn, more painful preparation, but such as he had habitually made, only now it was for a more perfect Festival.

His father, as much awestruck by his hopes as distressed by his penitence, still gave himself credit for having soothed him, and went to meet and forewarn the Vicar that poor Fitzjocelyn was inclined to despond, and was attaching such importance to the merest, foibles in a most innocent life, that he required the most tender and careful encouragement. He spoke in his usual tone of authoritative courtesy; and then, finding that his son wished to be left alone with Mr. Holdsworth, he went to the library to seek the only person to whom he could bear to talk.

'Mary,' he said, 'you were right. I have done so little to make that poor boy of mine happy, that he does not wish for life.'

Mrs. Ponsonby looked up surprised. 'Are you sure of what he meant?' she said. 'Was it not that this life has nothing to compare with that which is to come?'

'But what can be more unnatural?' said the Earl. 'At his age, with everything before him, nothing but what he felt as my harshness could so have checked hope and enjoyment. My poor Louis!' And, though eye and voice were steady and tearless, no words could express the anguish of his under-tone.

Mrs. Ponsonby adduced instances showing that, to early youth, with heart still untainted by the world, the joys of the Life Everlasting have often so beamed out as to efface all that earth could promise, but he could not be argued out of self-reproach for his own want of sympathy, and spoke mournfully of his cold manner, sternness to small faults, and denial of gratifications.

Mary the younger could not help rising from her corner to say, 'Indeed, Louis said the other day that you never had denied him any personal indulgence.'

'My dear, he never asked for personal indulgences,' said the Earl. His further speech was interrupted by a quick step, a slow opening of the door, and the entrance of James Frost, who grasped his outstretched hand with a breathless inquiry.

'He is very ill—' Lord Ormersfield paused, too much oppressed to say more.

'No better? What did the London surgeon say? what?'

'He says there is no time to be lost in attacking the inflammation. If we can subdue that, he may recover; but the state of the ankle weakens him severely. I believe myself that he is going fast,' said the Earl, with the same despairing calmness; and James, after gazing at him to collect his meaning, dropped into a chair, covered his face with his hands, and sobbed aloud.

Lord Ormersfield looked on as if he almost envied the relief of the outburst, but James's first movement was to turn on him, as if he were neglecting his son, sharply demanding, 'Who is with him?'

'He wished to be left with Mr. Holdsworth.'

'Is it come to this!' cried James. 'Oh, why did I not come down with him? I might have prevented all this!'

'You could not have acted otherwise,' said the Earl, kindly. 'Your engagement was already formed.'

'I could!' said James. 'I would not. I thought it one of your excuses for helping us.'

'It is vain to lament these things now,' said Lord Ormersfield. 'It is very kind in you to have come down, and it will give him great pleasure if he be able to see you.'

'If!' James stammered between consternation and anger at the doubt, and treated the Earl with a kind of implied resentment as if for injustice suffered by Louis, but it was affecting to see his petulance received with patience, almost with gratitude, as a proof of his affection for Louis. The Earl stood upright and motionless before the fire, answering steadily, but in an almost inward voice, all the detailed questions put by James, who, seated on one chair, with his hands locked on the back of the other, looked keenly up to him with his sharp black eyes, often overflowing with tears, and his voice broken by grief. When he had elicited that Louis had been much excited and distressed by the thought of his failings, he burst out, 'Whatever you may think, Lord Ormersfield, no one ever had less on his conscience!'

'I am sure of it.'

'I know of no one who would have given up his own way again and again without a murmur, only to be called fickle.'

'Yes, it has often been so,' meekly said Lord Ormersfield.

'Fickle!' repeated James, warming with the topic, and pouring out what had been boiling within for years. 'He was only fickle because his standard was too high to be reached! You thought him weak!'

'There may be weakness by nature strengthened by principle,' said Mrs. Ponsonby.

'True,' cried Jem, who, having taken no previous notice of her, had at first on her speaking bent his brows on her as if to extend to her the storm he was inflicting on poor, defenceless Lord Ormersfield, 'he is thought soft because of his easy way; but come to the point where harm displays itself, you can't move him a step farther—though he hangs back in such a quiet, careless fashion, that it seems as if he was only tired of the whole concern, and so it goes down again as changeableness.'

'You always did him justice,' said Lord Ormersfield, laying his hand on his cousin's shoulder, but James retreated ungraciously.

'I suppose, where he saw evil, he actually took a dislike,' said Mrs. Ponsonby.

'It is an absolute repugnance to anything bad. You,' turning again on the Earl, 'had an idea of his being too ready to run into all sorts of company; but I told you there was no danger.'

'You told me I might trust to his disgust to anything unrefined or dissipated. You knew him best.'

'There is that about him which men, not otherwise particular, respect as they might a woman or a child. They never show themselves in their true colours, and I have known him uphold them because he has never seen their worst side!'

'I have always thought he learnt that peculiar refinement from your grandmother.'

'I think,' said Mrs. Ponsonby, softly, 'that it is purity of heart which makes him see heaven so bright.'

'Sydney Calcott walked part of the way with me,' continued Jem, 'and showed more feeling than I thought was in him. He said just what I do, that he never saw any one to whom evil seemed so unable to cling. He spoke of him at school—said he was the friend of all the juniors, but too dreamy and uncertain for fellows of his own standing. He said, at first they did not know what to make of him, with his soft looks and cool ways—they could not make him understand bullying, for he could not be frightened nor put in a passion. Only once, one great lout tried forcing bad language on him, and then Fitzjocelyn struck him, fought him, and was thoroughly licked, to be sure: but Calcott said it was a moral victory—no one tried the like again—'

James was interrupted by Mr. Holdsworth's entrance. He said a few words apart to the Earl, who answered, with alarm, 'Not now; he has gone through enough.'

'I told him so, but he is very anxious, and begged me to return in the evening.'

'Thank you. You had better join us at dinner.'

The Vicar understood Lord Ormersfield better than did James, and said, pressing his hand, 'My Lord, it is heart-breaking, but the blessedness is more than we can feel.'

Mrs. Ponsonby and Mary were left to try to pacify James, who was half mad at his exclusion from the sickroom, and very angry with every hint of resignation—abusing the treatment of the doctors, calling Mr. Walby an old woman, and vehemently bent on prophesying the well-doing of the patient. Keenly sensitive, grief and suspense made him unusually irritable; and he seemed to have no power of waiting patiently, and trusting the event to wiser Hands.

Mrs. Ponsonby dared not entertain any such ardent wishes. Life had not afforded her so much joy that she should deem it the greatest good, and all that she had heard gave her the impression that Louis was too soft and gentle for the world's hard encounter,—most pure and innocent, sincere and loving at present, but rather with the qualities of childhood than of manhood, with little strength or perseverance, so that the very dread of taint or wear made it almost a relief to think of his freshness and sweetness being secured for ever. Even when she thought of his father, and shrank from such grief for him, she could not but see a hope that this affliction might soften the heart closed up by the first and far worse sorrow, and detach it from the interests that had absorbed it too exclusively. All this was her food for silent meditation. Mary sat reading or working beside her, paler perhaps than her wont, and betraying that her ear caught every sound on the stairs, but venturing no word except the most matter-of-fact remark, quietly giving force to the more favourable symptoms.

Not till after Mr. Walby's second visit, when there was a little respite in the hard life-and-death contest between the remedies and the inflammation, could Mrs. Frost spare a few moments for her grandson. She met him on the stairs—threw her arms round his neck, called him her poor Jemmy, and hastily told him that he must not make her cry. He looked anxiously in her face, and told her that he must take her place, for she was worn out.'

'No, thank you, my dear, I can rest by-and-by.'

It sounded very hopeless.

'Come, granny, you always take the bright side.'

'Who knows which is the bright side?' she said. 'Such as he are always the first. But there, dear Jem, I told you not to make too much of granny—' and hastily withdrawing her hand, she gave a parting caress to his hair as he stood on the step below her, and returned to her charge.

It would have been an inexpressible comfort to James to have had some one to reproach. His own wretchedness was like a personal injury, and an offence that he could resent would have been a positive relief. He was forced to get out of the way of Frampton coming up with a tray of lemonade, and glared at him, as if even a station on the stairs were denied, then dashed out of doors, and paced the garden, goaded by every association the scene recalled. It seemed a mere barbarity to deprive him of what he now esteemed as the charm of his life—the cousin who had been as a brother, ever seeking his sympathy, never offended by his sharp, imperious temper, and though often slighted or tyrannized over, meeting all in his own debonnaire fashion, and never forsaking the poor, hard-working student, so that he might well feel that the world could not offer him aught like Louis Fitzjocelyn.

He stood in the midst of the botanical garden, and, with almost triumphant satisfaction, prognosticated that now there would be regret that Louis's schemes had been neglected or sneered at, and when too late, his father might feel as much sorrow as he had time for. It was the bitterness, not the softness of grief, in which he looked forth into the dull blue east-windy haze deepening in the twilight, and presently beheld something dark moving along under the orchard bank beneath. 'Hollo! who's there?' he exclaimed, and the form, rearing itself, disclosed young Madison, never a favourite with him, and though, as a persecuted protege of Louis, having claims which at another time might have softened him, coming forward at an unlucky moment, when his irritation only wanted an object on which to discharge itself. It was plain that one who came skulking in the private grounds could intend no good, and James greeted him, harshly, with 'You've no business here!'

'I'm doing no harm,' said the boy, doggedly, for his temper was as stubborn as James's was excitable.

'No harm! lurking here in that fashion in the dark! You'll not make me believe that! Let me hear what brings you here! The truth, mind!'

'I came to hear how Lord Fitzjocelyn is,' said Tom, with brief bluntness and defiance.

'A likely story! What, you came to ask the apple-trees?' and James scornfully laughed. 'There was no back-door, I suppose! I could forgive you anything but such a barefaced falsehood, when you know it was your own intolerable carelessness that was the only cause of the accident!'

'Better say 'twas yourself!' cried Tom, hoarse with passion and shaking all over.

The provocation was intense enough to bring back James's real principle and self-restraint, and he spoke with more dignity. 'You seem to be beside yourself, Madison,' he said, 'you had better go at once, before any one finds you here. Lord Fitzjocelyn cared for you so much, that I should not wish for you to meet your deserts under present circumstances. Go! I wish to have no more of your tongue!'

The boy was bounding off, while James walked slowly after to see him beyond the grounds, and finding Warren the keeper, desired him to be on the look-out. Warren replied with the tidings that Madison had run away from his place, and that the police were looking out for him on the suspicion of having stolen Mr. Calcott's parcel, moralizing further on the depravity of such doings when my young Lord was so ill, but accounting for the whole by pronouncing poaching to be bred in the bone of the Marksedge people.

This little scene had done Jem a great deal of good, both by the exhalation of bitterness and by the final exertion of forbearance. He had, indeed, been under two great fallacies on this day,—soothing Charlotte for the grief that was not caused by Fitzjocelyn's illness, and driving to extremity the lad brimming over with sorrow not inferior to his own. Little did he know what a gentle word might have done for that poor, wild, tempestuous spirit!

Yet, James's heart smote him that evening, when, according to Louis's earnest wish, Mr. Holdsworth came again, and they all were admitted to the room, and he saw the feeble sign and summons to the Vicar to bend down and listen. 'Tell poor Madison, it was wrong in me not to go to see him. Give him one of my books, and tell him to go on well!'

That day had been one of rapid change, and the remedies and suffering had so exhausted Louis that he could scarcely speak, and seemed hardly conscious who was present. All his faculties were absorbed in the one wish, which late in the evening was granted. The scene was like an epitome of his life—the large irregular room, cumbered with the disorderly apparatus of all his multifarious pursuits, while there he lay on his little narrow iron bed, his features so fair and colourless as to be strangely like his mother's marble effigy—his eyes closed, and his brows often contracted with pain, so that there was a doubt how far his attention was free, but still with a calm, pure sweetness, that settled down more and more, as if he were being lulled into a sleep.

'He is asleep,' Mrs. Frost said, as they all rose up.

They felt what that sleep might become.

'We might as well wish to detain a snow-wreath,' thought Mr. Holdsworth.

CHAPTER VII
GOSSAMER

Chaos is come again.—Othello.

That sleep was not unto death. When James and Mary came simultaneously creeping to the door in the grey twilight of the morning, they heard that there had been less pain and more rest, and gradually throughout the day, there was a diminution of the dangerous symptoms, till the trembling hope revived that the patient might be given back again to life.

James was still sadly aggrieved at being forbidden the sick-room, and exceedingly envied Lord Ormersfield's seat there. He declared, so that Mary doubted whether it were jest or earnest, that the Earl only remained there because society expected it from their relative positions, and that it must retard poor Fitzjocelyn's recovery to be perpetually basilisked by those cold grey eyes. Mary stood up gallantly for the Earl, who had always been so kind to her, and, on her mother's authority, vouched for his strong though hidden, feelings; to which Jem replied, 'Aye! he was hiding a strong fear of being too late for the beginning of the Session.'

'I do not think it right to impute motives,' said Mary.

'I would not, Mary, if I could help it,' said James, 'but through the whole course of my life I have never seen a token that his lordship is worthy of his son. If he were an ordinary, practical, common-place block, apt to support his dignity, he might value him, but all the grace, peculiarity, and conventionality is a mere burthen and vexation, utterly wasted.'

Mary knew that she was a common-place block, and did not wonder at herself for not agreeing with James, but cherishing a strong conviction that the father and son would now leave off rubbing against each other; since no unprejudiced person could doubt of the strong affection of the father, nor of the warm gratitude of the son. In spite of the asperity with which James spoke of the Earl, she was beginning to like him almost as much as she esteemed him. This had not been the case in their childhood, when he used to be praised by the elders for his obedience to his grandmother and his progress in the Northwold Grammar School; but was terribly overbearing with his juniors, and whether he cuffed Louis or led him into mischief, equally distressed her. Grown up, he was peculiarly vif, quick and ready, unselfish in all his ways, and warmly affectionate—very agreeable companion where his sensitiveness was not wounded, and meriting high honour by his deeper qualities. Young as he was, he had already relieved his grandmother from his own maintenance: he had turned to the utmost account his education at the endowed school at Northwold; by sheer diligence, had obtained, first a scholarship and then a fellowship at Oxford; and now, by practising rigid economy, and spending his vacations in tuition, he was enabled to send his sister to a boarding-school. He had stolen a few days from his pupils on hearing of Fitzjocelyn's danger, but was forced to return as soon as the improvement became confirmed. On the previous day, he asked Mary to walk with him to the scene of the accident, and they discussed the cause with more coolness than they really felt, as they shuddered at the depth of the fall, and the size of the stones.

James declared it all the fault of that runaway scamp, young Madison, in whom Louis had always been deceived, and who had never been seen since the night of his apparition in the garden.

'Poor boy! I suppose that was the reason he ran away,' said Mary.

'A very good thing, too. He would never have been anything but a torment to Louis. I remember telling him he was setting the stones so as to break the neck of some one!'

'I think it would be of more use to build them up than to settle how they broke down,' said Mary. 'Do you think we could manage it safely?'

'A capital thought!' cried James, eagerly, and no sooner said than done. The two cousins set to work—procured some cement from the bricklayer in the village, and toiled at their masonry with right good-will as long as light and time served them, then made an appointment to meet at half-past six next morning, and finish their work.

When the rendezvous took place, they were rejoicing over Mrs. Frost's report of an excellent night, and over her own happy looks, from which James prognosticated that all her fatigue and watching had done no harm to her vigorous frame, for which gladness was always the best cordial. It was a joyous beginning on that spring morning, and seemed to add fresh sparkles to the dazzling dewdrops, and double merriment to the blackbirds and thrushes answering each other far and wide, around, as the sun drew up the grey veil of morning mist. 'They all seem holding a feast for his recovery!' exclaimed Mary, warming for once into poetry, as she trudged along, leaving green footmarks in the silver dew.

'Well they may,' said James; 'for who loves them better than he? I grudge myself this lovely morning, when he is lying there, and my poor Clara is caged up at that place—the two who would the most enjoy it.'

'Your going to see her will be as good as the spring morning.'

'Poor child! I dread it!' sighed Jem.

It was his first voluntary mention of his sister. He had always turned the conversation when Mrs. Ponsonby or Mary had tried to inquire for her, and Mary was glad to lead him on to say more.

'I remember her last when you were teaching her to run alone, and letting none of us touch her, because you said she was your child, and belonged to no one else.'

'I should not be so ungrateful, now that I am come to the sense of my responsibility in teaching her to go alone.'

'But she has Aunt Catherine,' said Mary, thinking that he was putting the natural guardian out of the question as much now as in the days referred to.

'My grandmother never had to do with any girl before, and does not profess to understand them. She let Clara be regularly a boy in school, at first learning the same lessons, and then teaching; and whatever I tried to impress in the feminine line, naturally, all went for nothing. She is as wild as a hare, and has not a particle of a girl about her!'

'But she is very young.'

'There it is again! She grows so outrageously. She is not sixteen, and there she is taller than granny already. It is getting quite absurd.'

'What advice do you want on that head?'

'Seriously, it is a disadvantage, especially to that sort of girl, who can't afford to look like a woman before her time. Well, as she must probably depend on herself, I looked out for as good a school as could be had for the means, and thought I had succeeded, and that she would be brought into some sort of shape. Granny was ready to break her heart, but thought it quite right.'

'Then, does it not answer?'

'That is just what I can't tell. You have been used to schools: I wish you could tell me whether it is a necessary evil, or Clara's own idiosyncrasy, or peculiar to the place.'

'Whether what is?'

'Her misery!'

'Misery! Why, there is nothing of that in her letters to my aunt. There is not a complaint.'

'She is a brave girl, who spares granny, when she knows it would be of no use to distress her. Judge now, there's the sort of letter that I get from her.'

Mary read.

> 'DEAREST JEMMY,—Write to me as quick as ever you can, and tell me how Louis is; and let me come home, or I shall run mad. It is no good telling me to command my feelings; I am sure I would if I could, for the girls are more detestable than ever; but what can one do when one cannot sleep nor eat? All the screaming and crying has got into one bump in my throat, because I can't get it out in peace. If I could only shy the inkstand at the English teacher's head! or get one moment alone and out of sight! Let me come home. I could at least run messages; and it is of no use for me to stay here, for I can't learn, and all the girls are looking at me. If they were but boys, they would have sense! or if I could but kick them! This will make you angry, but do forgive me; I can't help it, for I am so very unhappy. Louis is as much to me as you are, and no one ever was so kind; but I know he will get well—I know he will; only if I knew the pain was better, and could but hear every minute. You need not come to fetch me; only send me a telegraph, and one to Miss Brigham. I have money enough for a second-class ticket, and would come that instant. If you saw the eyes and heard the whispers of these girls, I am sure you would. I should laugh at such nonsense any other time, but now I only ask to be wretched quietly in a corner.
>
> 'Your affectionate, nearly crazy, sister,
> 'CLARA FROST DYNEVOR.'

Mary might well say that there was nothing more expedient than going to see Clara, and 'much,' said poor James, 'he should gain by that,' especially on the head that made him most uneasy, and on which he could only hint lightly—namely, whether the girls were 'putting nonsense in her head.'

'If they had done her any harm, she would never have written such a letter,' said Mary.

'True,' said Jem. 'She is a mere child, and never got that notion into her head for a moment; but if they put it in, we are done for! Or if the place were ever so bad, I can't remove her now, when granny is thus occupied. One reason why I made a point of her going to school was, that I thought doing everything that Fitzjocelyn did was no preparation for being a governess.'

'Oh! I hope it will not come to that! Mr. Oliver Dynevor talks of coming home in a very few years.'

'So few, that we shall be grey before he comes. No; Clara and I are not going to be bound to him for the wealth heaped up while my grandmother was left in poverty. We mean to be independent.'

Mary was glad to revert to Clara.

'I must do the best I can for her for the present,' said Jem,—'try to harden her against the girls, and leave her to bear it. Poor dear! it makes one's heart ache! And to have done it oneself, too! Then, in the holidays, perhaps, you will help me to judge. You will be her friend, Mary; there's nothing she needs so much. I thought she would have found one at school but they are not the right stamp of animal. She has been too much thrown on Louis; and though he has made a noble thing of her, that must come to an end, and the sooner the better.'

Certainly, it was a perplexity for a young elder brother; but there could not but remain some simple wonder in Mary's mind whether the obvious person, Mrs. Frost, had not better have been left to decide for her granddaughter.

The building operations gave full occupation to the powers of the two cousins, and in good time before breakfast, all was successfully completed,—a hand-rail affixed, and the passage cleared out, till it looked so creditable, as well as solid, that there was no more to wish for but that Louis should be able to see their handiwork.

James went away in the better spirits for having been allowed to shake Louis by the hand and exchange a few words with him. Mary augured that it would be the better for Clara and for the pupils.

All that further transpired from him was a cheerful letter to Mrs. Frost, speaking of Clara as perfectly well, and beginning to accommodate herself to her situation, and from this Mary gathered that he was better satisfied.

The days brought gradual improvement to the patient, under Mrs. Frost's tender nursing, and his father's constant assiduity; both of which, as he revived, seemed to afford him the greatest pleasure, and were requited with the utmost warmth and caressing sweetness towards his aunt, and towards his father with ever-fresh gratitude and delight. Lord Ormersfield was like another man, in the sick-room, whence he never willingly absented himself for an hour.

One day, however, when he was forced to go to Northwold on business, Louis put on a fit of coaxing importunity. Nothing would serve him but some of Jane Beckett's choice dried pears, in the corner of the oaken cupboard, the key of which was in Aunt Kitty's pocket, and no one must fetch them for him but Aunt Kitty herself, he was so absurdly earnest and grave about them, that Jane scolded him, and Mrs. Frost saw recovery in his arch eyes; understanding all the time that it was all an excuse for complimenting Jane, and sending her to air herself, visit the Faithfull sisters, and inspect the Lady of Eschalott. So she consented to accompany Lord Ormersfield, and leave their charge to Mrs. Ponsonby, who found Louis quite elated at the success of his manoeuvre—so much disposed to talk, and so solicitous for the good of his nurses, that she ventured on a bold stroke.

His chamber was nearly as much like a lumber-room as ever; for any attempt to clear away or disturb his possessions had seemed, in his half-conscious condition, to excite and tease him so much, that it had been at once relinquished. Although the room was large, it was always too much crowded with his goods; and the tables and chairs that had been brought in during his illness, had added to the accumulation which was the despair of Mrs. Beckett and Mr. Frampton. Mrs. Ponsonby thought it was time for Louis to make a sacrifice in his turn, and ventured to suggest that he was well enough to say where some of his things might be bestowed; and though he winced, she persevered in representing how unpleasant it must be to his father to live in the midst of so much confusion. The debonnaire expression passed over his face, as he glanced around, saying, 'You are right. I never reflected on the stretch of kindness it must have been. It shall be done. If I lose everything, it will not be soon that I find it out.'

It evidently cost him a good deal, and Mrs. Ponsonby proposed that Mary should come and deal with his treasures; a plan at which he caught so eagerly, that it was decided that no time was like the present, and Mary was called. He could move nothing but his hands; but they were eagerly held out in welcome: and his eyes glittered with the bright smile that once she had feared never to see again. She felt a moisture in her own which made her glad to turn aside to her task even while he complimented her with an allusion to the labours of Hercules. It did not seem uncalled-for, when she began by raising a huge sheet of paper that had been thrown in desperation to veil the confusion upon the table, and which proved to be the Ordnance map of the county, embellished with numerous streaks of paint. 'The outlines of the old Saxon wappentakes,' said Louis: 'I was trying to make them out in blue, and the Roman roads in red. That mark is spontaneous; it has been against some paint.'

Which paint was found in dried swamps in saucers, while cakes of lake and Prussian blue adhered to the drawing-board.

'The colour-box is probably in the walnut-press; but I advise you not to irritate that yet. Let me see that drawing, the design for the cottages that Frampton nipped in the bud—'

'How pretty and comfortable they do look!' exclaimed Mary, pleased to come to something that was within her sphere of comprehension. 'If they were but finished!'

'Ah! I thought of them when I was lying there in the dell! Had they been allowed to stand where I wanted them, there would have been no lack of people going home from work; but, "Quite impracticable" came in my way, and I had no heart to finish the drawing.'

'What a pity!' exclaimed Mary.

'This was Richardson's veto, two degrees worse than Frampton's; and I shall never be able to abuse Frampton again. I have seen him in his true light now, and never was any one more kind and considerate. Ha, Mary, what's that?'

'It looks like a rainbow in convulsions.'

'Now, Mary, did not I tell you that I could not laugh? It is a diagram to illustrate the theory of light for Clara.'

'Does she understand *that*?' cried Mary.

'Clara? She understands anything but going to school—poor child! Yes, burn that map of the strata,—not that—it is to be a painted window whenever I can afford one, but I never could make money stay with me. I never could think why—'

The *why* was evident enough in the heterogeneous mass—crumpled prints, blank drawing-paper, and maps heaped ruinously over and under books, stuffed birds, geological specimens, dislocated microscopes, pieces of Roman pavement, curiosities innumerable and indescribable; among which roamed blotting-books, memorandum-books, four pieces of Indian rubber, three pair of compasses, seven paper-knives, ten knives, thirteen odd gloves, fifteen pencils, pens beyond reckoning, a purse, a key, half a poem on the Siege of Granada, three parts of an essay upon Spade Husbandry, the dramatis personae of a tragedy on Queen Brunehault, scores of old letters, and the dust of three years and a half.

Louis owned that the arrangements conduced to finding rather than losing, and rejoiced at the disinterment of his long-lost treasures; but either he grew weary, or the many fragments, the ghosts of departed fancies, made him thoughtful; for he became silent, and only watched and smiled as Mary quietly and noiselessly completed her reforms, and arranged table and chairs for the comfort of his father and aunt. He thanked her warmly, and hoped that she would pursue her kind task another day,—a permission which she justly esteemed a great testimony to her having avoided annoying him. It was a great amusement to him to watch the surprised and pleased looks of his various nurses as each came in, and a real gratification to see his father settle himself with an air of comfort, observing that 'they were under great obligations to Mary.' Still, the sight of the arrangements had left a dreary, dissatisfied feeling with Louis: it might have been caught from Mary's involuntary look of disappointment at each incomplete commencement that she encountered,—the multitude of undertakings hastily begun, laid aside and neglected—nothing properly carried out. It seemed a mere waste of life, and dwelt on his spirits, with a weariness of himself and his own want of steadfastness—a sense of having disappointed her and disappointed himself, and he sighed so heavily several times, that his aunt anxiously asked whether he were in pain. He was, however, so much better, that no one was to sit up with him at night—only his father would sleep on a bed on the floor. As he bade him good night, Louis, for the first time, made the request that he might have his Bible given to him, as well as his little book; and on his father advising him not to attempt the effort of reading, he said, 'Thank you; I think I can read my two verses: I want to take up my old habits.'

'Have you really kept up this habit constantly?' asked his father, with wonder that Louis did not understand.

'Aunt Catharine taught it to us, he said. 'I neglected it one half-year at school; but I grew so uncomfortable, that I began again.'

The Earl gave the little worn volume, saying, 'Yes, Louis, there has been a thread running through your life.'

'Has there been one thread?' sadly mused Louis, as he found the weight of the thick book too much for his weak hands, and his eyes and head too dizzy and confused for more than one verse:—

'I am come that they might have life,
And that they might have it more abundantly."

The Bible sank in his hands, and he fell into a slumber so sound and refreshing, that when he opened his eyes in early morning, he did not at first realize that he was not awakening to health and activity, nor why he had an instinctive dread of moving. He turned his eyes towards the window, uncurtained, so that he could see the breaking dawn. The sky, deep blue above, faded and glowed towards the horizon into gold, redder and more radiant below; and in the midst, fast becoming merged in the increasing light, shone the planet Venus, in her pale, calm brilliance.

There was repose and delight in dwelling on that fair morning sky, and Louis lay dreamily gazing, while thoughts passed over his mind, more defined and connected than pain and weakness had as yet permitted. Since those hours in which he had roused his faculties to meet with approaching death, he had been seldom awake to aught but the sensations of the moment, and had only just become either strong enough, or sufficiently at leisure for anything like reflection. As he watched the eastern reddening, he could not but revert to the feelings with which he had believed himself at the gate of the City that needs neither sun nor moon to lighten it, and, for the first time, he consciously realized that he was restored to this world of life.

The sensation was not unmixed. His youthful spirit bounded at the prospect of returning vigour, his warm heart clung round those whom he loved, and the perception of his numerous faults made him grateful for a longer probation; but still he had a sense of having been at the borders of the glorious Land, and thence turned back to a tedious, doubtful pilgrimage.

There was much to occasion this state of mind. His life had been without great troubles, but with many mortifications; he had never been long satisfied with himself or his pursuits, his ardour had only been the prelude to vexation and self-abasement, and in his station in the world there was little incentive to exertion. He had a strong sense of responsibility, with a temperament made up of tenderness, refinement, and inertness, such as shrank from the career set before him. He had seen just enough of political life to destroy any romance of patriotism, and to make him regard it as little more than party spirit, and dread the hardening and deadening process on the mind. He had a dismal experience of his own philanthropy; and he had a conscience that would not sit down satisfied with selfish ease, pleasure, or intellectual pursuits. His smooth, bright, loving temper had made him happy; but the past was all melancholy, neglect, and futile enterprise; he had no attaching home—no future visions; and, on the outskirts of manhood, he shrank back from the turmoil, the temptations, and the roughness that awaited him—nay, from the mere effort of perseverance, and could almost have sighed to think how nearly the death-pang had been over, and the home of Love, Life, and Light had been won for ever:—

> 'I am come that they might have life,
> And that they might have it more abundantly.'

The words returned on him, and with them what his father had said, 'You have had a thread running through your life.' He was in a state between sleeping and waking, when the confines of reflection and dreaming came very near together, and when vague impressions, hardly noticed at the time they were made, began to tell on him without his own conscious volition. It was to him as if from that brightening eastern heaven, multitudes of threads of light were floating hither and thither, as he had often watched the gossamer undulating in the sunshine. Some were firm, purely white, and glistening here and there with rainbow tints as they tended straight upwards, shining more and more into the perfect day; but for the most part they were tangled together in inextricable confusion, intermingled with many a broken end, like fleeces of cobweb driven together by the autumn wind,—some sailing aimlessly, or with shattered tangled strands-some white, some dark, some anchored to mere leaves or sprays, some tending down to the abyss, but all in such a perplexed maze that the eye could seldom trace which were directed up, which downwards, which were of pure texture, which defiled and stained.

In the abortive, unsatisfactory attempt to follow out one fluctuating clue, not without whiteness, and heaving often upwards, but frail, wavering, ravelled, and tangled, so that scarcely could he find one line that held together, Louis awoke to find his father wondering that he could sleep with the sun shining full on his face.

'It was hardly quite a dream,' said Louis, as he related it to Mrs. Frost.

'It would make a very pretty allegory.'

'It is too real for that just now,' he said. 'It was the moral of all my broken strands that Mary held up to me yesterday.'

'I hope you are going to do more than point your moral, my dear. You always were good at that.'

'I mean it,' said Louis, earnestly. 'I do not believe such an illness—ay, or such a dream—can come for nothing.'

So back went his thoughts to the flaws in his own course; and chiefly he bewailed his want of sympathy for his father. Material obedience and submission had been yielded, but, having little cause to believe himself beloved, his heart had never been called into action so as to soften the clashings of two essentially dissimilar characters. Instead of rebelling, or even of murmuring, he had hid disappointment in indifference, taken refuge in levity and versatility, and even consoled himself by sporting with what he regarded as prejudice or unjust displeasure. All this cost him much regret and self-reproach at each proof of the affection so long veiled by reserve. Never would he have given pain, had he guessed that his father could feel; but he had grown up to imagine the whole man made up of politics and conventionalities, and his new discoveries gave him at least as much contrition as pleasure.

After long study of the debates, that morning, his father prepared to write. Louis asked for the paper, saying his senses would just serve for the advertisements, but presently he made an exclamation of surprise at beholding, in full progress, the measure which had brought Sir Miles Oakstead to Ormersfield, one of peculiar interest to the Earl. His blank look of wonder amused Mrs. Ponsonby, but seemed somewhat to hurt his father.

'You did not suppose I could attend to such matters now?' he said.

'But I am so much better!'

Fearing that the habit of reserve would check any exchange of feeling, Mrs. Ponsonby said, 'Did you fancy your father could not think of you except upon compulsion?'

'I beg your pardon, father,' said Louis, smiling, while a tear rose to his eyes, 'I little thought I was obstructing the business of the nation. What will Sir Miles do to me?'

'Sir Miles has written a most kind and gratifying letter,' said Lord Ormersfield, 'expressing great anxiety for you, and a high opinion of your powers.'

Louis had never heard of his own powers, except for mischief, and the colour returned to his cheeks, as he listened to the kind and cordial letter, written in the first shock of the tidings of the accident. He enjoyed the pleasure it gave his father far more than the commendation to himself; for he well knew, as he said, that 'there is something embellishing in a catastrophe,' and he supposed 'that had driven out the rose-coloured pastor.'

'There is always indulgence at your age,' said the Earl. 'You have created an impression which may be of great importance to you by-and-by.'

Louis recurred to politics. The measure was one which approved itself to his mind, and he showed all the interest which was usually stifled, by such subjects being forced on him. He was distressed at detaining his father when his presence might be essential to the success of his party, and the Earl could not bear to leave him while still confined to his bed. The little scene, so calm, and apparently so cold, seemed to cement the attachment of father and son, by convincing Louis of the full extent of his father's love; and his enthusiasm began to invest the Earl's grey head with a perfect halo of wisdom slighted and affection injured; and the tenor of his thread of life shone out bright and silvery before him, spun out of projects of devoting heart and soul to his father's happiness, and meriting his fondness.

The grave Earl was looking through a magnifying-glass no less powerful. He had not been so happy since his marriage; the consciousness of his own cold manner made him grateful for any demonstration from his son, and the many little graces of look and manner which Louis had inherited from his mother added to the charm. The sense of previous injustice enhanced all his good qualities, and it was easy to believe him perfect, while nothing was required of him but to lie still. Day and night did Lord Ormersfield wait upon him, grudging every moment spent away from him, and trying to forestall each wish, till he became almost afraid to express a desire, on account of the trouble it would cause. Mary found the Earl one day wandering among the vines in the old hothouse, in search of a flower, when, to her amusement, he selected a stiff pert double hyacinth, the special aversion of his son, who nevertheless received it most graciously, and would fain have concealed the headache caused by the scent, until Mrs. Frost privately abstracted it. Another day, he went, unasked, to hasten the birdstuffer in finishing the rose-coloured pastor; and when it came, himself brought it up-stairs, unpacked it, and set it up where Louis could best admire its black nodding crest and pink wings; unaware that to his son it seemed a memento of his own misdeeds—a perpetual lesson against wayward carelessness.

'It is like a new love,' said Mrs. Ponsonby; 'but oh! how much depends upon Louis after his recovery!'

'You don't mistrust his goodness now, mamma!'

'I could not bear to do so. I believe I was thinking of his father more than of himself. After having been so much struck by his religious feeling, I dread nothing so much as his father finding him deficient in manliness or strength of character.'

CHAPTER VIII
A TRUANT DISPOSITION

Gathering up each broken thread.
WHYTEHEAD.

'Tom Madison is come back,' said the Vicar, as he sat beside Fitzjocelyn's couch, a day or two after Lord Ormersfield had gone to London.

'Come back—where has he been?' exclaimed Louis.

'There!' said the Vicar, with a gesture of dismay; 'I forgot that you were to hear nothing of it! However, I should think you were well enough to support the communication.'

'What is it?' cried Louis, the blood rushing into his cheeks so suddenly, that Mr. Holdsworth felt guilty of having disregarded the precautions that he had fancied exaggerated by the fond aunt. 'Poor fellow—he has not—' but, checking himself, he added, 'I am particularly anxious to hear of him.'

'I wish there were anything more gratifying to tell you; but he took the opportunity of the height of your illness to run away from his place, and has just been passed home to his parish. After all your pains, it is very mortifying, but—'

'Pains! Don't you know how I neglected him latterly!' said Louis. 'Poor fellow—then—' but he stopped himself again, and added, 'You heard nothing of the grounds?'

'They were not difficult to find,' said Mr. Holdsworth. 'It is the old story. He was, as Mrs. Smith told me, 'a great trial'—more and more disposed to be saucy and disobedient, taking up with the most good-for-nothing boys in the town, haunting those Chartist lectures, and never coming home in proper time at night. The very last evening, he had come in at eleven o'clock, and when his master rebuked him, came out with something about the rights of man. He was sent to Little Northwold, about the middle of the day, to carry home some silver-handled knives of Mr. Calcott's, and returned no more. Smith fancied, at first, that he had made off with the plate, and set the police after him, but that proved to be an overhasty measure, for the parcel had been safely left. However, Miss Faithfull's servant found him frightening Mrs. Frost's poor little kitchen-maid into fits, and the next day James Frost detected him lurking suspiciously about the garden here, and set Warren to warn him off—'

Louis gave a kind of groan, and struck his hand against the couch in despair, then said, anxiously, 'What then?'

'No more was heard of him, till yesterday the police passed him home to the Union as a vagabond. He looks very ill and ragged; but he is in one of those sullen moods, when no one can get a word out of him. Smith declines prosecuting for running away, being only too glad of the riddance on any terms; so there he is at his grandfather's, ready for any sort of mischief.'

'Mr. Holdsworth,' said Louis, raising himself on his elbow, 'you are judging, like every one else, from appearances. If I were at liberty to tell the whole, you would see what a noble nature it was that I trifled with; and they have been hounding—Poor Tom! would it have been better for him that I had never seen him? It is a fearful thing, this blind treading about among souls, not knowing whether one does good or harm!'

'If you feel so,' said Mr. Holdsworth, hoping to lead him from the unfortunate subject, 'what must *we* do?'

'My position, if I live, seems to have as much power for evil, without the supernatural power for good. Doing hastily, or leaving undone, are equally fatal!'

'Nay, what hope can there be but in fear, and sense of responsibility?'

'I think not. I do more mischief than those who do not go out of their way to think of the matter at all!'

'Do you!' said the Vicar, smiling. 'At least, I know, for my own part, I prefer all the trouble and perplexity you give me, to a squire who would let me and my parish jog on our own way.'

'I dare say young Brewster never spoilt a Tom Madison.'

'The sight of self indulgence spoils more than injudicious care does. Besides, I look on these experiments as giving experience.'

'Nice experience of my best efforts!'

'Pardon me, Fitzjocelyn, have we seen your best?'

'I hope you will!' said Louis, vigorously. 'And to begin, will you tell this poor boy to come to me?'

Mr. Holdsworth had an unmitigated sense of his own indiscretion, and not such a high one of Fitzjocelyn's discretion as to make him think the interview sufficiently desirable for the culprit, to justify the possible mischief to the adviser, whose wisdom and folly were equally perplexing, and who would surely be either disappointed or deceived. Dissuasions and arguments, however, failed; and Mrs. Frost, who was appealed to as a last resource, no sooner found that her patient's heart was set on the meeting, than she consented, and persuaded Mr. Holdsworth that no harm would ensue equal to the evil of her boy lying there distressing himself.

Accordingly, in due time, Mr. Holdsworth admitted the lad, and, on a sign from Louis, shut himself out, leaving the runaway standing within the door, a monument of surly embarrassment. Raising himself, Louis said, affectionately, 'Never mind, Tom, don't you see how fast I am getting over it?'

The lad looked up, but apparently saw little such assurance in the thin pale cheeks, and feeble, recumbent form; for his face twitched all over, resumed the same sullen stolidity, and was bent down again.

'Come near, Tom,' continued Louis, with unabated kindness—'come and sit down here. I am afraid you have suffered a great deal,' as the boy shambled with an awkward footsore gait. 'It was a great pity you ran away.'

'I couldn't stay!' burst out Tom, half crying.

'Why not?'

'Not to have that there cast in my teeth!' he exclaimed, with blunt incivility.

'Did any one reproach you?' said Louis, anxiously. 'I thought no one knew it but ourselves.'

'You knew it, then, my Lord?' asked Tom, staring.

'I found out directly that there was no cement,' said Louis. 'I had suspected it before, and intended to examine whenever I had time.'

'Well! I thought, when I came back, no one did seem to guess as 'twas all along of me!' cried Tom. 'So sure I thought you hadn't known it, my Lord. And you never said nothing, my Lord!'

'I trust not. I would not consciously have accused you of what was quite as much my fault as yours. That would not have been fair play.'

'If I won't give it to Bill Bettesworth!' cried Tom.

'What has he done?'

'Always telling me that gentlefolks hadn't got no notion of fair play with the like of us, but held us like the dirt to be trampled on! But there—I'll let him know—'

'Who is he?'

'A young man what works with Mr. Smith,' returned Tom, his sullenness having given place to a frank, open manner, such as any one but Louis would have deemed too free and ready.

'Was he your great friend at Northwold?'

'A chap must speak to some one,' was Tom's answer.

'And what kind of a some one was he?'

'Why, he comes down Illershall way. He knows a thing or two, and can go on like an orator or a play-book—or like yourself, my Lord.'

'Thank you. I hope the thing or two were of the right sort.'

Tom looked sheepish.

'I heard something about bad companions. I hope he was not one. I ought to have come and visited you, Tom; I have been very sorry I did not. You'd better let me hear all about it, for I fear there must have been worse scrapes than this of the stones.'

'Worse!' cried Tom—'sure nothing could be worserer!'

'I wish there were no evils worse than careless forgetfulness,' said Louis.

'I didn't forget!' said Tom. 'I meant to have told you whenever you came to see me, but'—his eyes filled and his voice began to alter—'you never came, and she at the Terrace wouldn't look at me! And Bill and the rest of them was always at me, asking when I expected my aristocrat, and jeering me 'cause I'd said you wasn't like the rest of 'em. So then I thought I'd have my liberty too, and show I didn't care no more than they, and spite you all.'

'How little one thinks of the grievous harm a little selfish heedlessness may do!' sighed Louis, half aloud. 'If you had only looked to something better than me, Tom! And so you ran into mischief?'

Half confession, half vindication ensued, and the poor fellow's story was manifest enough. His faults had been unsteadiness and misplaced independence rather than any of the more degrading stamp of evils. The public-house had not been sought for liquor's sake, but for that of the orator who inflamed the crude imaginations and aspirations that effervesced in the youth's mind; and the rudely-exercised authority of master and foreman had only driven his fierce temper further astray. With sense of right sufficient to be dissatisfied with himself, and taste and principle just enough developed to loathe the evils round him, hardened and soured by Louis's neglect, and rendered discontented by Chartist preachers, he had come to long for any sort of change or break; and the tidings of the accident, coupled with the hard words which he knew himself to deserve but too well, had put the finishing stroke.

Hearing that the police were in pursuit of him, he had fancied it was on account of the harm done by his negligence. 'I hid about for a day,' he said: 'somehow I felt as if I could not go far off, till I heard how you were, my Lord, and I'd made up my mind that as soon as ever I heard the first stroke of the bell, I'd go and find the police, and his Lordship might hang me, and glad!'

Louis was nearer a tear than a smile.

'Then Mr. Frost finds me, and was mad at me. Nothing wasn't bad nough for me, and he sets Mr. Warren to see me off, so I had nothing for but to cut.'

'What did you think of doing?' sighed Louis.

'I made for the sea. If I could have got to them places in the Indies, such as that Philip went to, as you reads about in the verse-book—he as killed his wife and lost his son, and made friends with that there big rascal, and had the chest of gold—'

'Philip Mortham! Were you going in search of buccaneers?'

'I don't know, my Lord. Once you told me of some English Sir, as kills the pirates, and is some sort of a king. I thought, may be, now you'd tell me where they goes to dig for gold.'

'Oh, Tom, Tom, what a mess I have made of your notions!'

'Isn't there no such place?'

'It's a bad business, and what can you want of it?'

'I want to get shut of them as orders one about here and there, with never a civil word. Besides,' looking down, 'there's one I'd like to see live like a lady.'

'Would that make her happier?'

'I'll never see her put about, and slave and drudge, as poor mother did!' exclaimed Tom.

'That's a better spirit than the mere dislike to a master,' said Louis. 'What is life but obedience?'

'I'd obey fast enough, if folk would only speak like you do—not drive one about like a dog, when one knows one is every bit as good as they.'

'I'm sure I never knew that!'

Tom stared broadly.

'I never saw the person who was not my superior,' repeated Louis, quietly, and in full earnest. 'Not that this would make rough words pleasanter, I suppose. The only cure I could ever see for the ills of the world is, that each should heartily respect his neighbour.'

Paradoxes musingly uttered, and flying over his head, wore to Tom a natural and comfortable atmosphere; and the conversation proceeded. Louis found that geography had been as much at fault as chronology, and that the runaway had found himself not at the sea, but at Illershall, where he had applied for work, and had taken a great fancy to Mr. Dobbs, but had been rejected for want of a character, since the good superintendent made it his rule to keep up a high standard among his men. Wandering had succeeded, in which, moneyless, forlorn, and unable to find employment, he had been obliged to part with portions of his clothing to procure food; his strength began to give way, and he had been found by the police sleeping under a hedge; he was questioned, and sent home, crestfallen, sullen, and miserable, unwilling to stay at Marksedge, yet not knowing where to go.

His hankering was for Illershall, and Louis, thinking of the judicious care, the evening school, and the openings for promotion, decided at once that the experiment should be tried without loss of time. He desired Tom to bring him ink and paper, and hastily wrote:

> 'DEAR MR. DOBBS,—You would do me a great kindness by employing this poor fellow, and bearing with him. I have managed him very ill, but he would reward any care. Have an eye to him, and put him in communication with the chaplain. If you can take him, I will write more at length. If you have heard of my accident, you will excuse more at present.
>
> 'Yours very truly,
> 'FITZJOCELYN.'

Then arose the question, how Tom was to get to Illershall. He did not know; and Louis directed his search into the places where the loose money in his pocket might have been put. When it was found, Tom scrupled at the proposed half-sovereign. Three-and-fourpence would pay for his ticket. 'You will want a supper and a bed. Go respectably, Tom, and keep so. It will be some consolation for the mischief I have done you!'

'You done me harm!' cried Tom. 'Why, 'tis all along of you that I ain't a regularly-built scamp!'

'Very irregularly built, whatever you are!' said Louis. But I'll tell you what you shall do for me,' continued he, with anxious earnestness. 'Do you know the hollow ash-tree that shades over Inglewood stile? It has a stout sucker, with a honeysuckle grown into it—coming up among the moss, where the great white vase-shaped funguses grew up in the autumn.'

'I know him, my Lord,' said Tom, brightening at the detail, given with all a sick man's vivid remembrance of the out-of-doors world.

'I have fixed my mind on that stick! I think it has a bend at the root. Will you cut it for me, and trim it up for a walking-stick?'

'That I will, my Lord!'

'Thank you. Bring it up to me between seven and eight in the morning, if you please; and so I shall see you again—'

Mr. Holdsworth was already entering to close the conversation, which had been already over-long and exciting, for Louis, sinking back, mournfully exclaimed, 'The medley of that poor boy's mind is the worst of my pieces of work. I have made him too refined for one class, and left him too rough for another—discontented with his station, and too desultory and insubordinate to rise, nobleness of nature turning to arrogance, fact and fiction all mixed up together. It would be a study, if one was not so sorry!'

Nevertheless, Mr. Holdsworth could not understand how even Fitzjocelyn could have given the lad a recommendation, and he would have remonstrated, but that the long interview had already been sufficiently trying; so he did his best to have faith in his eccentric friend's good intentions.

In the early morning, Tom Madison made his appearance, in his best clothes, erect and open-faced, a strong contrast to the jaded, downcast being who had yesterday presented himself. The stick was prepared to perfection, and Louis acknowledged it with gratitude proportioned to the fancies that he had spent on it, poising it, feeling the cool grey bark, and raising himself in bed to try how he should lean on it. 'Hang it up there, Tom, within my reach. It seems like a beginning of independence.'

'I wish, my Lord,' blurted out Tom, in agitation, 'you'd tell me if you're to go lame for life, and then I should know the worst of it.'

'I suspect no one knows either the worst or the best,' said Louis, kindly. 'Since the pain has gone off, I have been content, and asked no questions. Mr. Walby says my ankle is going on so well, that it is a real picture, and a pleasure to touch it; and though I can't say the pleasure is mutual, I ought to be satisfied.'

'You'll only laugh at me!' half sobbed Tom, 'and if there was but anything I could do! I've wished my own legs was cut off—and serve me right—ever since I seen you lying there.'

'Thank you; I'm afraid they would have been no use to me! But, seriously, if I had been moderately prudent, it would not have happened. And as it is, I hope I shall be glad of that roll in Ferny dell to the end of my life.'

'I did go to see after mending them stones!' cried Tom, as if injured by losing this one compensation; 'but they are all done up, and there ain't nothing to do to them.'

'Look here, Tom: if you want to do anything for me, it is easily told, what would be the greatest boon to me. They tell me I've spoilt you, and I partly believe it, for I put more of my own fancies into you than of real good, and the way I treated you made you impatient of control: and then, because I could not keep you on as I should have wished,—as, unluckily, you and I were not made to live together on a desert island,—I left you without the little help I might have given. Now, Tom, if you go to the bad, I shall know it is all my fault—'

'That it ain't,' the boy tried to say, eagerly, but Louis went on.

'Don't let my bad management be the ruin of you. Take a turn from this moment. You know Who can help you, and Who, if you had thought of Him, would have kept you straight when I forgot. Put all the stuff out of your head about one man being equal to another. Equal they are; but some have the trial of ruling, others of obeying, and the last are the lucky ones. If we could only see their souls, we should know it. You'll find evening schools and lectures at Illershall; you'd better take to them, for you've more real liking for that sort of thing than for mischief; and if you finished up your education, you'd get into a line that would make you happier, and where you might do much good. There—promise me that you'll think of these things, and take heed to your Sundays.'

'I promise,' said Tom.

'And mind you write to me, Tom, and tell how you get on. I'll write, and let you know about your grandfather, and Marksedge news and all—'

The 'Thank you, my Lord,' came with great pleasure and alacrity.

'Some day, when you are a foreman, perhaps I may bring Miss Clara to see copper-smelting. Only mind, that you'll never go on soundly, nor even be fit to make your pretty tidy nest for any gentle bird, unless you mind one thing most of all; and that is, that we have had a new Life given us, and we have to begin now, and live it for ever and ever.'

As he raised himself, holding out his pale, slender hand from his white sleeve, his clear blue eyes earnestly fixed on the sky, his face all one onward look, something of that sense of the unseen passed into the confused, turbulent spirit of the boy, very susceptible of poetical impressions, and his young lord's countenance connected itself with all the floating notions left in his mind by parable or allegory. He did not speak, as Louis heartily shook his hardy red hand, and bade him good speed, but his bow and pulled forelock at the door had in them more of real reverence than of conventional courtesy.

Of tastes and perceptions above his breeding, the very sense of his own deficiencies had made him still more rugged and clownish, and removed him from the sympathies of his own class, while he almost idolized the two most refined beings whom he knew, Lord Fitzjocelyn and Charlotte Arnold. On an interview with her, his heart was set. He had taken leave of his half-childish grandfather, made up his bundle, and marched into Northwold, with three hours still to spare ere the starting of the parliamentary train. Sympathy, hope, resolution, and the sense of respectability had made another man of him; and, above all, he dwelt on the prospect held out of repairing the deficiencies of his learning. The consciousness of ignorance and awkwardness was very painful, and he longed to rub it off, and take the place for which he felt his powers. 'I will work!' thought he; 'I have a will to it, and, please God, when I come back next, it won't be as a rough, ignorant lout that I'll stand before Charlotte!'

'Louis,' said Mary Ponsonby, as she sat at work beside him that afternoon, after an expedition to the new house at Dynevor Terrace, 'I want to know, if you please, how you have been acting like a gentleman.'

'I did not know that I had been acting at all of late.'

'I could not help hearing something in Aunt Catharine's garden that has made me very curious.'

'Ha!' cried Louis, eagerly.

'I was sowing some annuals in our back garden, and heard voices through the trellis. Presently I heard, quite loud, 'My young Lord has behaved like a real gentleman, as he is, and no mistake, or I'd never have been here now.' And, presently, 'I've promised him, and I promise you, Charlotte, to keep my Church, and have no more to do with them things. I'll keep it as sacred as they keeps the Temperance pledge; for sure I'm bound to him, as he forgave me, and kept my secret as if I'd been his own brother: and when I've proved it, won't that satisfy you, Charlotte?'

'And what did Charlotte say?'

'I think she was crying; but I thought listening any more would be unfair, so I ran upstairs and threw up the drawing-room window to warn them.'

'Oh, Mary, how unfeeling!'

'I thought it could be doing no good!'

'That is so like prudent people, who can allow no true love under five hundred pounds a year! Did you see them? How did they look?'

'Charlotte was standing in an attitude, her hands clasped over her broom. The gentleman was a country-looking boy—'

'Bearing himself like a sensible, pugnacious cock-robin? Poor fellow, so you marred their parting.'

'Charlotte flew into the house, and the boy walked off up the garden. Was he your Madison, Louis? for I thought my aunt did not think it right to encourage him about her house.'

'And so he is to be thwarted in what would best raise and refine him. That great, bright leading star of a well-placed affection is not to be allowed to help him through all the storms and quicksands in his way.'

Good Mary might well open her eyes, but, pondering a little, she said, 'He need not leave off liking Charlotte, if that is to do him good; but I suppose the question is, what is safest for her?'

'Well, he is safe enough. He is gone to Illershall to earn her.'

'Oh! then I don't care! But you have not answered me, and I think I can guess the boy's secret that you have been keeping. Did you not once tell me that you trusted those stones in Ferny dell to him?'

'Now, Mary, you must keep his secret!'

'But why was it made one? Did you think it unkind to say that it was his fault?'

'Of course I did. When I thought it was all over with me, I could not go and charge the poor fellow with it, so as to make him a marked man. I was only afraid that thinking so often of stopping myself, I should bring it out by mistake.'

Mary looked down, and thought; then raised her eyes suddenly, and said, as if surprised, 'That was really very noble in you, Louis!' Then, thinking on, she said, 'But how few people would think it worth while!'

'Yes,' said Louis; 'but I had a real regard for this poor fellow, and an instinct, perhaps perverse, of shielding him; so I could not accuse him on my own account. Besides, I believe I am far more guilty towards him. His neglect only hurt my ankle—my neglect left him to fall into temptation.'

'Yet, by the way he talks of you—'

'Yes, he has the sort of generous disposition on which a little delicacy makes a thousand times more impression than a whole pile of benefits I hope and trust that he is going to repair all that is past. I wish I could make out whether good intentions overrule errors in detail, or only make them more fatal.'

Mary was glad to reason out the question. Abstract practical views interested her, and she had much depth and observation, more original than if she had read more and thought less. Of course, no conclusion was arrived at; but the two cousins had an argument of much enjoyment and some advantage to both.

Affairs glided on quietly till the Saturday, when Lord Ormersfield returned. Never had he so truly known what it was to come home as when he mounted the stairs, with steps unlike his usual measured tread, and beheld his son's look of animated welcome, and eager, outstretched hands.

'I was afraid,' said the Earl, presently, 'that you had not felt so well,' and he touched his own upper lip to indicate that the same feature in his son was covered with down like a young bird.

Louis blushed a little, but spoke indifferently. 'I thought it a pity not to leave it for the regulation moustache for the Yeomanry.'

'I wish I could think you likely to be fit to go out with the Yeomanry.'

'Every effort must be made!' cried Louis. 'What do they say in London about the invasion?'

It was the year 1847, when a French invasion was in every one's mouth, and Sydney Calcott had been retailing all sorts of facts about war-steamers and artillery, in a visit to Fitzjocelyn, whose patriotism had forthwith run mad, so that he looked quite baffled when his father coolly set the whole down as 'the regular ten years' panic.' There was a fervid glow within him of awe, courage, and enterprise, the outward symbol of which was that infant yellow moustache. He was obliged, however, to allow the subject to be dismissed, while his father told him of Sir Miles Oakstead's kind inquiries, and gave a message of greeting from his aunt Lady Conway, delivering himself of it as an unpleasant duty, and adding, as he turned to Mrs. Ponsonby, 'She desired to be remembered to you, Mary.'

'I have not seen her for many years. Is Sir Walter alive?'

'No; he died about three years ago.'

'I suppose her daughters are not come out yet?'

'Her own are in the school-room; but there is a step-daughter who is much admired.'

'Those cousins of mine,' exclaimed Louis, 'it is strange that I have never seen them. I think I had better employ some of my spare time this summer in making their acquaintance.'

Mrs. Ponsonby perceived that the Earl had become inspired with a deadly terror of the handsome stepdaughter; for he turned aside and began to unpack a parcel. It was M'Culloch's Natural Theology, into which Louis had once dipped at Mr. Calcott's, and had expressed a wish to read it. His father had taken some pains to procure this too-scarce book for him, and he seized on it with delighted and surprised gratitude, plunging at once into the middle, and reading aloud a most eloquent passage upon electricity. No beauty, however, could atone to Lord Ormersfield for the outrage upon method. 'If you would oblige me, Louis,' he said, 'you would read that book consecutively.'

'To oblige you, certainly,' said Louis, smiling, and turning to the first page, but his vivacious eagerness was extinguished.

M'Culloch is not an author to be thoroughly read without a strong effort. His gems are of the purest ray, but they lie embedded in a hard crust of reasoning and disquisition; and on the first morning, Louis, barely strong enough yet for a battle with his own volatility, looked, and owned himself, dead beat by the first chapter.

Mary took pity on him. She had been much interested by his account of the work, and would be delighted if he would read it with her. He brightened at once, and the regular habit began, greatly to their mutual enjoyment. Mary liked the argument, Louis liked explaining it; and the flood of allusions was delightful to both, with his richness of illustration, and Mary's actual experience of ocean and mountains. She brought him whatever books he wanted, and from the benevolent view of entertaining him while a prisoner, came to be more interested than her mother had ever expected to see her in anything literary. It was amusing to see the two cousins unconsciously educating each other—the one learning expansion, the other concentration, of mind. Mary could now thoroughly trust Louis's goodness, and therefore began by bearing with his vagaries, and gradually tracing the grain of wisdom that was usually at their root; and her eyes were opened to new worlds, where all was not evil or uninteresting that Aunt Melicent distrusted. Louis made her teach him Spanish; and his insight into grammar and keen delight in the majestic language and rich literature infected her, while he was amused by her positive distaste to anything incomplete, and playfully, though half murmuringly, submitted to his 'good governess,' and let her keep him in excellent order. She knew where all his property was, and, in her quaint, straightforward way, would refuse to give him whatever 'was not good for him.'

It was all to oblige Mary that, when he could sit up and use pen and pencil, he set to work to finish his cottage plans, and soon drew and talked himself into a vehement condition about Marksedge. Mary's patronage drew on the work, even to hasty learning of perspective enough for a pretty elevation intelligible to the unlearned, and a hopeless calculation of the expense.

The plans lay on the table when next his father came home, and their interest was explained.

'Did you draw all these yourself?' exclaimed the Earl. 'Where did you learn architectural drawing? I should have thought them done by a professional hand.'

'It is easy enough to get it up from books,' said Louis; 'and Mary kept me to the point, in case you should be willing to consider the matter. I would have written out the estimate; but this book allows for bricks, and we could use the stone at Inglewood more cheaply, to say nothing of beauty.'

'Well,' said Lord Ormersfield, considering, 'you have every right to have a voice in the management of the property. I should like to hear your views with regard to these cottages.'

Colouring deeply, and with earnest thanks, Fitzjocelyn stated the injury both to labourers and employers, caused by their distance from their work; he explained where he thought the buildings ought to stand, and was even guarded enough to show that the rents would justify the outlay. He had considered the matter so much, that he could even have encountered Richardson; and his father was only afraid that what was so plausible *must* be insecure. Caution contended with a real desire to gratify his son, and to find him in the right. He must know the wishes of the farmer, be sure of the cost, and be certain of the spot intended. His crippled means had estranged him from duties that he could not fulfil according to his wishes, and, though not a hard landlord, he had no intercourse with his tenants, took little interest in his estate, and was such a stranger to the localities, that Louis could not make him understand the nook selected for the buildings. He had seen the arable field called 'Great Courtiers,' and the farm called 'Small Profits,' on the map, but did not know their ups and downs much better than the coast of China.

'Mary knows them!' said Louis. 'She made all my measurements there, before I planned the gardens.'

'Mary seems to be a good friend to your designs,' said the Earl, looking kindly at her.

'The best!' said Louis. 'I begin to have some hope of my doings when I see her take them in hand.'

Lord Ormersfield thanked Mary, and asked whether it would be trespassing too much on her kindness to ask her to show him the place in question. She was delighted, and they set out at once, the Earl almost overpowering her by his exceeding graciousness, so that she was nearly ready to laugh when he complimented her on knowing her way through the bye-paths of his own park so much better than he did. 'It is a great pleasure to me that you can feel it something like home,' he said.

'I was so happy here as a child,' said Mary, heartily, 'that it must seem to me more of a home than any other place.'

'I hope it may always be so, my dear.'

He checked himself, as if he had been about to speak even more warmly; and Mary did the honours of the proposed site for the cottages, a waste strip fronting a parish lane, open to the south, and looking full of capabilities, all of which she pointed out after Louis's well-learned lesson, as eagerly as if it had been her own affair.

Lord Ormersfield gave due force to all, but still was prudent. 'I must find out,' he said, 'whether this place be in my hands, or included in Morris's lease. You see, Mary, this is an encumbered property, with every disadvantage, so that I cannot always act as you and Louis would wish; but we so far see our way out of our difficulties, that, if guided by good sense, he will be able to effect far more than I have ever done.'

'I believe,' was Mary's answer, 'this green is in the farmer's hands, but that he has no use for it.'

'I should like to be certain of his wishes. Farmers are so unwilling to increase the rates, that I should not like to consent till I know that it would be really a convenience to him.'

Mary suggested that there stood the farmhouse; and the Earl apologetically asked if she would dislike their proceeding thither, as he would not detain her long. She eagerly declared that Louis would be 'so glad,' and Lord Ormersfield turned his steps to the door, where he had only been once in his life, when he was a very young man, trying to like shooting.

The round-eyed little maid would say nothing but 'Walk in, sir,' in answer to inquiries if Mr. Norris were at home; and they walked into a parlour, chill with closed windows, and as stiff and fine as the lilac streamers of the cap that Mrs. Norris had just put on for their reception. Nevertheless, she was a sensible, well-mannered woman, and after explaining that her husband was close at hand, showed genuine warmth and interest in inquiring for Lord Fitzjocelyn. As the conversation began to flag, Mary had recourse to admiring a handsome silver tankard on a side table. It was the prize of a ploughing-match eight years ago, and brought out a story that evidently always went with it, how Mrs. Norris had been unwell and stayed at home, and had first heard of her husband's triumph by seeing the young Lord galloping headlong up the homefield, hurraing, and waving his cap. He had taken his pony the instant he heard the decision, and rushed off to be the first to bring the news to Mrs. Norris, wild with the honour of Small Profits. 'And,' said the farmer's wife, 'I always say Norris was as pleased with what I told him, as I was with the tankard!'

Norris here came in, an unpretending, quiet man, of the modern, intelligent race of farmers. There was anxiety at first in his eye, but it cleared off as he heard the cause of his landlord's visit, and he was as propitious as any cautious farmer could be. He was strong on the present inconveniences, and agreed that it would be a great boon to have a *few* families brought back, such as were steady, and would not burden the rates; but the *few* recurred so often as to show that he was afraid of a general migration of Marksedge. Lord Ormersfield thereupon promised that he should be consulted as to the individuals.

'Thank you, my Lord. There are some families at Marksedge that one would not wish to see nearer here; and I'll not say but I should like to have a voice in the matter, for they are apt to take advantage of Lord Fitzjocelyn's kindness.'

'I quite understand you. Nothing can be more reasonable. I only acted because my son was persuaded it was your wish.'

'It is so, my Lord. I am greatly obliged. He has often talked of it with me, and I had mentioned the matter to Mr. Richardson, but he thought your lordship would be averse to doing anything.'

'I have not been able to do all I could have wished,' said the Earl. 'My son will have it in his power to turn more attention to the property.'

'And he *is* a thorough farmer's friend, as they all say,' earnestly exclaimed Norris, with warmth breaking through the civil formal manner.

'True,' said Lord Ormersfield, gratified; 'he is very much attached to the place, and all connected with it.'

'I'm sure they're the same to him,' replied the farmer. 'As an instance, my Lord, you'll excuse it—do you see that boy driving in the cows? You would not look for much from him. Well, the morning the doctor from London came down, that boy came to his work, crying so that I thought he was ill. 'No, master,' said he, 'but what'll ever become of us when we've lost my young Lord?' And he burst out again, fit to break his heart. I told him I was sorry enough myself, but to go to his work, for crying would do no good. 'I can't help it, master,' says he, 'when I looks at the pigs. Didn't he find 'em all in the park, and me nutting—and helped me his own self to drive 'em out before Mr. Warren see 'em, and lifted the little pigs over the gap as tender as if they were Christians?'

'Yes, that's the way with them all,' interposed Mrs. Norris: 'he has the good word of high and low.'

Lord Ormersfield smiled: he smiled better than he used to do, and took leave.

'Fitzjocelyn will be a popular man,' he said.

Mary could not help being diverted at this moral deduced from the pig-story. 'Every one is fond of him,' was all she said.

'Talent and popularity,' continued the Earl. 'He will have great influence. The free, prepossessing manner is a great advantage, where it is so natural and devoid of effort.'

'It comes of his loving every one,' said Mary, almost indignantly.

'It is a decided advantage,' continued the Earl, complacently. 'I have no doubt but that he has every endowment requisite for success. You and your mother have done much in developing his character, my dear; and I see every reason to hope that the same influence continued will produce the most beneficial results.'

Mary thought this a magnificent compliment, even considering that no one but her mamma had succeeded in teaching Louis to read when a little boy, or in making him persevere in anything now: but then, when Lord Ormersfield did pay a compliment, it was always in the style of Louis XIV.

CHAPTER IX
THE FAMILY COMPACT

> Who, nurst with tender care,
> And to domestic bounds confined,
> Was still a wild Jack-hare
> COWPER.

'Mary,' said Mrs. Frost.

Mrs. Ponsonby was sitting by the open window of the library, inhaling the pleasant scents of July. Raising her eyes, she saw her aunt gazing at her with a look somewhat perplexed, but brim full of mischievous frolic. However, the question was only—'Where is that boy?'

'He is gone down with Mary to his cottage-building.'

'Oh! if Mary is with him, I don't care,' said Aunt Catharine, sitting down to her knitting; but her ball seemed restless, and while she pursued it, she broke out into a little laugh, and exclaimed, 'I beg your pardon, my dear, but I cannot help it. I never heard anything so funny!'

'As this scheme,' said Mrs. Ponsonby, with a little hesitation.

'Then you have the other side of it in your letter,' cried Mrs. Frost, giving way to her merriment. 'The Arabian Nights themselves, the two viziers laying their heads together, and sending home orders to us to make up the match!'

'My letter does not go so far,' said Mrs. Ponsonby, amused, but anxious.

'Yours is the lady's side. My orders are precise. Oliver has talked it over with Mr. Ponsonby, and finds the connexion would be agreeable; so he issues a decree that his nephew, Roland Dynevor—(poor Jem—he would not know himself!)—should enter on no profession, but forthwith pay his addresses to Miss Ponsonby, since he will shortly be in a position befitting the heir of our family!'

'You leave Prince Roland in happy ignorance,' said Mrs. Ponsonby, blushing a little.

'Certainly—or he would fly off like a sky-rocket at the first symptom of the princess.'

'Then I think we need not alter our plans. All that Mary's father tells me is, that he does not intend to return home as yet, though his successor is appointed, since he is much occupied by this new partnership with Oliver, and expects that the investment will be successful. He quite approves of our living at the Terrace, especially as he thinks I ought to be informed that Oliver has declared his intentions with regard to his nephew, and so if anything should arise between the young people, I am not to discourage it.'

'Mary is in request,' said Mrs. Frost, slyly, and as she met Mrs. Ponsonby's eyes full of uneasy inquiry. 'You don't mean that you have not observed at least his elder lordship's most decided courtship? Don't be too innocent, my dear.'

'Pray don't say so, Aunt Kitty, or you will make me uncomfortable in staying here. If the like ever crossed his mind, he must perceive that the two are just what we were together ourselves.'

'That might make him wish it the more,' Aunt Catharine had almost said, but she restrained it halfway, and said, 'Louis is hardly come to the time of life for a grande passion.'

'True. He is wonderfully young, and Mary not only seems much older, but is by no means the girl to attract a mere youth. I rather suspect she will have no courtship but from the elders.'

'In spite of her opportunities. What would some mammas—Lord Ormersfield's bugbear, for instance, Lady Conway—give for such a chance! Three months of a lame young Lord, and such a lame young Lord as my Louis!'

'I might have feared,' said Mrs. Ponsonby, 'if Mary were not so perfectly simple. Aunt Melicent managed to abstract all romance, and I never regretted it so little. She has looked after him merely because it came in her way as a form of kindness, and is too much his governess for anything of the other sort.'

'So you really do not wish for the other sort?' said Mrs. Frost, half mortified, as if it were a slight to her boy.

'I don't know how her father might take it,' said Mrs. Ponsonby, eager to disarm, her. 'With his grand expectations, and his view of the state of this property, he might make difficulties. He is fond of expressing his contempt for needy nobility, and I am afraid, after all that has passed, that this would be the last case in which he would make an exception.'

'Yet you say he is fond of Mary.'

'Very fond. If anything would triumph over his dislike, it would be his affection for her, but I had rather my poor Mary had not to put it to the proof. And, after all, I don't think it the safest way for a marriage, that the man should be the most attractive, and the woman the most—'

'Sensible! Say it, Mary—that is the charm in my nephew's eyes.'

'Your great-nephew is the point! No, no, Aunt Kitty; you are under a delusion. The kindness to Mary is no more than 'auld lang-syne,' and because he thinks her too impossible. He cannot afford for his son to marry anything but a grand unquestionable heiress. Mary's fortune, besides, depending on speculations, would be nothing to what Lady Fitzjocelyn ought to have.'

'For shame! I think better of him. I believe he would be unworldly when Louis's happiness was concerned.'

'To return to James,' said Mrs. Ponsonby, decidedly: 'I am glad that his uncle should have declared his intentions.'

'Oh, my dear, we are quite used to that. I am only glad that Jem takes no heed. We have had enough of that!—for my own part,' and the tears arose, 'I never expect that poor Oliver will think he has done enough in my lifetime. These things do so grow on a man! If I had but kept him at home!'

'It might have been the same.'

'There would have been something to divide his attention. His brother used to be a sort of idol; he seemed to love him the more for his quiet, easy ways, and to delight in waiting on him. I do believe he delays, because he cannot bear to come home without Henry!'

Mrs. Ponsonby preferred most topics to that of Mrs. Frost's sons, and was relieved by the sight of the young people returning across the lawn—Fitzjocelyn with his ash stick, but owing a good deal of support to Mary's firm, well-knit arm. They showed well together: even lameness could not disfigure the grace of his leisurely movements; and the bright changefulness and delicacy of his face contrasted well with the placid nobleness of her composed expression, while her complexion was heightened and her eyes lighted by exercise, so that she was almost handsome. She certainly had been looking uncommonly well lately. Was this the way they were to walk together through life?

But Mrs. Ponsonby had known little of married life save the troubles, and she was doubly anxious for her daughter's sake. She exceedingly feared unformed characters, and natures that had no root in themselves. Mary's husband must not lean on her for strength.

She was glad, as with new meaning, she watched their proceedings, to see how easily, and as a matter of course, Louis let Mary bring his footstool and his slipper, fetch his books, each at the proper time, read Spanish with him, and make him look out the words in the dictionary when he knew them by intuition, remind him of orders to be written for his buildings, and manage him as her pupil. If she ruled, it was with perfect calmness and simplicity, and the playfulness was that of brother and sister, not even with the coquettish intimacy of cousinhood.

The field was decidedly open to Roland Dynevor, alias James Frost.

Mrs. Ponsonby was loth to contemplate that contingency, though in all obedience, she exposed her daughter to the infection. He was expected on that afternoon, bringing his sister with him, for he had not withstood the united voices that entreated him to become Fitzjocelyn's tutor during the vacation, and the whole party had promised to remain for the present as guests at Ormersfield.

Louis, in high spirits, offered to drive Mrs. Ponsonby to meet the travellers at the station; and much did he inflict on her poor shattered nerves by the way. He took no servant, that there might be the more room, and perched aloft on the driving seat, he could only use his indefatigable tongue by leaning back with his head turned round to her. She kept a sharp lookout ahead; but all her warnings of coming perils only caused him to give a moment's attention to the horses and the reins, before he again turned backwards to resume his discourse. In the town, his head was more in the right direction, for he was nodding and returning greetings every moment; he seemed to have a bowing acquaintance with all the world, and when he drew up at the station, reached down several times to shake hands with figures whom his father would barely have acknowledged; exchanging good-humoured inquiries or congratulations with almost every third person.

Scarcely had the train dashed up before Mrs. Ponsonby was startled by a shout of 'He's there himself! Louis! Louis!' and felt, as well as saw, the springing ascent to the box of a tall apparition, in a scanty lilac cotton dress, an outgrown black mantle, and a brown straw bonnet, scarcely confining an overprofusion of fair hair. Louis let go the reins to catch hold of both hands, and cry, 'Well, old Giraffe! what have you done with Jem?'

'Seeing to the luggage! You won't let him turn me out! I must sit here!'

'You must have manners,' said Louis; 'look round, and speak rationally to Mrs. Ponsonby.'

'I never saw she was there!' and slightly colouring, the 'Giraffe' erected her length, turned round a small insignificant face slightly freckled, with hazel eyes, as light as if they had been grey; and stretched down a hand to be shaken by her new relation, but she was chiefly bent on retaining her elevation.

'There, Jem!' she cried exultingly, as he came forth, followed by the trunks and portmanteaus.

'Madcap!' he said; 'but I suppose the first day of the holidays must be privileged. Ha! Fitzjocelyn, you're the right man in the right place, whatever Clara is.'

So they drove off, James sitting by Mrs. Ponsonby, and taking care to inform her that, in spite of her preposterous height, Clara was only sixteen, he began to ask anxious questions as to Fitzjocelyn's recovery, while she looked up at the pair in front, and thought, from the appearance of things, that even Louis's tongue was more than rivalled, for the newcomer seemed to say a sentence in the time he took in saying a word. Poor Mrs. Ponsonby! she would not have been happier had she known in which pair of hands the reins were!

'And Louis! how are you?' cried Clara, as soon as this point had been gained; 'are you able to walk?'

'After a fashion.'

'And does your ankle hurt you?'

'Only if I work it too hard. One would think that lounging had become a virtue instead of a vice, to hear the way I am treated.'

'You look —' began Clara. 'But oh, Louis!' cried she, in a sort of hesitating wonder, 'what! a moustache?'

'Don't say a word:' he lowered his voice. 'Riding is against orders, but I cannot miss the Yeomanry, under the present aspect of affairs.'

'The invasion! A man in the train was talking of the war steamers, but Jem laughed. Do you believe in it?'

'It is a time when a display of loyalty and national spirit may turn the scale. I am resolved to let no trifle prevent me from doing my part,' he said, colouring with enthusiasm.

'You are quite right,' cried Clara. 'You ought to take your vassals, like a feudal chief! I am sure the defence of one's country ought to outweigh everything.'

'Exactly so. Our volunteer forces are our strength and glory, and are a happy meeting of all classes in the common cause. But say nothing, Clara, or granny will take alarm, and get an edict from Walby against me.'

'Dear granny! But I wish we were going home to the Terrace.'

'Thank you. How flattering!'

'You would be always in and out, and it would be so much more comfortable. Is Lord Ormersfield at home?'

'No, he will not come till legislation can bear London no longer.'

'Oh!'—with a sound of great relief.

'You don't know how kind he has been,' said Louis, eagerly. 'You will find it out when you are in the house with him.'

Clara laughed, but sighed. 'I think we should have had more fun at home.'

'What! than with me for your host? Try what I can do. Besides, you overlook Mary.'

'But she has been at school!'

'Well!'

'I didn't bargain for school-girls at home!'

'I should not have classed Mary in that category.'

'Don't ask me to endure any one who has been at school! Oh, Louis! if you could only guess—if you would only speak to Jem not to send me back to that place—'

'Aunt Kitty will not consent, I am sure, if you are really unhappy there, my poor Clara.'

'No! no! I am ordered not to tell granny. It would only vex her, and Jem says it must be. I don't want her to be vexed, and if I tell you, I may be able to keep it in!'

Out poured the whole flood of troubles, unequal in magnitude, but most trying to the high-spirited girl. Formal walks, silent meals, set manners, perpetual French, were a severe trial, but far worse was the companionship. Petty vanities, small disputes, fretful jealousies, insincere tricks, and sentimental secrets, seemed to Clara a great deal more contemptible than the ignorance, indolence, abrupt manners and boyish tastes which brought her into constant disgrace—and there seemed to be one perpetual chafing and contradiction, which made her miserable. And a further confidence could not help following, though with a warning that Jem must not hear it, for she did not mind, and he spent every farthing on her that he could afford. She had been teased about her dress, told that her friends were mean and shabby, and rejected as a walking companion, because she had no parasol, and that was vulgar.

'I am sure I wanted to walk with none of them,' said Clara, 'and when our English governess advised me to get one, I told her I would give in to no such nonsense, for only vulgar people cared about them. Such a scrape I got into! Well, then Miss Salter, whose father is a knight, and who thinks herself the great lady of the school, always bridled whenever she saw me, and, at last, Lucy Raynor came whispering up, to beg that I would contradict that my grandmamma kept a school, for Miss Salter was so very particular.'

'I should like to have heard your contradiction.'

'I never would whisper, least of all to Lucy Raynor, so I stood up in the midst, and said, as clear as I could, that my grandmother had always earned an honest livelihood by teaching little boys, and that I meant to do the same, for nothing would ever make me have anything to do with girls.'

'That spoilt it,' said Louis—'the first half was dignified.'

'What was the second?'

'Human nature,' said Louis.

'I see,' said Clara. 'Well, they were famously scandalized, and that was all very nice, for they let me alone. But you brought far worse on me, Louis.'

'I!'

'Ay! 'Twas my own fault, though, but I couldn't help it. You must know, they all are ready to bow down to the ninety-ninth part of a Lord's little finger; and Miss Brown—that's the teacher—always reads all the fashionable intelligence as if it were the Arabian Nights, and imparts little bits to Miss Salter and her pets; and so it was that I heard, whispered across the table, the dreadful accident to Viscount Fitzjocelyn!'

'Did nobody write to you?'

'Yes—I had a letter from granny, and another from Jem by the next morning's post, or I don't know what I should have done. Granny was too busy to write at first; I didn't three parts believe it before, but there was no keeping in at that first moment.'

'What did you do?'

'I gave one great scream, and flew at the newspaper. The worst was, that I had to explain, and then—oh! it was enough to make one sick. Why had I not said I was Lord Ormersfield's cousin? I turned into a fine aristocratic-looking girl on the spot! Miss Salter came and fondled, and wanted me to walk with her!'

'Of course; she had compassion on your distress—amiable feeling!'

'She only wanted to ask ridiculous questions, whether you were handsome.'

'What did you reply?'

'I told them not a word, except that my brother was going to be your tutor. When I saw Miss Salter setting off by this line, I made Jem take second-class tickets, that she might be ashamed of me.'

'My dear Giraffe, bend down your neck, and don't take such a commonplace, conventional view of your schoolfellows.'

'Conventional! ay, all agree because they know it by experience,' said Clara—'I'm sure I do!'

'Then take the other side—see the best.'

'Jem says you go too far, and are unreasonable with your theory of making the best of every one.'

'By no means. I always made the worst of Frampton, and now I know what injustice I did him. I never saw greater kindness and unselfishness than he has shown me.'

'I should like to know what best you would make of these girls!'

'You have to try that!'

'Can I get any possible good by staying?'

'A vast deal.'

'I'm sure Italian, and music, and drawing, are not a good compared with truth, and honour, and kindness.'

'All those things only grow by staying wherever we may happen to be, unless it is by our own fault.'

'Tell me what good you mean!'

'Learning not to hate, learning to mend your gloves. Don't jerk the reins, Clara, or you'll get me into a scrape.'

Clara could extract no more, nor did she wish it, for having relieved her mind by the overflow, she only wanted to forget her misfortunes. Her cousin Louis was her chief companion, they had always felt themselves on the same level of nonsense, and had unreservedly shared each other's confidences and projects; and ten thousand bits of intelligence were discussed with mutual ardour, while Clara's ecstasy became uncontrollable as she felt herself coming nearer to her grandmother. She finally descended with a bound almost as distressing to her brother as her ascent had been, and leapt at once to the embrace of Mrs. Frost, who stood there, petting, kissing her, and playfully threatening all sorts of means to stop her growth. Clara reared up her giraffe figure, boasting of having overtopped all the world present, except Louis! She made but a cold, abrupt response to her cousin Mary's greeting, and presently rushed upstairs in search of dear old Jane, with an impetus that made Mrs. Frost sigh, and say, 'Poor child! how happy she is;' and follow her, smiling, while James looked annoyed.

'Never mind, Jem,' said Louis, who had thrown himself at full length on the sofa, 'she deserves compensation. Let it fizz.'

'And undo everything! What do you say to that, Mary?'

'Mary is to say nothing,' said Louis, 'I mean that poor child to have her swing.'

'I shall leave you and James to settle that,' said Mary, quitting them.

'I am very anxious that Clara should form a friendship with Mary,' said James, gravely.

'Friendships can't be crammed down people's throats,' said Louis, in a weary indifferent tone.

'You who have been three months with Mary—!'

'Mary and I did not meet with labels round our necks that here were a pair of friends. Pray do you mean to send that victim of yours back to school?'

'Don't set her against it. I have been telling her of the necessity all the way home.'

'Is it not to be taken into consideration that a bad—not to say a base-style of girl seems to prevail there?'

'I can't help it, Fitzjocelyn,' cried Jem, ruffling up his hair, as he always did when vexed. 'Girls fit to be her companions don't go to school—or to no school within my means. This place has sound superiors, and she *must* be provided with a marketable stock of accomplishments, so there's no choice. I can trust her not to forget that she is a Dynevor.'

'Query as to the benefit of that recollection.'

'What do you mean?'

'That I never saw evils lessened by private self-exaltation.'

'Very philosophical! but as a matter of fact, what was it but the sense of my birth that kept me out of all the mischief I was exposed to at the Grammar School!'

'I always thought it had been something more respectable,' said Louis, his voice growing more sleepy.

'Pshaw! Primary motives being understood, secondary stand common wear the best.'

'As long as they don't eat into the primary.'

'The long and short of it is,' exclaimed James, impatiently, 'that we must have no nonsense about Clara. It is pain enough to me to inflict all this on her, but I would not do it, if I thought it were more than mere discomfort. Her principles are fixed, she is above these trumperies. But you have the sense to see that her whole welfare may depend on whether she gets fitted to be a valuable accomplished governess or a mere bonne, tossed about among nursery-maids. There's where poverty galls! Don't go and set my grandmother on! If she grew wretched and took Clara away, it would be mere condemning of her to rudeness and struggling!'

'Very well,' said Louis, as James concluded the brief sentences, uttered in the bitterness of his heart, 'one bargain I make. If I am to hold my tongue about school, I will have my own way with her in the holidays.'

'I tell you, Louis, that it is time to have done with childishness. Clara is growing up—I *won't* have you encourage her in all that wild flightiness—I didn't want to have had her here at all! If she is ever to be a reasonable, conformable woman, it is high time to begin. I can't have you undoing the work of six months! when Mary might make some hand of her, too—'

James stopped. Louis's eyes were shut, and he appeared to be completely asleep. If silence were acquiescence, it was at least gained; and so he went away, and on returning, intended to impress his lessons of reserve on Clara and her grandmother, but was prevented by finding Mrs. Ponsonby and her daughter already in the library, consulting over some letters, while Clara sat at her grandmother's knee in the full felicity of hearing all the Northwold news.

The tea was brought in, and there was an inquiry for Louis. He came slowly forward from the sofa at the dark end of the room, but disclaimed, of course, the accusation of fatigue.

'A very bad sign,' said James, 'that you have been there all this time without our finding it out. Decidedly, you have taken me in. You don't look half as well as you promised. You are not the same colour ten minutes together, just now white, and now—how you redden!'

'Don't, Jem!' cried Louis, as each observation renewed the tide of burning crimson in his cheek. 'It is like whistling to a turkey-cock. If I had but the blue variety, it might be more comfortable, as well as more interesting.'

Clara went into a choking paroxysm of laughter, which her brother tried to moderate by a look, and Louis rendered more convulsive by quoting

'Marked you his cheek of heavenly blue,'

and looked with a mischievous amusement at James's ill-suppressed displeasure at the merriment that knew no bounds, till even Mrs. Frost, who had laughed at first as much at James's distress as at Louis's travestie or Clara's fun, thought it time to check it by saying, 'You are right, Jem, he is not half so strong as he thinks himself. You must keep him in good order.'

'Take care, Aunt Kitty,' said Louis; 'you'll make me restive. A tutor and governess both! I appeal! Shall we endure it, Clara?'

'Britons never shall be slaves!' was the eager response.

'Worthy of the daughter of the Pendragons,' said Louis; 'but it lost half its effect from being stifled with laughing. You should command yourself, Clara, when you utter a sentiment. I beg to repeat Miss Frost Dynevor's novel and striking speech, and declare my adhesion, 'Britons never shall be slaves!' Liberty, fraternity, and equality! Tyrants, beware!'

'You ungrateful boy!' said Mrs. Frost; 'that's the way you use your good governess!'

'Only the way the nineteenth century treats all its good governesses,' said Louis.

'When it gets past them,' said Mary, smiling. 'I hope you did not think I was not ready to give you up to your tutor?'

Mary found the renunciation more complete than perhaps she had expected. The return of his cousins had made Fitzjocelyn a different creature. He did indeed read with James for two hours every morning, but this was his whole concession to discipline; otherwise he was more wayward and desultory than ever, and seemed bent on teazing James, and amusing himself by making Clara extravagantly wild and idle. Tired of his long confinement, he threw off all prudence with regard to health, as well as all struggle with his volatile habits; and the more he was scolded, the more he seemed to delight in making meekly ridiculous answers and going his own way. Sometimes he and Clara would make an appointment, at some unearthly hour, to see Mrs. Morris make cheese, or to find the sundew blossom open, or to sketch some effect of morning sun. Louis would afterwards be tired and unhinged the whole day, but never convinced, only capable of promoting Clara's chatter; and ready the next day to stand about with her in the sun at the cottages, to the increase of her freckles, and the detriment of his ankle. Their frolics would have been more comprehensible had she been more attractive; but her boisterous spirits were not engaging to any one but Louis, who seemed to enjoy them in proportion to her brother's annoyance, and to let himself down into nearly equal folly.

He gave some slight explanation to Mary, one day when he had been reminded of one of their former occupations—'Ah! I have no time for that now. You see there's nobody else to protect that poor Giraffe from being too rational.'

'Is that her great danger?' said Mary.

'Take my advice, Mary, let her alone. Follow your own judgment, and not poor Jem's fidgets. He wants to be 'father, mother both, and uncle, all in one,' and so he misses his natural vocation of elder brother. He wants to make a woman of her before her time; and now he has his way with her at school, he shall let her have a little compensation at home.'

'Is this good for her? Is it the only way she can be happy?'

'It is her way, at least; and if you knew the penance she undergoes at school, you would not grudge it to her. She is under his orders not to disclose the secrets of her prison-house, lest they should disquiet Aunt Catharine; and she will not turn to you, because—I beg your pardon, Mary—she has imbibed a distrust of all school-girls; and besides, Jem has gone and insisted on your being her friend more than human nature can stand.'

'It is a great pity,' said Mary, smiling, but grieved; 'I should not have been able to do her much good—but if I could only try!'

'I'll tell you,' said Louis, coming near, with a look between confidence and embarrassment; 'is it in the power of woman to make her dress look rather more like other people's without inflaming the blood of the Dynevors—cautiously, you know? Even my father does not dare to give her half-a-sovereign for pocket-money; but do ask your mother if she could not be made such that those girls should not make her their laughingstock.'

'You don't mean it!'

'Aye, I do; and she has not even told James, lest he should wish to spend more upon her. She glories in it, but that is hardly wholesome.'

'Then she told you?'

'Oh, yes! We always were brothers! It is great fun to have her here! I always wished it, and I'm glad it has come before they have made her get out of the boy. He will be father to the woman some day; and that will be soon enough, without teasing her.'

Mary wished to ask whether all this were for Clara's good, but she could not very well put such a question to him; and, after all, it was noticeable that, noisy and unguarded as Clara's chatter was, there never was anything that in itself should not have been said: though her manner with Louis was unceremonious, it was never flirting; and refinement of mind was as evident in her rough-and-ready manner as in his high-bred quietness. This seemed to account for Mrs. Frost's non-interference, which at first amazed her niece; but Aunt Catharine's element was chiefly with boys, and her love for Clara, though very great, showed itself chiefly in still regarding her as a mere child, petting her to atone for the privations of school, and while she might assent to the propriety of James's restrictions, always laughing or looking aside when they were eluded.

James argued and remonstrated. He said a great deal, always had the advantage in vehemence, and appeared to reduce Louis to a condition of quaint debonnaire indifference; and warfare seemed the normal state of the cousins, the one fiery and sensitive, the other cool and impassive, and yet as appropriate to each other as the pepper and the cucumber, to borrow a bon mot from their neighbour, Sydney Calcott.

If Jem came to Mary brimful of annoyance with Louis's folly, a mild word of assent was sufficient to make him turn round and do battle with the imaginary enemy who was always depreciating Fitzjocelyn. To make up for Clara's avoidance of Mary, he rendered her his prime counsellor, and many an hour was spent in pacing up and down the garden in the summer twilight; while she did her best to pacify him by suggesting that thorough relaxation would give spirits and patience for Clara's next half year, and that it might be wiser not to overstrain his own undefined authority, while the lawful power, Aunt Catharine, did not interfere. Surely she might safely be trusted to watch over her own granddaughter; and while Clara was so perfectly simple, and Louis such as he was, more evil than good might result from inculcating reserve. At any rate, it was hard to meddle with the poor child's few weeks of happiness, and to this James always agreed; and then he came the next day to relieve himself by fighting the battle over again. So constantly did this occur, that Aunt Kitty, in her love of mischief, whispered to Mrs. Ponsonby that she only hoped the two viziers would not quarrel about the three thousand sequins, three landed estates, and three slaves.

Still, Louis's desertion had left unoccupied so many of the hours of Mary's time that he had previously absorbed, that her mother watched anxiously to see whether she would feel the blank. But she treated it as a matter of course. She had attended to her cousin when he needed her, and now that he had regained his former companion, Clara, she resigned him without effort or mortification, as far as could be seen. She was forced to fall back on other duties, furnishing the house, working for every one, and reading some books that Louis had brought before her. The impulse of self-improvement had not expired with his attention, and without any shadow of pique she was always ready to play the friend and elder sister whenever he needed her, and to be grateful when he shared her interests or pursuits. So the world went till Lord Ormersfield's return caused Clara's noise to subside so entirely, that her brother was sufficiently at ease to be exceedingly vivacious and entertaining, and Mrs. Ponsonby hoped for a great improvement in the state of affairs.

CHAPTER X
THE BETTER PART OF VALOUR

>   For who is he, whose chin is but enriched
>   With one appearing hair, that will not follow
>   These culled and choice-drawn cavaliers 'gainst France?
>   Work, work your thoughts, and therein see a siege.
>   King Henry V.

The next forenoon, Mary met James in the park, wandering in search of his pupil, whom he had not seen since they had finished their morning's work in the study. Some wild freak with Clara was apprehended, but while they were conferring, Mary exclaimed, 'What's that?' as a clatter and clank met her ear.

'Only the men going out to join old Brewster's ridiculous yeomanry,' said Jem.

'Oh, I should like to see them,' cried Mary, running to the top of a bank, whence she could see into the hollow road leading from the stables to the lodge. Four horsemen, the sun glancing on their helmets, were descending the road, and a fifth, at some distance ahead, was nearly out of sight. 'Ah,' she said, 'Louis must have been seeing them off. How disappointed he must be not to go!'

'I wish I was sure—' said James, with a start. 'I declare his folly is capable of anything! Why did I not think of it sooner?'

Clara here rushed upon them with her cameleopard gallop, sending her voice before her, 'Can you see them?'

'Scarcely,' said Mary, making room for her.

'Where's Louis'!' hastily demanded her brother.

'Gone to the yeomanry meeting,' said Clara, looking in their faces in the exultation of producing a sensation.

James was setting off with a run to intercept him, but it was too late; and Clara loudly laughed as she said, 'You can't catch him.'

'I've done with him!' cried James. 'Can madness go further?'

'James! I am ashamed of you,' cried the Giraffe, with great stateliness. 'Here are the enemy threatening our coasts, and our towns full of disaffection and sedition; and when our yeomanry are lukewarm enough to go off grouse-shooting instead of attending to their duty, what is to become of the whole country if somebody does not make an exertion? The tranquillity of all England may depend on the face our yeomanry show.'

'On Lieutenant Fitzjocelyn's yellow moustache! Pray how long have you been in the secret of these heroic intentions?'

'Ever since I came home.'

'We all knew that he meant to go out if he could,' said Mary, in a tone calculated to soothe Jem, and diminish Clara's glory in being sole confidante, 'but we did not think him well enough. I hope it will do him no harm.'

'Exertions in a good cause can do no harm!' boldly declared Clara; then, with sudden loss of confidence, 'do you really think it will?'

'Just cripple him for life,' said James.

'Mr. Walby wished him not to attempt riding,' said Mary. 'He thinks any strain on the ankle just now might hurt him very much; but it may be over caution.'

'Mr. Walby is an old woman,' said Clara. 'Now, Jem, you said so yourself. Besides, it is all for his duty! Of course, he would risk anything for the good of his country.'

'Don't say another word, Clara,' exclaimed James, 'or you will drive me distracted with your folly. One grain of sense, and even you would have stopped it; but neither you nor he could miss a chance of his figuring in that masquerade dress! Look at the sun, exactly like a red-hot oven! We shall have him come home as ill as ever!'

Clara had another milder and more sorrowful version of the scolding from her grandmother, but Lord Ormersfield escaped the day's anxiety by being so busy with Richardson, that he never emerged from the study, and did not miss his son.

It was an exceedingly sultry day, and the hopeful trusted that Louis would be forced to give in, before much harm could be done; but it was not till five o'clock that the hoofs were heard on the gravel; and Jem went out to revenge himself with irony for his uneasiness.

'I hope you are satisfied,' he said, 'dulce est pro patria mori.'

Louis was slowly dismounting, and as he touched the ground gave a slight cry of pain, and caught at the servant's arm for support.

'No more than I expected,' said James, coming to help him; and at the same moment Lord Ormersfield was heard exclaiming—

'Fitzjocelyn—! what imprudence!'

'Take care,' hastily interrupted James, finding Louis leaning helplessly against him, unable to speak or stand, and his flushed cheek rapidly changing to deadly white.

They lifted him up the steps into the hall, where he signed to be laid down on the seat of the cool north window, and trying to smile, said 'it was only the hot sun, and his foot aching *rather*; it would soon go off.' And when, with much pain and difficulty, Frampton had released his swollen foot from the regulation-boot, into which he had foolishly thrust it, he went on more fluently. 'He had thought it his duty, especially when Mr. Shaw, the captain of his troop, had chosen to go away—he had believed it could do no harm—he was sure it was only a little present discomfort, and in the present crisis—'

He addressed his aunt, but his eyes were on his father; and when he heard not a single word from him, he suddenly ceased, and presently, laying his head down on the window-sill, he begged that no one would stand and watch him, he should come into the library in a few minutes.

The few minutes lasted, however, till near dinnertime, when he called to Mary, as she was coming downstairs, and asked her to help him into the library; he could remain no longer exposed to Frampton's pity, as dinner went in.

He dragged himself along with more difficulty than he had found for weeks, and sank down on the sofa with a sigh of exhaustion; while Clara, who was alone in the room, reared herself up from an easy-chair, where she had been sitting in an attitude that would have been despair to her mistress.

'Ha, Clara!' said Louis, presently; 'you look as if you had been the object of invective?'

'I don't care,' exclaimed Clara, 'I know you were in the good old cause.'

'Conde at Jarnac, Charles XII. at Pultowa—which?' said Louis. 'I thought of both myself—only, unluckily, I made such frightful blunders. I was thankful to my men for bringing me off, like other great commanders.'

'Oh, Louis! but at least you were in your place—you set the example.'

'Unluckily, these things descend from the sublime to the other thing, when one is done up, and beginning to doubt whether self-will cannot sometimes wear a mask.'

'I'm sure they are all quite cross enough to you already, without your being cross to yourself.'

'An ingenious and elegant impersonal,' said Louis.

Clara rushed out into the garden to tell the stiff old rose-trees that if Lord Ormersfield were savage now, he would be more horrid than ever.

Meanwhile, Louis drew a long sigh, murmuring, 'Have I gone and vexed him again? Mary, have I been very silly?'

The half-piteous doubt and compunction had something childish, which made her smile as she answered: 'You had better have done as you were told.'

'The surest road to silliness,' said Louis, whose tendency was to moralize the more, the more tired he was, 'is to think one is going to do something fine! It is dismal work to come out at the other end of an illusion.'

'With a foot aching as, I am afraid, yours does.'

'I should not mind that, but that I made such horrid mistakes!'

These weighed upon his mind so much, that he went on, half aloud, rehearsing the manoeuvres and orders in which he had failed, from the difficulty of taking the command of his troop for the first time, when bewildered with pain and discomfort. The others came in, and James looked rabid; Louis stole a glance now and then at his father, who preserved a grave silence, while Clara stood aloof, comparing the prostrate figure in blue and silver to all the wounded knights in history or fiction.

He was past going in to dinner, and the party were 'civil and melancholy,' Mrs. Frost casting beseeching looks at her grandson, who sat visibly chafing at the gloom that rested on the Earl's brow, and which increased at each message of refusal of everything but iced water. At last Mrs. Frost carried off some grapes from the dessert to tempt him, and as she passed through the open window—her readiest way to the library—the Earl's thanks concluded with a disconsolate murmur 'quite ill,' and 'abominable folly;' a mere soliloquy and nearly inaudible, but sufficient spark to produce the explosion.

'Fitzjocelyn's motives deserve no such name as folly,' James cried, with stammering eagerness.

'I know you did not encourage him,' said Lord Ormersfield.

'I did,' said a young, clear voice, raised in alarm at her own boldness; 'Jem knew nothing of it, but I thought it right.'

Lord Ormersfield made a little courteous inclination with his head, which annihilated Clara upon the spot.

'I doubt whether I should have done right in striving to prevent him,' said James. 'Who can appreciate the moral effect of heroism?'

'Heroism in the cause of a silver jacket!'

'Now, that is the most unfair thing in the world!' cried James, always most violent when he launched out with his majestic cousin. 'There is not a man living more careless of his appearance. You do him justice, Mrs. Ponsonby?'

'Yes, I do not believe that vanity had anything to do with it. A man who would bear what he has done to-day would do far more.'

'If it had been for any reasonable cause,' said the Earl.

'You may not understand it, Lord Ormersfield,' exclaimed James, 'but I do. In these times of disaffection, a sound heart, and whole spirit, in our volunteer corps may be the saving of the country; and who can tell what may be the benefit of such an exhibition of self-sacrificing zeal. The time demands every man's utmost, and neither risk nor suffering can make him flinch from his duty.'

'My dear Jem,' said a voice behind him at the window, 'I never see my follies so plainly as when you are defending them. Come and help me up stairs; Granny is ordering me up; a night's rest will set all smooth.'

It was not a night's rest, neither did it set things smooth. In vain did Louis assume a sprightly countenance, and hold his head and shoulders erect and stately; there was no concealing that he was very pale, and winced at every step. His ankle had been much hurt by the pressure of the stirrup, and he was not strong enough to bear with impunity severe pain, exertion, and fatigue on a burning summer day. It was evident that his recovery had been thrown back for weeks.

His father made no reproaches, but was grievously disappointed. His exaggerated estimate of his son's discretion had given place to a no less misplaced despondency, quite inaccessible to Mrs. Ponsonby's consolations as to the spirit that had prompted the performance. He could have better understood a youth being unable to forego the exhibition of a handsome person and dress, than imagine that any one of moderate sense could either expect the invasion, or use these means of averting it. If imagination was to be allowed for, so much the worse. A certain resemblance to the childish wilfulness with which his wife had trifled with her health, occurred to him, increasing his vexation by gloomy shadows of the past.

His silent mortification and kind anxiety went to his son's heart. Louis was no less disappointed in himself, in finding his own judgment as untrustworthy as ever, since the exploit that had been a perpetual feast to his chivalrous fancy had turned out a mere piece of self-willed imprudence, destroying all the newly-bestowed and highly-valued good opinion of his father; and even in itself, incompetently executed. 'He had made a fool of himself every way.' That had been James's first dictum, and he adopted it from conviction.

In the course of the day, goodnatured, fat Sir Gilbert Brewster, the colonel of the yeomanry, who had been seriously uneasy at his looks, and had tried to send him home, rode over to inquire for him, complimenting him on being 'thorough game to the last.' Louis relieved his mind by apologies for his blunders, whereupon he learnt that his good colonel had never discovered them, and now only laughed at them, and declared that they were mere trifles to what the whole corps, officers and men, committed whenever they met, and no one cared except one old sergeant who had been in the Light Dragoons. Louis's very repentance for them was another piece of absurdity. He smiled, indeed, but seemed to give himself up as a hopeless subject. His spirits flagged as they had not done throughout his illness, and, unwell, languid, and depressed, he spent his days without an attempt to rally. He was only too conscious of his own inconsistency, but he had not energy enough to resume any of the habits that Mary had so diligently nursed, neglected even his cottage-building, would not trouble himself to consider the carpenter's questions, forgot messages, put off engagements, and seemed to have only just vigour enough to be desultory, tease James, and spoil Clara.

Lord Ormersfield became alarmed, and called in doctors, who recommended sea air, and James suggested a secluded village on the Yorkshire coast, where some friends had been reading in the last long vacation. This was to be the break-up of the party; Mrs. Frost and the two Marys would resort to Dynevor Terrace, Clara would return to school, and James undertook the charge of Louis, who took such exceedingly little heed to the arrangements, that Jem indignantly told him that he cared neither for himself nor anybody else.

CHAPTER XI
A HALTING PROPOSAL

Shallow. Will you upon good dowry, marry her?
Slender. I will do a greater thing than that, upon your request.
        Merry Wives of Windsor.

The first thing that Louis did appear to care for was a letter that arrived about three days previous to their departure, addressed to 'Lord Fitsgosling, Hawmsfield Park, Northwold.' Rather too personal, as he observed, he must tell his correspondent that it hurt his feelings. The correspondent was Tom Madison, whose orthography lagged behind his other attainments, if his account might be trusted of 'they lectures on Kemistry.' His penmanship was much improved, and he was prospering, with hopes of promotion and higher wages, when he should have learnt to keep accounts. He liked Mr. Dobbs and the chaplain, and wished to know how to send a crown per post to 'old granfer up at Marksedge; because he is too ignorant to get a border sinned. Please, my lord, give my duty to him and all enquiring friends, and to Schirlt, up at the Teras.'

Highly amused, Louis lay on the uppermost step from the library window, in the cool summer evening, laughing over the letter. 'There, Aunt Kitty, he said, 'I commit that tender greeting to your charge,' and as she looked doubtful, 'Yes, do, there's a good aunt and mistress.'

'I am afraid I should not be a good mistress; I ought not to sanction it.'

'Better sanction it above board than let it go on by stealth,' said Louis. 'You are her natural protector.'

'So much the more reason against it! I ought to wish her to forget this poor boy of yours.'

'Ay, and light Hymen's torch with some thriving tallow chandler, who would marry a domestic slave as a good speculation, without one spark of the respectful chivalrous love that—'

'Hush! you absurd boy.'

'Well, then, if you won't, I shall go to Jane. The young ladies are all too cold and too prudent, but Jane has a soft spot in her heart, and will not think true love is confined within the rank that keeps a gig. I did think Aunt Kitty had been above vulgar prejudices.'

'Not above being coaxed by you, you gosling, you,' said Aunt Kitty; 'only you must come out of the dew, the sun is quite gone.'

'Presently,' said Louis, as she retreated by the window.

'I would not have been too cold or too prudent!' said Clara.

'I well believe it!'

'You will be one if you are not the other,' said Mary, gathering her work up, with the dread of one used to tropical dews. 'Are not you coming in?'

'When I can persuade myself to write a letter of good advice, a thing I hate.'

'Which,' asked Mary; 'giving or receiving it?'

'Receiving, of course.'—'Giving, of course,' said Clara and Louis at the same instant.

'Take mine, then,' said Mary, 'and come out of the damp.'

'Mary is so tiresome about these things!' cried Clara, as their cousin retreated. 'Such fidgetting nonsense.'

'I once argued it with her,' said Louis, without stirring; 'and she had the right side, that it is often more self-denying to take care of one's health, than to risk it for mere pleasure or heedlessness.'

'There's no dew!' said Clara; 'and if there was, it would not hurt, and if it did, I should be too glad to catch a cold, or something to keep me at home. Oh, if I could only get into a nice precarious state of health!'

'You would soon wish yourself at school, or anywhere else, so that you could feel some life in your limbs,' half sighed Louis.

'I've more than enough! Oh! how my feet ache to run! and my throat feels stifled for want of making a noise, and the hatefulness of always sitting upright, with my shoulders even! Come, you might pity me a little this one night, Louis: I know you do, for Jem is always telling me not to let you set me against it.'

'No, I don't pity you. Pity is next akin to contempt.'

'Nonsense, Louis. Do be in earnest.'

'I have seldom seen the human being whom I could presume to pity: certainly not you, bravely resisting folly and temptation, and with so dear and noble a cause for working.'

'You mean, the hope of helping to maintain grandmamma.'

'Which you will never be able to do, unless you pass through this ordeal, and qualify yourself for skilled labour.'

'I know that,' said Clara; 'but the atmosphere there seems to poison, and take the vigour out of all they teach. Oh, so different from granny teaching me my notes, or Jem teaching me French—'

'Growling at you—'

'He never growled half as much as, I deserved. I cared to learn of him; but I don't care for anything now,—no, not for drawing, which you taught me! There's no heart in it! The whole purpose is to get amazing numbers of marks and pass each other. All dates and words, and gabble gabble!'

'Ay! there's an epitome of the whole world: all ambition, and vanity, and gabble gabble,' said Louis, sadly. 'And what is a gosling, that he should complain?'

'You don't mean that in reality. You are always merry.'

'Some mirth is because one does not always think, Clara; and when one does think deeply enough, there is better cheerfulness.'

'Deeply enough,' said Clara. 'Ah! I see. Knowing that the world of gabble is not what we belong to, only a preparation? Is that it!'

'It is what I meant.'

'Ah I but how to make that knowledge help us.'

'There's the point. Now and then, I think I see; but then I go off on a wrong tack: I get a silly fit, and a hopeless one, and lose my clue. And yet, after all, there is a highway; and wayfaring men, though fools, shall not err therein,' murmured Louis, as he gazed on the first star of evening.

'Oh! tell me how to see my highway at school!'

'If I only kept my own at home, I might. But you have the advantage—you have a fixed duty, and you always have kept hold of your purposes much better than I.'

'My purpose!' said Clara. 'I suppose that is to learn as fast as I can, that I may get away from that place, and not be a burthen to granny and Jem. Perhaps Jem will marry and be poor, and then I shall send his sons to school and college.'

'And pray what are your social duties till that time comes?'

'That's plain enough,' said Clara: 'to keep my tone from being deteriorated by these girls. Why, Louis, what's that for?' as, with a bow and air of alarm, he hastily moved aside from her.

'If you are so much afraid of being deteriorated—'

'Nonsense! If you only once saw their trumpery cabals, and vanities, and mean equivocations, you would understand that the only thing to be done is to keep clear of them; take the learning I am sent for, but avoid them!'

'And where is the golden rule all this time?' said Louis, very low.

'But ought not one to keep out of what is wrong?'

'Yes, but not to stand aloof from what is not wrong. Look out, not for what is inferior to yourself, but what is superior. Ah! you despair; but, my Giraffe, will you promise me this? Tell me, next Christmas, a good quality for every bad one you have found in them. You shake your head. Nay, you must, for the credit of your sex. I never found the man in whom there was not something to admire, and I had rather not suppose that women are not better than men. Will you promise?'

'I'll try, but—'

'But, mind, it takes kind offices to bring the blossoms out. There—that's pretty well, considering our mutual sentiments as to good advice.'

'Have you been giving me good advice?'

'Not bad, I hope.'

'I thought only people like—like Mary—could give advice.'

'Ah! your blindness about Mary invalidates your opinion of your schoolfellows. It shows that you do not deserve a good friend.'

'I've got you; I want no other.'

'Quite wrong. Not only is she full of clear, kind, solid sense, like a pillar to lean on, but she could go into detail with you in your troubles. You have thrown away a great opportunity, and I am afraid I helped you. I shall hold you in some esteem when you are—to conclude sententiously—worthy of her friendship.'

Clara's laugh was loud enough to bring out the Earl, to summon them authoritatively out of the dew. Louis sat apart, writing his letter; Clara, now and then, hovering near, curious to hear how he had corrected Tom's spelling. He had not finished, when the ladies bade him good-night;

and, as he proceeded with it, his father said, 'What is that engrossing correspondence, Louis?'

'Such a sensible letter, that I am quite ashamed of it,' said Louis.

'I wonder at the time you chose for writing, when you are so soon to part with our guests.'

'I have no excuse, if you think it uncivil. I never have spirit to set about anything till the sun is down.'

His father began at once to speak softly: 'No, I intended no blame; I only cannot but wonder to see you so much engrossed with Clara Dynevor.'

'Poor child! she wants some compensation.'

'I have no doubt of your kind intentions; but it would be safer to consider what construction may be placed on attentions so exclusive.'

Louis looked up in blank, incredulous amazement, and then almost laughingly exclaimed, 'Is that what you mean? Why, she is an infant, a baby—'

'Not in appearance—'

'You don't know her, father,' said Louis. 'I love her with all my heart, and could not do more. Why, she is, and always has been, my she-younger-brother!'

'I am aware,' said the Earl, without acknowledging this peculiar relationship, 'that this may appear very ridiculous, but experience has shown the need of caution. I should be concerned that your heedless good-nature should be misconstrued, so as to cause pain and disappointment to her, or to lead you to neglect one who has every claim to your esteem and gratitude.'

Louis was bewildered. 'I have been a wretch lately,' he said, 'but I did not know I had been a bear.'

'I did not mean that you could be deficient in ordinary courtesy; but I had hoped for more than mere indifferent civility towards one eminently calculated—' Lord Ormersfield for once failed in his period.

'Are we talking at cross purposes?' exclaimed Fitzjocelyn. 'What have I been doing, or not doing?'

'If my meaning require explanation, it is needless to attempt any.— Is your ankle painful to-night?'

Not a word more, except about his health, could Louis extract, and he went to his room in extreme perplexity. Again and again did he revolve those words. Quick as were his perceptions on most points, they were slow where self-consciousness or personal vanity might have sharpened them; and it was new light to him that he had come to a time of life that could attach meaning to his attentions.

Whom had he been neglecting? What had his father been hoping? Who was eminently calculated, and for what?

It flashed upon him all at once. 'I see! I see!' he cried, and burst into a laugh.

Then came consternation, or something very like it. He did not want to feel embarked in manhood. And then his far-away dream of a lady-love had been so transcendently fair, so unequalled in grace, so perfect in accomplishments, so enthusiastic in self-devoted charity, all undefined, floating on his imagination in misty tints of glory! That all this should be suddenly brought down from cloudland, to sink into Mary Ponsonby, with the honest face and downright manner for whom romance and rapture would be positively ridiculous!

Yet the notion would not be at once dismissed. His declaration that he would do anything to gratify his father had been too sincere for him lightly to turn from his suggestion, especially at a moment when he was full of shame at his own folly, and eagerness to retain the ground he had lost in his father's opinion, and, above all, to make him happy. His heart thrilled and glowed as he thought of giving his father real joy, and permanently brightening and enlivening that lonely, solitary life. Besides, who could so well keep the peace between him and his father, and save him by hints and by helpfulness from giving annoyance? He had already learnt to depend on her; she entered into all his interests, and was a most pleasant companion—so wise and good, that the most satisfactory days of his life had been passed under her management, and he had only broken from it to 'play the fool.' He was sick of his own volatile Quixotism, and could believe it a relief to be kept in order without trusting to his own judgment. She had every right to his esteem and affection, and the warm feeling he had for her could only be strengthened by closer ties. The unworldliness of the project likewise weighed with him. Had she been a millionaire or a Duke's daughter, he would not have spent one thought on the matter; but he was touched by seeing how his father's better feelings had conquered all desire for fortune or connexion.

And then Mary could always find everything he wanted!

'I will do it!' he determined. 'Never was son more bound to consider his father. Of course, she will make a much better wife than I deserve. Most likely, my fancies would never have been fulfilled. She will save me from my own foolishness. What ought a man to wish for more than a person sure to make him good? And—well, after all, it cannot be for a long time. They must write to Lima. Perhaps they will wait till her father's return, or at least till I have taken my degree.'

This last encouraging reflection always wound up the series that perpetually recurred throughout that night of broken sleep; and when he rose in the morning, he felt as if each waking had added a year to his life, and looked at the glass to see whether he had not grown quite elderly.

'No, indeed! I am ridiculously youthful, especially since I shaved off my moustache in my rage at the Yeomanry mania! I must systematically burn my cheeks, to look anything near her age!' And he laughed at himself, but ended with a long-drawn sigh.

He was in no state of mind to pause: he was tired of self-debate, and was in haste to render the step irrevocable, and then fit himself to it; and he betook himself at once to the study, where he astonished his father by his commencement, with crimson cheeks—'I wished to speak to you. Last night I did not catch your meaning at once.'

'We will say no more about it,' was the kind answer. 'If you cannot turn your thoughts in that direction, there is an end of the matter.'

'I think,' said Louis, 'that I could.'

'My dear boy,' said the Earl, with more eagerness than he could quite control, 'you must not imagine that I wish to influence your inclinations unduly; but I must confess that what I have seen for the last few months, has convinced me that nothing could better secure your happiness.'

'I believe so,' said Louis, gazing from the window.

'Right,' cried the Earl, with more gladness and warmth than his son had ever seen in him; 'I am delighted that you appreciate such sterling excellence! Yes, Louis,' and his voice grew thick, 'there is nothing else to trust to.'

'I know it,' said Louis. 'She is very good. She made me very happy when I was ill.'

'You have seen her under the most favourable circumstances. It is the only sort of acquaintance to be relied on. You have consulted your own happiness far more than if you had allowed yourself to be attracted by mere showy gifts.'

'I am sure she will do me a great deal of good,' said Louis, still keeping his eyes fixed on the evergreens.

'You could have done nothing to give me more pleasure!' said the Earl, with heartfelt earnestness. 'I know what she is, and what her mother has been to me. That aunt of hers is a stiff, wrongheaded person, but she has brought her up well—very well, and her mother has done the rest. As to her father, that is a disadvantage; but, from what I hear, he is never likely to come home; and that is not to be weighed against what she is herself. Poor Mary! how rejoiced she will be, that her daughter at least should no longer be under that man's power! It is well you have not been extravagant, like some young men, Louis. If you had been running into debt, I should not have been able to gratify your wishes now; but the property is so nearly disencumbered, that you can perfectly afford to marry her, with the very fair fortune she must have, unless her father should gamble it away in Peru.'

This was for Lord Ormersfield the incoherency of joy, and Louis was quite carried along by his delight. The breakfast-bell rang, and the Earl rising and drawing his son's arm within his own, pressed it, saying, 'Bless you, Louis!' It was extreme surprise and pleasure to Fitzjocelyn, and yet the next moment he recollected that he stood committed.

How silent he was—how unusually gentle and gracious his father to the whole party! quite affectionate to Mary, and not awful even to Clara. There was far too much meaning in it, and Louis feared Mrs. Ponsonby was seeing through all.

'A morning of Greek would be insupportable,' thought he; and yet he felt as if the fetters of fate were being fast bound around him, when he heard his father inviting James to ride with him.

He wandered and he watched, he spoke absently to Clara, but felt as if robbed of a protector, when she was summoned up-stairs to attend to her packing, and Mary remained alone, writing one of her long letters to Lima.

'Now or never,' thought he, 'before my courage cools. I never saw my father in such spirits!'

He sat down on an ottoman opposite to her, and turned over some newspapers with a restless rustling.

'Can I fetch anything for you?' asked Mary, looking up.

'No, thank you. You are a great deal too good to me, Mary.'

'I am glad,' said Mary, absently, anxious to go on with her letter; but, looking up again at him—'I am sure you want something.'

'No—nothing—but that you should be still more good to me.'

'What is the matter?' said Mary, suspecting that he was beginning to repent of his lazy fit, and wanted her to hear his confession.

'I mean, Mary,' said he, rising, and speaking faster, 'if you—if you would take charge of me altogether. If you would have me, I would do all I could to make you happy, and it would be such joy to my father, and—' (rather like an after-thought) 'to me.'

Her clear, sensible eyes were raised, and her colour deepened, but the confusion was on the gentleman's side—she was too much amazed to feel embarrassment, and there was a pause, till he added, 'I know better than to think myself worthy of you; but you will take me in hand—and, indeed, Mary, there is no one whom I like half so well.'

Poor Louis! was this his romantic and poetical wooing!

'Stop, if you please, Louis!' exclaimed Mary. 'This is so very strange!' And she seemed ready to laugh.

'And—what do you say, Mary?'

'I do not know. I cannot tell what I ought to say,' she returned, rising. 'Will you let me go to mamma?'

She went; and Louis roamed about restlessly, till, on the stairs, he encountered Mrs. Frost, who instantly exclaimed, 'Why, my dear, what is the matter with you?'

'I have been proposing to Mary,' said he, in a very low murmur, his eyes downcast, but raised the next moment, to see the effect, as if it had been a piece of mischief.

'Well—proposing what?'

'Myself;' most innocently whispered.

'You!—you!—Mary!—And—' Aunt Catharine was scarcely able to speak, in the extremity of her astonishment. 'You are not in earnest!'

'She is gone to her mother,' said Louis, hanging over the baluster, so as to look straight down into the hall; and both were silent, till Mrs. Frost exclaimed, 'My dear, dear child, it is an excellent choice! You must be very happy with her!'

'Yes, I found my father was bent on it.'

'That was clear enough,' said his aunt, laughing, but resuming a tone of some perplexity. 'Yet it takes me by surprise: I had not guessed that you were so much attracted.'

'I do like her better than any one. No one is so thoroughly good, no one is likely to make me so good, nor my father so happy.'

There was some misgiving in Mrs. Frost's tone, as she said, 'Dear Louis, you are acting on the best of motives, but—'

'Don't, pray don't, Aunt Kitty,' cried Louis, rearing himself for an instant to look her in the face, but again throwing half his body over the rail, and speaking low. 'I could not meet any one half so good, or whom I know as well. I look up to her, and—yes—I do love her heartily—I would not have done it otherwise. I don't care for beauty and trash, and my father has set his heart on it.'

'Yes, but—' she hesitated. 'My dear, I don't think it safe to marry, because one's father has set his heart on it.'

'Indeed,' said Louis, straightening himself, 'I do think I am giving myself the best chance of being made rational and consistent. I never did so well as when I was under her.'

'N—n—no—but—'

'And think how my father will unbend in a homelike home, where all should be made up to him,' he continued, deep emotion swelling his voice.

'My dear boy! And you are sure of your own feeling?'

'Quite sure. Why, I never saw any one,' said he, smiling—'I never cared for any one half so much, except you, Aunt Kitty, no, I didn't. Won't that do?'

'I know I should not have liked your grandpapa—your uncle, I mean-to make such comparisons.'

'Perhaps he had not got an Aunt Kitty,' said Louis.

'No, no! I can't have you so like a novel. No, don't be anxious. It can't be for ever so long, and, of course, the more I am with her, the better I must like her. It will be all right.'

'I don't think you know anything about it,' said Mrs. Frost, 'but there, that's the last I shall say. You'll forgive your old aunt.'

He smiled, and playfully pressed her hand, adding, 'But we don't know whether she will have me.'

Mary had meantime entered her mother's room, with a look that revealed the whole to Mrs. Ponsonby, who had already been somewhat startled by the demeanour of the father and son at breakfast.

'Oh, mamma, what is to be done?'

'What do you wish, my child?' asked her mother, putting her arm round her waist.

'I don't know yet,' said Mary. 'It is so odd!' And the disposition to laugh returned for a moment.

'You were not at all prepared.'

'Oh no! He seems so young. And,' she added, blushing, 'I cannot tell, but I should not have thought his ways were like the kind of thing.'

'Nor I, and the less since Clara has been here.'

'Oh,' said Mary, without a shade on her calm, sincere brow, 'he has Clara so much with him because he is her only friend.'

The total absence of jealousy convinced Mrs. Ponsonby that the heart could hardly have been deeply touched, but Mary continued, in a slightly trembling voice, 'I do not see why he should have done this, unless—'

'Unless that his father wished it.'

'Oh,' said Mary, somewhat disappointed, 'but how could Lord Ormersfield possibly—'

'He has an exceeding dread of Louis's making as great a mistake as he did,' said Mrs. Ponsonby; 'and perhaps he thinks you the best security.'

'And you think Louis only meant to please him?'

'My dear, I am afraid it may be so. Louis is very fond of him, and easily led by a strong character.'

She pressed her daughter closer, and felt rather than heard a little sigh; but all that Mary said was, 'Then I had better not think about it.'

'Nay, my dear, tell me first what you think of his manner.'

'It was strange, and a little debonnaire, I think,' said Mary, smiling, but tears gathering in her eyes. 'He said I was too good for him. He said he would make me happy, and that he and his father would be very happy.' A great tear fell. 'Something about not being worthy.' Mary shed a few more tears, while her mother silently caressed her; and, recovering her composure, she firmly said, 'Yes, mamma, I see it is not the real thing. It will be kinder to him to tell him to put it out of his head.'

'And you, my dear?'

'Oh, mamma, you know you could not spare me.'

'If this were the real thing, dearest—'

'No,' whispered Mary, 'I could not leave you alone with papa.'

Mrs. Ponsonby went on as if she had not heard: 'As it is, I own I am relieved that you should not wish to accept him. I cannot be sure it would be for your happiness.'

'I do not think it would be right,' said Mary, as if that were her strength.

'He is a dear, noble fellow, and has the highest, purest principles and feelings. I can't but love him almost as if he were my own child: I never saw so much sweetness and prettiness about any one, except his mother; and, oh! how far superior he is to her! But then, he is boyish, he is weak—I am afraid he is changeable.'

'Not in his affections,' said Mary, reproachfully.

'No, but in purposes. An impulse leads him he does not know where, and now, I think, he is acting on excellent motives, without knowing what he is doing. There's no security that he might not meet the person who—'

'Oh, mamma!'

'He would strive against temptation, but we have no right to expose him to it. To accept him now, it seems to me, would be taking too much advantage of his having been left so long to our mercy, and it might be, that he would become restless and discontented, find out that he had not chosen for himself—regret—and have his tone of mind lowered—'

'Oh, stop, mamma, I would not let it be, on any account.'

'No, my dear, I could not part with you where we were not sure the 'real thing' was felt for you. If he had been strongly bent on it, he would have conducted matters differently; but he knows no better.'

'You and I don't part,' said Mary.

Neither spoke till she renewed her first question,

'What is to be done?'

'Shall I go and speak to him, my dear?'

'Perhaps I had better, if you will come with me.'

Then, hesitating—'I will go to my room for a moment, and then I shall be able to do it more steadily.'

Mrs. Ponsonby's thoughts were anxious during the five minutes of Mary's absence; but she returned composed, according to her promise, whatever might be the throbbings beneath. As Mrs. Ponsonby opened the door, she saw Louis and his aunt together, and was almost amused at their conscious start, the youthful speed with which the one darted into the further end of the corridor, and the undignified haste with which the other hopped down stairs.

By the time they reached the drawing-room, he had recovered himself so as to come forward in a very suitable, simple manner, and Mary said, at once, 'Louis, thank you; but we think it would be better not—'

'Not!' exclaimed Fitzjocelyn.

'Not,' repeated Mary; 'I do not think there is that between us which would make it right.'

'There would be!' cried Louis, gaining ardour by the difficulty, 'if you would only try. Mrs. Ponsonby, tell her we would make her happy.'

'You would try,' said Mrs. Ponsonby, kindly; 'but I think she is right. Indeed, Louis, you must forgive me for saying that you are hardly old enough to make up your mind—'

'Madison is younger,' said Louis, boyishly enough to make her smile, but earnestly proceeding, 'Won't you try me? Will you not say that if I can be steady and persevering—'

'No,' said Mrs. Ponsonby; 'it would not be fair towards either of you to make any conditions.'

'But if without them, I should do better—Mary, will you say nothing?'

'We had better not think of it,' said Mary, her eyes on the ground.

'Why? is it that I am too foolish, too unworthy?'

She made a great effort. 'Not that, Louis. Do not ask any more; it is better not; you have done as your father wished—now let us be as we were before.'

'My father will be very much disappointed,' said Louis, with chagrin.

'I will take care of your father,' said Mrs. Ponsonby, and as Mary took the moment for escaping, she proceeded to say some affectionate words of her own tender feeling towards Louis; to which he only replied by saying, sadly, and with some mortification, 'Never mind; I know it is quite right. I am not worthy of her.'

'That is not the point; but I do not think you understand your own feelings, or how far you were actuated by the wish to gratify your father.'

'I assure you,' cried Louis, 'you do not guess how I look up to Mary; her unfailing kindness, her entering into all my nonsense—her firm, sound judgment, that would keep me right—and all she did for me when I was laid up. Oh! why cannot you believe how dear she is to me?'

'*How dear* is just what I do believe; but still this is not enough.'

'Just what Aunt Kitty says,' said Louis, perplexed, yet amused at his own perplexity.

'You will know better by-and-by,' she answered, smiling: 'in the meantime, believe that you are our very dear cousin, as ever.' And she shook hands with him, detecting in his answering smile a little relief, although a great deal of disappointment.

Mary had taken refuge in her room, where a great shower of tears would have their course, though she scolded herself all the time. 'Have done! have done! It is best as it is. He does not really wish it, and I could not leave mamma. We will never think of it again, and we will be as happy as we were before.'

Her mother, meanwhile, was waiting below-stairs, thinking that she should spare Louis something, by taking the initiative in speaking to his father; and she was sorry to see the alacrity with which the Earl came up to her, with a congratulatory 'Well, Mary!' She could hardly make him comprehend the real state of the case; and then his resignation was far more trying than that of the party chiefly concerned. Her praise of Fitzjocelyn had little power to comfort. 'I see how it is,' he said, calmly: 'do not try to explain it away; I acquiesce—I have no doubt you acted wisely for your daughter.'

'Nothing would have delighted me more, if he were but a few years older.'

'You need not tell me the poor boy's failings,' said his father, sadly.

'It is on account of no failing; but would it not be a great mistake to risk their happiness to fulfil our own scheme?'

'I hoped to secure their happiness.'

'Ay, but is there not something too capricious to find happiness without its own free will and choice? Did you never hear of the heart?'

'Oh! if she be attached elsewhere'—and he seemed so much relieved, that Mrs. Ponsonby was sorry to be obliged to contradict him in haste, and explain that she did not believe Fitzjocelyn's heart to be yet developed; whereupon he was again greatly vexed. 'So he has offered himself without attachment. I beg your pardon, Mary; I am sorry your daughter should have been so treated.'

'Do not misunderstand me. He is strangely youthful and simple, bent on pleasing you, and fancying his warm, brotherly feeling to be what you desire.'

'It would be the safest foundation.'

'Yes, if he were ten years older, and had seen the world; but in these things he is like a child, and it would be dangerous to influence him. Do not take it to heart; you ought to be contented, for I saw nothing so plainly as that he loves nobody half so well as you. Only be patient with him.'

'You are the same Mary as ever,' he said, softened; and she left him, hoping that she had secured a favourable audience for his son, who soon appeared at the window, somewhat like a culprit.

'I could not help it!' he said.

'No; but you may set a noble aim before you—you may render yourself worthy of her esteem and confidence, and in so doing you will fulfil my fondest hopes.'

'I asked her to try me, but they would make no conditions. I am sorry this could not be, since you wished it.'

'If you are not sorry on your own account, there are no regrets to be wasted on mine.'

'Candidly, father,' said Louis, 'much as I like her, I cannot be sorry to keep my youth and liberty a little longer.'

'Then you should never have entered on the subject at all,' said Lord Ormersfield, beginning to write a letter; and poor Louis, in his praiseworthy effort not to be reserved with him, found he had been confessing that he had not only been again making a fool of himself, but, what was less frequent and less pardonable, of his father likewise. He limped out at the window, and was presently found by his great-aunt, reading what he called a raving novel, to see how he ought to have done it. She shook her head at him, and told him that he was not even decently concerned.

'Indeed I am,' he replied. 'I wished my father to have had some peace of mind about me, and it does not flatter one's vanity.'

Dear, soft-hearted Aunt Kitty, with all her stores of comfort ready prepared, and unable to forgive, or even credit, the rejection of her Louis, without a prior attachment, gave a hint that this might be his consolation. He caught eagerly at the idea. 'I had never once thought of that! It can't be any Spaniard out in Peru—she has too much sense. What are you looking so funny about? What! is it nearer home? That's it, then! Famous! It would be a capital arrangement, if that terrible old father is conformable. What an escape I have had of him! I am sure it is a most natural and proper preference—'

'Stop! stop, Louis, you are going too fast. I know nothing. Don't say a word to Jem, on any account: indeed, you must not. It is all going on very well now; but the least notion that he was observed, or that it was his Uncle Oliver's particular wish, and there would be an end of it.'

She was just wise enough to keep back the wishes of the other vizier, but she had said enough to set Louis quite at his ease, and put him in the highest spirits. He seemed to have taken out a new lease of boyishness, and, though constrained before Mary, laughed, talked, and played pranks, so as unconsciously to fret his father exceedingly.

Clara's alert wits perceived that so many private interviews had some signification; and Mrs. Frost found her talking it over with her brother, and conjecturing so much, that granny thought it best to supply the key, thinking, perhaps, that a little jealousy would do Jem no harm. But the effect on him was to produce a fit of hearty laughter, as he remembered poor Lord Ormersfield's unaccountable urbanity and suppressed exultation in the morning's ride. 'I honour the Ponsonbys,' he said, 'for not choosing to second his lordship's endeavours to tyrannize over that poor fellow, body and soul. Poor Louis! he is fabulously dutiful.'

But Clara, recovering from her first stupor of wonder, began scolding him for presuming to laugh at anything so cruel to Louis. It was not the part of a friend! And with tears of indignation and sympathy starting from her eyes, she was pathetically certain that, though granny and Jem were so unfeeling as to laugh, his high spirits were only assumed to hide his suffering. 'Poor Louis! what had he not said to her about Mary last night! Now she knew what he meant! And as to Mary, she was glad she had never liked her, she had no patience with her: of course, she was far too prosy and stupid to care for anything like Louis, it was a great escape for him. It would serve her right to marry a horrid little crooked clerk in her father's office; and poor dear, dear Louis must get over it, and have the most beautiful wife in the world. Don't you remember, Jem, the lady with the splendid dark eyes on the platform at Euston Square, when you so nearly made us miss the train, with the brow that you said—'

'Hush, Clara, don't talk nonsense.'

CHAPTER XII
CHILDE ROLAND

> A house there is, and that's enough,
> From whence one fatal morning issues
> A brace of warriors, not in buff,
> But rustling in their silks and tissues.
> The heroines undertook the task;
> Thro' lanes unknown, o'er stiles they ventured,—
> Rapped at the door, nor stayed to ask,
> But bounce into the parlour entered.
>   Gray's Long Story.

'No carmine? Nor scarlet lake in powder?'

'Could procure some, my Lord.'

'Thank you, the actinia would not live. I must take what I can find. A lump of gamboge—'

'If you stay much longer, he will not retain his senses,' muttered James Frost, who was leaning backwards against the counter, where the bewildered bookseller of the little coast-town of Bickleypool was bustling, in the vain endeavour to understand and fulfil the demands of that perplexing customer, Lord Fitzjocelyn.

'Some drawing-paper. This is hardly absorbent enough. If you have any block sketch-books?—'

'Could procure some, my Lord.'

James looked at his watch, while the man dived into his innermost recesses. 'The tide!' he said.

'Never mind, we shall only stick in the mud.'

'How could you expect to find anything here? A half-crown paint-box is their wildest dream.'

'Keep quiet, Jem, go and look out some of those library books, like a wise man.'

'A wise man would be at a loss here,' said James, casting his eye along the battered purple backs of the circulating-library books.

'Wisdom won't condescend! Ah! thank you, this will do nicely. Those colours—yes; and the Seaside Book. I'll choose one or two. What is most popular here?'

James began to whistle; but Louis, taking up a volume, became engrossed beyond the power of hints, and hardly stepped aside to make way for some ladies who entered the shop. A peremptory touch of the arm at length roused him, and holding up the book to the shopman, he put it into his pocket, seized his ash-stick, put his arm into his cousin's, and hastened into the street.

'Did you ever see—' began Jem.

'Most striking. I did not know you had met with her. What an idea—the false self conjuring up phantoms—'

'What are you talking of? Did you not see her?'

'Elizabeth Barrett. Was she there?'

'Is that her name? Do you know her?'

'I had heard of her, but never—'

'How?—where? Who is she?'

'I only saw her name in the title-page.'

'What's all this? You did not see her?'

'Who? Did not some ladies come into the shop?'

'Some ladies! Is it possible? Why, I touched you to make you look.'

'I thought it was your frenzy about the tide. What now?—'

James made a gesture of despair. 'The loveliest creature I ever saw. You may see her yet, as she comes out. Come back!'

'Don't be so absurd,' said Fitzjocelyn, laughing, and, with instinctive dislike of staring, resisting his cousin's effort to wheel him round. 'What, you will?' withdrawing his arm. 'I shall put off without you, if you don't take care.'

And, laughing, he watched Jem hurry up the sloping street and turn the corner, then turned to pursue his own way, his steps much less lame and his looks far more healthful than they had been a month before. He reached the quay—narrow, slippery, and fishy, but not without beauty, as the green water lapped against the hewn stones, and rocked the little boats moored in the wide bay, sheltered by a richly-wooded promontory. 'Jem in a fit of romance! Well, whose fault will it be if we miss the tide? I'll sit in the boat, and read that poem again.— Oh! here he comes, out of breath. Well, Jem, did the heroine drop glove or handkerchief? Or, on a second view, was she minus an eye?'

'You were,' said James, hurrying breathlessly to unmoor the boat.

'Let me row,' said Louis; 'your breath and senses are both lost in the fair vision.'

'It is of no use to talk to you—'

'I shall ask no questions till we are out of the harbour, or you will be running foul of one of those colliers—a tribute with which the Fair Unknown may dispense.'

The numerous black colliers and lighters showed that precautions were needful till they had pushed out far enough to make the little fishy town look graceful and romantic; and the tide was ebbing so fast, that Louis deemed it prudent to spend his strength on rowing rather than on talking.

James first broke silence by exclaiming—'Do you know where Beauchastel is?'

'On the other side of the promontory. Don't you remember the spire rising among the trees, as we see it from the water?'

'That church must be worth seeing. I declare I'll go there next Sunday.'

Another silence, and Louis said—'I am curious to know whether you saw her.'

'She was getting into the carriage as I turned the corner; so I went back and asked Bull who they were.'

'I hope she was the greengrocer's third cousin.'

'Pshaw! I tell you it was Mrs. Mansell and her visitors.'

'Oho! No wonder Beauchastel architecture is so grand. What an impudent fellow you are, Jem!'

'The odd thing is,' said James, a little ashamed of Louis having put Mansell and Beauchastel together, as he had not intended, 'that it seems they asked Bull who we were. I thought one old lady was staring hard at you, as if she meant to claim acquaintance, but you shot out of the shop like a sky-rocket.'

'Luckily there's no danger of that. No one will come to molest us here.'

'Depend on it, they are meditating a descent on his lordship.'

'You shall appear in my name, then.'

'Too like a bad novel: besides, you don't look respectable enough for my tutor. And, now I think of it, no doubt she was asking Bull how he came to let such a disreputable old shooting-jacket into his shop.'

The young men worked up an absurd romance between them, as merrily they crossed the estuary, and rowed up a narrow creek, with a whitewashed village on one side, and on the other a solitary house, the garden sloping to the water, and very nautical—the vane, a union-jack waved by a brilliant little sailor on the top of a mast, and the arbour, half a boat set on end; whence, as James steered up to the stone steps that were one by one appearing, there emerged an old, grizzly, weather-beaten sailor, who took his pipe from his mouth, and caught hold of the boat.

'Thank you, Captain!' cried Fitzjocelyn. 'I've brought home the boat safe, you see, by my own superhuman exertions—no thanks to Mr. Frost, there!'

'That's his way, Captain,' retorted Jem, leaping out, and helping his cousin: 'you may thank me for getting him home at all! But for me, he would have his back against the counter, and his head in a book, this very moment.'

'Ask him what he was after,' returned Louis.

'Which of us d'ye think most likely to lag, Captain Hannaford?' cried Jem, preventing the question.

'Which would you choose to have on board?'

'Ye'd both of ye make more mischief than work,' said the old seaman, who had been looking from one to the other of the young men, as if they were performing a comedy for his special diversion.

'So you would not enter us on board the Eliza Priscilla?' cried Louis.

'No, no,' said the old man, shrewdly, and with an air of holding something back; whereupon they both pressed him, and obtained for answer, 'No, no, I wouldn't sail with you'—signing towards Fitzjocelyn—'in my crew: ye'd be more trouble than ye're worth. And as to you, sir, if I wouldn't sail with ye, I'd like still less to sail under you.'

He finished with a droll, deprecating glance, and Louis laughed heartily; but James was silent, and as soon as they had entered the little parlour, declared that it would not do to encourage that old skipper—he was waylaying them like the Ancient Mariner, and was actually growing impudent.

'An old man's opinion of two youngsters is not what I call impudence,' began Louis, with an emphasis that made Jem divert his attack.

Those two cousins had never spent a happier month than in these small lodgings, built by the old retired merchant-seaman evidently on the model of that pride of his heart, the Eliza Priscilla, his little coasting trader, now the charge of his only surviving son; for this was a family where drowning was like a natural death, and old Captain Hannaford looked on the probability of sleeping in Ebbscreek churchyard, much as Bayard did at the prospect of dying in his bed. His old deaf wife kept the little cabin-like rooms most exquisitely neat; and the twelve-years-old Priscilla, the orphan of one of the lost sons, waited on the gentlemen with an old-fashioned, womanly deportment and staid countenance that, in the absence of all other grounds of distress, Louis declared was quite a pain to him.

The novelty of the place, the absence of restraint, the easy life, and, above all, the freshness of returning health, rendered his spirits exceedingly high, and he had never been more light-hearted and full of mirth. James, elated at his rapid improvement, was scarcely less full of liveliness and frolic, enjoying to the utmost the holiday, which perhaps both secretly felt might be the farewell to the perfect carelessness of boyish relaxation. Bathing, boating, fishing, dabbling, were the order of the day, and withal just enough quarrelling and teasing to add a little spice to their pleasures. Louis was over head and ears in maritime natural history; but Jem, backed by Mrs. Hannaford, prohibited his 'messes' from making a permanent settlement in the parlour; though festoons of seaweed trellised the porch, ammonites heaped the grass-plat, tubs of sea-water flanked the approach to the front door; and more than one bowl, with inmates of a suspicious nature, was often deposited even on the parlour table.

On the afternoon following the expedition to Bickleypool, Louis was seated, with an earthenware pan before him, coaxing an actinia with raw beef to expand her blossom, to be copied for Miss Faithfull. Another bowl stood near, containing some feathery serpulas; and the weeds were heaped on the locker of the window behind him, and on the back of the chair which supported his lame foot. The third and only remaining chair accommodated James, with a book placed on the table; and a semicircle swept round it, within which nothing marine might extend.

Louis was by turns drawing, enticing his refractory sitter, exhorting her to bloom, and complimenting her delicate beauty, until James, with a groan, exclaimed, 'Is silence impossible to you, Fitzjocelyn? I would go into the garden, but that I should be beset by the intolerable old skipper!'

'I beg your pardon—I thought you never heard nor heeded me.'

'I don't in general, but this requires attention; and it is past all bearing to hear how you go on to that Jelly!'

'Read aloud, then: it will answer two purposes.'

'This is Divinity—Hooker,' said James, sighing wearily.

'So much the better. I read some once; I wish I had been obliged to go on.'

'You are the oddest fellow!—After all, I believe you have a craving after my profession.'

'Is that a discovery?' said Louis, washing the colour out of his brush. 'The only person I envy is a country curate—except a town one.'

'Don't talk like affectation!' growled James.

'Do you know, Jem,' said Louis, leaning back, and drawing the brush between his lips, 'I am persuaded that something will turn up to prevent it from being your profession.'

'Your persuasions are wrong, then!'

'That fabulous uncle in the Indies—'

'You know I am determined to accept nothing from my uncle, were he to lay it at my feet—which he never will.'

'Literally or metaphorically?' asked Louis, softly.

'Pshaw!'

'You Dynevors don't resemble my sea-pink. See how she stretches her elegant fringes for this very unpleasant bit of meat! There! I won't torment you any more; read, and stop my mouth!'

'You are in earnest?'

'You seem to think that if a man cannot be a clergyman, he is not to be a Christian.'

'Then don't break in with your actinias and stuff!'

'Certainly not,' said Louis, gravely.

The first interruption came from James himself. Leaping to his feet with a sudden bound, he exclaimed, 'There they are!' and stood transfixed in a gaze of ecstasy.

'You have made me smudge my lake,' said Louis, in the mild tone of 'Diamond, Diamond!'

'I tell you, there they are!' cried James, rushing into wild activity.

'One would think it the Fair Unknown,' said Louis, not troubling himself to look round, nor desisting from washing out his smudge.

'It is! it is!—it is all of them! Here they come, I tell you, and the place is a very merman's cave!'

'Take care—the serpula—don't!' as James hurriedly opened the door leading to the stairs—disposed of the raw meat on one step and the serpulas on another, and hurled after them the heap of seaweed, all but one trailing festoon of 'Luckie Minnie's lines,' which, while his back was turned, Louis by one dexterous motion wreathed round the crown of his straw hat; otherwise never stirring, but washing quietly on, until he rose as little Priscilla opened the door, and stood aside, mutely overawed at the stream of flounced ladies that flowed past, and seemed to fill up the entire room. It was almost a surprise to find that, after all, there were only three of them!

'I knew I was not mistaken,' said a very engaging, affectionate voice. 'It is quite shocking to have to introduce myself to you—Lady Conway—'

'My aunt!' cried Louis, with eager delight—'and my cousin!' he added, turning with a slight blush towards the maiden, whom he felt, rather than saw, to be the worthy object of yesterday's rapture.

'Not quite,' she answered, not avoiding the grasp of his hand, but returning it with calm, distant politeness.

'Not quite,' repeated Lady Conway. 'Your real cousins are no farther off than Beauchastel—'

'Where you must come and see them,' added the third lady—a portly, cordial, goodnatured dame, whom Lady Conway introduced as Mrs. Mansell, who had known his mother well; and Louis making a kind of presentation of his cousin James, the two elder ladies were located on two of the chairs: the younger one, as if trying to be out of the way, placed herself on the locker. Jem stood leaning on the back of the other chair; and Louis stood over his aunt, in an ecstasy at the meeting—at the kind, warm manner and pleasant face of his aunt—and above all, at the indescribable pleasure imparted by the mere presence of the beautiful girl, though he hardly dared even to look at her; and she was the only person whose voice was silent in the chorus of congratulation, on the wonderful chance that had brought the aunt and nephew together. The one had been a fortnight at Beauchastel, the other a month at Ebbscreek, without guessing at each other's neighbourhood, until Lady Conway's attention had been attracted at the library by Louis's remarkable resemblance to her sister, and making inquiries, she had learnt that he was no other than Lord Fitzjocelyn. She was enchanted with the likeness, declaring that all she wished was to see him look less delicate, and adding her entreaties to those of Mrs. Mansell, that the two young men would come at once to Beauchastel.

Louis looked with wistful doubt at James, who, he knew, could not brook going to fine places in the character of tutor; but, to his surprise and pleasure, James was willing and eager, and made no demur, except that Fitzjocelyn could not walk so far, and the boat was gone out. Mrs. Mansell then proposed the ensuing Monday, when, she said, she and Mr. Mansell should be delighted to have them to meet a party of shooting gentlemen—of course they were sportsmen. Louis answered at once for James; but for himself, he could not walk, nor even ride the offered shooting-pony; and thereupon ensued more minute questions whether his ankle were still painful.

'Not more than so as to be a useful barometer. I have been testing it by the sea-weeds. If I am good for nothing else, I shall be a walking weather-glass, as well as a standing warning against man-traps.'

'You don't mean that you fell into a man-trap!' exclaimed Mrs. Mansell, in horror. 'That will be a warning for Mr. Mansell! I have such a dread of the frightful things!'

'A trap ingeniously set by myself,' said Louis. 'I was only too glad no poor poacher fell into it.'

'Your father told me that it was a fall down a steep bank,' exclaimed Lady Conway.

'Exactly so; but I suppose he thought it for my credit to conceal that my trap consisted of a flight of stone stops, very solid and permanent, with the trifling exception of cement.'

'If the truth were known,' said James, 'I believe that a certain scamp of a boy was at the bottom of those steps.'

'I'm the last person to deny it,' said Louis, quietly, though not without rising colour, 'there was a scamp of a boy at the bottom of the steps, and very unpleasant he found it—though not without the best consequences, and among them the present—' And he turned to Lady Conway with a pretty mixture of gracefulness and affection, enough to win the heart of any aunt.

Mrs. Mansell presently fell into raptures at the sight of the drawing materials, which must, she was sure, delight Isabel, but she was rather discomfited by the sight of the 'subject,'—called it an odious creature, then good-humouredly laughed at herself, but would not sit down again, evidently wishing to escape from close quarters with such monsters. Lady Conway likewise rose, and looked into the basin, exclaiming, in her turn, 'Ah! I see you understand these things! Yes, they are very interesting!

Virginia will be delighted; she has been begging me for an aquarium wherever we go. You must tell her how to manage it. Look, Isabel, would not she be in ecstasies?'

Miss Conway looked, but did not seem to partake in the admiration. 'I am perverse enough never to like what is the fashion,' she said.

'I tried to disgust Fitzjocelyn with his pets on that very ground,' said James; 'but their charms were too strong for him.'

'Fashion is the very testimony to them,' said Louis. 'I think I could convince you.'

He would perhaps have produced his lovely serpula blossoms, but he was forced to pass on to his aunt and Mrs. Mansell, who had found something safer for their admiration, in the shape of a great Cornu ammonis in the garden.

'He can throw himself into any pursuit,' said James, as he paused at the door with Miss Conway; but suddenly becoming aware of the slimy entanglement round his hat, he exclaimed, 'Absurd fellow!' and pulled it off rather petulantly, adding, with a little constraint, 'Recovery does put people into mad spirits! I fancy the honest folks here look on in amaze.'

Miss Conway gave a very pretty smile of sympathy and consolation, that shone like a sunbeam on her beautiful pensive features and dark, soft eyes. Then she began to admire the view, as they stood on the turf, beside Captain Hannaford's two small cannon, overlooking the water towards Bickleypool, with a purple hill rising behind it. A yacht was sailing into the harbour, and James ran indoors to fetch a spy-glass, while Lady Conway seized the occasion of asking her nephew his tutor's name.

Louis, who had fancied she must necessarily understand all his kindred, was glad to guard against shocks to Jem's sensitive pride, and eagerly explained the disproportion between his birth and fortune, and his gallant efforts to relieve his grandmother from her burthens. He was pleased to find that he had touched all his auditors, and to hear kind-hearted Mrs. Mansell repeat her special invitation to Mr. Frost Dynevor with double cordiality.

'If you must play practical jokes,' said James, as they watched the carriage drive off, 'I wish you would choose better moments for them.'

'I thought you would be more in character as a merman brave,' said Louis.

'I wonder what character you thought you appeared in?'

'I never meant you to discover it while they were here, nor would you, if you were not so careful of your complexion. Come, throw it at my head now, as you would have done naturally, and we shall have fair weather again!'

'I am only concerned at the impression you have made.'

'Too late now, is it? You don't mean to be bad company for the rest of the day. It is too bad, after such a presence as has been here. She is a poem in herself. It is like a vision to see her move in that calm, gliding way. Such eyes, so deep, so tranquil, revealing the sphere apart where she dwells! An ideal! How can you be savage after sitting in the same room, and hearing that sweet, low voice?'

Meantime the young lady sat back in the carriage, dreamily hearing, and sometimes answering, the conversation of her two elders, as they returned through pretty forest-drives into the park of Beauchastel, and up to the handsome, well-kept house; where, after a few words from Mrs. Mansell, she ascended the stairs.

'Isabel!' cried a bright voice, and a girl of fourteen came skating along the polished oak corridor. 'Come and have some tea in the school-room, and tell us your adventures!' And so saying, she dragged the dignified Isabel into an old-fashioned sitting-room, where a little pale child, two years younger, sprang up, and, with a cry of joy, clung round the elder sister.

'My white bind-weed,' said Isabel, fondly caressing her, 'have you been out on the pony?'

'Oh I yes, we wanted only you. Sit down there.'

And as Isabel obeyed, the little Louisa placed herself on her lap, with one arm round her neck, and looked with proud glee at the kind, sensible-faced governess who was pouring out the tea.

'The reconnoitring party!' eagerly cried Virginia.

'Did you find the cousin?'

'Yes, we did.'

'Oh! Then what is he like?'

'You will see when he comes on Monday.'

'Coming—oh! And is he so very handsome?'

'I can see how pretty a woman your Aunt Louisa must have been.'

'News!' laughed Virginia; 'when mamma is always preaching to me to be like her!'

'Is he goodnatured?' asked Louisa.

'I had not full means of judging,' said Isabel, more thoughtfully than seemed justified by the childish question. 'His cousin is coming too,' she added; 'Mr. Frost Dynevor.'

'Another cousin!' exclaimed Virginia.

'No; a relation of Lord Ormersfield—a person to be much respected. He is heir to a lost estate, and of a very grand old family. Lord Fitzjocelyn says that he is exerting himself to the very utmost for his grandmother and orphan sister; denying himself everything. He is to be a clergyman. There was a book of divinity open on the table.'

'He must be very good!' said Louisa, in a low, impressed voice, and fondling her sister's hand. 'Will he be as good as Sir Roland?'

'Oh! I am glad he is coming!' cried Virginia. 'We have so wished to see somebody very good!'

A bell rang—a signal that Lady Conway would be in her room, where she liked her two girls to come to her while she was dressing. Louisa reluctantly detached herself from her sister, and Virginia lingered to say, 'Dress quickly, please, please, Isabel. I know there is a new bit of Sir Roland done! Oh! I hope Mr. Dynevor is like him!'

'Not quite,' said Isabel, smiling as they ran away. 'Poor children, I am afraid they will be disappointed; but long may their craving be to see 'somebody very good!'

'I am very glad they should meet any one answering the description,' said the governess. 'I don't gather that you are much delighted with the object of the expedition.'

'A pretty boy—very pretty. It quite explains all I have ever heard of his mother.'

'As you told the children.'

'More than I told the children. Their aunt never by description seemed to me my ideal, as you know. I would rather have seen a likeness to Lord Ormersfield, who—though I don't like him—has something striking in the curt, dry, melancholy dignity of his manner.'

'And how has Lord Fitzjocelyn displeased you?'

'Perhaps there is no harm in him—he may not have character enough for that; but talk, attitudes, everything betrays that he is used to be worshipped—takes it as a matter of course, and believes nothing so interesting as himself.'

'Don't you think you may have gone with your mind made up?'

'If you mean that I thought myself uncalled for, and heartily detested the expedition, you are right; but I saw what I did not expect.'

'Was it very bad?'

'A very idle practical joke, such as I dislike particularly. A quantity of wet sea-weed wound round Mr. Dynevor's hat.'

Miss King laughed. 'Really, my dear, I don't think you know what young men like from each other.'

'Mr. Dynevor did not like it,' said Isabel, 'though he tried to pass it off lightly as the spirits of recovery. Those spirits—I am afraid he has too much to suffer from them. There is something so ungenerous in practical wit, especially from a prosperous man to one unprosperous!'

'Well, Isabel, I won't contradict, but I should imagine that such things often showed people to be on the best of terms.'

Isabel shook her head, and left the room, to have her dark hair braided, with little heed from herself, as she sat dreamily over a book. Before the last bracelet was clasped, she was claimed by her two little sisters, who gave her no peace till her desk was opened, and a manuscript drawn forth, that they might hear the two new pages of her morning's work. It was a Fouque-like tale, relieving and giving expression to the yearnings for holiness and loftiness that had grown up within Isabel Conway in the cramped round of her existence. The story went back to the troubadour days of Provence, where a knight, the heir of a line of shattered fortunes, was betrothed to the heiress of the oppressors, that thus all wrongs might be redressed. They had learnt to love, when Sir Roland discovered that the lands in dispute had been won by sacrilege. He met Adeline at a chapel in a little valley, to tell the whole. They agreed to sacrifice themselves, that restitution should be made; the knight to go as a crusader to the Holy Land; the lady, after waiting awhile to tend her aged father, to enter a convent, and restore her dower to the church. Twice had Isabel written that parting, pouring out her heart in the high-souled tender devotion of Roland and his Adeline; and both feeling and description were beautiful and poetical, though unequal. Louisa used to cry whenever she heard it, yet only wished to hear it again and again, and when Virginia insisted on reading it to Miss King, tears had actually been surprised in the governess's eyes. Yet she liked still better Adeline's meek and patient temper, where breathed the feeling Isabel herself would fain cherish—the deep, earnest, spiritual life and high consecrated purpose that were with the Provencal maiden through all her enforced round of gay festivals, light minstrelsy, tourneys, and Courts of Love. Thus far had the story gone. Isabel had been writing a wild, mysterious ballad, reverting to that higher love and the true spirit of self-sacrifice, which was to thrill strangely on the ears of the thoughtless at a contention for the Golden Violet, and which she had adapted to a favourite air, to the extreme delight of the two girls. To them the Chapel in the valley, Roland and his Adeline, were very nearly real, and were the hidden joy of their hearts,—all the more because their existence was a precious secret between the three sisters and Miss King, who viewed it as such an influence on the young ones, that, with more meaning than she could have explained, she called it their Telemaque. The following-up of the teaching of Isabel and Miss King might lead to results as little suspected by Lady Conway as Fenelon's philosophy was by Louis XIV.

Lady Conway was several years older than her beautiful sister, and had married much later. Perhaps she had aimed too high, and had met with disappointments unavowed; for she had finally contented herself with becoming the second wife of Sir Walter Conway, and was now his serene, goodnatured, prosperous widow. Disliking his estate and neighbourhood, and thinking the daughters wanted London society and London masters, she shut up the house until her son should be of age, and spent the season in Lowndes-square, the autumn either abroad, in visits, or at watering-places.

Beauchastel was an annual resort of the family. Isabel was more slenderly portioned than her half-sisters; and she was one of the nearest surviving relations of her mother's cousin, Mr. Mansell, whose large comfortable house was always hospitable; and whose wife, a great dealer in goodnatured confidential gossip, used to throw out hints to her great friend Lady Conway, that much depended on Isabel's marriage—that Mr. Mansell had been annoyed at connexions formed by others of his relations—but though he had decided on nothing, the dear girl's choice might make a great difference.

Nothing could be more passive than Miss Conway. She could not remember her mother, but her childhood had been passed under an admirable governess; and though her own Miss Longman had left her, Miss King, the successor, was a person worthy of her chief confidence. At two-and-twenty, the school-room was still the home of her affections, and her ardent love was lavished on her little sisters and her brother Walter.

Going out with Lady Conway was mere matter of duty and submission. She had not such high animal spirits as to find enjoyment in her gaieties, and her grave, pensive character only attained to walking through her part; she had seen little but the more frivolous samples of society, scorned and disliked all that was worldly and manoeuvring, and hung back from levity and coquetry with utter distaste. Removed from her natural home, where she would have found duties and seen various aspects of life, she had little to interest or occupy her in her unsettled wanderings; and to her the sap of life was in books, in dreams, in the love of her brother and sisters, and in discussions with Miss King; her favourite vision for the future, the going to live with Walter at Thornton Conway when he should be of age. But Walter was younger than Louisa, and it was a very distant prospect.

Her characteristic was a calm, serene indifference, in which her stepmother acquiesced, as lovers of peace do in what they cannot help; and the more willingly, that her tranquil dignity and pensive grace exactly suited the style of her tall queenly figure, delicate features, dark soft languid eyes, and clear olive complexion, just tinged with rosebud pink.

What Louis said of her to his tutor on the Monday night of their arrival was beyond the bounds of all reason; and it was even more memorable that Jem was neither satirical nor disputatious, assented to all, and if he sighed, it was after his door was shut.

A felicitous day ensued, spent by James in shooting, by Fitzjocelyn, in the drawing-room; whither Mrs. Mansell had requested Isabel's presence, as a favour to herself. The young lady sat at work, seldom raising her eyes, but this was enough for him; his intense admiration and pleasure in her presence so exhilarated him, that he rattled away to the utmost. Louisa was at first the excuse. In no further doubt of his good-nature, she spent an hour in the morning in giving him anagrams to guess; and after she had repaired to the schoolroom, he went on inventing fresh ones, and transposing the ivory letters, rambling on in his usual style of pensive drollery. Happiness never set him off to advantage, and either there was more froth than ordinary, or it appeared unusually ridiculous to an audience who did not detect the under-current of reflection. His father would have been in despair, Mrs. Ponsonby or Mary would have interposed; but the ladies of Beauchastel laughed and encouraged him, — all but Isabel, who sat in the window, and thought of Adeline, 'spighted and angered both,' by a Navarrese coxcomb, with sleeves down to his heels, and shoes turned up to his knees. She gave herself great credit for having already created him a Viscount.

In the afternoon, Louis drove out lionizing with his aunt; but though the ponies stopped of themselves at all the notable views; sea, hill, and river were lost on him. Lady Conway could have drawn out a far less accessible person, and her outpouring of his own sentiments made him regard her as perfect.

She consulted him about her winter's resort. Louisa required peculiar care, and she had thought of trying mineral baths—what was thought of Northwold? what kind of houses were there? The Northwold faculty themselves might have taken a lesson from Fitzjocelyn's eloquent analysis of the chemical properties of the waters, and all old Mr. Frost's spirit would seem to have descended on him when he dilated on the House Beautiful.

Lodgers for Miss Faithfull! what jubilee they would cause! And such lodgers! No wonder he was in ecstasy. All the evening the sound of his low, deliberate voice was unceasing, and his calm announcements to his two little cousins were each one more startling than the last; while James, to whom it was likewise all sunshine, was full of vivacity, and a shrewd piquancy of manner that gave zest to all he said, and wonderfully enlivened the often rather dull circle at Beauchastel.

Morning came; and when the ladies descended to breakfast, it was found that Lord Fitzjocelyn had gone out with the sportsmen. The children lamented, and their elders pronounced a young gentleman's passion for shooting to be quite incalculable. When, late in the day, the party returned, it was reported that he did not appear to care much for the sport; but had walked beside Mr. Mansell's shooting-pony, and had finally gone with him to see his model farm. This was a sure road to the old squire's heart, and no one was more delighted with the guest. For Aunt Catharine's sake, Louis was always attracted by old age, and his attentive manners had won Mr. Mansell's heart, even before his inquiries about his hobby had completed the charm. To expound and to listen to histories of agricultural experiments that really answered, was highly satisfactory to both, and all the evening they were eager over the great account-book which was the pride of the squire's heart; while Virginia and Louisa grumbled or looked imploring, and Isabel marvelled at there being any interest for any one in old Mr. Mansell's conversation.

'What is the meaning of this?' asked James, as they went up stairs.

Louis shrugged like a Frenchman, looked debonnaire, and said 'Good-night.'

Again he came down; prepared for shooting, though both pale and lame; but he quietly put aside all expostulations, walking on until, about fifty yards from the house, a pebble, turning under the injured foot, caused such severe pain that he could but just stagger to a tree and sit down.

There was much battling before Mr. Mansell would consent to leave him, or he to allow James to help him back to the house, before going on to overtake the party.

Very irate was Jem, at folly that seemed to have undone the benefits of the last month, and at changeableness that was a desertion of the queen to whom all homage was due. He was astonished that Louis turned into the study, a room little inhabited in general, and said, 'Make haste—you will catch the others; don't fall in with the ladies.'

'I mean to send your aunt to you.'

'Pray don't. Can't you suppose that peace is grateful after having counted every mortal hour last night?'

'Was that the reason you were going to walk ten miles without a leg to stand upon? Fitzjocelyn! is this systematic?'

'What is?' said Louis, wearily.

'Your treatment of—your aunt.'

'On what system should aunts be treated?'

'Of all moments to choose for caprice! Exactly when I thought even you were fixed!'

'Pur troppo,' sighed Louis.

'Ha!' cried Jem, 'you have not gone and precipitated matters! I thought you could never amaze me again; but even you might have felt she was a being to merit rather more time and respect!'

'Even I am not devoid of the organ of veneration.'

His meek tone was a further provocation; and with uplifted chin, hair ruffled like the crest of a Shetland pony, flashing eyes, and distinct enunciation, James exclaimed, 'You will excuse me for not understanding you. You come here; you devote yourself to your aunt and cousins—you seem strongly attracted; then, all on a sudden, you rush out shooting—an exercise for which you don't care, and when you can't walk: you show the most pointed neglect. And after being done-up yesterday, you repeat the experiment to-day, as if for the mere object of laming yourself for life. I could understand pique or temper, but you have not the—'

'The sense,' said Louis; 'no, nor anything to be piqued at.'

'If there be a motive,' said James, 'I have a right to demand not to be trifled with any longer.'

'I wish you could be content to shoot your birds, and leave me in peace: you will only have your fun spoilt, like mine, and go into a fury. The fact is, that my father writes in a state of perturbation. He says, I might have understood, from the tenor of his conduct, that he did not wish me to be intimate with my aunt's family! He cannot know anything about them, for it is all one warning against fashion and frivolity. He does not blame us—especially not you.'

'I wish he did.'

'But he desires that our intercourse should be no more than propriety demands, and plunges into a discourse against first impressions, beauty, and the like.'

'So that's the counterblast!'

'You ought to help me, Jem,' said Louis, dejectedly.

'I'll help you with all my heart to combat your father's prejudices.'

'An hour's unrestrained intercourse with these people would best destroy them,' said Louis; 'but, in the mean time—I wonder what he means.'

'He means that he is in terror for his darling scheme.'

'Mrs. Ponsonby was very right,' sighed Louis.

'Ay! A pretty condition you would be in, if she had not had too much principle to let you be a victim to submission. That's what you'll come to, though! You will never know the meaning of passion; you will escape something by it, though you will be twisted round his lordship's finger, and marry his choice. I hope she will have red hair!'

'Negative and positive obedience stand on different grounds,' said Louis, with such calmness as often fretted James, but saved their friendship. 'Besides, till I had this letter, I had no notion of any such thing.'

James's indignation resulted in fierce stammering; while Louis deliberately continued a viva voce self-examination, with his own quaint naivete, betraying emotion only by the burning colour of cheek and brow.

'No; I had no such notion. I only felt that her presence had the gladdening, inspiring, calming effect of moonlight or starlight. I reverenced her as a dream of poetry walking the earth. Ha! now one hears the sound of it—that is like it! I did not think it was such a confirmed case. I should have gone on in peace but for this letter, and never thought about it at all.'

'So much the better for you!'

'My father is too just and candid not to own his error, and be thankful.'

'And you expect her to bear with your alternations in the mean time?'

'Towards her I have not alternated. When I have made giggle with Clara under the influence of the starry sky, did you suppose me giggling with Lyra or the Pleiades! I should dread to see the statue descend; it seemed irreverence even to gaze. The lofty serenity keeps me aloof. I like to believe in a creature too bright and good for human nature's daily food. Our profane squinting through telescopes at the Lady Moon reveals nothing but worn-out volcanoes and dry oceans, black gulfs and scorched desolation; but verily that may not be Lady Moon's fault—only that of our base inventions.

So I would be content to mark her—Isabel, I mean—queenly, moonlike name!—walk in beauty and tranquillity unruffled, without distorting my vision by personal aims at bringing her down to my level. There—don't laugh at me, Jem.'

'No, I am too sorry for you.'

'Why!' he exclaimed, impatient of compassion; 'do you think it desperate?'

'I see your affection given to a most worthy object, and I know what your notions of submission will end in.'

'Once for all, Jem,' said Fitzjocelyn, 'do you know how you are using my father? No; Isabel Conway may be the happiness or the disappointment of my life—I cannot tell. I am sure my father is mistaken, and I believe he may be convinced; but I am bound not to fly in the face of his direct commands, and, till we can come to an understanding, I must do the best I can, and trust to—'

The last word was lost, as he turned to nurse his ankle, and presently to entreat James to join the sportsmen; but Jem was in a mood to do nothing pleasing to himself nor to any one else. A sacrifice is usually irritating to the spectators, who remonstrate rather than listen to self-reproach; and Louis had been guilty of three great offences—being in the right, making himself ridiculous, and submitting tamely—besides the high-treason to Isabel's beauty. It was well that the Earl was safe out of the way of the son of the Pendragons!

Fitzjocelyn was in pain and discomfort enough to make James unwilling to leave him; though his good-will did not prevent him from keeping up such a stream of earplugs and sinister auguries, that it was almost the climax of good-temper that enabled Louis to lie still, trying to read a great quarto Park's Travels, and abstaining from any reply that could aggravate matters. As the one would not go to luncheon, the other would not; and after watching the sound of the ladies' setting out for their drive, Louis said that he would go and lie on the turf; but at that moment the door was thrown open, and in ran Virginia. Explanations were quickly exchanged—how she had come to find Vertot's Malta for Isabel, and how he had been sent in by hurting his foot.

'Were you going to stay in all day?' said Virginia. 'Oh, come with us! We have the pony-carriage; and we are going to a dear old ruin, walking and driving by turns. Do, pray, come; there's plenty of room.'

There could be no objection to the school-room party, and it was no small relief to escape from James and hope he was amused; so Fitzjocelyn allowed himself to be dragged off in triumph, and James was acceding to his entreaty that he would go in search of the shooting-party, when, as they reached the hall-door, they beheld Miss Conway waiting on the steps.

There was no receding for her any more than for Louis, so she could only make a private resolution against the pony-carriage, and dedicate herself to the unexceptionable company of little sister, governess and tutor; for James had resigned the shooting, and attached himself to the expedition. It was an excellent opportunity of smoothing his cousin's way, and showing that all was not caprice that might so appear: so he began to tell of his most advantageous traits of character, and to explain away his whimsical conduct, with great ardour and ingenuity. He thought he should be perfectly satisfied if he could win but one smile of approbation from that gravely beautiful mouth; and it came at last, when he told of Fitzjocelyn's devoted affection to Mrs. Frost and his unceasing kindness to the old ladies of Dynevor Terrace. Thus gratified, he let himself be led into abstract questions of principle,—a style of discussion frequent between Miss King and Isabel, but on which the latter had never seen the light of a man's mind thrown except through books. The gentlemen whom she had met were seldom either deep or earnest, except those too much beyond her reach; and she had avoided anything like confidence or intimacy: but Mr. Dynevor could enlighten and vivify her perplexed reflections, answer her inquiries, confirm her opinion of books, and enter into all that she ventured with diffidence to express. He was enchanted to find that no closer approach could dim the lustre of Louis's moon, and honoured her doubly for what she had made herself in frivolous society. He felt sure that his testimony would gain credit where Fitzjocelyn's would be regarded as love-blinded, and already beheld himself forcing full proof of her merits on the reluctant Earl, beholding Louis happy, and Isabel emancipated from constraint.

A five miles' walk gave full time for such blissful discoveries; for Miss Conway was resolute against entering the pony-carriage, and walked on, protesting against ever being fatigued; while Louis was obliged to occupy his seat in the carriage, with a constant change of companions.

'I think, my dear,' said Miss King, when the younger girls had gone to their mother's toilette, 'that you will have to forgive me.'

'Meaning,' said Isabel, 'that you are bitten too! Ah! Miss King, you could not withstand the smile with which he handed you in!'

'Could you withstand such an affectionate account of your cruel, tyrannical practical joker?'

'Facts are stubborn things. Do you know what Mr. Dynevor is doing at this moment? I met him in the gallery, hurrying off to Ebbscreek for some lotion for Lord Fitzjocelyn's ankle. I begged him to let Mrs. Mansell send; but no-no one but himself could find it, and his cousin could not bear strangers to disarrange his room. If anything were wanting, it would be enough to see how simply and earnestly such a man has been brought to pamper—nay, to justify, almost to adore, the whims and follies of this youth.'

'If anything were wanting to what? To your dislike.'

'It would not be so active as dislike, unless—' Isabel spoke with drooping head, and Miss King did not ask her to finish, but said, 'He has not given you much cause for alarm.'

'So; he is at least a thorough gentleman. It may be conceit, or wrong self-consciousness, but from the moment the poor boy was spied in the shop, I had a perception that mamma and Mrs. Mansell marked him down. Personally he would be innocent, but, through all his chatter, I cannot shake off the fancy that I am watched, or that decided indifference is not needed to keep him at a distance.'

'I wish you could have seen him without knowing him!'

'In vain, dear Miss King! I can't bear handsome men. I see his frivolity and shallowness; and for amiability, what do you think of keeping his cousin all the morning from shooting for such a mere nothing, and then sending him off for a ten miles' walk?

'For my part, I confess that I was struck with the good sense and kindness he showed in our tete-a-tete—I thought it justified Mr. Dynevor's description.'

'Yes, I have no doubt that there is some good in him. He might have done very well, if he had not always been an idol.'

Isabel was the more provoked with Lord Fitzjocelyn, when, by-and-by, he appeared in the drawing-room, and related the result of his cousin's mission. Jem, who would know better than himself where to find his property, had not chosen to believe his description of the spot where he had left the lotion, and, in the twilight, Louis had found his foot coiled about by the feelers and claws of a formidable monster—no other than a bottled scorpion, a recent present from Captain Hannaford. He did not say how emblematic the scorpion lotion was of that which Jem had been administering to his wounded spirit all the morning, but he put the story in so ludicrous a light that Isabel decided that Mr. Dynevor was ungenerously and ungratefully treated as a butt; and she turned away in displeasure from the group whom the recital was amusing, to offer her sympathy to the tutor, and renew the morning's conversation.

CHAPTER XIII
FROSTY, BUT KINDLY

> Go not eastward, go not westward,
> For a stranger whom we know not.
> Like a fire upon the hearthstone,
> Is a neighbour's homely daughter;
> Like the moonlight or the starlight,
> Is the handsomest of strangers.
>   Legend of Hiawatha.

'What a laboured production had the letter been! How many copies had the statesman written! how late had he sat over it at night! how much more consideration had he spent on it than on papers involving the success of his life! A word too much or too little might precipitate the catastrophe, and the bare notion of his son's marriage with a pupil of Lady Conway renewed and gave fresh poignancy to the past.

At first his anxieties were past mention; but he grew restless under them, and the instinct of going to Mrs. Ponsonby prevailed. At least, she would know what had transpired from James, or from Fitzjocelyn to Mrs. Frost.

She had heard of ecstatic letters from both the cousins, and Mary had been delighted to identify Miss Conway with the Isabel of whom one of her school friends spoke rapturously, but the last letter had beenfrom James to his grandmother, declaring that Lord Ormersfield was destroying the happiness of the most dutiful of sons, who was obedient even to tameness, and so absurd that there was no bearing him. His lordship must hear reason, and learn that he was rejecting the most admirable creature in existence, her superiority of mind exceeding even her loveliness of person. He had better beware of tyranny; it was possible to abuse submission, and who could answer for the consequences of thwarting strong affections? All the ground Fitzjocelyn had gained in the last six weeks had been lost; and for the future, James would not predict.

'An uncomfortable matter,' said Mrs. Ponsonby, chiefly for the sake of reading her daughter's feelings. 'If it were not in poor Louis's mind already, his father and James would plant it there by their contrary efforts.'

'Oh! I hope it will come right,' said Mary. 'Louis is too good, and his father too kind, for it not to end well. And then, mamma, he will be able to prove, what nobody will believe—that he is constant.'

'You think so, do you?' said her mother, smiling.

Mary blushed, but answered, 'where he really cared, he would be constant. His fancy might be taken, and he might rave, but he would never really like what was not good.—If he does think about Miss Conway, we may trust she is worthy of him. Oh! I should like to see her!'

Mary's eyes lighted up with an enthusiasm that used to be a stranger to them. It was not the over-acted indifference nor the tender generosity of disappointment: it seemed more to partake of the fond, unselfish, elder-sisterly affection that she had always shown towards Louis, and it set her mother quite at ease.

Seeing Lord Ormersfield riding into the terrace, Mary set out for a walk, that he might have his tete-a-tete freely with her mother. On coming home, she met him on the stairs; and he spoke with a sad softness and tone of pardon that alarmed her so much, that she hastened to ask her mother whether Louis had really avowed an attachment.

'Oh no,' said Mrs. Ponsonby; 'he has written a very right-minded letter, on the whole, poor boy! though he is sure the Conways have only to be known to be appreciated. Rather too true! It is in his Miss Fanny hand, stiff and dispirited; and his father has worked himself into such a state of uneasiness, that I think it will end in his going to Ebbscreek at once.'

'O mamma, you won't let him go and torment Louis?'

'Why, Mary, have you been learning of James? Perhaps he would torment him more from a distance; and besides, I doubt what sort of counsellor James is likely to make in his present mood.'

'I never could see that James made any difference to Louis,' said Mary. 'I know people think he does, because Louis gives up wishes and plans to him; but he is not led in opinions or principles, as far as I can see.'

'Not unless his own wishes went the same way.'

'At least, Lord Ormersfield will see Miss Conway!'

'I am afraid that will do no good. It will not be for the first time. Lady Conway has been his dread from the time of his own marriage; and if she should come to Northwold, he will be in despair. I do think he must be right; she must be making a dead set at Louis.'

'Not Miss Conway,' said Mary. 'I know she must be good, or he would not endure her for a moment.'

'Mary, you do not know the power of beauty.'

'I have heard of it,' said Mary; 'I have seen how Dona Guadalupe was followed. But those people were not like Louis. No, mamma; I think James might be taken in, I don't think Louis could be—unless he had a very grand dream of his own before his eyes; and then it would be his own dream, not the lady that he saw; and by-and-by he would find it out, and be so vexed!'

'And, I trust, before he had committed himself!'

'Mamma, I won't have you think Miss Conway anything but up to his dreams! I know she is. Only think what Jane Drummond says of her!'

When the idea of going to see how matters stood had once occurred to the Earl, he could not stay at home: the ankle and the affections preyed on him by turns, and he wrote to Sir Miles Oakstead to fix an earlier day for the promised visit, as well as to his son, to announce his speedy arrival. Then he forgot the tardiness of cross-country posts, and outran his letter, so that he found no one to meet him at Bickleypool; and on driving up to the gate at Ebbscreek, found all looking deserted. After much knocking, Priscilla appeared, round-eyed and gasping, and verified his worst fears with 'Gone to Bochattle.' However, she explained that only one gentleman was gone to dine there; the other was rowing him round the point, with grandfather;—they would soon be back—indeed they ought, for the tide was so low, they would have to land down by the shingle bar.

She pointed out where the boat must come in; and thither the Earl directed his steps, feeling as if he were going to place himself under a nutmeg-grater, as he thought how James Frost would receive the implied distrust of his guardianship.

The sunset gleam was fading on the sleepy waves that made but a feint of breaking, along the shining expanse of moist uncovered sand, when two figures were seen progressing from the projecting rocks, casting long shadows before them. Lord Ormersfield began to prepare a mollifying address—but, behold! Was it the effect of light so much to lengthen Jem's form? nay, was it making him walk with a stick? A sudden, unlooked-for hope seized the Earl. The next minute he had been recognised; and in the grasping hands and meeting eyes, all was forgotten, save the true, fond affection of father and son.

'I did not expect this pleasure. They told me you were dining out.'

'Only rowing Jem to the landing-place. I told him to make my excuses. It is a dinner to half the neighbourhood, and my foot is always troublesome if I do not lay it up in the evening.'

'I am glad you are prudent,' said his father, dismissing his fears in his gratification, and proceeding to lay his coming to the score of his foot.

Fitzjocelyn did not wish to see through the plea—he was much too happy in his father's unusual warmth and tenderness, and in the delights of hospitality. Mrs. Hannaford was gone out, and eatables were scarce; but a tea-dinner was prepared merrily between Priscilla, the Captain, and Louis, who gloried in displaying his school-fagging accomplishments with toast, eggs, and rashers—hobbled between parlour and kitchen, helping Priscilla, joking with the Captain, and waiting on his father so eagerly and joyously as to awaken a sense of adventure and enjoyment in the Earl himself. No meal, with Frampton behind his chair, had ever equalled Fitzjocelyn's cookery or attendance; and Louis's reminiscences of the penalties he had suffered from his seniors for burnt toast, awoke like recollections of schoolboy days, hitherto in utter oblivion, and instead of the intended delicate conversation, father and son found themselves laughing over a 'tirocinium or review of schools.'

Still, the subject must be entered on; and when Lord Ormersfield had mentioned the engagement to go to Oakstead, he added, 'All is well, since I have found you here. Let me tell you that I never felt more grateful nor more relieved than by this instance of regard for my wishes.'

Though knowing the fitful nature of Louis's colour, he would have been better satisfied not to have called up such an intensity of red, and to have had some other answer than, 'I wish you saw more of them.'

'I see them every year in London.'

'London gives so little scope for real acquaintance,' ventured Louis again, with downcast eyes.

'You forget that Lady Conway is my sister-in-law.' Louis would have spoken, but his father added, 'Before you were born, I had full experience of her. You must take it on trust that her soft, prepossessing manners belong to her as a woman of the world who cannot see you without designs on you.'

'Of course,' said Louis, 'I yield to your expressed wishes; but my aunt has been very kind to me: and,' he added, after trying to mould the words to their gentlest form, 'you could not see my cousins without being convinced that it is the utmost injustice—'

'I do not censure them,' said his father, as he hesitated between indignation and respect, 'I only tell you, Louis, that nothing could grieve me more than to see your happiness in the keeping of a pupil of Lady Conway.'

He met a look full of consternation, and of struggles between filial deference and the sense of injustice. All Louis allowed himself to say was, however, 'Surely, when I am her own nephew! when our poverty is a flagrant fact—she may be acquitted of anything but caring for me for—for my mother's sake.'

There was a silence that alarmed Louis, who had never before named his mother to the Earl. At last, Lord Ormersfield spoke clearly and sternly, in characteristic succinct sentences, but taking breath between each. 'You shall have no reason to think me prejudiced. I will tell you facts. There was a match which she desired for such causes as lead her to seek you. The poverty was greater, and she knew it. On one side there was strong affection; on that which she influenced there was—none whatever. If there were scruples, she smothered them. She worked on a young innocent mind to act out her deceit, and without a misgiving on—on his part that his feelings wore not returned, the marriage took place.'

'It could not have been all her own fault,' cried Louis. 'It must have been a willing instrument—much to blame—'

His father cut him short with sudden severity, such as startled him. 'Never say so, Louis. She was a mere child, educated for that sole purpose, her most sweet and docile nature wasted and perverted.'

'And you know this of your own knowledge?' said Fitzjocelyn, still striving to find some loophole to escape from such testimony.

The Earl paused, as if to collect himself, then repeated the words, slowly and decidedly, 'Of my own knowledge. I could not have spoken thus otherwise.'

'May I ask how it ended?'

'As those who marry for beauty alone have a right to expect. There was neither confidence nor sympathy. She died early. I—we—those who loved her as their own life—were thankful.'

Louis perceived the strong effort and great distress with which these words were uttered, and ventured no answer, glancing hastily through all his connexions to guess whose history could thus deeply affect his father; but he was entirely at a loss; and Lord Ormersfield, recovering himself, added, 'Say no more of this; but, believe me, it was to spare you from her manoeuvres that I kept you apart from that family.'

'The Northwold baths have been recommended for Louisa,' said Fitzjocelyn. 'Before we knew of your objections, we mentioned Miss Faithfull's lodgings.'

What the Earl was about to utter, he suppressed.

'You cannot look at those girls and name manoeuvring!' cried Louis.

'Poor things.'

After a silence, Lord Ormersfield added, with more anxiety than prudence, 'Set my mind at rest, Louis. There can have been no harm done yet, in so short a time.'

'I—don't—know—' said Louis, slowly. 'I have seldom spoken to her, to be sure. She actually makes me shy! I never saw anything half so lovely. I cannot help her reigning over my thoughts. I shall never believe a word against her, though I cannot dispute what you say of my aunt. She is of another mould, I wish you could let me hope that—'

A gesture of despair from his father cut him short.

'I will do whatever you please,' he concluded.

'You will find that time conquers the fancy,' said the Earl, quickly. 'I am relieved to find that you have at least not committed yourself: it would be no compliment to Mary Ponsonby.'

Louis's lip curled somewhat; but he said no more, and made no objections to the arrangements which his father proceeded to detail. Doubtful of the accommodations of Ebbscreek, Lord Ormersfield had prudently retained his fly, and though Louis, intending to sleep on the floor, protested that there was plenty of room, he chose to return to the inn at Bickleypool. He would call for Louis to-morrow, to take him for a formal call at Beauchastel; and the day after they would go together to Oakstead, leaving James to return home, about ten days sooner than had been previously concerted.

Lord Ormersfield had not been gone ten minutes, before James's quick bounding tread was heard far along the dry woodland paths. He vaulted over the gate, and entered by the open window, exclaiming, as he did so, 'Hurrah! The deed is done; the letter is off to engage the House Beautiful.'

'Doom is doom!' were the first words that occurred to Louis. 'The lion and the prince.'

'What's that?'

'There was once a king,' began Louis, as if the tale were the newest in the world, 'whose son was predestined to be killed by a lion. After much consideration, his majesty enclosed his royal highness in a tower, warranted wild-beast proof, and forbade the chase to be mentioned in his hearing. The result was, that the locked-up prince died of look-jaw in consequence of tearing his hand with a nail in the picture of the lion.'

'I shall send that apologue straight to Ormersfield.'

'You may spare that trouble. My father has been with me all the evening.'

'Oh! his double-ganger visits you. That accounts for your freaks.'

'Double-gangers seldom come in yellow-bodied flys.'

'His lordship in propria persona. You don't mean it.'

'He is sleeping at the 'George' at Bickleypool. There is a letter coming to-morrow by the post, to say he is coming to-day, with every imaginable civility to you; but I am to go to the rose-coloured pastor's with him on Wednesday.'

'So there's an end of our peace and comfort!'

'I am afraid we have sadly discomposed his peace.'

'Did you discover whether his warnings have the slightest foundation?'

'He told me a history that somewhat accounts for his distrust of my aunt. I think there must be another side to it, and nothing can be more unjust than to condemn all the family, but it affected him so exceedingly that I do not wonder at his doing so. He gave no names, but I am sure it touched him very nearly. Can you tell who it could have been?' And he narrated enough to make James exclaim, 'It ought to touch him nearly. He was talking of himself.'

'Impossible!—my mother!' cried Louis, leaping up.

'Yes—his own version of his married life.'

'How do you know? You cannot remember it,' said Louis, though too well convinced, as he recollected the suppressed anguish, and the horror with which all blame of the young wife had been silenced.

'I have heard of it again and again. It was an unhappy, ill-assorted marriage: she was gay, he was cold.'

'My Aunt Catharine says so?'

'As far as she can blame anything. Your mother was a sweet blossom in a cold wind. She loved and pitied her with all her heart. Your aunt was talking, this very evening, of your father having carried her sister to Ormersfield, away from all her family, and one reason of her desire to go to Northwold is to see those who were with her at last.'

Louis was confounded. 'Yes! I see,' he said. 'How obtuse not to read it in his own manner! How much it explains!' and he silently rested his brow on his hands.

'Depend upon it, there are two sides to the story. I would not be a pretty, petted, admired girl in his keeping.'

'Do you think it mends matters with me to fasten blame on either?' said Louis, sadly. 'No; I was realizing the perception of such a thread of misery woven into his life, and thinking how little I have felt for him.'

'Endowing him with your own feelings, and then feeling for him!'

'No. I cannot estimate his feeling. He is of harder, firmer stuff than I; and for that very reason, I suspect, suffering is a more terrific thing. I heard the doctors saying, when I bore pain badly, that it would probably do the less future harm: a bad moral, but I believe it is true of the mental as of the physical constitution.' Answering something between a look and a shrug of James, he mused on, aloud—'I understand better what the wreck of affection must have been.'

'For my part,' said James, 'I do not believe in the affection that can tyrannize over and blight a woman.'

'Nay, James! I cannot doubt. My very name—my having been called by it, are the more striking in one so fond of usage and precedent. Things that passed between him and Mrs. Ponsonby while I was ill—much that I little regarded and ill requited—show what force of love and grief there must have been. The cold, grave manner, is the broken, inaccessible edge of the cliff rent asunder.'

'If romance softens the rough edge, you are welcome to it! I may as well go to bed!'

'Not romance—the sad reality of my poor father's history. I trust I shall never treat his wishes so lightly—'

Impatient of one-sided sympathy, James exclaimed, 'As if you did not give way to him like a slave!'

'Yes, like a slave,' said Louis, gravely. 'I wish to give way like a son who would try to comfort him for what he has undergone.'

'Now, I should have thought your feeling would have been for your mother!'

'If my mother could speak to me,' said Louis, with trembling lips, 'she would surely bid me to try my utmost, as far as in me lies, to bring peace and happiness to my father. I cannot tell where the errors may have been, and I will never ask. If she was as like to me as they say, I could understand some of them! At least, I know that I am doubly bound to give as little vexation to him as possible, and I trust that you will not make it harder to me. You lost your father so early, that you can hardly estimate—'

'The trial?' said James, willing to give what had passed the air of a joke.

'Exactly so—Good night.'

CHAPTER XIV
NEW INHABITANTS

Sometimes a troop of damsels glad—
Sometimes a curly shepherd lad,
Or long-haired page in crimson clad,
    Goes by to towered Camelot;
And sometimes, through the mirror blue,
The knights come riding two and two.
She hath no loyal knight and true—
    The Lady of Shalott.
    TENNYSON.

'Oakstead, Oct. 14th, 1847.

'My Dear Aunt,—I find that Fitzjocelyn is writing to you, but I think you will wish for a fuller account of him than can be obtained from his own letters. Indeed, I should be much obliged if you would kindly exercise your influence to persuade him that he is not in a condition to be imprudent with impunity. Sir Miles Oakstead was absolutely shocked to see the alteration in his appearance, as well as in his spirits; and although both our kind host and hostess are most solicitous on his account, it happens unfortunately that they are at this juncture quite alone, so that he is without companions of his own age. I must not, however, alarm you. The fact is, that circumstances have occurred which, though he has acted in the most exemplary manner, have harassed and distressed him a good deal, and his health suffers from the difficulty of taking sufficient exercise. James will triumph when he hears that I regret having shortened his stay by the sea-side; for neither the place nor the weather seems to agree with him: he has had a recurrence of wakeful nights, and is very languid. Poor boy! yesterday he wandered out alone in the rain, lost his way, and came home so fatigued that he slept for three hours on the sofa, but to-day he seems better—has more colour, and has been less silent. We go to Leffingham Castle from Monday till Thursday, when I shall take him to London for Hastings to decide whether it be fit for him to return to Christchurch after the vacation, according to his own most anxious wish. With my love to Mary Ponsonby and her daughter, and best remembrances to James,

'Your affectionate nephew,
'ORMERSFIELD.'

The same envelope contained another letter of many sheets, beginning in a scrawl:—

'Scene—Rose-coloured Pastor's Nest. Tables, chairs, books, papers, despatch-boxes. The two ex-ministers writing and consulting. Viscount F. looking on like a colt running beside its parent at plough, thinking that harness leaves deep marks, and that he does not like the furrow.

'October 13th, 1847.—That correct date must be a sign that he is getting into harness.

'Well, dear Aunt Kitty, to make a transition from the third to the first person, like Mrs. Norris, you have in this short scene an epitome of the last fortnight. Lady Oakstead is an honourable matron, whom I pity for having me in her way; a man unable to be got rid of by the lawful exercises of shooting and riding, and with a father always consulting her about him, and watching every look and movement, till the blood comes throbbing to my temples by the mere attraction of his eyes. To be watched into a sense of impatience and ingratitude, is a trial of life for which one is not prepared. My father and Sir Miles are very busy; I hang here an anomaly, sitting with them as being less in their way than in Lady Oakstead's, and wondering what I shall be twenty years hence. I am sick of the only course of life that will content my father, and I can see no sunshine likely to brighten it. But, at least, no one's happiness is at stake but my own. Here is a kind, cordial letter from Lady Conway, pressing me to join her at Scarborough, make expeditions, &c. My father is in such a state about me, that I believe I could get his consent to anything, but I suppose it would not be fair, and I have said nothing to him as yet. On Monday we go to Leffingham, which, I hear, is formality itself. After that, more state visits, unless I can escape to Oxford. My father fancies me not well enough; but pray unite all the forces of the Terrace to impress that nothing else will do me any good. Dragging about in this dreary, heartless way is all that ails me, and reading for my degree would be the best cure. I mean to work hard for honours, and, if possible, delude myself with hopes of success. Work is the need. Here, there is this one comfort. There is no one to talk to, no birds in last year's nest, sons absent, daughters disposed of, but, unluckily, the Pastoress, under a mistaken sense of kindness, has asked the Vicar's son to walk with me, and he is always lying in wait,—an Ensign in a transition state between the sheepish schoolboy and the fast man, with an experience of three months of depot. Having roused him from the pristine form, I regret the alternative.

'Did I ever write so savage a letter? Don't let it vex you, or I won't send it. What a bull! There is such a delectable Scotch mist, that no one will suspect me of going out; and I shall actually cheat the Ensign, and get a walk in solitude to hearten me for the dismal state dinner party of the evening.

'October 14th.—Is it in the book of fate that I should always treat this rose-coloured pastor like a carrion crow? I have done it again! And it has but brought out more of my father's marvellous kindness and patience.

'I plunged into the Scotch mist unsuspected and unpursued. The visible ebullition of discontent had so much disgusted me that I must needs see whether anything could be done with it, and fairly face the matter, as I can only do in a walk. Pillow counsel is feverish and tumultuous; one is hardly master of oneself. The soft, cool, mist-laden air, heavy but incense-breathing, was a far more friendly adjunct in the quiet decay of nature—mournful, but not foul nor corrupt, because man had not spoilt it. It suited me better than a sunny, glaring day, such as I used to revel in, and the brightness of which, last spring, made me pine to be in the free air. Such days are past with me; I had better know that they are, and not strive after them. Personal happiness is the lure, not the object, in this world. I have my Northwold home, and I am beginning to see that my father's comfort depends on me as I little imagined, and sufficiently to sweeten any sacrifice. So I have written to refuse Scarborough, for there is no use in trying to combine two things, pleasing my father and myself. I wish the determination may last; but mine have never been good for much, and you must help me.

'Neither thinking nor fog conduced to seeing where I was going; and when my ankle began to give out, and I was going to turn, I ran into a hedge, which, looming through the mist, I had been taking for a fine range of distant mountains—rather my way of dealing with other objects. Being without a horse on whose neck to lay the reins, I could only coast the hedge, hoping it might lead me back to Oakstead Park, which I had abandoned in my craving for space and dread of being dogged by the Ensign. But the treacherous hedge led me nowhere but to a horsepond; and when I had struggled out of the adjacent mire, and attained a rising ground, I could only see about four yards square of bare down, all the rest being grey fog. Altogether, the scene was worth something. I heard what I thought the tinkling of a sheep bell through the cloud, which dulled the sound like cotton wool; I pursued the call, when anon, the veil began to grow thin, and revealed, looking just like a transparency, a glimpse of a little village in a valley almost under my feet, trees, river, church-spire and all, and the bell became clearer, and showed me what kind of flock it was meant for. I turned that way, and had just found a path leading down the steep, when down closed the cloud—a natural dissolving view—leaving me wondering whether it had been mirage or imagination, till presently, the curtain drew up in earnest. Out came, not merely form, but colour, as I have seen a camera clear itself—blue sky, purple hills, russet and orange woods, a great elm green picked out with yellow, a mass of brown oaks, a scarlet maple, a beech grove, skirting a brilliant water meadow, with a most reflective stream running through it, and giving occasion for a single arched bridge, and a water mill, with a wheel draperied with white foam; two swans disporting on the water (I would not declare they were not geese), a few cottony flakes of mist hanging over damp corners, the hill rising green, with the bright whitewashed cottages of this district, on the side a rich, red, sandstone-coloured church, late architecture, tower rather mouldering—all the more picturesque; churchyard, all white headstones and ochreous sheep, surmounted by a mushroom-shaped dark yew tree, railed in with intensely white rails, the whole glowing in the parting coup-de-soleil of a wet day, every tear of every leaf glistening, and everything indescribably lustrous. It is a picture that one's mental photograph ought to stamp for life, and the cheering and interest it gave, no one but you can understand. I wished for you, I know. It looks so poor in words.

'After the service, I laid hold of the urchin whose hearty stare had most reminded me of Tom Madison, and gave him a shilling to guide me back to Oakstead, a wise measure, for down came the cloud, blotting all out like the Castle of St. John, and by the time I came home, it was pitch dark and raining hard, and my poor father was imagining me at the foot of another precipice. I was hoping to creep up in secret, but they all came out, fell upon me, Lady Oakstead sent me tea, and ordered me to rest; and so handsomely did I obey, that when next I opened my eyes, and saw my father waiting, as I thought, for me to go down to dinner with him, I found he had just come up after the ladies had quitted the diningroom. So kind and so little annoyed did he seem, that I shook myself, to be certified that I had broken no more bones, but it was all sheer forbearance and consideration—enough to go to one's heart—when it was the very thing to vex him most. With great penitence, I went down, and the first person I encountered was the very curate I had seen in my *mist*erious village, much as if he had walked out of a story book. On fraternizing, I found him to be a friend of Holdsworth. Lady Oakstead is going to take me, this afternoon, to see his church, &c., thoroughly; and behold, I learn from him that she is a notable woman for doing good in her parish, never so happy as in trotting to cottages, though her good deeds are always in the background. Thereupon, I ventured to attack her this morning on cottage garniture, and obtained the very counsel I wanted about ovens and piggeries, we began to get on together, and she is to put me up to all manner of information that I want particularly. I must go now, not to keep her waiting, never mind the first half of my letter—I have no time to cancel it now. I find my father wants to put in a note: don't believe a word that he says, for I am much better to-day, body and mind.

Goosey, goosey gander,
Where shall we wander,

Anywhere, everywhere, to remain still 'Your most affectionate, 'FITS GOSLING.'

Dear Aunt Kitty! One of her failings was never to be able to keep a letter to herself. She fairly cried over her boy's troubles; and Mrs. Ponsonby would not have known whether to laugh or cry but for James's doleful predictions, which were so sentimental as to turn even his grandmother to the laughing party, and left him no sympathizer but Mary, who thought it very hard and cruel to deride Louis when he was trying so earnestly to be good and suffering so much. Why should they all—Aunt Catharine herself—be merry over his thinking the spring-days of his life past away, and trying so nobly and patiently to resign himself?

'It is the way of the world, Mary,' said James. 'People think they are laughing at the mistaking a flock of sheep for the army of Pentapolin of the naked arm, when they are really sneering at the lofty spirit taking the weaker side. They involve the sublime temper in the ridiculous accident, and laugh both alike to scorn.'

'Not mamma and Aunt Catharine,' said Mary. 'Besides, is not half the harm in the world done by not seeing where the sublime is invaded by the ridiculous?'

'I see nothing ridiculous in the matter,' said James. 'His father has demanded an unjustifiable sacrifice. Fitzjocelyn yields and suffers.'

'I do believe Lord Ormersfield must relent; you see how pleased he is, saying that Louis's conduct is exemplary.'

'He would sacrifice a dozen sons to one prejudice!'

'Perhaps Miss Conway will overcome the prejudice. I am sure, if he thinks Louis's conduct exemplary, Louis must have the sort of happiness he used to wish for most, and his father would do his very best to gratify him.'

That sentence was Mary's cheval de bataille in her discussions with James, who could never be alone with her without broaching the subject. The two cousins often walked together during James's month at Northwold. The town church was not very efficiently served, and was only opened in the morning and late evening on Sundays, without any afternoon prayers, and James was often in the habit of walking to Ormersfield church for the three o'clock service, and asking Mary to join him. Their return was almost always occupied in descriptions of Miss Conway's perfections, and Mary learnt to believe that two beings, evidently compounded of every creature's best, must be destined for each other.

'How well it is,' she thought, 'that I did not stand in the way. Oh! how unhappy and puzzled I should be now. How thankful I am that dear mamma understood all for us so well! How glad I am that Louis is waiting patiently, not doing anything self-willed. As long as his father says he is exemplary, it must make one happy, and mamma will convince Lord Ormersfield. It will all turn out well; and how delightful it will be to see him quite happy and settled!'

Mary and her mother had by this time taken root at Dynevor Terrace, and formed an integral part of the inhabitants. Their newspaper went the round of the houses, their name was sent to the Northwold book-club and enrolled among the subscribers to local charities, and Miss Mercy Faithfull found that their purse and kitchen would bear deeper hauls than she could in general venture upon. Mary was very happy, working under her, and was a welcome and cheerful visitor to the many sick, aged, and sorrowful to whom she introduced her.

If Mary could only have induced Aunt Melicent to come and see with her own eyes, to know Mrs. Frost and the Faithfull sisters, and, above all, to see mamma in her own house, she thought one of her most eager wishes would have been fulfilled. But invite as she and her mother might, they could not move Miss Ponsonby from Bryanstone Square. Railroads and country were both her dread; and she was not inclined, to overcome her fears on behalf of a sister-in-law whom she forgave, but could not love.

'You must give it up, my dear,' said Mrs. Ponsonby. 'I let the time for our amalgamation pass. Melicent and I were not tolerant of each other. Since she has given you back to me, I can love and respect her as I never did before; but a little breach in youth becomes too wide in age for either repentance or your affection, my dear, to be able to span it.'

Mary saw what a relief it was that the invitations were not accepted, and though she was disappointed, she blamed herself for having wished otherwise. Tranquillity was such a boon to that wearied spirit, each day was so much gain that went by without the painful, fluttered look of distress, and never had Mrs. Ponsonby had so much quiet enjoyment with her daughter and her aunt. Mary was perfectly contented in seeing her better, and had no aims beyond the present trivial, commonplace life, with so many to help by little ordinary services, and her mother serene and comfortable. Placid, and yet active, she went busily through the day, and did not forget the new pleasures to which Louis had opened her mind. She took up his books without a pang, and would say, briskly and unblushingly, to her mother, how strange it was that before she had been with him, she had never liked at all, what she now cared for so much.

The winter portended no lack of excitement. Miss Faithfull's rooms were engaged. When Miss Mercy ran in breathless to Mrs. Frost with the tidings, she little knew what feelings were excited; the hope and fear, the doubt and curiosity; the sense of guilt towards the elder nephew, in not preventing what she could not prevent, the rejoicing on behalf of the younger nephew; the ladylike scorn of the motives that brought the lodgers; yet the warm feeling towards what was dear to Louis and admired by Jem.

What a flapping and battering of carpets on the much-enduring stump! What furious activity of Martha! What eager help of little Charlotte, who was in a perfect trepidation of delight at the rumour that a real beauty, fit for a heroine, was coming! What trotting hither and thither of Miss Mercy! What netting of blinds and stitching of chintz by Miss Salome! What envy and contempt on the part of other landladies on hearing that Miss Faithfull's apartments were engaged for the whole winter! What an anxious progress was Miss Mercy's, when she conducted Mrs. Frost and Mary to a final inspection! and what was her triumph when Mary, sitting down on the well-stuffed arm-chair, pronounced that people who would not come there did not understand what comfort was.

Every living creature gazed—Mrs. Frost through her blind, Mary behind her hydrangea in the balcony, Charlotte from her attic window,—when the lodgers disembarked in full force—two ladies, two children, one governess, three maids, two men, two horses, one King Charles's spaniel! Let it be what it might, it was a grand windfall for the Miss Faithfulls.

Mary's heart throbbed as the first carriage thundered upon the gravel, and a sudden swelling checked her voice as she was about to exclaim 'There she is!' when the second lady emerged, and moved up the garden path. She was veiled and mantled; but accustomed as was Mary's eye to the Spanish figure and walk, the wonderful grace of movement and deportment struck her as the very thing her eye had missed ever since she left Peru. What the rest of the strangers were like, she knew not; she had only eyes for the creature who had won Louis's affection, and doubtless deserved it, as all else that was precious.

'So they are come, Charlotte,' said Mrs. Frost, as the maiden demurely brought in the kettle.

'Yes, ma'am;' and stooping to put the kettle on, and growing carnation-coloured over the fire. 'Oh, ma'am, I never saw such a young lady. She is all one as the king's sister in The Lord of the Isles!'

While the object of all this enthusiasm was arriving at the Terrace, she was chiefly conscious that Sir Roland was sinking down on the ramparts of Acre, desperately wounded in the last terrible siege; and she was considering whether palmer or minstrel should carry the tidings of his death to Adeline. It was her refuge from the unpleasant feelings, with which she viewed the experiment of the Northwold baths upon Louisa's health. As the carriage stopped, she cast one glance at the row of houses, they struck her as dreary and dilapidated; she drew her mantle closer, shivered, and walked into the house. 'Small rooms, dingy furniture-that is mamma's affair,' passed through her mind, as she made a courteous acknowledgment of Miss Mercy's greeting, and stood by the drawing-room fire. 'Roland slowly awoke from his swoon; a white-robed old man, with a red eight-pointed cross on his breast, was bending over him. He knew himself to be in—I can't remember which tower the Hospitallers defended. I wonder whether Marianne can find the volume of Vertot.'

'Isabel, Isabel!' shrieked Virginia, who, with Louisa, had been roaming everywhere, 'here is a discovery in the school-room! Come!'

It was an old framed print of a large house, as much of a sham castle as the nature of things would permit; and beneath were the words 'Cheveleigh, the seat of Roland Dynevor, Esquire.'

'There!' cried Virginia; 'you see it is a castle, a dear old feudal castle! Think of that, Isabel! Why, it is as good as seeing Sir Roland himself, to have seen Mr. Dynevor Frost disinherited. Oh! if his name were only Roland, instead of that horrid James!'

'His initials are J. R.,' said Isabel. 'It is a curious coincidence.'

'It only wants an Adeline to have the castle now,' said Louisa. 'Oh! there shall be an heiress, and she shall be beautiful, and he shan't go crusading—he shall marry her.'

The sisters had not been aware that the school-room maid, who had been sent on to prepare, was busy unpacking in a corner of the room. 'They say, Miss Louisa,' she interposed, 'that Mr. Frost is going to be married to a great heiress—his cousin, Miss Ponsonby, at No. 7.'

Isabel requited the forwardness by silently leaving the room with the sisters, and Virginia apologized for not having been more cautious than to lead to such subjects. 'It is all gossip,' she said, angrily; 'Mr. Dynevor would never marry for money.'

'Nay, let us find in her an Adeline,' said Isabel.

The next day, Miss Mercy had hurried into No. 7, to declare that the ladies were all that was charming, but that their servants gave themselves airs beyond credence, especially the butler, who played the guitar, and insisted on a second table; when there was a peal of the bell, and Mary from her post of observation 'really believed it was Lady Conway herself;' whereupon Miss Mercy, without listening to persuasions, popped into the back drawing room to effect her retreat.

Lady Conway was all eagerness and cordiality, enchanted to renew her acquaintance, venturing so early a call in hopes of prevailing on Mrs. Ponsonby to come out with her to take a drive. She conjured up recollections of Mary's childhood, declared that she looked to her for drawing Isabel out, and was extremely kind and agreeable. Mary thought her delightful, with something of Louis's charm of manner; and Mrs. Ponsonby believed it no acting, for Lady Conway was sincerely affable and affectionate, with great warmth and kindness, and might have been all that was excellent, had she started into life with a different code of duty.

So there was to be an intimacy. For Fitzjocelyn's sake, as well as for the real good-nature of the advances, Mrs. Ponsonby would not shrink back more than befitted her self-respect. Of that quality she had less than Mrs. Frost, who, with her innate punctilious spirit, avoided all favours or patronage. It was curious to see the gentle old lady fire up with all the dignity of the Pendragons, at the least peril of incurring an obligation, and, though perfectly courteous, easy, and obliging, she contrived to keep at a greater distance than if she had been mistress of Cheveleigh. There, she would have remembered that both she and Lady Conway were aunts to Louis; at Northwold, her care was to become beholden for nothing that she could not repay.

Lady Conway did her best, when driving out with Mrs. Ponsonby, to draw her into confidence. There were tender reminiscences from her heart of poor sweet Louisa, tearful inquiries respecting her last weeks, certainties that Mrs. Ponsonby had been of great use to her; for, poor darling, she had been thoughtless—so much to turn her head. There was cause for regret in their own education—there was then so much less attention to essentials. Lady Conway could not have borne to bring up her own girls as she herself and her sisters had grown up; she had chosen a governess who made religion the first object, and she was delighted to see them all so attached to her; she had never had any fears of their being too serious—people had learnt to be reasonable now, did not insist on the impracticable, did not denounce moderate gaieties, as had once been done to the alarm of poor Louisa.

Sweetest Louisa's son! She could not speak too warmly of him, and she declared herself highly gratified by Mr. Mansell's opinion of his modesty, attention, and good sense. Mr. Mansell was an excellent judge, he had such as opinion of Lord Ormersfield's public character.

And, at a safe interval, she mentioned the probability that Beauchastel might be settled on Isabel, if she should marry so as to please Mr. Mansell: he cared for connexion more than for wealth; if he had a weakness, it was for rank.

Mrs. Ponsonby thought it fair that the Earl should be aware of these facts. He smiled ironically.

He left his card with his sister-in-law, and, to have it over while Louis was safe at Oxford, invited the party to spend a day at Ormersfield, with Mrs. Frost to entertain them. He was far too considerate of the feelings that he attributed to the Ponsonbys to ask them to come; and as three out of the six in company were more or less in a state of haughtiness and coolness, Lady Conway's graces failed entirely; and poor innocent Virginia and Louisa protested that they had never spent so dull a day, and that they could not believe their cousin Fitzjocelyn could belong to such a tiresome place.

Isabel, who had undergone more dull days than they had, contrived to get through it by torturing Adeline with utter silence of all tidings from the East, and by a swarm of suitors, with the fantastic Viscount foremost. She never was awake from her dream until Mr. Holdsworth came to dinner, and was so straightforward and easy that he thawed every one.

Afterwards, he never failed to return an enthusiastic reply to the question that all the neighbourhood were asking each other—namely, whether they had seen Miss Conway.

No one was a more devoted admirer than the Lady of Eschalott, whose webs had a bad chance when there was one glimpse of Miss Conway to be obtained from the window, and the vision of whose heart was that Mrs. Martha might some day let her stand in the housemaid's closet, to behold her idol issue forth in the full glory of an evening dress—a thing Charlotte had read of, but never seen anything nearer to it than Miss Walby coming to tea, and her own Miss Clara in the scantiest of all white muslins.

But Mrs. Martha was in an unexampled state of vixenish crossness, and snapped venomously at mild Mrs. Beckett for the kindest offers of sparing Charlotte to assist her in her multiplied labours. She seemed to be running after time all day long, with five dinners and teas upon her hands, poor woman, and allowing herself not the slightest relaxation, except to rush in for a few seconds to No. 7, to indulge herself by inveighing against the whole of the fine servants; and yet she was so proud of having lodgers at all, that she hated them for nothing so much as for threatening to go away.

The object of her bitterest invectives was the fastidious butler, Mr. Delaford, who by her account could do nothing for himself, grudged her mistresses their very sitting-room, drank wine with the ladies' maids like a gentleman, and ordered fish for the second table; talked of having quitted a duke, and submitting to live with Lady Conway because he compassionated unprotected females, and my Lady was dependent on him for the care of Sir Walter in the holidays. To crown his offences, he never cleaned his own plate, but drew sketches and played the guitar! Moreover, Mrs. Martha had her notions that he was making that sickly Frenchified maid of Miss Conway's much too fond of him; and as to his calling himself Mr. Delaford—why, Mrs. Martha had a shrewd suspicion that he was some kin to her first cousin's brother-in-law's shopman's wife in Tottenham-court-road, whose name she knew was Ford, and who had been picked out of a gutter! The establishment of such a fact appeared as if it would be the triumph of Mrs. Martha's life. In the meantime, she more than hinted that she would wear herself to the bone rather than let Charlotte Arnold into the house; and Jane, generally assenting, though seldom going all lengths, used to divert the conversation by comparisons with Mr. Frampton's politeness and consideration. He never came to No. 5 to give trouble, only to help.

The invectives produced on Charlotte's mind an effect the reverse of what was intended. Mr. Delaford, a finer gentleman than Mr. Frampton and Mr. Poynings, must be a wonder of nature. The guitar—redolent of serenades and Spanish cloaks—oh! but once to see and hear it! The very rudeness of Mrs. Martha's words, so often repeated, gave her a feeling in favour of their object. She had known Mrs. Martha unjust before. Poor Tom! if he had only been a Spaniard, he would have sung about the white dove—his pretty thought—in a serenade, but then he might have poignarded Mr. James in his passion, which would have been less agreeable—she supposed he had forgotten her long ago—and so much the better!

It was a Sunday evening. Every one was gone to church except Charlotte, who was left to keep house. Though November, it was not cold, the day had been warm and showery, and the full moon had risen in the most glorious brightness, riding in a sky the blue of which looked almost black by contrast with her brilliancy. Charlotte stood at the back door, gazing at the moon walking in brightness, and wandered into the garden, to enjoy what to her was beyond all other delights, reading Gessner's Death of Abel by moonlight. There was quite sufficient light, even if she had not known the idyll almost by heart; and in a trance of dreamy, undefined delight, she stood beside the dark ivy-covered wall, each leaf glistening in the moonbeams, which shed a subdued pearliness over her white apron and collar, paled but gave a shadowy refinement to her features, and imparted a peculiar soft golden gloss to the fair braids of hair on her modest brow.

A sound of opening the back gate made her give one of her violent starts; but before she could spring into the shelter of the house, she was checked by the civil words, 'I beg your pardon, I was mistaken—I took this for No. 8.'

'Three doors off—' began Charlotte, discovering, with a shy thrill of surprise and pleasure, that she had been actually accosted by the great Mr. Delaford; and the moonlight, quite as becoming to him as to her, made him an absolute Italian count, tall, dark, pale, and whiskered. He did not go away at once, he lingered, and said softly, 'I perceive that you partake my own predilection for the moonlight hour.'

Charlotte would have been delighted, had it not been a great deal harder to find an answer than if the old Lord had asked her a question; but she simpered and blushed, which probably did just as well. Mr. Delaford supposed she knew the poet's lines—

'How sweet the moonlight sleeps on yonder bank—'

'Oh yes, sir—so sweet!' exclaimed the Lady of Eschalott, under her breath, though yonder bank was only represented by the chequer-work of Mrs. Ponsonby's latticed trellis; and Mr. Delaford proceeded to quote the whole passage, in a deep mellow voice, but with a great deal of affectation; and Charlotte gasped, 'So beautiful!'

'I perceive that you have a fine taste for poetry,' said Mr. Delaford, so graciously, that Charlotte presumed to say, 'Oh, sir! is it true that you can play the guitar?'

He smiled upon her tone of veneration, and replied, 'a trifle—a little instrumental melody was a great resource. If his poor performance would afford her any gratification, he would fetch his guitar.'

'Oh, sir—thank you—a psalm-tune, perhaps. It is Sunday—if you would be so kind.'

He smiled superciliously as he regretted that his music was not of that description, and Charlotte felt ready to sink into the earth at the indignity she had done the guitar in forgetting that it could accompany anything but such songs as Valancourt sang to Emily. She begged his pardon humbly; and he declared that he had a great respect for a lady's scruples, and should be happy to meet her another evening. 'If Mrs. Beckett would allow her,' said Charlotte, overpowered with gratitude: 'there would be the moon full to-morrow—how delightful!' He could spare a short interval between the dinner and the tea; and with this promise he took leave.

Honest little Charlotte told Mrs. Beckett the whole story, and all her eager wishes for to-morrow evening; and Jane sighed and puzzled herself, and knew it would make Martha very angry, but could not help being goodnatured. Jane had a great deference for Martha's strong, rough character; but then Martha had never lived in a great house, and did not know 'what was what,' nor the difference between 'low people' and upper servants. So Jane acted chaperon as far as her easy discretion went, and had it to say to her own conscience, and to the angry Martha, that he never said one word that need offend any young woman.

There was a terrible storm below-stairs in the House Beautiful at the idea of Delaford taking up with Mrs. Frost's little kitchen-maid—Delaford, the lady's-maid killer par excellence, wherever Lady Conway went, and whose coquetries whitened the cheeks of Miss Conway's poor Marianne, the object of his attentions whenever he had no one else in view. He had not known Charlotte to be a kitchen-maid when he first beheld her, and her fair beauty and retiring grace had had full scope, assisted by her veneration for himself; and now the scorn of the grand Mrs. Fanshawe, and the amusement of teasing Marianne, only made him the more bent on patronizing 'the little rustic,' as he called her. He was deferential to Mrs. Beckett, who felt herself in her element in discussing plate, china, and large establishments with him; and he lent books, talked poetry, and played the guitar to Charlotte, and even began to take her portrait, with her mouth all on one side.

Delaford was an admirable servant, said the whole Conway family; he was trusted as entirely as he represented, and Lady Conway often gave him charge over her son in sports and expeditions beyond ladies' management: he was, in effect, nearly the ruler of the household, and never allowed his lady to go anywhere if he did not approve. If it had not been for the 'little rustic's' attractions, perhaps he might have made strong demonstrations against the House Beautiful. Little did Miss Faithfull know the real cause of her receiving or retaining her lodgers.

CHAPTER XV
MOTLEY THE ONLY WEAR

> For better far than passion's glow,
> Or aught of worldly choice,
> To listen His own will to know,
> And, listening, hear his voice.
>   The Angel of Marriage—REV. I. WILLIAMS.

The friendships that grew up out of sight were far more effective than anything that Lady Conway could accomplish on the stage. Miss King and the Miss Faithfulls found each other out at once, and the governess was entreated to knock at the door at the bottom of the stairs whenever her pupils could spare her.

Then came eager wishes from her pupils to be admitted to the snuggery, and they were invited to see the curiosities. Isabel believed the 'very good' was found, and came with her sisters. She begged to be allowed to help in their parish work, under Miss Mercy Faithfull's guidance; and Sir Roland stood still, while she fancied she was learning to make little frocks, but really listening to their revelations of so new a world. She went out with Miss Mercy—she undertook a class and a district, and began to be happier than ever before; though how much of the absolute harder toil devolved on Miss King, neither she nor the governess understood.

This led to intercourse with Mary Ponsonby; and Isabel was a very different person in that homely, friendly parlour, from the lofty, frigid Miss Conway of the drawing-room. Cold hauteur melted before Mary's frank simplicity, and they became friends as fast as two ladies could beyond the age of romantic plunges, where on one side there was good-will without enthusiasm, on the other enthusiasm and reserve. They called each other 'Miss Conway' and 'Miss Ponsonby,' and exchanged no family secrets; but they were, for all that, faster friends than young ladies under twenty might imagine.

One winter's day, the crisp, exhilarating frost had lured them far along the high road beyond Mr. Calcott's park palings, talking over Isabel's favourite theme, what to wish for her little brother, when the sound of a large clock striking three made Isabel ask where she was.

'It was the stable clock at Ormersfield,' said Mary, 'did you not know we were on that road?'

'No, I did not.' And Isabel would have turned, but Mary begged her to take a few steps up the lane, that they might see how Lord Fitzjocelyn's new cottages looked. Isabel complied, and added, after a pause, 'Are you one of Lord Fitzjocelyn's worshippers?'

'I should not like to worship any one,' said Mary, looking straightforward. 'I am very fond of him, because I have known him all my life. And he is so good!'

'Then I think I may consider you exempt! It is the only fault I have to find with Northwold. You are the only person who does not rave about him—the only person who has not mentioned his name.'

'Have I not? I think that was very unkind of me—'

'Very kind to me,' said Isabel.

'I meant, to him,' said Mary, blushing; 'if you thought that I did not think most highly of him—'

'Don't go on! I was just going to trust to you for a calm, dispassionate statement of his merits, and I shall soon lose all my faith in you.'

'My mother—' began Mary; but just then Lord Ormersfield came forth from one of the cottages, and encountered the young ladies. He explained that Fitzjocelyn was coming home next week, and he had come to see how his last orders had been executed, since Frampton and the carpenter had sometimes chosen to think for themselves. He was very anxious that all should be right, and, after a few words, revealed a perplexity about ovens and boilers, in which Mary's counsel would be invaluable. So, with apologies and ceremonies to Miss Conway, they entered, and Isabel stood waiting in the dull kitchen, smelling of raw plaster, wondering at the extreme eagerness of the discussion with the mason over the yawning boiler, the Earl referring to his son's letter, holding it half-a-yard off, and at last giving it to Mary to decipher by the waning light.

So far had it waned, that when the fixtures had all been inspected, Lord Ormersfield declared that the young ladies must not return alone, and insisted on escorting them home. Every five minutes some one thought of something to say: there was an answer, and by good luck a rejoinder; then all died away, and Mary pondered how her mother would in her place have done something to draw the two together, but she could not. She feared the walk had made Isabel more adverse to all connected with Ormersfield than even previously; for the Ormersfield road was avoided, and the question as to Fitzjocelyn's merits was never renewed.

Mary thought his cause would be safest in the hands of his great champion, who was coming home from Oxford with him, and was to occupy his vacation in acting tutor to little Sir Walter Conway. Louis came, the day after his return, with his father, to make visits in the Terrace, and was as well-behaved and uninteresting as morning calling could make him. He was looking very well—his general health quite restored, and his ankle much better; though he was still forbidden to ride, and could not walk far.

'You must come and see me, Aunt Kitty,' he said; 'I am not available for coming in to see you. I'm reading, and I've made a resignation of myself,' he added, with a slight blush, and debonnaire shrug, glancing to see that his father was occupied with James.

They were to dine with Lady Conway on the following Tuesday. In the interim, no one beheld them except Jem, who walked to Ormersfield once or twice for some skating for his little pupil Walter, and came back reporting that Louis had sold himself, body and soul, to his father.

Clara came home, a degree more civilized, and burning to confide to Louis that she had thought of his advice, had been the less miserable for it, and had much more on which to consult him. She could not conceive why even grandmamma would not consent to her accompanying the skaters; though she was giving herself credit for protesting that she was not going on the ice, only to keep poor Louis company, while the others were skating.

She was obliged to defer her hopes of seeing him until Tuesday, when she had been asked to drink tea in the school-room, and appear in the evening. Mrs. Frost had consented, as a means of exempting herself from the party. And Clara's incipient feminine nature began to flutter at her first gaiety. The event was magnified by a present from Jem, of a broad rose-coloured sash and white muslin dress, with a caution that she was not to consider the tucks up to the waist as a provision for future growth.

She flew to exhibit the finery to the Miss Faithfulls, and to consult on the making-up, and, to her consternation, was caught by Miss Conway kneeling on the floor, being measured by Miss Salome. To Isabel, there was a sort of touching novelty in the simplicity that could glory in pink ribbon when embellished by being a brother's gift; she looked on with calm pleasure at such homely excitement, and even fetched some bows of her own, for examples, and offered to send Marianne down with patterns.

Clara was enchanted to recognise in Miss Conway the vision of the Euston-square platform. The grand, quiet style of beauty was exactly fitted to impress a mind like hers, so strongly imbued with sentiments like those of Louis, and regarding Isabel as necessarily Louis's destiny, she began to adore her accordingly, with a girl-reverence, quite as profound, far more unselfish, and little less ardent than that of man for woman. That a female vision of perfection should engross Clara's imagination, was a step towards softening her; but, poor child! the dawn of womanhood was to come in a painful burst.

Surprised at her own aspect, with her light hair dressed by Jane and wreathed with ivy leaves by grandmamma, and her skirts so full that she could not refrain from making a gigantic cheese, she was inspected and admired by granny and Jane, almost approved by Jem himself; and, exalted by the consciousness of being well-dressed, she repaired to the school-room tea at the House Beautiful.

Virginia and Louisa were, she thought, very poor imitations of Louis's countenance—the one too round, the other too thin and sallow; but both they, their brother, and Miss King were so utterly unlike anything at school, that she was at once at ease, and began talking with Walter over schoolboy fun, in which he could not be a greater proficient than herself. Walter struck up a violent friendship for her on the spot, and took to calling her 'a fellow,' in oblivion of her sex; and Virginia and Louisa fell into ecstasies of laughter, which encouraged Clara and Walter to compete with each other which should most astonish their weak minds.

In the drawing-room, Lady Conway spoke so graciously, that Clara, was quite distressed at looking over her head. Mary looked somewhat oppressed, saying her mother had not been so well that day; and she was disposed to keep in the background, and occupy herself with Clara; but it was quite contrary to the Giraffe's notions to be engrossed by any one when Louis was coming. As if she had divined Mary's intentions of keeping her from importuning him, she was continually gazing at the door, ready at once to claim his attention.

At first, the gentlemen only appeared in a black herd at the door, where Mr. Calcott had stopped Lord Ormersfield short, in his eagerness to impress on him the views of the county on a police-bill in course of preparation for the next session. The other magistrates congregated round; but James Frost and Sydney Calcott had slipped past, to the piano where Lady Conway had sent Miss Calcott and Isabel. 'Why did not Fitzjocelyn, come too?' was murmured by the young group in the recess opposite the door; and when at last he became visible, leaning against the wall, listening to the Squire, Virginia declared he was going to serve them just as he used at Beauchastel.

'Oh, no! he shan't—I'll rescue him!' exclaimed Clara; and leaping up to her cameleopard attitude, she sprang forward, and, with a voice audible in an unlucky lull of the music, she exclaimed, 'Louis! Louis! don't you see that I am here?'

As he turned, with a look of surprise and almost rebuke, her own words came back to her ears as they must have sounded to others; her face became poppy-coloured, nothing light but her flaxen eyebrows; and she scarcely gave her hand to be shaken. 'No, I did not know you were coming,' he said; and almost partaking her confusion, as he felt all eyes upon her, he looked in vain for a refuge for her.

How welcome was Mary's kind face and quiet gesture, covering poor Clara's retreat as she sank into a dark nook, sheltered by the old black cabinet! Louis thanked Mary by a look, as much as to say, 'Just like you,' and was glad to perceive that James had not been present. He had gone to ask Miss Faithfull to supply the missing stanzas of a Jacobite song, and just then returned, saying that she knew them, but could not remember them.

Fitzjocelyn, however, capped the fragment, and illustrated it with some anecdotes that interested Miss Conway. James had great hopes that she was going to see him to the best advantage, but still there was a great drawback in the presence of Sydney Calcott. Idolized at home, successful abroad, young Calcott had enough of the prig to be a perpetual irritation to Jem Frost, all the more because he could never make Louis resent, nor accept, as other than natural, the goodnatured supercilious patronage of the steady distinguished senior towards the idle junior.

Jacobite legends and Stuart relics would have made Miss Conway oblivious of everything else; but Sydney Calcott must needs divert the conversation from that channel by saying, 'Ah! there Fitzjocelyn is in his element. He is a perfect handbook to the byways of history.'

'For the diffusion of useless knowledge?' said Louis.

'Illustrated by the examination, when the only fact you could adduce about the Argonauts was that Charles V. founded the order of the Golden Fleece.'

'I beg your pardon; it was his great-grandfather. I had read my Quentin Durward too well for that.'

'I suspect,' said Isabel, 'that we had all rather be examined in our Quentin Durward than our Charles V.

'Ah!' said young Calcott, 'I had all my dates at my fingers' ends when I went up for the modern history prize. Now my sister could beat me.'

'A proof of what I always say,' observed Louis, 'that it is lost labour to read for an examination.'

'From personal experience?' asked Sydney.

'A Strasburg goose nailed down and crammed before a fire, becomes a Strasburg pie,' said Louis.

Never did Isabel look more bewildered, and Sydney did not seem at once to catch the meaning. James added, 'A goose destined to fulfil the term of existence is not crammed, but the pie stimulus is not required to prevent it from starving.'

'Is your curious and complimentary culinary fable aimed against reading or against examinations?' asked Sydney.

'Against neither; only against the connecting preposition.'

'Then you mean to find a superhuman set of students?'

'No; I'm past that. Men and examinations will go on as they are; the goose will run wild, the requirements will be increased, he will nail himself down in his despair; and he who crams hardest, and has the hottest place will gain.'

'Then how is the labour lost?' asked Isabel.

'You are new to Fitzjocelyn's paradoxes,' said Sydney; as if glorying in having made Louis contradict himself.

'The question is, what is lost labour?' said Louis.

Both Sydney Calcott and Miss Conway looked as if they thought he was arguing on after a defeat. 'Calcott is teaching her his own obtuseness!' thought James, in a pet; and he exclaimed, 'Is the aim to make men or winners of prizes?'

'The aim of prizes is commonly supposed to be to make men,' loftily observed Sydney.

'Exactly so; and, therefore, I would not make them too analogous to the Strasburg system,' said Louis. 'I would have them close, searching, but not admitting of immediate cramming.'

'Pray how would you bring that about?'

'By having no subject on which superficial knowledge could make a show.'

'Oh! I see whither you are working round! That won't do now, my dear fellow; we must enlarge our field, or we shall lay ourselves open to the charge of being narrow-minded.'

'You have not strength of mind to be narrow-minded!' said Louis, shaking his head. 'Ah! well, I have no more to say; my trust is in the narrow mind, the only expansive one—'

He was at that moment called away; Lord Ormersfield's carriage had been announced, and his son was not in a quarter of the room where he wished to detain him. James could willingly have bitten Sydney Calcott for the observation, 'Poor Fitzjocelyn! he came out strong to-night.'

'Very clever,' said Isabel, wishing to gratify James.

'Oh yes, very; if he had ever taken pains,' said Sydney. 'There is often something in his paradoxes. After all, I believe he is reading hard for his degree, is he not, Jem? His feelings would not be hurt by the question, for he never piqued himself upon his consistency.'

Luckily for the general peace, the Calcott household was on the move, and Jem solaced himself on their departure by exclaiming, 'Well done, Strasburg system! A high-power Greek-imbibing machine, he may be, but as to comprehending Fitzjocelyn—'

'Nay,' said Isabel, 'I think Lord Fitzjocelyn ought to carry about a pocket expositor, if he will be so very startling. He did not stay to tell us what to understand by narrow minds.'

'Did you ever hear of any one good for anything, that was not accused of a narrow mind?' exclaimed James.

'If that were what he meant,' said Isabel,—'but he said his trust was in the narrow mind—'

'In what is popularly so called,' said James.

'I think,' said Mary, leaning forward, and speaking low, 'that he did not mean it to be explained away. I think he was going to say that the heart may be wide, but the mind must be so far narrow, that it will accept only the one right, not the many wrong.'

'I thought narrowness of mind consisted in thinking your own way the only right one,' said Isabel.

'Every one says so,' said Mary, 'and that is why he says it takes strength of mind to be narrow-minded. Is not the real evil, the judging people harshly, because their ways are not the same; not the being sure that the one way is the only right! Others may be better than ourselves, and may be led right in spite of their error, but surely we are not to think all paths alike—

'And is that Lord Fitzjocelyn's definition of a narrow mind?' said Isabel. 'It sounds like faith and love. Are you sure you did not make it yourself, Miss Ponsonby?'

'I could not,' said Mary, blushing, as she remembered one Sunday evening when he had said something to that effect, which had insensibly overthrown the theory in which she had been bred up, namely, that all the sincere were right, and yet that, practically every one was to be censured, who did not act exactly like Aunt Melicent.

She rose to take leave, and Clara clung to her, emerging from the shade of her cabinet with colour little mitigated since her disappearance. James would have come with them, but was detained by Lady Conway for a few moments longer than it took them to put on their shawls; and Clara would not wait. She dragged Mary down the steps into the darkness, and groaned out, 'O Mary, he can never speak to me again!'

'My dear! he will not recollect it. It was very awkward, but new places and new people often do make us forget ourselves.'

'Everybody saw, everybody heard! O, I shall never bear to meet one of them again!'

'I think very few saw or heard—' began Mary.

'He did! I did! That's enough! The rest is nothing! I have been as bad as any one at school! I shall never hold up my head there again as I have done, and Louis! Oh!'

'Dear child, it will not be remembered. You only forgot how tall you were, and that you were not at home. He knows you too well to care.'

James shouted from behind to know why they had not been let into the house; and as Clara rushed in at the door and he walked on with Mary to leave her at home and fetch his grandmother, who had been spending the evening with Mrs. Ponsonby, he muttered, 'I don't know which is most intolerable! He neglects her, talks what, if it be not nonsense, might as well be; and as if she were not ready enough to misunderstand, Sydney Calcott must needs thrust in his wits to embroil her understanding. Mary! can't you get her to see the stuff he is made of?'

'If she cannot do that for herself, no persuasion of mine will make her,' said Mary.

'No! you do not half appreciate him either! No one does! And yet you could, if you tried, do something with her! I see she does not think you prejudiced. You made an impression to-night.'

Mary felt some consternation. Could it depend on her? She could speak naturally, and from her heart in defence of Louis when occasion served; but something within her forbade the thought of doing so on a system. Was that something wrong! She could not answer; but contented herself with the womanly intuition that showed her that anything of persuasion in the present state of affairs would be ineffectual and unbecoming.

Meantime, Clara had fled to her little room, to bid her childhood farewell in a flood of bitter tears.

Exaggerated shame, past disdain of the foibles of others, the fancy that she was publicly disgraced and had forfeited Louis's good opinion, each thought renewed her sobs; but the true pang was the perception that old times were passed for ever. He might forgive, he would still be friend and cousin; but womanhood had broken on her, and shown that perfect freedom was at an end. Happy for her that she wept but for the parting from a playfellow! Happy that her feelings were young and undeveloped, free from all the cruel permanence that earlier vanity or self-consciousness might have given; happy that it could be so freely washed away! When she had spent her sobs, she could resolve to be wise and steady, so as to be a fit governess to his children; and the tears flowed at the notion of being so distant and respectful to his lordship. But what stories she could tell them of his boyhood! And in the midst of—'Now, my dears, I will tell you about your papa when he was a little boy,' she fell asleep.

That party was a thing to be remembered with tingling cheeks for life, and Clara dreaded her next meeting with Louis; but the days passed on without his coming to the Terrace, and the terror began to wear off, especially as she did not find that any one else remembered her outbreak. Mary guarded against any unfavourable impression by a few simple words to Isabel and Miss King as to the brotherly terms that had hitherto prevailed, and poor Clara's subsequent distress. Clara came in for some of the bright tints in which her brother was viewed at the House Beautiful; Walter was very fond of her, and she had been drawn into a friendship for Virginia, cemented in the course of long walks, when the schoolroom party always begged for Mr. and Miss Dynevor, because no one else could keep Walter from disturbing Louisa's nerves by teasing her pony or sliding on dubious ice.

As Mrs. Ponsonby often joined in Lady Conway's drive, Mary and Isabel were generally among the walkers; and Mary was considered by Louisa as an inestimable pony-leader, and an inexhaustible magazine of stories about sharks, earthquakes, llamas, and icebergs.

James and Miss Conway generally had either book or principle to discuss, and were usually to be found somewhat in the rear, either with or without Miss King. One day, however, James gave notice that he should not be at their service that afternoon; and as soon as Walter's lessons had been despatched, he set out with rapid steps for Ormersfield Park, clenching his teeth together every now and then with his determinate resolution that he would make Louis know his own mind, and would 'stand no nonsense.'

'Ah! James, good morning,' said the Earl, as he presented himself in the study. 'You will find Louis in his room. I wish you would make him come out with you. He is working harder than is good for him.'

He spoke of his son far differently from former times; but Jem only returned a judiciously intoned 'Poor fellow.'

Lord Ormersfield looked at him anxiously, and, hesitating, said, 'You do not think him out of spirits?'

'Oh, he carries it off very well. I know no one with so strong a sense of duty,' replied Jem, never compassionate to the father.

Again the Earl paused, then said, 'He may probably speak more unreservedly to you than to me.'

'He shuns the topic. He says there is no use in aggravating the feelings by discussion. He would fain submit in heart as well as in will.'

Lord Ormersfield sighed, but did not appear disposed to say more; and, charitably hoping that a dagger had been implanted in him, Jem ran upstairs, and found Louis sitting writing at a table, which looked as if Mary had never been near it.

'Jem! That's right! I've not seen you this age.'

'What are you about?'

'I wanted particularly some one to listen. It is an essay on the Police—'

'Is this earnest?'

'Sober earnest. Sir Miles and all that set are anxious to bring the matter forward, and my father has been getting it up, as he does whatever he may have to speak upon. His eyes are rather failing for candle-light work, so I have been helping him in the evening, till it struck me that it was a curious subject to trace in history,—the Censors, the attempts in Germany and Spain, to supply the defective law, the Spanish and Italian dread of justice. I became enamoured of the notion, and when I have thrown all the hints together, I shall try to take in my father by reading them to him as an article in the Quarterly.'

'Oh, very well. If your soul is there, that is an end of the matter.'

'Of what matter?'

'Things cannot run on in this way. It is not a thing to lay upon me to go on working in your cause with her when you will not stir a step in your own behalf.'

'I am very much obliged to you, but I never asked you to work in my cause. I beg your pardon, Jem, don't fly into a Welsh explosion. No one ever meant more kindly and generously—' He checked himself in amaze at the demonstration he had elicited; but, as it was not accompanied with words, he continued, 'No one can be more grateful to you than I; but, as far as I can see, there is nothing for it but to be thankful that no more harm has been done, and to let the matter drop;' and he dropped his hand with just so much despondency as to make Jem think him worth storming at, instead of giving him up; and he went over the old ground of Louis being incapable of true passion and unworthy of such a being if he could yield her without an effort, merely for the sake of peace.

'I say, Jem,' said Louis, quietly, 'all this was bad enough on neutral ground; it is mere treason under my father's own roof, and I will have no more of it.'

'Then,' cried James, with a strange light in his eyes, 'you henceforth renounce all hopes—all pretensions?'

'I never had either hope or pretension. I do not cease to think her, as I always did, the loveliest creature I ever beheld. I cannot help that; and the state I fell into after being with her on Tuesday, convinced me that it is safest to stay here and fill up time and thought as best I may.'

'For once, Fitzjocelyn,' said James, with a gravity not natural to him, 'I think better of your father than you do. I would neither treat him as so tyrannical nor so prejudiced as your conduct supposes him.'

'How? He is as kind as possible. We never had so much in common.'

'Yes. Your submission so far, and the united testimony of the Terrace, will soften him. Show your true sentiments. A little steadiness and perseverance, and you will prevail.'

'Don't make me feverish, Jem.'

A summons to Lord Fitzjocelyn to come down to a visitor in the library cut short the discussion, and James took leave at once, neither cousin wishing to resume the conversation.

The darts had not been injudiciously aimed. The father and son were both rendered uneasy. They had hitherto been unusually comfortable together, and though the life was unexciting, Louis's desire to be useful to his father, and the pressing need of working for his degree, kept his mind fairly occupied. Though wistful looks might sometimes be turned along the Northwold road, when he sallied forth in the twilight for his constitutional walk, he did not analyse which number of the Terrace was the magnet, and he avoided testing to the utmost the powers of his foot. The affection and solicitude shown for him at home claimed a full return; nor had James been greatly mistaken in ascribing something to the facility of nature that yielded to force of character. But Jem had stirred up much that Louis would have been contented to leave dormant; and the hope that he had striven to excite came almost teazingly to interfere with the passive acquiescence of an indolent will. Perturbed and doubtful, he was going to seek counsel as usual of the open air, as soon as the visitor was gone, but his father followed him into the hall, asking whither he was going.

'I do not know. I had been thinking of trying whether I can get as far as Marksedge.'

Marksedge would be fatal to the ankle, solitude to the spirits, thought the Earl; and he at once declared his intention of walking with his son as far as he should let him go.

Louis was half vexed, half flattered, and they proceeded in silence, till conscious of being ruffled, and afraid of being ungracious, he made a remark on the farm that they were approaching, and learnt in return that the lease was nearly out, the tenant did not want a renewal, and that Richardson intended to advertise.

He breathed a wish that it were in their own hands, and this led to a statement of the condition of affairs, the same to which a year before he had been wilfully deaf, and to which he now attended chiefly for the sake of gratifying his father, though he better understood what depended on it. At least, it was making the Earl insensible to the space they were traversing, and the black outlines of Marksedge were rising on him before he was aware. Then he would have turned, but Louis pleaded that having come so far, he should be glad to speak to Madison's grandfather, and one or two other old people, and he prevailed.

Lord Ormersfield was not prepared for the real aspect of the hamlet.

'Richardson always declared that the cottages were kept in repair,' he said.

'Richardson never sees them. He trusts to Reeves.'

'The people might do something themselves to keep the place decent.'

'They might; but they lose heart out of sight of respectability. I will just knock at this door—I will not detain you a moment.'

The dark smoky room, damp, ill-paved floor, and cracked walls produced their effect; and the name and voice of the inmate did more. Lord Ormersfield recognised a man who had once worked in the garden, and came forward and spoke, astonished and shocked to find him prematurely old. The story was soon told; there had been a seasoning fever as a welcome to the half-reclaimed moorland; ague and typhus were frequent visitors, and disabling rheumatism a more permanent companion to labourers exhausted by long wet walks in addition to the daily toil. At an age less than that of the Earl himself, he beheld a bowed and broken cripple.

Fitzjocelyn perceived his victory, and forebore to press it too hastily, lest he should hurt his father's feelings; and walked on silently, thinking how glad Mary would be to hear of this expedition, and what a pity it was that the unlucky passage of last August should have interfered with their comfortable friendship. At last the Earl broke silence by saying, 'It is very unfortunate;' and Louis echoed, 'Very.'

'My poor Uncle Dynevor! He was, without exception, the most wrongheaded person I ever came in contact with, yet so excessively plausible and eager that he carried my poor father entirely along with him. Louis! nothing is so ruinous as to surrender the judgment.'

Fully assenting, Louis wondered whether Marksedge would serve no purpose save the elucidation of this truism, and presently another ensued.

'Mischief is sooner done than repaired. As I have been allowing you, there has never been ready money at command.'

'I thought there were no more mortgages to be paid off. The rents of the Fitzjocelyn estate and the houses in the lower town must come to something.'

He was then told how these, with his mother's fortune, had been set apart to form a fund for his establishment, and for the first time he was shown the object of arrangements against which he had often in heart rebelled. His first impulse was to exclaim that it was a great pity, and that he could not bear that his father should have denied himself on his account.

'Do you think these things are sacrifices to me?' said the Earl. 'My habits were formed long ago.'

'Mine have been formed on yours,' said Louis. 'I should be encumbered by such an income as you propose unless you would let me lay it out in making work for the men and improving the estate, and that I had rather you undertook, for I should be certain to do something preposterous, and then be sorry.'

'Mrs. Ponsonby judged rightly. It was her very advice.'

'Then!' cried Louis, as if the deed were done.

'You would not find the income too large in the event of your marriage.'

'A most unlikely event!'

His father glanced towards him. If there had been a symptom of unhappiness, relenting was near, but it so chanced that Marksedge was reigning supreme, and he was chiefly concerned to set aside the supposition as an obstacle to his views. The same notion as James Frost's occurred to the Earl, that it could not be a tenacious character which could so easily set aside an attachment apparently so fervent, but the resignation was too much in accordance with his desires to render him otherwise than gratified, and he listened with complacency to Louis's plans. Nothing was fixed, but there was an understanding that all should have due consideration.

This settled, Louis's mind recurred to the hint which his father had thrown out, and he wondered whether it meant that the present compliance might be further stretched, but he thought it more likely to be merely a reference to ordinary contingencies. Things were far too comfortable between him and his father to be disturbed by discussion, and he might ultimately succeed better by submitting, and leaving facts and candour to remove prejudice.

To forget perplexity in the amusement of a mystification, he brought down his essay, concealing it ingeniously within a review flanked by blue-books, and, when Lord Ormersfield was taking out a pair of spectacles with the reluctance of a man not yet accustomed to them, he asked him if he would like to hear an article on the Police question.

At first the Earl showed signs of nodding, and said there was nothing to the purpose in all the historical curiosities at the outset, so that Louis, alarmed lest he should absolutely drop asleep, skipped all his favourite passages, and came at once to the results of the recent inquiries. The Earl was roused. Who could have learnt those facts? That was telling—well put, but how did he get hold of it. The very thing he had said himself—What Quarterly was it? Surely the Christmas number was not out. Hitherto Louis had kept his countenance and voice, but in an hiatus, where he was trying to extemporize, his father came to look over his shoulder to see what ailed the book, and, glancing upwards with a merry debonnaire face, he made a gesture as if convicted.

'Do you mean that this is your own composition?'

'I beg your pardon for the pious fraud!'

'It is very good! Excellently done!' said Lord Ormersfield. 'There are redundancies—much to betray an unpractised hand—but—stay, let me hear the rest—' Very differently did he listen now, broad awake, attacking the logic of every third sentence, or else double shotting it with some ponderous word, and shaking his head at Utopian views of crime to be dried up at the fountain head. Next, he must hear the beginning, and ruthlessly picked it to pieces, demolishing all the Vehme Gericht and Santissima Hermandad as irrelevant, and, when he had made Louis ashamed and vexed with the whole production, astonishing him by declaring that it would tell, and advising him to copy it out fair with these *little* alterations.

These *little* alterations would, as he was well aware, evaporate all the spirit, and though glad to have pleased his father, his perseverance quailed before the task; but he said no more than thank you. The next day, before he had settled to anything, Lord Ormersfield came to his room, saying, 'You will be engaged with your more important studies for the next few hours. Can you spare the paper you read to me last night?'

'I can spare it better than you can read it, I fear,' said Louis, producing a mass of blotted MS in all his varieties of penmanship, and feeling a sort of despair at the prospect of being brought to book on all his details.

His father carried it off, and they did not meet again till late in the day, when the first thing Louis heard was, 'I thought it worth while to have another opinion on your manuscript before re-writing it. I tried to read it to Mrs. Ponsonby, but we were interrupted, and I left it with her.'

Presently after. 'I have made an engagement for you. Lady Conway wishes that you should go to luncheon with her to-morrow. I believe she wants to consult you about some birth-day celebration.'

Louis was much surprised, and somewhat entertained.

'When will you have the carriage?' pursued the Earl.

'Will not you come?'

'No, I am not wanted. In fact, I do not see how you can be required, but anything will serve as an excuse. In justice, however, I should add that our friends at the Terrace are disposed to think well of the younger part of the family.'

Except for the cold constraint of the tone, Louis could have thought much ground gained, but he was sure that his holiday would be damped by knowing that it was conceded at the cost of much distress and uneasiness.

Going to Northwold early enough for a call at No. 5, he was greeted by Mrs. Frost with, 'My dear! what have you been about? I never saw your father so much pleased in his life! He came in on purpose to tell me, and I thought it exceedingly kind. So you took him in completely. What an impudent rogue you always were!'

'I never meant it to go beyond the study. I was obliged to write it down in self-defence, that I might know what he was talking of.'

'I believe he expects you to be even with Sydney Calcott after all. It is really very clever. Where did you get all those funny stories?'

'What! you have gone and read it!'

'Ah, ha! Mrs. Ponsonby gave us a pretty little literary soiree. Don't be too proud, it was only ourselves, except that Mary brought in Miss Conway. Jem tried to read it, but after he had made that Spanish Society into 'Hammer men dead,' Mary got it away from him, and read through as if it had been in print.'

'What an infliction!'

'It is very disrespectful to think us so frivolous. We only wished all reviews were as entertaining.'

'It is too bad, when I only wanted to mystify my father.'

'It serves you right for playing tricks. What have you been doing to him, Louis? You will turn him into a doting father before long.'

'What have you done with Clara?'

'She goes every day to read Italian with Miss Conway, and the governess is so kind as to give her drawing lessons. She is learning far more than at school, and they are so kind! I should hardly know how to accept it, but Jem does not object, and he is really very useful there, spends a great deal of time on the boy, and is teaching the young ladies Latin.'

'They are leaving you lonely in the holidays! You ought to come to Ormersfield, your nephews would take better care of you.'

'Ah! I have my Marys. If I were only better satisfied about the dear old one. She is far less well than when she came.'

'Indeed! Is Mary uneasy?'

'She says nothing, but you know how her eye is always on her, and she never seems to have her out of her thoughts. I am afraid they are worried about Lima. From what Oliver says, I fear Mr. Ponsonby goes on worse than ever without either his family or his appointment to be a restraint.'

'I hope they do not know all! Mary would not believe it, that is one comfort!'

'Ah, Louis! there are things that the heart will not believe, but which cut it deeply! However, if that could be any comfort to them, he wishes them to spare nothing here. He tells them they may live at the rate of five thousand pounds a-year, poor dears. Indeed, he and Oliver are in such glory over their Equatorial steam navigation, that I expect next to hear of a crash.'

'You don't look as if it would be a very dreadful sound.'

'If it would only bring my poor Oliver back to me!'

'Yes—nothing would make Jem so civil to him as his coming floated in on a plank, wet through, with a little bundle in one hand and a parrot in the other.'

Mrs. Frost gave one of her tender laughs, and filled up the picture. 'Jane would open the door, Jane would know Master Oliver's black eyes in a moment—'No, no. *I* must see him first! If he once looked up I could not miss him, whatever colour he may have turned. I wonder whether he would know me!'

'Don't you know that you grow handsomer every year, Aunt Kitty?'

'Don't flatter, sir.'

'Well, I most go to my aunt.'

He tarried to hear the welcome recital of all the kind deeds of the house of Conway. He presently found Lady Conway awaiting him in the drawing-room, and was greeted with great joy. 'That is well! I hoped to work on your father by telling him I did not approve of young men carrying industry too far—'

'That is not my habit.'

'Then it is your excuse for avoiding troublesome relations! No, not a word! I know nothing about the secret that occupied Isabel at Mrs. Ponsonby's select party. But I really wanted you. You are more au fait as to the society here than the Ponsonbys and Dynevors. Ah! when does that come off?'

'What is to come off?'

'Miss Ponsonby and Mr. Dynevor. What a good creature he is!'

'I cannot see much likelihood of it, but you are more on the scene of action.'

'She could do much better, with such expectations, but on his account I could not be sorry. It is shocking to think of that nice young sister being a governess. I think it a duty to give her every advantage that may tend to form her. With her connexions and education, I can have no objection to her as a companion to your cousins, and with a few advantages, though she will never be handsome, she might marry well. They are a most interesting family. Isabel and I are most anxious to do all in our power for them.'

'Clara is obliged,' said Louis, with undetected irony, but secret wonder at the dexterity with which the patronage must have been administered so as not to have made the interesting family fly off at a tangent.

Isabel made her appearance in her almost constant morning dress of soft dove-coloured merino entirely unadorned, and looking more like a maiden in a romance than ever. She had just left Adeline standing on the steps of a stone cross, exhorting the Provencals to arm against a descent of Moorish corsairs, and she held out her hand to Fitzjocelyn much as Adeline did, when the fantastic Viscount professed his intention of flying instead of fighting, and wanted her to sit behind him on his courser.

Lady Conway pronounced her council complete, and propounded the fete which she wished to give on the 12th of January in honour of Louisa's birthday. Isabel took up a pencil, and was lost in sketching wayside crosses, and vessels with lateen sails, only throwing in a word or two here and there when necessary. Dancing was still, Lady Conway feared, out of the question with Fitzjocelyn.

'And always will be, I suspect. So much for my bargain with Clara to dance with her at her first ball!'

'You like dancing?' exclaimed Isabel, rejoiced to find another resemblance to the fantastic Viscount.

'Last year's Yeomanry ball was the best fun in the world!'

'There, Isabel,' said Lady Conway, 'you ought to be gratified to find a young man candid enough to allow that he likes it! But since that cannot be, I must find some other plan—'

'What cannot be?' exclaimed Louis. 'You don't mean to omit the dancing—'

'It could not be enjoyed without you. Your cousins and friends could not bear to see you sitting down—'

Isabel's lips were compressed, and the foam of her waves laughed scornfully under her pencil.

'They must get accustomed to the melancholy spectacle,' said Louis. 'I do not mean to intermit the Yeomanry ball, if it take place while I am at home. The chaperons are the best company, after all. Reconsider it, my dear aunt, or you will keep me from coming at all.'

Lady Conway was only considering of tableaux, and Louis took fire at the notion: he already beheld Waverley in his beloved Yeomanry suit, Isabel as Flora, Clara as Davie Gellatley—the character she would most appreciate. Isabel roused herself to say that tableaux were very dull work to all save the actors, and soon were mere weariness to them. Her stepmother told her she had once been of a different mind, when she had been Isabel Bruce, kneeling in her cell, the ring before her. 'I was young enough then to think myself Isabel,' was her answer, and she drew the more diligently because Fitzjocelyn could not restrain an interjection, and a look which meant, 'What an Isabel she must have been!'

She sat passive while Lady Conway and Louis decked up a scene for Flora MacIvor; but presently it appeared that the Waverley of the piece was to be, according to Louis, not the proper owner of the Yeomanry uniform, but James Frost. His aunt exclaimed, and the rehearsals were strong temptation; but he made answer, 'No—you must not reckon on me: my father would not like it.'

The manful childishness, the childish manfulness of such a reply, were impenetrable. If his two-and-twenty years did not make him ashamed of saying so, nothing else could, and it covered a good deal. He knew that his father's fastidious pride would dislike his making a spectacle of himself, and thought that it would be presuming unkindly on to-day's liberty to involve himself in what would necessitate terms more intimate than were desired.

The luncheon silenced the consultation, which was to be a great secret from the children; but afterwards, when it was resumed, with the addition of James Frost, Fitzjocelyn was vexed to find the tableaux discarded; not avowedly because he excluded himself from a share, but because the style of people might not understand them. The entertainment was to be a Christmas-tree—not so hackneyed a spectacle in the year 1848 as in 1857—and Louis launched into a world of couplets for mottoes. Next came the question of guests, when Lady Conway read out names from the card-basket, and Fitzjocelyn was in favour of everybody, till Jem, after many counter-statements, assured Lady Conway that he was trying to fill her rooms with the most intolerable people in the world.

'My aunt said she wanted to give pleasure.'

'Ah! there's nothing so inconvenient to one's friends as good nature. Who cares for what is shared indiscriminately?'

'I don't think I can trust Fitzjocelyn with my visiting-list just yet,' said Lady Conway. 'You are too far above to be sensible of the grades beneath, with your place made for you.'

'Not at all,' said Louis. 'Northwold tea-parties were my earliest, most natural dissipation; and I spoke for these good people for my own personal gratification.'

'Nay, I can't consent to your deluding Lady Conway into Mrs. Walby.'

'If there be any one you wish me to ask, my dear Fitzjocelyn—' began Lady Conway.

'Oh no, thank you; Jem is quite right. I might have been playing on your unguarded innocence; but I am the worst person in the world to consult; for all the county and all the town are so kind to me, that I don't know whom I could leave out. Now, the Pendragon there will help you to the degree of gentility that may safely be set to consort together.'

'What an unkind fling!' thought Isabel.

Louis took leave, exclaiming to himself on the stairs, 'There! if comporting oneself like a donkey before the object be a token, I've done it effectually. Didn't I know the exclusiveness of the woman? Yet, how could I help saying a word for the poor little Walbys? and, after all, if they were there, no one would speak to them but Aunt Kitty and I. And Isabel, I am sure she scorned the fastidious nonsense; I saw it in her eye and lip.'

After a quarter of an hour spent in hearing her praises from Miss Faithfull, he betook himself to Mrs. Ponsonby's, not quite without embarrassment, for he had not been alone with the mother and daughter since August.

'I am glad you did not come before,' said Mary, heartily; 'I have just done:' and she returned to her writing-table, while her mother was saying,

'We like it very much.'

'You have not been copying that wretched concern!' exclaimed Louis. 'Why, Mary, you must have been at it all night. It is a week's work.'

'Copying is not composing,' said Mary.

'But you have mended it, made it consecutive! If I had guessed that my father meant to trouble any one with it!'

'If you take pains with it, it may be very valuable,' said Mrs. Ponsonby. 'We have marked a few things that you had better revise before it goes to Oakstead.'

'Goes to Oakstead!' said Louis, faintly.

'Your father talks of sending it, to see if Sir Miles does not think it might tell well in one of the Reviews.'

'I hope not. I should lose all my faith in anonymous criticism, if they admitted such a crude undergraduate's omnium gatherum! Besides, what an immense task to make it presentable!'

'Is that the root of your humility?'

'Possibly. But for very shame I must doctor it, if Mary has wasted so much time over it. It does not look so bad in your hand!'

'It struck me whether you had rendered this Spanish story right.'

'Of course not. I never stuck to my dictionary.'

A sound dose of criticism ensued, tempered by repetitions of his father's pleasure, and next came some sympathy and discussion about the farm and Marksedge, in which the ladies took their usual earnest part, and Mary was as happy as ever in hearing of his progress. He said no word of their neighbours; but he could not help colouring when Mary said, as he wished her good-bye, 'We like the party in the House Beautiful so much! Miss Conway is such an acquisition to me! and they are doing all you could ever have wished for Clara.'

Mary was glad that she had said it. Louis was not so glad. He thought it must have been an effort, then derided his vanity for the supposition.

CHAPTER XVI
THE FRUIT OF THE CHRISTMAS-TREE

> Age, twine thy brows with fresh spring flowers,
> And call a train of laughing hours;
> And bid them dance, and bid them sing:
> And thou, too, mingle in the ring.
> WORDSWORTH

The 12th of January was the last day before James and Louis meant to return to Oxford, Jem taking Clara on from thence to school. It was to be the farewell to Christmas—one much enjoyed in Dynevor Terrace. Fitzjocelyn's absence was almost a relief to Clara; she could not make up her mind to see him till she could hope their last encounter had been forgotten; and in the mean time, her anticipations were fixed on the great 12th. She was aware of what the entertainment would consist, but was in honour bound to conceal her knowledge from Virginia and Louisa, who on their side affected great excitement and curiosity, and made every ostentation of guessing and peeping. Gifts were smuggled into the house from every quarter—some to take their chance, some directed with mottoes droll or affectionate. Clara prepared a few trifles, in which she showed that school had done something for her fingers, and committed her little parcels to her brother's care; and Miss Mercy was the happiest of all, continually knocking at the locked door of the back drawing-room with gilded fir cones, painted banners, or moss birds'-nests, from Miss Salome.

Miss King and Isabel had undertaken the main business. When roused from her pensive stillness, Isabel could be very eager, active, and animated; and she worked with the exhilaration that she could freely enjoy when unrestrained by perceiving that she was wanted to produce an effect. What woman's height and hand could not perform fell to the share of James, who, with his step-ladder and dexterous hands, was invaluable. Merrily, merrily did the three work, laughing over their suspended bonbons, their droll contrivances, or predicting the adaptations of their gifts; and more and more gay was the laugh, the tutor more piquant, the governess more keen and clever, the young lady more vivacious, as the twilight darkened, and the tree became more laden, and the streamers and glass balls produced a more brilliant effect.

Proudly, when the task was accomplished, did they contemplate their work, and predict the aspect of their tinsel and frippery when duly lighted up. Then, as they dispersed to dress, James ran home, and hastily tapped at his sister's door.

'What is the matter?' she cried. 'Have the tassels come off my purse?'

'Nothing of the kind, but—' he came quite in, and looked round restlessly, then hastily said, 'You gave me nothing for Miss Conway.'

'I wished it very much,' said Clara, 'but I could not bear to do anything trumpery for her. Oh, if one could give her anything worth having!'

'Clara, I had thought—but I did not know if you would like to part with it—'

'I had thought of it too,' said Clara; 'but I thought you would not like it to be given away.'

Pulling out a drawer, she opened an odd little box of queer curiosities, whence she took a case containing an exquisite ivory carving, a copy of the 'Madonna della Sedia,' so fine that a magnifier alone could fully reveal the delicacy and accuracy of the features and expression. It was mounted as a bracelet clasp, and was a remnant of poor Mr. Dynevor's treasures. It had been given to Mrs. Henry Frost, and had descended to her daughter.

'Should you be willing?' wistfully asked James.

'That I should! I have longed to give her what she would really care for. She has been so very kind—and her kindness is so very sweet in its graciousness! I shall always be the happier for the very thinking of it.'

'I am glad—' began Jem, warmly; but, breaking off, he added—'This would make us all more comfortable. It would lessen the weight of obligation, and that would be satisfactory to you.'

'I don't know. I like people to be so kind, that I can't feel as if I would pay them off, but as if I could do nothing but love them.'

'You did not imagine that I rate this as repayment!'

'Oh! no, no!'

'No! it is rather that nothing can be too precious—' then pausing—'You are sure you are willing, Clary?'

'Only too glad. I like it to be something valuable to us as well as in itself. If I only had a bit of black velvet, I could set it up.'

In ten minutes, Jem had speeded to a shop and back again, and stood by as Clara stitched the clasp to the ribbon velvet; while there was an amicable dispute, he insisting that the envelope should bear only the initials of the true donor, and she maintaining that 'he gave the black velvet.' She had her way, and wrote, 'From her grateful C. F. D. and J. R. F. D.;' and as James took the little packet, he thanked her with an affectionate kiss—a thing so unprecedented at an irregular hour, that Clara's heart leapt up, and she felt rewarded for any semblance of sacrifice.

He told his grandmother that he had agreed with his sister that they could do no otherwise than present the ivory clasp; and Mrs. Frost, who had no specially tender associations with it, was satisfied to find that they had anything worth offering on equal terms.

She was to be of the party, and setting forth, they, found the House Beautiful upside down—even the Faithfull parlour devoted to shawls and bonnets, and the two good old sisters in the drawing-room; Miss Salome, under the protection of little Louisa, in an easy chair, opposite the folding doors. Small children were clustered in shy groups round their respective keepers. Lady Conway was receiving her guests with the smile so engaging at first sight, Isabel moving from one to the other with stately grace and courtesy, Virginia watching for Clara, and both becoming merged in a mass of white skirts and glossy heads, occupying a wide area. Mrs. Frost was rapturously surrounded by half-a-dozen young men, Sydney Calcott foremost, former pupils enchanted to see her, and keeping possession of her all the rest of the evening. She was a dangerous person to invite, for the Northwold youth had no eyes but for her.

The children were presently taken down to tea in the dining-room by Miss King and Miss Mercy; and presently a chorus of little voices and peals of laughter broke out, confirming the fact, whispered by Delaford to his lady, that Lord Fitzjocelyn had arrived, and had joined the downstairs party.

While coffee went round in the drawing-room, Isabel glided out to perform the lighting process.

'Oh, Mr. Dynevor!' she exclaimed, finding him at her side, 'I did not mean to call you away.'

'Mere unreason to think of the performance alone,' said James, setting up his trusty ladder. 'What would become of that black lace?'

'Thank you, it may be safer and quicker.'

'So far the evening is most successful,' said Jem, lighting above as she lighted below.

'That it is! I like Northwold better than any place I have been in since I left Thornton Conway. There is so much more heartiness and friendliness here than in ordinary society.

'I think Fitzjocelyn's open sympathies have conduced—'

Isabel laughed, and he checked himself, disconcerted.

'I beg your pardon,' she said; 'I was amused at the force of habit. If I were to say the Terrace chimneys did not smoke, you would say it was Lord Fitzjocelyn's doing.'

'Do not bid me do otherwise than keep him in mind.'

Down fell the highest candle: the hot wax dropping on Isabel's arm caused her to exclaim, bringing Jem down in horror, crying, 'I have hurt you! you are burnt!'

'Oh no, only startled. There is no harm done, you see,' as she cracked away the cooled wax—'not even a mark to remind me of this happy Christmas.'

'And it has been a happy Christmas to you,' he said, remounting.

'Most happy. Nothing has been so peaceful or satisfactory in my wandering life.'

'Shall I find you here at Easter?'

'I fear not. Mamma likes to be in London early; but perhaps she may leave the school-room party here, as Louisa is gaining so much ground, and that would be a pledge of our return.'

'Too much joy,' said James, almost inaudibly.

'I hope Walter may spend his holidays here,' she pursued. 'It is a great thing for him to be with any one who can put a few right notions into his head.'

Jem abstained from, as usual, proposing Fitzjocelyn for his example, but only said that Walter was very susceptible of good impressions.

'And most heartily we thank you for all you have done for him,' said Isabel, doubting whether Walter's mother appreciated the full extent of it; 'indeed, we have all a great deal to thank you for. I hope my sisters and I may be the better all our lives for the helps and explanations you have given to us. Is that the last candle? How beautiful! We must open.'

'Miss Conway—'

'Yes'—she paused with her hand on the key.

'No, no—do not wait,' taking the key himself. 'Yet—yes, I must—I must thank you for such words—'

'My words?' said Isabel, smiling. 'For thanking you, or being happy here?'

'Both! both! Those words will be my never-failing charm. You little guess how I shall live on the remembrance. Oh, if I could only convey to you what feelings you have excited—'

The words broke from him as if beyond his control, and under the pressing need of not wasting the tapers, he instinctively unlocked the door as he spoke, and cut himself short by turning the handle, perhaps without knowing what he was about.

Instantly Lady Conway and Miss King each pushed a folding leaf, Isabel and James drew back on either side, and the spectators beheld the tall glistening evergreen, illuminated with countless little spires of light, glancing out among the dark leaves, and reflected from the gilt fir-cones, glass balls, and brilliant toys.

'Sister! sister!' cried Miss Mercy, standing by Miss Faithfull's chair, in the rear of the throng, and seizing her hand in ecstasy; 'it is like a dream! like what we have read of! Oh, the dear little children! So very kind of Lady Conway! Could you have imagined—?' She quite gasped.

'It is very pretty, but it was a nicer Christmas-tree last year at Lady Runnymede's,' said Louisa, with the air of a critic. 'There we had coloured lamps.'

'Little fastidious puss!' said Louis, 'I thought you keeping in the background out of politeness; but I see you are only blasee with Christmas-trees. I pity you! I could no more be critical at such a moment than I could analyse the jewels in Aladdin's cave.'

'Oh, if you and Miss Faithfull talk, Cousin Fitzjocelyn, you will make it seem quite new.'

'You will deride the freshness of our simplicity,' said Louis, but presently added, 'Miss Salome, have we not awakened to the enchanted land? Did ever mortal tree bear stars of living flame? Here are realized the fabled apples of gold—nay, the fir-cones of Nineveh, the jewel-fruits of Eastern story, depend from the same bough. Yonder lamps shine by fairy spell.'

'Now, Cousin Fitzjocelyn, do you think I suppose you so silly—'

'Soft! The Dryad of the Enchanted Bower advances. Her floating robes, her holly crown, beseem her queenly charms.'

'As if you did not know that it is only Isabel!'

'Only! May the word be forgiven to a sister! Isabel! The name is all-expressive.'

'She is looking even more lovely than usual,' said Miss Faithfull. 'I never saw such a countenance.'

'She has a colour to-night,' added Miss Mercy, 'which does, as you say, make her handsomer than ever. Dear! dear! I hope she is not tired. I am so sorry I did not help her to light the tree!'

'I do not think it is fatigue,' said her sister. 'I hope it is animation and enjoyment—all I have ever thought wanting to that sweet face.'

'You are as bad as my prosaic cousin,' said Louis, 'disenchanting the magic bower and the wood-nymph into fir, wax, and modern young ladyhood.'

'There, cousin, it is you who have called her a modern young lady.'

Before Louisa had expressed her indignation, there was a call for her.

'The Sovereign of the Bower beckons,' said Louis. 'Favoured damsel, know how to deserve her smiles. Fairy gifts remain not with the unworthy.'

As he put her forward, some one made way for her. It was Mary, and he blushed at perceiving that she must have heard all his rhodomontade. As if to make amends, he paused, and asked for Mrs. Ponsonby.

'Much more comfortable to-night, thank you;' and the pleasant, honest look of her friendly eyes relieved him by not reproaching him.

'I wish she were here. It is a prettier, more visionary sight than I could have conceived.'

'I wish she could see it; but she feared the crowd. Many people in a room seem to stifle her. Is Lord Ormersfield here?'

'No, it would not be his element. But imagine his having taken to walking with me! I really think he will miss me.'

'Really?' said Mary, amused.

'It is presumptuous; but he does not see well at night, and is not quite broken in to his spectacles. Mary, I hope you will walk over to see after him. Nothing would be so good for him as walking you back, and staying to dinner with you. Go right into the library; he would be greatly pleased.

Can't you make some book excuse? And you have the cottages to see. The people inaugurated the boilers with Christmas puddings.'

'Mr. Holdsworth told us how pleased they were. And the Norrises?'

'Mrs. Norris is delighted; she has found a woman to wash, and says it will save her a maid. The people can get milk now: I assure you they look more wholesome already! And Beecher has actually asked for two more houses in emulation. And Richardson found himself turned over to me!'

'Oh, that's right.'

'I've been at the plans all the afternoon. I see how to contrive the fireplace in the back room, that we could not have in the first set, and make them cheaper, too. My father has really made a point of that old decrepit Hailes being moved from Marksedge; and Mary, he, and Richardson mean Inglewood to be made over to me for good. I am to put in a bailiff, and do as I can with it—have the profits or bear the losses. I think I have an idea—'

In spite of her willingness to hear the idea, Mary could not help asking, 'Have you sent off the Police article?'

'Hush, Mary; it is my prime object to have it well forgotten.'

'Oh! did not Sir Miles like it?'

'He said it wanted liveliness and anecdote. So the Santissima Hermandad, and all the extraneous history, were sent to him; and then he was well content, and only wanted me to leave out all the Christian chivalry—all I cared to say—'

'You don't mean not to finish? Your father was so pleased, Isabel so much struck! It is a pity—'

'No, no; you may forgive me, Mary—it is not pure laziness. It was mere rubbish, without the point, which was too strong for the two politicians; rubbish, any way. Don't tell me to go on with it; it was a mere trial, much better let it die away. I really have no time; if I don't mind my own business, I shall be a plucked gosling; and that would go to his, lordship's heart. Besides, I must get these plans done. Do you remember where we got the fire-bricks for the ovens?'

Mary was answering, when Walter came bursting through the crowd. 'Where is he? Fitzjocelyn, it is your turn.'

'Here is a curious specimen for our great naturalist,' said Mrs. Frost, a glow in her cheeks, and her voice all stifled mirth and mischief.

It was a large nest of moss and horsehair, partly concealed under the lower branches, and containing two huge eggs streaked and spotted with azure and vermilion, and a purple and yellow feather, labelled, 'Dropped by the parent animal in her flight, on the discovery of the nest by the crew of H.M.S. Flying Dutchman. North Greenland, April 1st, 1847. Qu.? Female of Equus Pegasus. Respectfully dedicated to the Right Honourable Viscount Fitzjocelyn.'

'A fine specimen,' said the Viscount at once, with the air of a connoisseur, by no means taken by surprise. 'They are not very uncommon; I found one myself about the same date in the justice-room. I dare say Mr. Calcott recollects the circumstance.'

'Oh, my dear fellow,' exclaimed Sydney, instead of his father; 'you need not particularize. You always were a discoverer in that line.'

'True,' said Louis, 'but this is unique. North Greenland—ah! I thought it was from a Frosty country. Ha, Clara?'

'Not I; I know nothing of it,' cried Clara, in hurry and confusion, not yet able to be suspected of taking liberties with him.

'No?' said Louis, turning about his acquisition; 'I thought I knew the female that laid these eggs. The proper name is, I fancy, Glacies Dynevorensis—var. Catharina—perhaps—'

Walter and Louisa had brought their mother to see the nest, the point of which she comprehended as little as they; and not understanding how much amusement was betokened by her nephew's gravity, she protested that none of her party had devised it, nor even been privy to it, and that Mr. Dynevor must bear the blame, but he was very busy detaching the prizes from the tree, and hastily denied any concern with it. Aunt Catharine was obliged to console Lady Conway, and enchant Louis by owning herself the sole culprit, with no aid but Miss Mercy's. Together they had disposed the nest in its right locality, as soon as the Earl's absence was secure.

'I had not courage for it before him,' she laughed. 'As for this fellow, I knew he would esteem it a compliment.'

'As a tribute to his imagination?' said Isabel, who, in her mood of benevolence, could be struck with the happy understanding between aunt and nephew revealed by such a joke, so received.

'It would be a curious research,' said Louis, 'whether more of these nidifications result from over-imagination or the want of it.'

'Often from want of imagination, and no want of cowardice,' said Isabel.

'That sort of nest has not illuminated eggs like these,' said Louis. 'They are generally extremely full of gunpowder, and might be painted with a skull and crossbones. I say, Clara, has Aunt Kitty considered the consequences?

She has sacrificed her ostrich eggs! I can never part with these original productions of her genius.'

He exhibited his mare's nest with his own gay bonhommie to all who were curious, and presently, when every one's attention had been again recalled to the wonders which Isabel was distributing, and he had turned aside to dispose of his treasure, he heard a sound of soliloquy half aloud, 'I wonder whether she has it!' from Clara, who stood a little apart.

'What?' asked Louia.

'My ivory clasp with the Madonna,' said Clara. 'Jem and I thought it the only thing worthy of Miss Conway.'

'Hem!' said Louis; 'it is not your fault, Clara; but it would be graceful to learn to receive a favour.'

'A favour, but not a grand thing like this,' said Clara, showing a beautiful little case of working implements.

'Hardly worth, even intrinsically, your mother's bracelet,' said Louis. 'But I am not going to talk treason to the family doctrine, though it is very inconvenient to your friends.'

'Then you think we ought not to have done it?'

'That depends on what I can't decide.'

'What's that?'

'Whether you give it out of love or out of pride.'

'I think we gave it out of one, and excused it by the other.'

'Very satisfactory. To reward you, here is something for you to do. I shall never get at Aunt Kitty to-night. I see the midshipman, young Brewster, will not relinquish her; so will you or will she administer this letter to the Lady of Eachalott?'

'You don't mean that is Tom Madison!' exclaimed Clara. 'Why, it is like copper-plate. No more Fitsgoslings!'

'No, indeed! Is he not a clever fellow? He has just reached the stage of civilization that breaks out in dictionary words. I have been, in return, telling him the story of the Irish schoolmaster who puzzled the magistrate's bench by a petition about a small cornuted animal, meaning a kid. But I should think it would be very edifying to Charlotte to see herself commemorated as the individual at the Terrace, and his grandfather as his aged relative. He sends the old man ten shillings this time, for he is promoted. Don't you think I may be proud of him? Is Mary gone home? She must hear about him.'

As he turned away in search of Mary, Clara felt a soft hand on her shoulder, and Isabel beckoned her to follow into the back drawing-room, where the tree was burnt out and deserted.

'I may thank *you*,' said Isabel, in a low, sweet voice, pressing her hand.

'And Jem,' said Clara; 'he thought of it first.'

'It is the most beautiful Christmas gift; but I do not like for you to part with it, my dear.'

'We both wished it, and grandmamma gave leave. We longed for you to have something we prized like this, for it belonged to my mamma. It is Jem's present too, for he went out and bought the black velvet.'

'Clasp it on for me, dear Clara. There!' and Isabel kissed the fingers which obeyed. 'It shall never leave my arm.'

Clara's face burnt with surprise and pleasure amounting to embarrassment, as Isabel expressed hopes of meeting again, and engaged her to write from school. She looked for her brother to take his share of thanks; but he was determinately doing his duty in cutting chicken and cake for those who desired supper, and he did not come in their way again till all the guests were gone, and good-night and good-bye were to be said at once.

Lady Conway was warm in expressing her hopes that Walter would enjoy the same advantages another holidays, and told Mr. Dynevor she should write to him. But Jem made little answer, nothing like a promise. Clara thought he had become stiff from some unknown affront, perhaps some oppressive present, for he seemed to intend to include all the young ladies in one farewell bow. But Isabel advanced with outstretched hand and flushing cheek, and her murmured 'Thank you' and confiding pressure drew from him such a grasp as could not easily be forgotten.

Clara's heart was all the lighter because she was sure that Fitzjocelyn had forgiven, and, what was more, forgotten. She had spoken naturally to him once more, and was ready for anything now—even though they had missed all confidential discussions upon school.

She gave Charlotte Tom Madison's letter. The little maiden took it, and twirled it about rather superciliously. 'What business had my young Lord,' she thought, 'to fancy she cared for that poor fellow? Very likely he was improved, and she was glad of it, but she knew what was genteel now. Yes, she would read it at once; there was no fear that it would make her soft and foolish—she had got above that!'

CHAPTER XVII
THE RIVALS

'Which king, Bezonian?'—Henry IV.

Sir Roland of Provence remained in suspense whether to be a novice or an irrevocably pledged Hospitalier. The latter was most probable; and when Adeline's feelings had been minutely analysed, Miss Conway discovered that she had better not show her morning's work to her sisters.

Clara and Louis pronounced Jem to be as savage as a bear all through the journey. Clara declared it was revenge for having been civil and amiable all through the vacation; and Louis uttered a theatrical aside, that even *that* could not have been maintained if he had not occasionally come to Ormersfield to relieve himself a little upon their two lordships.

Laugh as he might, Fitzjocelyn was much concerned and perplexed by his cousin's ill-humour, when it appeared more permanent than could be puffed off in a few ebullitions. Attempts to penetrate the gloom made it heavier, and Louis resolved to give it time to subside. He waited some days before going near James, and when he next walked to his college found him engaged with pupils. He was himself very busy, and had missed his cousin several times before he at length found him alone.

'Why, Jem, old fellow, what are you about? You've not been near my rooms this term. Are you renouncing me in anticipation of my plucking?'

'You won't be plucked unless you go out of your senses for the occasion.'

'No thanks to your advice and assistance if I am not. But it would conduce to my equanimity, Jem, to know whether we are quarrelling, as in that case I should know how to demean myself.'

'I've no quarrel with you. You have far more reason—But,' added Jem, catching himself up, 'don't you know I have no leisure for trifling? The Ordination is the second week in March.'

'The Ordination!'

'Ay—you know it! My fellowship depends on it.'

'I never liked to contemplate it.' He sat down and mused, while James continued his occupation. Presently he said, 'Look here. Sir Miles Oakstead asked me if I had any clever Oxford friend to recommend. If he comes into office, he—'

'I'll be no great man's hanger-on.'

'This matter is not imminent. You are barely four-and-twenty. Wait a year or two; even a few months would—'

'You have tried my forbearance often enough,' broke in James; 'my object is—as you very well know—to maintain myself and mine without being liable to obnoxious patronage. If you think I should disgrace the office, speak out!'

Louis, without raising his eyes, only answered with a smile.

'Then, what do you mean? As to your notions of a vocation, ninety-nine out of a hundred are in my case. I have been bred up to this—nothing else is open—I mean to do my duty; and surely that is vocation—no one has a right to object—'

'No one; I beg your pardon,' meekly said Louis, taking up his stick to go; but both knew it was only a feint, and James, whose vehemence was exhausting itself, resumed, in an injured tone, 'What disturbs you? what is this scruple of yours!—you, who sometimes fancy you would have been a curate yourself!'

'I have just inclination enough to be able to perceive that you have none.'

'And is every one to follow his bent?'

'This is not a step to be taken against the grain, even for the best earthly motives. Jem! I only beg you to ask advice. For the very reason that you are irreproachable, you will never have it offered.'

'The present time, for instance?' said James, laughing as best he might.

'That is nothing. I have no faith in my own judgment, but, thinking as I do of the profession and of you, I cannot help believing that my distaste for seeing you in it must be an instinct.'

'Give me your true opinion and its grounds candidly, knowing that I would not ask another man living.'

'Nor me, if I did not thrust it on you.'

'Now for it! Let us hear your objection.'

'Simply this. I do not see that anything impels you to take Holy Orders immediately, except your wish to be independent, and irrevocably fixed before your uncle can come home. This seems to me to have a savour of something inconsistent with what you profess. It might be fine anywhere else, but will it not bear being brought into the light of the sanctuary? No, I cannot like it. I have no doubt many go up for ordination far less fit than you, but—Jem, I wish you would not. If you would but wait a year!'

'No, Fitzjocelyn, my mind is made up. I own that I might have preferred another course, and Heaven knows it is not that I think myself worthy of this; but I have been brought up to this, and I will not waver. It is marked out for me as plainly as your earldom for you, and I will do my duty in it as my appointed calling. There lies my course of honest independence: you call it pride—see what those are who are devoid of it: there lie my means of educating my sister, providing for my grandmother. I can see no scruple that should deter me.'

Fitzjocelyn having said his say, it was his turn and his nature to be talked down.

'In short,' concluded James, walking about the room, 'there is no alternative. Waiting for a College living is bad enough, but nothing else can make happiness even possible.'

'One would think you meant one sort of happiness,' said Louis, with a calm considering tone, and look of inquiry which James could not brook.

'What else?' he cried. 'Fool and madman that I am to dwell on the hopeless—'

'Why should it be hopeless?—' began Louis.

'Hush! you are the last person with whom I could discuss this subject,' he said, trying to be fierce, but with more sorrow than anger. 'I must bear my burthen alone. Believe me, I struggled hard. If you and I be destined to clash, one comfort is, that even I could never quarrel with you.'

'I have not the remotest idea of your meaning.'

'So much the better. No, so much the worse. You are not capable of feeling what I do for her, or you would have hated me long ago. Do not stay here! I do not know that I can quite bear the sight of you—But don't let me lose you, Louis.'

James wrung the hand of his cousin; and no sooner was he alone, than he began to pace the room distractedly.

'Poor Jem!' soliloquized Fitzjocelyn. 'At least, I am glad the trouble is love, not the Ordination. But as to his meaning! He gives me to understand that we are rivals—It is the most absurd thing I ever knew—I declare I don't know whether he means Mary or Isabel. I suppose he would consider Mary's fortune a barrier—No, she is too serene for his storms—worthy, most worthy—but she would hate to be worshipped in that wild way. Besides, I am done for in that quarter. No clashing there—! Nay, the other it can never be—after all his efforts to lash me up at Christmas. Yet, he was much with her, he made Clara sacrifice the clasp to her. Hm! She is an embodied romance, deserving to be raved about; while for poor dear Mary, it would be simply ridiculous. I wish I could guess—it is too absurd to doubt, and worse to ask; and, what's more, he would not stand it. If I did but know! I'm not so far gone yet, but that I could leave the field to him, if that would do him any good. Heigh ho! it would be en regle to begin to hate him, and be as jealous as Bluebeard; but there! I don't know which it is to be about, and one can't be jealous for two ladies at once, luckily, for it would be immensely troublesome, unless a good, hearty quarrel would be wholesome to revive his spirits. It is a bad time for it, though! Well, I hope he does not mean Mary—I could not bear for her to be tormented by him. That other creature might reign over him like the full moon dispersing clouds. Well! this is the queerest predicament I ever heard of!' And on he wandered, almost as much diverted by the humour of the doubt, as annoyed by the dilemma.

He had no opportunity for farther investigation: James removed himself so entirely from his society, that he was obliged to conclude that the prevailing mood was that of not being quite able to bear the sight of him. His consolation was the hope of an opening for some generous proceeding, though how this should be accomplished was not visible, since it was quite as hard to be generous with other people's hearts as to confer a benefit on a Pendragon. At any rate, he was so confident of Jem's superiority, as to have no fear of carrying off the affection of any one whom his cousin wished to win.

James was ordained, and shortly after went to some pupils for the Easter vacation, which was spent by Louis at Christchurch, in studying hard. The preparation for going up for his degree ended by absorbing him entirely, as did every other pursuit to which he once fairly devoted himself, and for the first time he gave his abilities full scope in the field that ought long ago to have occupied them. When, finally, a third class was awarded to him, he was conscious that it might have been a first, but for his past waste of time.

He was sorry to leave Oxford: he had been happy there in his own desultory fashion; and the additional time that his illness had kept him an undergraduate, had been welcome as deferring the dreaded moment of considering what was to come next. He had reached man's estate almost against his will.

He was to go to join his father in London; and he carried thither humiliation for having, by his own fault, missed the honours that too late he had begun to value as a means of gratifying his father.

The Earl, however, could hardly have taken anything amiss from Louis. After having for so many years withheld all the lassez-aller of paternal affection, when the right chord had once been touched, his fondness for his grown-up son had the fresh exulting pride, and almost blindness that would ordinarily have been lavished on his infancy. Lord Ormersfield's sentiments were few and slowly adopted, but they had all the permanence and force of his strong character, and his affection for Fitzjocelyn partook both of parental glory in a promising only son, and of that tenderness, at once protecting and dependent, that fathers feel for daughters. This was owing partly to Louis's gentle and assiduous attentions during the last vacation, and also to his long illness, and remarkable resemblance to his mother, which rendered fondness of him a sort of tribute to her, and restored to the Earl some of the transient happiness of his life.

It was a second youth of the affections, but it was purchased by a step towards age. The anxiety, fatigue, and various emotions of the past year had told on the Earl, and though still strong, vigorous, and healthy, the first touch of autumn had fallen on him—he did not find his solitary life so self-sufficing as formerly, and craved the home feeling of the past Christmas. So the welcome was twice as warm as Louis had expected; and as he saw the melancholy chased away, the stern grey eyes lighted up, and the thin, compressed lips relaxed into a smile, he forgot his aversion to the well-appointed rooms in Jermyn Street, and sincerely apologized that he had not brought home more credit to satisfy his father.

'Oakstead was talking it over with me,' was the answer; 'and we reckoned up many more third-class men than first who have distinguished themselves.'

'Many thanks to Sir Miles,' said Louis, laughing. 'My weak mind would never have devised such consolation.'

'Perhaps the exclusive devotion to study which attains higher honours may not be the beat introduction to practical life.'

'It is doing the immediate work with the whole might.'

'You do work with all your might.'

'Ay! but too many irons in the fire, and none of them red-hot through, have been my bane.'

'You do not set out in life without experience; I am glad your education is finished, Louis!' said his father, turning to contemplate him, as if the sight filled up some void.

'Are you?' said Louis, wearily. 'I don't think I am. It becomes my duty—or yours, which is a relief—to find out the next stage.'

'Have you no wishes?'

'Not at the present speaking, thank you. If I went out and talked to any one, I might have too many.'

'No views for your future life?'

'Thus far: to do as little harm as may be—to be of some use at home—and to make turnips grow in the upland at Inglewood, I have some vague fancy to see foreign parts, especially now they are all in such a row—it would be such fun—but I suppose you would not trust me there now. Here I am for you to do as you please with me—a gracious permission, considering that you did not want it. Only the first practical question is how to get this money from Jem to Clara. I should like to call on her, but I suppose that would hardly be according to the proprieties.'

'I would walk to the school with you, if you wish to see her. My aunt will be glad to hear of her, if we go home to-morrow.'

'Are you thinking of going home?' exclaimed Louis, joyfully coming to life.

'Yes; but for a cause that will grieve you. Mrs. Ponsonby is worse, and has written to ask me to come down.'

'Materially worse?'

'I fear so. I showed my aunt's letter to Hastings, who said it was the natural course of the disease, but that he thought it would have been less speedy. I fear it has been hastened by reports from Peru. She had decided on going out again; but the agitation overthrew her, and she has been sinking ever since,' said Lord Ormersfield, mournfully.

'Poor Mary!'

'For her sake I must be on the spot, if for no other cause. If I had but a home to offer her!'

Louis gave a deep sigh, and presently asked for more details of Mrs. Ponsonby's state.

'I believe she is still able to sit up and employ herself at times, but she often suffers dreadfully. They are both wonderfully cheerful. She has little to regret.'

'What a loss she will be! Oh, father! what will you do without her?'

'I am glad that you have known her. She has been more than a sister to me. Things might have been very different, if that miserable marriage had not separated us for so many years.'

'How could it have happened? How was it that she—so good and wise—did not see through the man?'

'She would, if she had been left to herself; but she was not. My mother discovered, when too late, that there had been foolish, impertinent jokes of that unfortunate trifler, poor Henry Frost, that made her imagine herself suspected of designs on me.'

'Mary would never have attended to such folly!' cried Louis.

'Mary is older. Besides, she loved the man, or thought she did. I believe she thinks herself attached to him still. But for Mary's birth, there would have been a separation long ago. There ought to have been; but, after my father's death, there was no one to interfere! What would I not have given to have been her brother! Well! I never could see why one like her was so visited—!' Then rousing himself, as though tender reminiscences were waste of time, he added, 'There you see the cause of the caution I gave you with regard to Clara Dynevor. It is not fair to expose a young woman to misconstructions and idle comments, which may goad her to vindicate her dignity by acting in a manner fatal to her happiness. Now,' he added, having drawn his moral, 'if we are to call on Clara, this would be the fittest time. I have engaged for us both to dine at Lady Conway's this evening: I thought you would not object.'

'Thank you; but I am sure you cannot wish to go out after such news.'

'There is not sufficient excuse for refusing. There is to be no party, and it would be a marked thing to avoid it.'

Louis hazarded a suggestion that the meeting with Clara would be to little purpose if they were all to sit in state in the drawing-room; and she was asked for on the plea of going to see the new Houses of Parliament. The Earl of Ormersfield's card and compliments went upstairs, and Miss Frost Dynevor appeared, with a demure and astonished countenance, which changed instantly to ecstasy when she saw that the Earl was not alone. Not at all afraid of love, but only of misconstructions, he goodnaturedly kept aloof, while Clara, clinging to Louis's arm, was guided through the streets, and in and out among the blocks of carved stone on the banks of the Thames, interspersing her notes of admiration and his notes on heraldry with more comfortable confidences than had fallen to their lot through the holidays.

His first hope was that Clara might reveal some fact to throw light on the object of her brother's affections, but her remarks only added to his perplexity. Once, when they had been talking of poor Mary, and lamenting her fate in having to return to her father, Louis hazarded the conjecture that she might find an English home.

'There is her aunt in Bryanston Square,' said Clara. 'Or if she would only live with us! You see I am growing wise, as you call it: I like her now.'

'That may be fortunate,' said Louis. 'You know her destination according to Northwold gossip.'

'Nonsense! Jem would scorn an heiress if she were ten times prettier. He will never have an escutcheon of pretence like the one on the old soup tureen that the Lady of Eschalott broke, and Jane was so sorry for because it was the last of the old Cheveleigh china.'

Louis made another experiment. 'Have you repented yet of giving away your clasp?'

'No, indeed! Miss Conway always wears it. She should be richly welcome to anything I have in the world.'

'You and Jem saw much more of them than I did.'

'Whose fault was that? Jem was always raving about your stupidity in staying at home.'

He began to question whether his interview with James had been a dream. As they were walking back towards the school, Clara went on to tell him that Lady Conway had called and taken her to a rehearsal of a concert of ancient music, and that Isabel had taken her for one or two drives into the country.

'This must conduce to make school endurable,' said Louis.

'I think I hate it more because I hate it less.'

'Translate, if you please.'

'The first half-year, I scorned them all, and they scorned me; and that was comfortable—'

'And consistent. Well?'

'The next, you had disturbed me; I could not go on being savage with the same satisfaction, and their tuft-hunting temper began to discharge itself in such civility to me, that I could not give myself airs with any peace.'

'Have you made no friends?'

One and a half. The whole one is a good, rough, stupid girl, who comes to school because she can't learn, and is worth all the rest put together. The half is Caroline Salter, who is openly and honestly purse-proud, has no toad-eating in her nature, and straight-forwardly contemns high-blood and no money. We fought ourselves into respect for one another; and now, I verily believe, we are fighting ourselves into friendship. She is the only one that is proud, not vain; so we understand each other. As to the rest, they adore Caroline Halter's enamelled watch one day; and the next, I should be their 'dearest' if I would but tell them what we have for dinner at Ormersfield, and what colour your eyes are!'

'The encounters have made you so epigrammatic and satirical, that there is no coming near you.'

'Oh, Louis! if you knew all, you would despise me as I do myself! I do sometimes get drawn into talking grandly about Ormersfield; and though I always say what I am to be, I know that I am as vain and proud as any of them: I am proud of being poor, and of the Pendragons, and of not being silly! I don't know which is self-respect, and which is pride!'

'I have always had my doubts about that quality of self-respect. I never could make out what one was to respect.'

'Oh, dear! les voila!' cried Clara, as, entering Hanover Square, they beheld about twenty damsels coming out of the garden in couples. 'I would not have had it happen for the whole world!' she added, abruptly withdrawing the arm that had clung to him so trustfully across many a perilous crossing.

She seemed to intend to slip into the ranks without any farewells, but the Earl, with politeness that almost confounded the little elderly governess, returned thanks for having been permitted the pleasure of her company, and Louis, between mischief and good-nature, would not submit to anything but a hearty, cousinly squeeze of the hand, nor relinquish it till he had forced her to utter articulately the message to grandmamma that she had been muttering with her head averted. At last it was spoken sharply, and her hand drawn petulantly away, and, without looking back at him, her high, stiff head vanished into the house, towering above the bright rainbow of ribbons, veils, and parasols.

The evening would have been very happy, had not Lord Ormersfield looked imperturbably grave and inaccessible to his sister-in-law's blandishments. She did not use the most likely means of disarming him when she spoke of making a tour in the summer. It had been a long promise that Isabel and Virginia should go to see their old governess at Paris; but if France still were in too disturbed a state, they might enjoy themselves in Belgium, and perhaps her dear Fitzjocelyn would accompany them as their escort.

His eyes had glittered at the proposal before he recollected the sorrow that threatened his father, and began to decline, protesting that he should be the worst escort in the world, since he always attracted accidents and adventures. But his aunt, discovering that he had never been abroad, became doubly urgent, and even appealed to his father.

'As far as I am concerned, Fitzjocelyn may freely consult his own inclinations,' said the Earl, so gravely, that Lady Conway could only turn aside the subject by a laugh, and assurance that she did not mean to give him up. She began to talk of James Frost, and her wishes to secure him a second time as Walter's tutor in the holidays.

'You had better take him with you,' said Louis; 'he would really be of use to you, and how he would enjoy the sight of foreign parts!'

Isabel raised her head with a look of approbation, such as encouraged him to come a little nearer, and apeak of the pleasure that her kindness had given to Clara.

'There is a high spirit and originality about Clara, which make her a most amusing companion.'

Isabel replied, 'I am very glad of an hour with her, especially now that I am without my sisters.'

'She must be such a riddle to her respectable school-fellows, that intercourse beyond them must be doubly valuable.'

'Poor child! Is there no hope for her but going out as a governess?'

'Unluckily, we have no Church patronage for her brother; the only likely escape—unless, indeed, the uncle in Peru, whom I begin to regard as rather mythical, should send an unavoidable shower of gold on them.'

'I hope not,' said Isabel, 'I could almost call their noble poverty a sacred thing. I never saw anything so beautiful as the reverent affection shown to Mrs. Dynevor on Walter's birthday, when she was the Queen of the Night, and looked it, and her old pupils vied with each other in doing her honour. I have remembered the scene so often in looking at our faded dowagers here.'

'I would defy Midas to make my Aunt Catharine a faded dowager,' said Louis.

'No; but he could have robbed their homage of half—nay, all its grace.'

They talked of Northwold, and Isabel mentioned various details of Mrs. Ponsonby, which she had learnt from Miss King, and talked of Mary with great feeling and affection. Never had Louis had anything so like a conversation with Isabel, and he was more bewitched than ever by the enthusiasm and depth of sensibilities which she no longer concealed by coldness and reserve. In fact, she had come to regard him as an accessory of Northwold, and was delighted to enjoy some exchange of sympathy upon Terrace subjects—above all, when separated from the school-room party. Time had brought her to perceive that the fantastic Viscount did not always wear motley, and it was almost as refreshing as meeting with Clara, to have some change from the two worlds in which she lived. In her imaginary world, Adeline had just been rescued from the Corsairs by a knight hospitalier, with his vizor down, and was being conducted home by him, with equal probabilities of his dying at her feet of a concealed mortal wound, or conducting her to her convent gate, and going off to be killed by the Moors. The world of gaiety was more hollow and wearisome than ever; and the summons was as unwelcome to her as to Fitzjocelyn, when Lord Ormersfield reminded him that the ladies were going to an evening party, and that it was time to take leave.

'Come with us, Fitzjocelyn,' said his aunt. 'They would be charmed to have you;' and she mentioned some lions, whose names made Louis look at his father.

'I will send the carriage for you,' said the Earl; but Louis had learnt to detect the tone of melancholy reluctance in that apparently unalterable voice, and at once refused. Perhaps it was for that reason that Isabel let him put on her opera-cloak and hand her down stairs. 'I don't wonder at you,' she said; 'I wish I could do the same.'

'I wished it at first,' he answered; 'but I could not have gone without a heavy heart.'

'Are you young enough to expect to go to any gaieties without a heavy heart?'

'I am sorry for you,' said he, in his peculiar tone: 'I suppose I am your elder.'

'I am almost twenty-*four*,' she said, with emphasis.

'Indeed! That must be the age for care, to judge by the change it has worked in Jem Frost.'

The words were prompted by a keen, sudden desire to mark their effect; but he failed to perceive any, for they were in a dark part of the entry, and her face was turned away.

'Fitzjocelyn,' said the Earl, on the way home, 'do not think it necessary to look at me whenever you receive an invitation. It makes us both appear ridiculous, and you are in every respect your own master.'

'I had rather not, thank you,' said Louis, in an almost provokingly indifferent tone.

'It is full time you should assume your own guidance.'

'How little he knows how little that would suit him!' thought Louis, sighing despondingly. 'Am I called on to sacrifice myself in everything, and never even satisfy him?'

CHAPTER XVIII
REST FOR THE WEARY

> Therefore, arm thee for the strife
> All throughout this mortal life,
> Soldier now and servant true,
> Earth behind, and heaven in view.
>   REV. I. WILLIAMS.

The first impression on arriving at Northwold was, that the danger had been magnified. Mrs. Frost's buoyant spirits had risen at the first respite; and though there was a weight on Mary's brow, she spoke cheerfully, and as if able to attend to other interests, telling Louis of her father's wish for some good workmen to superintend the mines, and asking him to consult his friends at Illershall on the subject.

Lord Ormersfield came down encouraged by his visit to the invalid, whom he had found dressed and able to converse nearly as usual. She begged him to come to dinner the next day, and spend the evening with her, promising with a smile that if he would bring Louis, their aunt should chaperon Mary.

When the Earl went upstairs after dinner, the other three closed round the fire, and talked in a tranquil, subdued strain, on various topics, sometimes grave, sometimes enlivened by the playfulness inherent in two of the party. Aunt Kitty spoke of her earlier days, and Louis and Mary ventured questions that they would have ordinarily deemed intrusive. Yet it was less the matter than the manner of their dialogue—the deep, unavowed fellow-feeling and mutual reliance—which rendered it so refreshing and full of a kind of repose. Louis felt it like the strange bright stillness, when birds sing their clearest, fullest notes, and the horizon reach of sky beams with the softest, brightest radiance, just ere it be closed out by the thunder-cloud, whose first drops are pausing to descend; and to Mary it was peace—peace which she was willing gratefully to taste to the utmost, from the instinctive perception that the call had come for her to brace all her powers of self-control and fortitude; while to the dear old aunt, besides her enjoyment of her darling's presence, each hour was a boon that she could believe the patient or the daughter, relieved and happy.

Louis was admitted for a few minutes' visit to the sick-chamber, and went up believing that he ought to be playful and cheerful; but he was nearly overcome by Mrs. Ponsonby's own brightness, as she hoped that her daughter and aunt had made themselves agreeable.

'Thank you, I never was so comfortable, not even when my foot was bad.'

'I believe you consider that a great compliment.'

'Yes, I never was so much off my own mind, nor on other people's:' and the recollection of all he owed to Mrs. Ponsonby's kindness rushing over him, he looked so much affected, that Mary was afraid of his giving way, and spoke of other matters; her mother responded, and he came away quite reassured, and believing Mrs. Frost's augury that at the next call, the invalid would be in the drawing-room.

On the way home, however, his father overthrew such hopes, and made him aware of the true state of the case,—namely, that this was but the lull before another attack, which, whether it came within weeks or days, would probably be the last.

'Does Mary know?'

'She does. She bears up nobly.'

'And what is to become of her?'

The Earl sighed deeply. 'Lima is her destiny. Her mother is bent on it, and says that she wishes it herself; but on one thing I am resolved: she shall not go alone! I have told her mother that I will go with her, and not leave her without seeing what kind of home that man has for her. Mary—the mother, I mean—persists in declaring that he has real affection for his child, and that her presence will save him.'

'If anything could—' broke out Louis.

'It should! it ought; but I do not trust him. I know Robert Ponsonby as his wife has never chosen to know him. This was not a time for disguise, and I told her plainly what I thought of risking her daughter out there. But she called it Mary's duty—said that he was fully to be trusted where his child was concerned, and that Mary was no stranger at Lima, but could take care of herself, and had many friends besides Oliver Dynevor there. But I told her that go with her I would!'

'You to take the voyage! Was not she glad?'

'I think she was relieved; but she was over-grateful and distressed, and entreating me to be patient with him. She need not fear. I never was a hasty man; and I shall only remember that she bears his name, and that he is Mary's father—provided always that it is fit Mary should remain with him. Miserable! I can understand that death may well come as a friend—But her daughter!' he exclaimed, giving way more than he might have done anywhere but in the dark; 'how can she endure to leave her to such a father—to such prospects!'

'She knows it is not only to such a father that she leaves her,' murmured Louis.

'Her words—almost her words,' said the Earl, between earnestness and impatience; 'but when these things come to pressing realities, it is past me how such sayings are a consolation.'

'Not if they were no more than sayings.'

There was silence. Louis heard an occasional groaning sigh from his father, and sat still, with feelings strongly moved, and impelled to one of his sudden and impetuous resolutions.

The next morning, he ordered his horse, saying he would bring the last report from the Terrace.

That afternoon, Mrs. Ponsonby observed a tremulousneas in Mary's hand, and a willingness to keep her face turned away; and, on more minute glances, a swelling of the eyelids was detected.

'My dear,' said Mrs. Ponsonby, 'you should take a walk to-day. Pray go out with the Conways.'

'Oh no, thank you, mamma.'

'If the cousins come in from Ormersfield, I shall tell Louis to take you to look at his farm. It would be very good for you—My dear, what is it?' for Mary's ears and neck, all that she could see, were crimson.

'Oh, mamma! he has been doing it again. I did not mean to have told you—' said Mary, the strong will to be calm forcing back the tears and even the flush.

'Nay, dear child, nothing can hurt me now. You must let me share all with you to the last. What did you say to him?'

'I told him that I could not think of such things now,' said Mary, almost indignantly.

'And he?'

'He begged my pardon, and said he only did it because he thought it might be a relief to you.'

'Only; did he say 'only?'

'I am not sure. At least,' she added, with a deep sigh, 'I thought he meant only—'

'And you, my dearest, if you had not thought he meant *only*?'

'Don't ask me, mamma; I cannot think about it!'

'Mary, dearest, I do wish to understand you.'

'Is it of any use for me to ask myself?' said Mary.

'I think it is. I do not say that there might not be insuperable obstacles; but I believe we ought to know whether you are still indifferent to Louis.'

'Oh, that I never was! Nobody could be!'

'You know what I mean,' said her mother, slightly smiling.

'Mamma, I don't know what to say,' replied Mary, after a pause. 'I had thought it wrong to let my thoughts take that course; but when he spoke in his own soft, gentle voice, I felt, and I can't help it, that—he—could—comfort—me—better—than—any one.'

Not hesitating, but slowly, almost inaudibly, she brought out the words; and, as the tears gushed out irrepressibly with the last, she hastened from the room, and was seen no more till she had recovered composure, and seemed to have dismissed the subject.

Louis kept this second attempt a secret; he was not quite sure how he felt, and did not wish to discuss his rejection. At breakfast, he received a note from Mrs. Ponsonby, begging him to come to the Terrace at three o'clock; and the hope thus revived made him more conversational than he had been all the former day.

He found that Mary was out walking, and he was at once conducted to Mrs. Ponsonby's room, where he looked exceedingly rosy and confused, till she began by holding out her hand, and saying, 'I wish to thank you.'

'I am afraid I vexed Mary,' said Louis, with more than his usual simplicity; 'but do you think there is no hope? I knew it was a bad time, but I thought it might make you more at ease on her account.'

'You meant all that was most kind.'

'I thought I might just try,' pursued he, disconsolately, 'whether she did think me any steadier. I hope she did not think me very troublesome. I tried not to harass her much.'

'My dear Louis, it is not a question of what you call steadiness. It is the old story of last summer, when you thought us old ones so much more romantic than yourself.'

'You are thinking of Miss Conway,' said Louis, blushing, but with curious naivete. 'Well, I have been thinking of that, and I really do not believe there was anything in it. I did make myself rather a fool at Beauchastel, and Jem would have made me a greater one; but you know my father put a stop to it. Thinking her handsomer than other people can't be love, can it?'

'Not alone, certainly.'

'And actually,' he pursued, 'I don't believe I ever think of her when I am out of the way of her! No, indeed! if I had not believed that was all over, do you think I could have said what I did yesterday?'

'Not unless you believed so.'

'Well, but really you don't consider how little I have seen of her. I was in awe of her at first, and since, I have kept away on purpose. I never got on with her at all till the other evening. I don't believe I care for her one bit. Then,' suddenly pausing, and changing his tone, 'you don't trust me after all.'

'I do. I trust your principle and kindness implicitly, but I think the very innocence of your heart prevents you from knowing what you are about.'

'It is very hard,' said Louis; 'every one will have it that I must be in love, till I shall have to believe so myself, and when I know it cannot come to good.'

'You are making yourself more simple than you really are,' said Mra. Ponsonby, half provoked.

Louis shut his eyes, and seemed to be rousing his faculties; then, taking a new turn, he earnestly said, 'You know that the promises must settle the question, and keep my affections fast.'

'Ah, Louis! there is the point. Others, true and sincere as yourself, have broken their own hearts, and those of others, from having made vows in wilful ignorance of latent feelings. It would be a sin in me to allow you to bind yourself to Mary, with so little comprehension as you have of your own sentiments.'

'Then I have done wrong in proposing it.'

'What would have been wrong in some cases, was more of blindness—ay, and kindness—in you. Louis, I cannot tell you my gratitude for your wish to take care of my dear girl,' she said, with tears in her eyes. 'I hope you fully understand me.'

'I see I have made a fool of myself again, and that you have a right to be very angry with me.'

'Not quite,' said Mrs. Ponsonby, smiling, 'but I am going to give you some advice. Settle your mind as to Miss Conway. Your father is beginning to perceive that his distrust was undeserved; he has promised me not to object in case it should be for your true happiness; and I do believe, for my own part, that, in some respects, she is better fitted for his daughter-in-law than my poor Mary.'

'No one ever was half as good as Mary!' cried Louis. 'And this is what you tell me!'

'Mind, I don't tell you to propose to her, nor to commit yourself in any way: I only tell you to put yourself in a position to form a reasonable judgment of your own feelings. That is due to her, to yourself, and to your wife, be she who she may.'

Louis sighed, and presently added, smiling, 'I am not going to rave about preferences for another; but I do want to know whether anything can be done for poor Jem Frost.'

'Ha! has he anything of this kind on his mind?'

'He does it in grand style—disconsolate, frantic, and frosty; but he puzzles me completely by disclosing nothing but that he has no hope, and thinks me his rival. Can nothing be done?'

'No, Louis,' said Mrs. Ponsonby, decidedly; 'I have no idea that there is anything in that quarter. What may be on his mind, I cannot tell: I am sure that he is not on Mary's.'

Louis rose. 'I have tired you,' he said, 'and you are very patient with my fooleries.'

'You have been very patient with many a lecture of mine, Louis.'

'There are very few who would have thought me worth lecturing.'

'Ah, Louis! if I did not like you so well for what you are, I should still feel the right to lecture you, when I remember the night I carried you to your father, and tried to make him believe that you would be his comfort and blessing. I think you have taught him the lesson at last!'

'You have done it all,' said Louis, with deep feeling.

'And now, may I say what more I want to see in you? If you could acquire more resolution, more manliness—will you pardon my saying so?'

'Ah! I have always found myself the identical weak man that all books give up as a hopeless case,' said Louis, accepting the imputation more easily than she could have supposed possible.

'No,' she said, vigorously, 'you have not come to your time of life without openings to evil that you could not have resisted if you had been really weak.'

'Distaste—and rather a taste for being quizzed,' said Louis.

'Those are not weakness. Your will is indolent, and you take refuge in fancying that you want strength. Rouse yourself, not to be drifted about—make a line for yourself.'

'My father will have me walk in no line but his own.'

'You have sense not to make duty to him an excuse for indolence and dislike of responsibility. You have often disappointed yourself by acting precipitately; and now you are throwing yourself prone upon him, in a way that is unwise for you both.'

'I don't know what to do!' said Louis. 'When I thought the aim of my life was to be to devote myself to his wishes, you—ay, and he too—tell me to stand alone.'

'It will be a disappointment to him, if you do not act and decide for yourself—yes, and worse than disappointment. He knows what your devotional habits are; and if he sees you wanting in firmness or energy, he will set down all the rest as belonging to the softer parts of your nature.'

'On the contrary,' exclaimed Louia, indignantly, 'all the resolution I ever showed came from nothing else!'

'I know it. Let him see that these things make a man of you; and, Louis—you feel what a difference it might make!'

Louis bowed his head thoughtfully.

'You, who are both son and daughter to him, may give up schemes and pleasures for his sake, and may undertake work for which you have no natural turn; but, however you may cross your inclinations, never be led contrary to your judgment. Then, and with perseverance, I think you will be safe.'

'Perseverance—your old lesson.'

'Yes; you must learn to work over the moment when novelty is gone and failure begins, even though your father should treat the matter as a crotchet of your own. If you know it is worth doing, go on, and he will esteem you and it.'

'My poor private judgment! you work it hard! when it has generally only run me full-drive into some egregious blunder!'

'Not your true deliberate judgment, exercised with a sense of responsibility. Humility must not cover your laziness. You have such qualities and such talents as must be intended to do good to others, not to be trifled away in fitful exertions. Make it your great effort to see clearly, and then to proceed steadfastly, without slackening either from weariness or the persuasions of others.'

'And you won't let me have the one person who can see clearly, and keep me steady?'

'To be your husband, instead of your wife! No, Louis; you must learn to take yourself on your own hands, and lean neither on your father, nor on any one else on earth, before you can be fit for Mary, or—'

'And if I did?' began Louis.

'You would make a man of yourself,' she said, interrupting him. 'That is the first thing—not a reed shaken with the wind. You can do it; there is nothing that Grace cannot do.'

'I know there is not,' said Louis, reverently.

'And, oh! the blessing that you would so bring on yourself and on your dear father! You have already learnt to make him happier than I ever looked to see him; and you must be energetic and consistent, that so he may respect, not you, but the Power which can give you the strength.'

Louis's heart was too full to make any answer. Mrs. Ponsonby lay back in her chair, as though exhausted by the energy with which she had spoken the last words; and there was a long silence. He thought he ought to go, and yet could not resolve to move. At last she spoke—'Good-bye, Louis. Come what may, I know Mary will find in you the—all that I have found your father.'

'Thank you, at least, for saying that,' said Louis. 'If you would only hold out a hope—I wish it more than ever now! I do not believe that I should ever do as well with any one else! Will you not give me any prospect?'

'Be certain of your own heart, Louis! Nay,' as she saw his face brighten, 'do not take that as a promise. Let me give you a few parting words, as the motto I should like to leave with you—'Quit yourselves like men; be strong.' And so, Louis, whatever be your fixed and resolute purpose, so it be accordant with the Will of Heaven, you would surely, I believe, attain it, and well do you know how I should rejoice to see'—She broke off, and said, more feebly, 'I must not go on any longer. Let me wish you good-bye, Louis: I have loved you only less than my own child!'

Louis knelt on one knee beside her, held her hand, and bowed down his face to hide the shower of tears that fell, while a mother's kiss and a mother's blessing were on his brow.

He went down stairs, and out of the house, and took his horse from the inn stables, without one word to any one. The ostlers said to each other that the young Lord was in great trouble about the lady at the Terrace.

Mary came home; and if she knew why that long walk had been urged on her, she gave no sign. She saw her mother worn and tired, and she restrained all perception that she was conscious that there had been agitation. She spoke quietly of the spring flowers that she had seen, and of the people whom she had met; she gave her mother her tea, and moved about with almost an increase of the studied quietness of the sick-room. Only, when Mrs. Frost came in for an hour, Mary drew back into a corner with her knitting, and did not speak.

'Mary,' said her mother, when she came back from lighting her aunt down stairs, 'come to me, my child.'

Mary came, and her mother took both her hands. They were chilly; and there was a little pulse on Mary's temple that visibly throbbed, and almost seemed to leap, with fearful rapidity.

'Dear child, I had no power to talk before, or I would not have kept you in suspense. I am afraid it will not do.'

'I was sure of it,' said Mary, almost in a whisper. 'Dear mamma, you should not have vexed and tired yourself.'

'I comforted myself,' said Mrs. Ponsonby; 'I said things to him that I had longed to say, and how beautifully he took them! But I could not feel that he knew what he was about much better than he did the first time.'

'It would not be right,' said Mary, in her old tone.

'I think your father might have been persuaded. I would have written, and done my utmost—'

'Oh, mamma, anything rather than you should have that worry!'

'And I think things will be different—he is softened, and will be more so. But it is foolish to talk in this way, and it may be well that the trial should not be made; though that was not the reason I answered Louis as I did.'

'I suppose it will be Miss Conway,' said Mary, trying to smile.

'At least, it ought to be no one else till he has seen enough of her to form a judgment without the charm of prohibition; and this he may do without committing himself, as they are so nearly connected. I must ask his father to give him distinct permission, and then I shall have done with these things.'

Mary would not break the silence, nor recall her to earthly interests; but she returned to the subject, saying, wistfully, 'Can you tell me that you are content, dear child?'

'Quite content, thank you, mamma—I am certain it is right,' said Mary. 'It would be taking a wrong advantage of his compassion. I fall too far short of what would be wanted to make him happy.'

She spoke firmly, but her eyes were full of tears. Her mother felt as if no one could fail of happiness with Mary, but, controlling the impulse, said, 'It is best, dearest; for you could not bear to feel yourself unable to make him happy, or to fancy he might have more peace without you. My dear, your prospect is not all I could have wished or planned, but this would be too cruel.'

'It is my duty to go to papa,' said Mary. 'What would be selfish could not turn out well.'

'If you could be sure of his feelings—if he were only less strangely youthful—No,' she added, breaking off, as if rebuking herself, 'it is not to be thought of, but I do not wonder at you, my poor Mary—I never saw any one so engaging, nor in whom I could place such confidence.'

'I am so glad!' said Mary, gratefully. 'You used not to have that confidence.'

'I feared his being led. Now I feel as sure as any one can dare of his goodness. But I have been talking to him about self-reliance and consistency. He is so devoid of ambition, and so inert and diffident when not in an impetuous fit, that I dread his doing no good as well as no evil.'

Mary shook her head. Did she repress the expression of the sense that her arm had sometimes given him steadiness and fixed his aim?'

'The resemblance to his mother struck me more than ever,' continued Mrs. Ponsonby. 'There is far more mind and soul, but almost the same nature—all bright, indolent sweetness, craving for something to lean on, but he shows what she might have been with the same principles. Dear boy! may he do well!'

'He will be very happy with Miss Conway,' said Mary. 'She will learn to appreciate all he says and does—her enthusiasm will spur him on. I shall hear of them.'

The unbreathed sigh seemed to be added to the weight of oppression on Mary's patient breast; but she kept her eye steady, her brow unruffled.

All the joys did indeed appear to be passing from her with her mother, and she felt as if she should never know another hour of gladness, nor of rest in full free open-hearted confidence, but she could not dwell either on herself or on the future, and each hour that her mother was spared to her was too precious to be wasted or profaned by aught that was personal.

Mrs. Ponsonby herself realized the weary soon to be at rest, the harassed well nigh beyond the reach of troubling. She treated each earthly care and interest as though there were peace in laying it down for the last time. At intervals, as she was able, she wrote a long letter to her husband, to accompany the tidings of her death; and she held several conversations with Mary on her conduct for the future. She hoped much from Mary's influence, for Mr. Ponsonby was fond of his daughter, and would not willingly display himself in his worst colours before her; and Mary's steadiness of spirits and nerves might succeed, where her own liability to tears and trembling had always been a provocation. Her want of judgment in openly preferring her own relations to his uncongenial sister had sown seeds of estrangement and discord which had given Mrs. Ponsonby some cause for self-reproach, and she felt great hope that her daughter would prevail where she had failed. There was little danger that he would not show Mary affection enough to make her home-duties labours of love; and at her age, and with her disposition, she could both take care of herself, and be an unconscious restraint on her father. The trust and hope that she would be the means of weaning her father from evil, and bringing him home a changed man, was Mrs. Ponsonby's last bright vision.

As to scruples on Lord Ormersfield becoming Mary's escort on the voyage, Mrs. Ponsonby perceived his determination to be fixed beyond remonstrance. Perhaps she could neither regret that her daughter should have such a protector, nor bear to reject his last kindness; and she might have lingering hopes of the consequences of his meeting her husband, at a time when the hearts of both would be softened.

These matters arranged, she closed out the world. Louis saw her but once again, when other words than their own were spoken, and when the scene brought back to him a like one which had seemed his own farewell to this earth. His thread of life was lengthened—here was the moment to pray that it might be strengthened. Firm purpose was wakening within him, and the battle-cry rang again in his ears—'Quit yourselves like men; be strong!'

His eye sought Mary. She looked, indeed, like one who could 'suffer and be strong.' Her brow was calm, though as if a load sat on her, borne too patiently to mar her peace. The end shone upon her, though the path might be hid in gloom: one step at a time was enough, and she was blest above all in her mother's good hope.

A hush was on them all, as though they were watching while a tired, overtasked child sank to rest.

There was a space of suffering, when Mary and Miss Mercy did all that love could do, and kept Mrs. Frost from the sight of what she could neither cheer nor alleviate, and when all she could do was to talk over the past with Lord Ormersfield.

Then came a brief interval of relief and consciousness, precious for ever to Mary's recollection. The last words of aught beneath were—'My dearest love to your father. Tell him I know now how much he has to forgive.'

The tender, impulsive, overhasty spirit had wrought for itself some of the trials that had chastened and perfected it, even while breaking down the earthly tabernacle, so as to set free the weary soul, to enter into Rest!

CHAPTER XIX
MOONSHINE

> He talked of daggers and of darts,
>   Of passions and of pains,
> Of weeping eyes and wounded hearts,
>   Of kisses and of chains:
> But still the lady shook her head,
>   And swore by yea and nay,
> My whole was all that he had said,
>   And all that he could say.
>   W. MACKWORTH PRAED.

Mary's strength gave way. She was calm and self-possessed as ever, she saw Lord Ormersfield, wrote to her aunt, made all necessary arrangements, and, after the funeral, moved to Mrs. Frost's house. But, though not actually ill, she was incapable of exertion, could not walk up stairs without fatigue; and after writing a letter, or looking over papers, Aunt Catharine would find her leaning back, so wan and exhausted, that she could not resist being laid down to rest on the sofa.

She shrank from seeing any fresh face, and the effort of talking to the Earl resulted in such weariness and quiet depression, that Mrs. Frost dared not press her to admit any one else, except Louis, who rode to the Terrace almost every day; but when the kind aunt, believing there must be solace in the sight of her boy, begged to bring him in, Mary answered, with unusual vehemence, 'Pray don't: tell him I cannot see any one.' And when Mrs. Frost returned from a sorrowful talk with Louis, she believed that Mary had been weeping.

Louis was sad enough. Out of the few friends of his childhood he could ill afford to lose one, and he grieved much for his father, to whom the loss was very great. The Earl strove, in his old fashion, to stifle sorrow in letters of business, but could not succeed: the result was, that he would discuss the one, Mary's past, and the other, Mary's future, till time waxed so short that he gladly accepted his son's assistance. Conversations with Richardson and orders to Frampton devolved on Louis, and the desire to do no mischief caused him to employ his intellect in acquiring a new habit of attention and accuracy.

His reverence for Mary was doubled, and he was much concerned at his exclusion, attributing it to his mistimed proposals, and becoming sensible that he had acted boyishly and without due respect. With a longing desire to do anything for her, he dared not even send her a greeting, a flower, or a book, lest it should appear an intrusion; and but for his mournful looks, his aunt would have been almost vexed at his so often preventing her from going to make another attempt to induce his cousin to see him.

Mary first roused herself on finding that Lord Ormersfield was taking it for granted that she would wait to hear from her father before sailing for Peru. The correspondence which had passed since her mother had begun to decline, had convinced her that he expected and wished for her without loss of time, and the vessel whose captain he chiefly trusted was to sail at the end of May. She entreated to be allowed to go alone, declaring that she had no fears, and would not endure that the Earl should double Cape Horn on her account; but he stood fast—he would not be deprived of the last service that he could render to her mother, and he had not reliance enough on her father to let her go out without any guardian or friend.

Recent letters from Mr. Ponsonby and from Oliver Dynevor reiterated requests for an intelligent man conversant with mining operations, and Oliver had indicated a person whom he remembered at Chevleigh; but, as his mother said, he forgot that people grew old in the Eastern hemisphere, and the application was a failure. Finding that Mary regarded it as her charge, Fitzjocelyn volunteered to go to Illershall to consult his friend Mr. Dobbs; and his first meeting with Mary was spent in receiving business-like instructions as to the person for whom he should inquire.

There were some who felt dubious when he was seen walking back from the station with a young man who, in spite of broadcloth and growth, was evidently Tom Madison.

'I could not help it, Mary,' said Louis, 'it was not my fault that Dobbs would recommend him.'

Mr. Dobbs had looked this way and that, and concluded with, 'Well, Lord Fitzjocelyn, I do not know who would answer your purpose better than the young fellow you sent here a year ago.'

It appeared that Tom had striven assiduously both to learn his business and to improve himself; and, having considerable abilities, already brightened and sharpened by Louis, his progress had been surprising. He had no low tastes, and was perfectly to be relied on for all essential points; but Mr. Dobbs owned that he should be relieved by parting with him, as he was not liked by his fellows, and was thought by the foremen to give himself airs. Quarrels and misunderstandings had arisen so often, that he himself had been obliged to exert an influence on his behalf, which he feared might make him obnoxious to the accusation of partiality. He considered that the lad had worth, substance, and promise far beyond his fellows; but his blunt, haughty manners, impatience of rough jokes, and rude avoidance of the unrefined, made him the object of their dislike, so that it was probable that he would thrive much better abroad and in authority; and at his age, he was more likely to adapt himself to circumstances, and learn a new language, than an older man, more used to routine.

The vision of the land for digging gold and silver seemed about to be realized, just as Tom had been growing learned enough to despise it. Enterprise and hopes of fortune made him wild to go; and Mary after reading Dobbs's letter, and laying before Louis the various temptations of Lima, found that he thought England to the full as dangerous for his protege. She, therefore, sent for the young man, and decided as dispassionately as she could, upon taking him.

The Ormersfield world was extremely indignant; Frampton and Gervas prophesied that no good would come of such a choice, and marvelled at the Vicar, who gave the lad lodging in his house, and spent the evenings in giving him such mathematical instruction and teaching of other kinds, as he thought most likely to be useful to him.

To his surprise, however, Tom was much more grave and sober-minded under his promotion than could have been expected. Louis, who had undertaken his outfit, was almost disappointed to find him so much out of heart, and so little responsive to cheerful auguries; and at last a little hint at bantering about the individual at the Terrace explained his despondence.

It was all over. Charlotte had hardly spoken to him while he was waiting at No. 5, and Miss Faithfull's Martha had told him there had been nothing but walking and talking with Lady Conway's fine butler, and that Charlotte would never have nothing more to say to him! Now! Just as he might have spoken! Was it not enough to knock the heart out of it all! He never wished to go near No. 5 again.

Louis strongly advised him at least to know his fate, and declared that for his part, he would never take any Mrs. Martha's word, rather than that of the lady herself. Speak out, and, of course, Montrose's famous motto came in, and was highly appreciated by Tom, though he still shook his head ruefully, as he recollected what a lout he had been at his last meeting with

Charlotte, and how little he could compare with such a fine gentleman as had been described, 'And she always had a taste for gentility.'

'Well, Tom, I would not wish to see a better gentleman any day, than you have stuff enough in you to make; and, if Charlotte be a girl worth having, she'll value that more than French polish. You're getting polished, too, Tom, and will more as you get better and sounder, and that polish will be true and not French.'

Meantime Charlotte had been in twenty states of mind. Had Tom striven at once to return to the former terms, the Lady of Eschalott might have treated it as mere natural homage, compared him with Delaford's delicate flatteries, and disclaimed him. She had been chilling and shy at the first meeting, expecting him to presume on his promotion, but when he was gone, came no more, except for necessary interviews with Miss Ponsonby, and then merely spoke civilly, and went away directly, her heart began to fail her. Neglect mortified her; she was first affronted, sure she did not care, and resolved to show that she did not; but then the vexation became stronger, she wondered if he had heard of Delaford, was angry at her intercourse with the butler being deemed an offence, and finally arrived at a hearty longing for a return to old times. Vanity or affection, one or the other, demanded Tom's allegiance.

And Tom came at last. He did not come by moonlight—he did not come at all romantically; but as she was washing vegetables, he stood by the scullery door, and made no elegant circumlocutions. Would she be his wife, some time or other? and he would try to be worthy of her.

Fitzjocelyn had judged her rightly! Sound true love had force enough to dispel every illusion of sentimental flattery. Charlotte burst into a flood of tears, and, sobbing behind her apron, confessed that she never liked nobody like Tom, but she was afraid he would think she had been false to him, for she did like Mr. Delaford's talk, all about poetry and serenades; but she never would heed him no more, not if he went down on his knees to her.

Tom was a great deal more likely to perform that feat.

He stood his ground when Mrs. Beckett came in, and told her all about it, and the good old soul mingled her tears with Charlotte's, wished them joy, and finished washing the greens. Nevertheless Mrs. Frost thought the kitchen-clock was very slow.

Their 'walking together' was recognised. Martha was very angry with Jane, and predicted that the young vagabone would never be heard of more; and that the only benefit would be, that it would settle the girl's mind, and hinder her from encouraging any more followers. And even Mrs. Frost had her doubts. Her prudent counsel interfered with Tom's wish to carry out poor little Charlotte as his wife; and they had to content themselves with a betrothal until they should have 'saved something,' exchanging brooches, each with a memorial lock of hair. During the remaining week, the Lady of Eschalott neither ate nor slept, and though she did her work, her tears never seemed to cease. She defended herself by averring that Miss Ponsonby's pillow was soaked every morning; but if Mary's heavy eyelids corroborated her, her demeanour did not. Mary was busy in dismantling the house and in packing up; speaking little, but always considerate and self-possessed, and resolute in avoiding all excitement of feeling. She would not go to Ormersfield, as the Earl proposed, even for one day, and a few books connected with the happy lessons of last summer, were given into Mrs. Frost's keeping, with the steady, calm word, 'I had better not take them.' She made no outpouring even to that universal, loving confidante, Aunt Catharine; and the final parting did not break down her self-restraint, though, as the last bend of her head was given, the last chimney of Northwold disappeared, her sensation of heartache almost amounted to sickening.

She was going to Bryanston Square. Her aunt had been as kind as possible, and had even offered to come to Northwold to fetch her home; but Mary had been too considerate to allow her to think of so dreadful a journey, and had in fact, been glad to be left only to her own Aunt Catharine. The last letters which had passed between Mrs. Ponsonby and Annt Melicent had been such as two sincere Christian women could not fail to write in such circumstances as must soften down all asperities, alleviate prejudice and variance, and be a prelude to that perfect unity when all misunderstandings shall end for ever; and thus Mary had the comfort of knowing that the two whom she loved so fondly, had parted with all mutual affection and cordial honour.

She really loved the little prim stiff figure who stood on the stairs to welcome her. The house had been her home for ten of the most home-forming years of her life, and felt familiar and kindly; it was very quiet, and it was an unspeakable comfort to be with one who talked freely of her father with blind partiality and love, and did not oppress her with implied compassion for her return to him.

Yet Mary could not help now and then being sensible that good Aunt Melicent was not the fountain of wisdom which she used to esteem her. Now and then a dictum would sound narrow and questionable, objections to books seemed mistaken, judgments of people hard, and without sufficient foundation; and when Mary tried to argue, she found herself decidedly set down, with as much confident superiority as if she had been still sixteen years old. Six years spent in going to the other side of the world, and in seeing so many varieties of people, did not seem to Aunt Melicent to have conferred half so much experience as sleeping every night in Bryanston Square, daily reading the Morning Post, and holding intercourse with a London world of a dozen old ladies, three curates, and a doctor.

The worst of it was, that a hurt and angry tenderness was always excited in Mary's mind by the manner of any reference to Northwold or Ormersfield. It seemed to be fixed, beyond a doubt, that everything there must have been wrong and fashionable; and even poor dear Aunt Kitty was only spoken of with a charitable hope that affliction had taught her to see the error of her days of worldly display.

It was allowed that there was nothing objectionable in Clara Frost, who was subdued by the sight of Mary's deep mourning, and in silent formal company could be grave and formal too. But there was a severe shock in a call from Lady Conway and Isabel; and on their departure Mary was cross-examined, in the hope that they had been outrageously gay at Northwold, and for want of any such depositions, was regaled with histories of poor Lady Fitzjocelyn's vanities, which had not lost by their transmission through twenty-two years and twice as many mouths.

Still more unpleasant was the result of a visit from the Earl and his son to appoint the day of starting for Liverpool. Louis was in no mood to startle any one; he was very sad at heart, and only anxious to be inoffensive; but his air was quite enough to give umbrage, and cause the instant remark, 'I never saw such a puppy!'

Nothing but such angry incoherency occurred to Mary, that she forcibly held her peace, but could not prevent a burning crimson from spreading over her face. She went and stood at the window, glad that Miss Ponsonby had just taken up the newspaper, which she daily read from end to end, and then posted for Lima.

By and by came a little dry cough, as she went through the presentations at the levee, and read out 'Viscount Fitzjocelyn, by the Earl of Ormersfield.'

Mary's mind made an excursion to the dear Yeomanry suit, till her aunt, having further hunted them out among the Earls and Viscounts summed up at the end, severely demanded whether she had known of their intention.

'I knew he was to be presented.'

'Quite the young man of fashion. No doubt beginning that course, as if the estate were not sufficiently impoverished already. I am not surprised at the report that Lord Ormersfield was very anxious to secure your fortune for his son.'

This was too much, and Mary exclaimed, 'He never believes in any fortune that depends on speculation.'

'Oh, so there was nothing in it!' said Miss Ponsonby, who would have liked the satisfaction of knowing that her niece had refused to be a Countess, and, while Mary was debating whether her silence were untruthful, her bent head and glowing cheek betrayed her. 'Ah! my dear, I will ask no questions; I see you have been annoyed. It always happens when a girl with expectations goes among needy nobility.'

'You would not say that, if you knew the circumstances,' said Mary, looking down.

'I won't distress you, my dear; I know you are too wise a girl to be dazzled with worldly splendours, and that is enough for me.'

The poor old furniture at Ormersfield!

Mary held her tongue, though reproaching herself for cruel injustice to all that was dearest to her, but how deny her refusal, or explain the motives.

Not that her aunt wanted any explanation, except her own excellent training, which had saved her niece from partaking her mother's infatuation for great people. She had a grand secret to pour into the bosom of her intimates in some tete-a-tete tea-party by-and-by, and poor Mary little guessed at the glorification of her prudence which was flowing from her aunt's well-mended pen, in a long letter to Mr. Ponsonby. She thought it right that he should be informed, she said, that their dear Mary had conducted herself according to their fondest wishes; that the relations, among whom she had unfortunately been thrown, had formed designs on her fortune, such as they had every reason to expect; that every solicitation had been employed, but that Mary had withstood all that would have been most alluring to girls brought up to esteem mere worldly advantages. It was extremely gratifying, the more so as the young gentleman in question might be considered as strikingly handsome to the mere outward eye, which did not detect the stamp of frivolity, and the effect of an early introduction to the world of fashion and dissipation. She trusted that their dear young heiress would have a better fate, owing to her own wisdom, than being chosen to support the extravagance of a young titled adventurer.

Having worked herself up into enthusiastic admiration of her own work, Miss Ponsonby was kinder than ever to her niece, and pitied her for being harassed with Lord Fitzjocelyn's company to Liverpool.

Mary was not as much relieved as she had expected, when her hand had been released from his pressure, and she had seen the last glimpse of his returning boat.

Henceforth her imagination was to picture him only with Isabel Conway.

And so Viscount Fitzjocelyn was left with more liberty than he knew what to do with. He was disinclined to begin the pursuit of Miss Conway, as if this would involve a want of delicacy and feeling, and he had no other object. The world was before him, but when he drove to the Liverpool Station, he was unwilling to exert his mind to decide for what ticket to ask.

The bias was given by the recollection of a message from his father to Frampton. It would be less trouble to go home than to write, and, besides, Aunt Catharine was alone. She was his unfailing friend, and it would be a great treat to have her to himself.

Home then he went, where he spent the long summer days in listless, desultory, busy idleness, often alone, dreaming over last year, often passing his evenings with his aunt, or bringing her to see his designs; dining out whenever he was invited, and returning odd uncertain answers when Mr. Calcott asked him what he was going to do.

Mr. Holdsworth was going to leave James in charge of his parish, and take a walking tour in Cornwall, and perversely enough, Louis's fancy fixed on joining him; and was much disappointed when Mrs. Frost proved, beyond dispute, that an ankle, which a little over haste or fatigue always rendered lame, would be an unfair drag upon a companion, and that if he went at all, it must not be on his own feet.

At last, Lady Conway made a descent upon Northwold. Paris had become so tranquil that she had no hesitation in taking her two elder daughters to make their promised visit; and such appeals were made to Louis to join them, that it became more troublesome to refuse than to comply, and, at the shortest notice, he prepared to set out as the escort of the Conway family.

'Now for it!' he thought. 'If she be the woman, I cannot fail to find it out, between the inns and the sights!'

Short as the notice was, the Lady of Eschalott could have wished it shorter. No sooner had Mr. Delaford set foot in the House Beautiful, than Mrs. Martha announced to him that he would be happy to hear that Charlotte Arnold was going to be married to a very respectable young man, whom she had known all his life, and to whom Mr. Dynevor and Miss Ponsonby had given an appointment to the gold mines, out of respect for Lord Fitzjocelyn. Mr. Delaford gravely declared himself glad to hear it.

But Delaford's purpose in life was, that no maiden should fail of being smitten with his charms; and he took Charlotte's defection seriously to heart.

His first free moment was devoted to a call in Number 5, but Charlotte was scouring in the upper regions, and Mrs. Beckett only treated him to another edition of the gold mines, in which, if they became silver, the power and grandeur of Mr. Oliver were mightily magnified. Mr. Delaford thrummed his most doleful tunes on the guitar that evening, but though the June sun was sinking beauteously, Charlotte never put her head out. However, the third time, he found her, and then she was coy and blushing, reserved and distant, and so much prettier, and more genuine than all his former conquests, that something beyond vanity became interested.

He courted the muses, and walked in with a pathetic copy of verses, which, some day or other, might serve to figure in the county newspaper, complaining of desertion and cruelty.

Charlotte sat at the little round table; Jane was upstairs, and without her guardian, she felt that she must guard herself. He laid the verses down before her with a most piteous countenance.

'Please don't, Mr. Delaford,' she said; 'I asked Mrs. Beckett to tell you—'

'She has transfixed my breast,' was the commencement, and out poured a speech worthy of any hero of Charlotte's imagination, but it was not half so pleasant to hear as to dream of, and the utmost she could say was a reiteration of her 'please don't!'

At last she mustered courage to say, 'I can't listen, sir. I never ought to have done it. I am promised now, and I can't.'

A melodramatic burst of indignation frightened her nearly out of her senses, and happily brought Jane down. He was going the next day, but he returned once more to the charge, very dolorous and ill-used; but Charlotte had collected herself and taken counsel by that time. 'I never promised you anything, sir,' she said. 'I never knew you meant nothing.'

'Ah! Miss Arnold, you cannot interpret the heart!' and he put his hand upon it.

'Nor I don't believe you meant it, neither!' continued Charlotte, with spirit. 'They tell me 'tis the way you goes on with all young women as have the ill-luck to believe you, and that 'tis all along of your hard-heartedness that poor Miss Marianne looks so dwining.'

'When ladies will throw themselves at a gentleman's head, what can a poor man do? Courtesy to the sex is my motto; but never, never did I love as I love you!' said Delaford—'never have I spoken as I do now! My heart and hand are yours, fairest Charlotte!'

'For shame, Mr. Delaford; don't you know I am promised?'

He went on, disregarding—'My family is above my present situation, confidential though it be; but I would at once quit my present post—I would open an extensive establishment for refreshment at some fashionable watering-place. My connexions could not fail to make it succeed. You should merely superintend—have a large establishment under you—and enjoy the society and amusements for which you are eminently fitted. We would have a library of romance and poetry—attend the theatre weekly—and,'—(finishing as if to clench the whole) 'Charlotte, do you know what my property consists of? I have four hundred pounds and expectations!'

If Charlotte had not been guarded, what would have been the effect of the library of poetry and romance?

But her own poetry, romance, and honest heart, all went the same way, and she cried out—'I don't care what you have, not I. I've promised, and I'll be true—get along with you!'

The village girl, hard pressed, was breaking out.

'You bid me go. Cruel girl! your commands shall be obeyed. I go abroad! You know the disturbed state of the Continent.—In some conflict for liberty, where the desperate poniard is uplifted—there—'

'Oh! don't talk so dreadful. Pray—'

'Do you bid me pause? At a word from you. You are the arbitress of my destiny.'

'No; I've nothing to do—do go! Only promise you'll not do nothing dangerous—'

'Reject me, and life is intolerable. Where the maddened crowd rise upon their tyrants, there in thickest of the fray—'

'You'll be the first to take to your heels, I'll be bound! Ain't you ashamed of yourself, to be ranting and frightening a poor girl that fashion?' cried the friendly dragon Martha, descending on them.

'Do you apply that language to me, ma'am?'

'That I do! and richly you deserve it, too, sir! See if your missus doesn't hear of your tricks, if I find you at this again.'

The 'sex' fairly scolded the courteous Delaford off the field; and though she turned her wrath on Charlotte for having encouraged him, and wondered what the poor young man over the seas would think of it, her interposition had never been so welcome. Charlotte cried herself into tranquillity, and was only farther disturbed by a dismal epistle, conveyed by the shoe-boy on the morning of departure, breathing the language of despair, and yet announcing that she had better think twice of the four hundred pounds and expectations, for that it was her destiny that she and no other should be the bride of Delaford.

'If I could only know he would do nothing rash!' sighed Charlotte.

Jane comforted her; Martha held that he was the last man in the world who would do anything rash. Miss Conway's Marianne, who was left behind, treated Charlotte as something ignominious, but looked so ill, miserable, and pining, that Miss Mercy was persuaded she was going into a decline, and treated her with greater kindness than she had met since she was a child.

In the meantime, Fitzjocelyn had begun with a fit of bashfulness. The knowledge that this was the crisis, and that all his friends looked to the result of the expedition, made him feel as if he were committing himself whenever he handed Isabel in or out of a carriage, and find no comfort except in Virginia's chattering.

This wore off quickly; the new scene took effect on his impressible mind, and the actual sights and sounds drove out all the rest. His high spirits came back, he freely hazarded Mrs. Frost's old boarding-school French, and laughed at the infinite blunders for which Virginia took him to task, was excessively amused at Delaford's numerous adventures, and enjoyed everything to the utmost. To Miss Conway he turned naturally as the person best able to enter into the countless associations of every scene; and Isabel, becoming aware of his amount of knowledge, and tone of deep thought, perceived that she had done Mr. Frost Dynevor injustice in believing his friendship blind or unmerited.

They were on most comfortable terms. They had walked all over Versailles together, and talked under their breath of the murdered Queen; they had been through the Louvre, and Isabel, knowing it well of old, found all made vivid and new by his enthusiastic delight; they had marvelled together at the poor withered 'popular trees,' whose name had conferred on them the fatal distinction of trees of liberty; they had viewed, like earnest people, the scenes of republican Paris, and discussed them with the same principles, but with sufficient difference in detail for amicable argument. They had thought much of things and people, and not at all of each other.

Only Isabel thought she would make the Viscount into a Vidame, both as more quaint and less personal, and involving slight erasures, and Louis was surprised to find what was the true current of his thoughts. With Isabel propitious, without compunction in addressing her, with all the novelty and amusement before him, he found himself always recurring to Mary, trying all things by Mary's judgment, wondering whether he should need approval of his theories in Mary's eyes, craving Mary's sympathies, following her on her voyage, and imagining her arrival. Was it the perverse spirit of longing after the most unattainable?

He demanded of himself whether it were a fatal sign that he regretted the loss of Isabel, when she went to spend a few days with her old governess. Miss Longman had left the Conway family in order to take care of the motherless children of a good-for-nothing brother, who had run too deeply into debt to be able to return to England. He was now dead, but she was teaching English, and obtaining advantages of education for her nieces, which detained her at Paris; and as she had a bed to offer her former pupil, Isabel set her heart on spending her last three days in the unrestrained intercourse afforded by a visit to her. Louis found that though their party had lost the most agreeable member, yet it was not the loss of the sun; and that he was quite as ready to tease his aunt and make Virginia laugh, as if Isabel had been looking on with a smile of wonder and commiseration for their nonsense.

CHAPTER XX
THE FANTASTIC VISCOUNT

Search for a jewel that too casually
Hath left mine arm: it was thy master's. Shrew me
If I would lose it for a revenue
Of any king's in Europe!—Cymbeline.

'My dear Fitzjocelyn, what is to be done? Have you heard? Delaford says these horrid creatures are rising! There was an attack on the Hotel de Ville last night! A thousand people killed, at least!—The National Guard called out!'

'One of the lions of Paris, my dear aunt; Virginia is seeing it in style.'

'Seeing it! We must go at once. They will raise those horrid barricades;—we shall be closed in. And Isabel gone to that governess! I wish I had never consented! How could I come here at all? Fitzjocelyn, what is to be done?'

'Drive round that way, if you are bent on going,' said Louia, coolly. 'Meantime, Virginia, my dear, I will thank you for some coffee.'

'How can you talk of such things?' cried his aunt. 'It is all those savage wretches, mad because the national workshops are closed. Delaford declares they will massacre all the English.'

'Poor wretches, I believe they are starving. I think you are making yourself ill—the most pressing danger. Come, Virginia, persuade your mamma to sit down to breakfast, while I go to reconnoitre. Where are the passports?'

Virginia had lost all terror in excitement, but neither she nor her mother could bear to let him go out, to return they knew not when. The carriage had already been ordered, but Lady Conway was exceedingly frightened at the notion of driving anywhere but direct to the railway station; she was sure that they should encounter something frightful if they went along the Boulevards.

'Could not Delaford go to fetch Isabel?' suggested Virginia, 'he might take a carriage belonging to the hotel.'

Delaford was summoned, and desired to go to fetch Miss Conway, but though he said, 'Yes, my Lady,' he looked yellow and white, and loitered to suggest whether the young lady would not be alarmed.

'I will go with you,' said Louis. 'Order the carriage, and I shall be ready.'

Lady Conway, to whom his presence seemed protection, was almost remonstrating, but he said, 'Delaford is in no state to be of use. He would take bonjour for a challenge. Let me go with him, or he will take care the young lady is alarmed. When we are all together, we can do as may seem best, and I shall be able better to judge whether we are to fight or fly.'

Outside the door he found Delaford, who begged to suggest to his lordship that my Lady would be alarmed if she were left without either of them, he could hardly answer it to himself that she should remain without any male protector.

'Oh yes, pray remain to defend her,' said Louis, much amused, and hastening down-stairs he ordered the carriage to drive to Rue — —, off the Boulevard St. Martin.

He thought there were signs boding tempest. Shops were closed, and men in blouses were beginning to assemble in knots—here and there the red-cap loomed ominously in the far end of narrow alleys, and in the wider streets the only passengers either seemed in haste like himself, or else were National Guards hurrying to their alarm-post.

He came safely to Miss Longman's apartments, where he found all on the alert—the governess and her nieces recounting their experiences of February, which convinced them that there was more danger in returning than in remaining. Miss Longman was urgent to keep Isabel and Lord Fitzjocelyn for at least a few hours, which she declared would probably be the duration of any emeute, but they knew this would cause dreadful anxiety, and when Fitzjocelyn proposed returning alone, Isabel insisted on accompanying him, declaring that she had no fears, and that her mother would be miserable if her absence should detain them. Perhaps she was somewhat deceived by the cool, almost ludicrous, light in which he placed the revolution, as a sort of periodical spasm, and Miss Longman's predictions that the railway would be closed, only quickened her preparations.

After receiving many entreaties to return in case of alarm, they took leave, Louis seating himself beside the driver, as well to keep a look-out, as to free Miss Conway from fears of a tete-a-tete. Except for such a charge of ladies, he would have been delighted at the excitement of an emeute; but he was far from guessing how serious a turn affairs were taking.

The dark blue groups were thickening into crowds; muskets and pikes were here and there seen, and once he recognised the sinister red flag. A few distant shots were heard, and the driver would gladly have hastened his speed, but swarms of haggard-looking men began to impede their progress, and strains of 'Mourir pour la patrie' now and then reached their ears.

Close to the Porte St. Denis they were brought to a full stop by a dense throng, above whose heads were seen a line of carriages, the red flag planted on the top. Many hands were seizing the horses' heads, and Louis leapt down, but not before the door had been opened, and voices were exclaiming, 'Descendez citoyenne; au nom de la nation, descendez.' The mob were not uncivil, they made way for Louis, and bade him reassure her that no harm was intended, but the carriage was required for the service of the nation.

Isabel had retreated as far as she could from their hands, but she showed no signs of quailing; her eyes were bright, her colour high, and the hand was firm which she gave to Louis as she stepped out. There was a murmur of admiration, and more than one bow and muttered apology about necessity and the nation, as the crowd beheld the maiden in all her innate nobleness and dignity.

'Which way?' asked Louis, finding that the crowd were willing to let them choose their course.

'Home,' said Isabel, decidedly, 'there is no use in turning back.'

They pressed on past the barricade for which their carriage had been required, a structure of confiscated vehicles, the interstices filled up with earth and paving stones, which men and boys were busily tearing up from the trottoirs, and others carrying to their destination. They were a gaunt, hungry, wolfish-looking race, and the first words that Isabel spoke were words of pity, when they had passed them, and continued their course along the Boulevards, here in desolate tranquillity. 'Poor creatures, they look as if misery made them furious! and yet how civil they were.'

'Were you much alarmed? I wish I could have come to you sooner.'

'Thank you; I knew that you were at hand, and their address was not very terrific, poor things. I do not imagine there was any real danger.'

'I wish I knew whether we are within or without the barricades. If within, we shall have to cross another. We are actually becoming historical!'

He broke off, amazed by Isabel's change of countenance, as she put her hand to the arm he held, hastily withdrew it, and exclaimed, 'My bracelet! oh, my bracelet!' turning round to seek it on the pavement.

'The ivory clasp?' asked Louis, perceiving its absence.

'Oh yes!' she cried, in much distress, 'I would not have lost it for all the world.'

'You may have left it at Miss Longman's.'

'No, no, I was never without it!'

She turned, and made a few retrograde steps, searching on the ground, as if conscious only of her loss, shaking off his hand when he touched her arm to detain her.

A discovery broke on, him. Well that he could bear it!

'Hark!' he said, 'there is cannon firing! Miss Conway, you cannot go back. I will do my utmost to recover your clasp, but we must not stay here.'

'I had forgotten. I beg your pardon, I did not think!' said Isabel, with a species of rebuked submission, as if impressed by the calmness that gave authority to his manner; and she made no remark as he made her resume his arm, and hurried her on past houses with closed doors and windows.

Suddenly there was the sound of a volley of musketry far behind. 'Heaven help the poor wretches,' said Louis; and Isabel's grasp tightened on his arm.

Again, again—the dropping sound of shot became continual. And now it was in front as well as in the rear; and the booming of cannon resounded from the heart of the city. They were again on the outskirts of a crowd.

'It is as I thought,' said Louis, 'we are between both. There is nothing for it but to push on, and see whether we can cross the barricades; are you afraid to encounter it!'

'No,' said Isabel.

'There is a convent not far off, I think. We might find shelter for you there. Yet they might break in. It might not be easy to meet. I believe you are safer with me. Will you trust in me?'

'I will not have you endanger yourself for me. Dispose of me as you will—in a convent, or anywhere. Your life is precious, your safety is the first thing.'

'You are speaking in irony.'

'I did not mean it: I beg your pardon.' But she coloured and faltered. 'You must distinctly understand that this is only as Englishman to Englishwoman.'

'As Englishman to Englishwoman,' repeated Louis, in her own formula. 'Or rather,' he added, lowering his voice, 'trust me, for the sake of those who gave the clasp.'

He was answered by her involuntary pressure of his arm, and finally, to set her at ease, he said, hurriedly, 'If it went wrong with me, it would be to Lima that I should ask you to send my love.'

There was no time for more. They were again on the freshly-torn ground, whence the pavement had been wrenched. The throng had thickened behind them, and seemed to be involving them in the vortex. Above their heads Louis could see in front between the tall houses, the summit of another barricade complete, surmounted with the red flag, and guarded by a fierce party of ruffians.

All at once, tremendous yells broke out on all sides. The rattle of a drum, now and then, might be distinguished, shouts and shrieks resounded, and there was a sharp fire of musketry from the barricade, and from the adjoining windows; there was a general rush to the front, and Louis could only guard Isabel by pressing her into the recess of the closed doorway of one of the houses, and standing before her, preventing himself from being swept away only by exerting all his English strength against the lean, wild beings who struggled past him, howling and screaming. The defenders sprang upon the barricade, and thrust back and hurled down the National Guards, whose heads were now and then seen as they vainly endeavoured to gain the summit. This desperate struggle lasted for a few minutes, then cries of victory broke out, and there was sharp firing on both sides, which, however, soon ceased; the red flag and the blouses remaining still in possession. Isabel had stood perfectly silent and motionless through the whole crisis, and though she clung to her protector's arm, it was not with nervous disabling terror, even in the frightful tumult of the multitude. There was some other strength with her!

'You are not hurt?' said Louis, as the pressure relaxed.

'Oh no! thank God! You are not?'

'Are you ready? We must make a rush before the next assault.'

A lane opened in the throng to afford passage for the wounded. Isabel shrank back, but Louis drew her on hastily, till they had attained the very foot of the barricade, where a space was kept clear, and there was a cry 'Au large, or we shall fire.'

'Let us pass, citizens,' said Louis, hastily rehearsing the French he had been composing. 'You make not war on women. Let me take this young lady to her mother.'

Grim looks were levelled at them by the fierce black-bearded men, and their mutterings of belle made her cling the closer to her guardian.

'Let her pass, the poor child!' said more than one voice.

'Hein!—they are English, who take the bread out of our mouths.'

'If you were a political economist,' said Louis, gravely, fixing his eyes on the shrewd-looking, sallow speaker, I would prove to you your mistake; but I have no time, and you are too good fellows to wish to keep this lady here, a mark for the Garde Nationale.'

'He is right there,' said several of the council of chiefs, and a poissarde, with brawny arms and a tall white cap, thrusting forward, cried out, 'Let them go, the poor children. What are they doing here? They look fit to be set up in the church for waxen images!'

'Take care you do not break us,' exclaimed Louis, whose fair cheek had won this tribute; and his smile, and the readiness of his reply, won his admission to the first of the steps up the barricade.

'Halte la!' cried a large-limbed, formidable-looking ruffian on the summit, pointing his musket towards them; 'none passes here who does not bring a stone to raise our barricade for the rights of the Red Republic, and cry, La liberte, l'egalite, et la, fraternite, let it fit his perfidious tongue as it may.'

'There's my answer,' said Louis, raising his right arm, which was dripping; with blood, 'you have made me mount the red flag!'

'Ha!' cried the friendly fishwife, 'Wounded in the cause of the nation! Let him go.'

'He has not uttered the cry!' shouted the rest.

Louis looked round with his cool, pensive smile.

'Liberty!' he said, 'what *we* mean by liberty is freedom to go where we will, and say what we will. I wish you had it, my poor fellows. Fraternity—it is not shooting our brother. Egalite—I preach that too, but in my own fashion, not yours. Let me pass—si cela vou est egal.'

His nonchalant intrepidity—a quality never lost on the French—raised an acclamation of le brave Anglais. No one stirred a hand to hinder their mounting to the banquette, and several hands were held out to assist in surmounting the parapet of this extempore fortification. Isabel bowed her thanks, and Louis spoke them with gestures of courtesy; and shouts of high applause followed them as they sped along the blood-stained street.

The troops were re-forming after the repulse, and the point was to pass before the attack could be renewed, as well as not to be mistaken for the insurgents.

They were at once challenged, but a short explanation to the officer was sufficient, and they were suffered to turn into the Rue Richelieu, where they were only pursued by the distant sounds of warfare.

'Oh, Lord Fitzjocelyn!' cried Isabel, as he slackened his pace, and gasped for breath.

'You are sure you are not hurt?' he said.

'Oh no, no; but you—'

'It is very little,' he said—'a stray shot—only enough to work on their feelings. What good-natured rogues they were. I will only twist my handkerchief round to stop the blood. Thank you.'

Isabel tried to help him, but she was too much afraid of hurting him to draw the bandage tight.

They dashed on, finding people on the watch for tidings, and meeting bodies of the National Guard, and when at length they reached the Place Vendome, they found the whole establishment watching for them, and Virginia flew to meet them on the stairs, throwing her arms round her sister, while Lady Conway started forward with the agitated joy, and almost anger, of one who felt injured by the fright they had made her suffer.

'There you are! What has kept you! Delaford said they were slaughtering every one on the Boulevards!'

'I warned you of the consequences of taking me,' said Louis, dropping into a chair.

'Mamma! he is all over blood!' screamed Virginia.

Lady Conway recoiled, with a slight shriek.

'It is a trifle,' said Louis;' Isabel is safe. There is all cause for thankfulness. We could never have got through if she had not been every inch a heroine.'

'Oh, Lord Fitzjocelyn, if I could thank you!'

'Don't,' said Louis, with so exactly his peculiar droll look and smile, that all were reassured.

Isabel began to recount their adventure.

'In the midst of those horrid wretches! and the firing!' cried Lady Conway. 'My dear, how could you bear it? I should have died of fright!'

'There was no time for fear,' said Isabel, with a sort of scorn; 'I should have been ashamed to be frightened when Lord Fitzjocelyn took it so quietly. I was only afraid lest you should repeat their horrid war-cry. I honour your refusal.'

'Of course one would not in their sense, poor things, and on compulsion,' said Louis, his words coming the slower from the exhaustion which made him philosophize, rather than exert himself. 'In a true sense, it is the war-cry of our life.'

'How can you talk so!' cried Lady Conway. 'Delaford says the ruffians are certain to overpower the Guard. We must go directly. Very likely this delay of yours may prevent us from getting off at all.'

'I will find out whether the way be open,' said Louis, 'when I have-'

His words failed him, for as he rose, the handkerchief slipped off, a gush of blood came with it, and he was so faint that he could hardly reach the sofa.

Lady Conway screamed, Virginia rang the bells, Isabel gave orders that a surgeon should be called.

'Spirits from the vasty deep,' muttered Louis, in the midst of his faintness, 'the surgeons have graver work on hand.'

'For heaven's sake, don't talk so!' cried his aunt, without daring to look at him; 'I know your arm is broken!'

'Broken bones are a very different matter, experto crede. This will be all right when I can stop the bleeding,' and steadying himself with difficulty, he reached the door, and slowly repaired to his own room, while the girls sent Fanshawe and Delaford to his assistance.

Lady Conway, unable to bear the sight of blood, was in a state of nervous sobbing, which Virginia's excited restlessness did not tend to compose; and Isabel walked up and down the room, wishing that she could do anything, looking reproachfully at her mother, and exalting to the skies the courage, presence of mind, and fortitude of the wounded knight.

Presently, Delaford came down with a message from Lord Fitzjocelyn that it was of no use to wait for him, for as the butler expressed it, 'the haemorrhage was pertinacious,' and he begged that the ladies would depart without regard to him. 'In fact,' said Delaford, 'it was a serious crisis, and there was no time to be lost; an English gentleman, Captain Lonsdale, who had already offered his services, would take care of his lordship, and my Lady had better secure herself and the young ladies.'

'Leave Fitzjocelyn!' cried Virginia.

'Is it very dangerous, Delaford?' asked Lady Conway.

'I would not be responsible for the consequences of remaining, my Lady,' was the answer. 'Shall I order the horses to be brought out?'

'I don't know. Is the street full of people? Oh! there is firing! What shall I do? Isabel, what do you say!'

Isabel was sitting still and upright; she hardly raised her eyelids, as she tranquilly said, 'Nothing shall induce me to go till he is better.'

'Isabel! this is most extraordinary! Do you know what you are saying?'

Isabel did not weaken her words by repetition, but signed to Delaford to leave them, and he never ventured to disregard Miss Conway. Virginia hung about her, and declared that she was quite right; and Lady Conway, in restless despair, predicted that they would all be massacred, and that her nephew would bleed to death, and appealed to every one on the iniquity of all the doctors in Paris for not coming near him.

Poor Louis himself was finding it very forlorn to be left to Fanshawe, whose one idea was essences, and Delaford, who suggested nothing but brandy. Some aunts and cousins he had, who would not have left him to their tender mercies. He was growing confused and feeble, speculating upon arteries, and then starting from a delusion of Mary's voice to realize his condition, and try to waken his benumbed faculties.

At last, a decided step was heard, and he saw standing by him a vigorous, practical-looking Englishman, and a black-eyed, white-hooded little Soeur de Charite. Captain Lonsdale, on hearing the calls for surgical aid, had without a word, hurried out and secured the brisk little Sister, who, with much gesticulation, took possession of the arm, and pronounced it a mere trifle, which would have been nothing but for the loss of blood, the ball having simply passed through the fleshy part of the arm, avoiding the bone. Louis, pleased with this encounter as a result of the adventure, was soon in condition to rise, though with white cheeks and tottering step, and to present to Lady Conway her new defender.

The sight of a bold, lively English soldier was a grand consolation, even though he entirely destroyed all plans of escape by assuring her that there was a tremendous disturbance in the direction of the Northern Railway, and that the only safe place for ladies was just where she was. He made various expeditions to procure intelligence, and his tidings were cheerful enough to counteract the horrible stories that Delaford was constantly bringing in, throughout that Saturday, the dreadful 24th of June, 1848.

It was late before any one ventured to go to bed; and Louis, weak and weary, had wakened many times from dreamy perceptions that some wonderful discovery had been made, always fixing it upon Mary, and then finding himself infinitely relieved by recollecting that it did not regard her. He was in the full discomfort of the earlier stage of this oft-repeated vision, when his door was pushed open, and Delaford's trembling voice exclaimed, 'My Lord, I beg your pardon, the massacre is beginning.'

'Let me know when it is over,' said Louis, nearly in his sleep.

Delaford reiterated that the city was bombarded, thousands of armed men were marching on the hotel, and my Lady ought to be informed. A distant cannonade, the trampling of many feet, and terrified voices on the stairs, finally roused Louis, and hastily rising, he quitted his room, and found all the ladies on the alert. Lady Conway was holding back Virginia from the window, and by turns summoning Isabel to leave it, and volubly entreating the master of the hotel to secure it with feather-beds to defend them from the shot.

'Oh, Fitzjocelyn!' she screamed, 'tell him so—tell him to take us to the cellars. Why will he not put the mattresses against the windows before they fire?'

'I should prefer a different relative position for ourselves and the beds,' said Louis, in his leisurely manner, as he advanced to look out. 'These are the friends of order, my dear aunt; you should welcome your protectors. Their beards and their bayonets by gaslight are a grand military spectacle.'

'They will fire! There will be fighting here! They will force their way in. Don't, Virginia—I desire you will not go near the window.'

'We are all right. You are as safe as if you were in your own drawing-room,' said Captain Lonsdale, walking in, and with his loud voice drowning the panic, that Louis's cool, gentle tones only irritated.

Isabel looked up and smiled, as Louis stood by her, leaving his aunt and Virginia to the martial tones of their consoler.

'I could get no one to believe me when I said it was only the soldiers,' she observed, with some secret amusement.

'The feather-bed fortress was the leading idea,' said Louis. 'Some ladies have a curious pseudo presence of mind.'

'Generally, I believe,' said Isabel, 'a woman's presence of mind should be to do as she is told, and not to think for herself, unless she be obliged.'

'Thinking for themselves has been fatal to a good many,' said Louis, relapsing into meditation—'this poor Paris among the rest, I fancy. What a dawn for a Sunday morning! How cold the lights look, and how yellow the gas burns. We may think of home, and be thankful!' and kneeling with one knee on a chair, he leant against the shutter, gazing out and musing aloud.

'Thankful, indeed!' said Isabel, thoughtfully.

'Yes—first it was thinking not at all, and then thinking not in the right way.'

Isabel readily fell into the same strain. 'They turned from daylight and followed the glare of their own gas,' said she.

So they began a backward tracing of the calamities of France; and, as Louis's words came with more than usual slowness and deliberation, they had only come to Cardinal de Richelieu, when Captain Lonsdale exclaimed, 'I am sorry to interrupt you, Lord Fitzjocelyn, but may I ask whether you can afford to lose any more blood?'

'Thank you; yes, the bandage is loosened, but I was too comfortable to move,' said Louis, sleepily, and he reeled as he made the attempt, so that he could not have reached his room without support.

The Captain had profited sufficiently by the Sister's example to be able to staunch the blood, but not till the effusion had exhausted Louis so much that all the next day it mattered little to him that the city was in a state of siege, and no one allowed to go out or come in. Even a constant traveller like Captain Lonsdale, fertile in resource, and undaunted in search of all that was to be seen, was obliged to submit, the more willingly that Fitzjocelyn needed his care, and the ladies' terror was only kept at bay by his protection. He sat beside the bed where lay Louis in a torpid state, greatly disinclined to be roused to attend when his aunt would hasten into the room, full of some horrible rumour brought in by Delaford, and almost petulant because he would not be alarmed. All he asked of the Tricolor or of the Drapeau Rouge for the present was to let him alone, and he would drop into a doze again, while the Captain was still arguing away her terror.

More was true than he would allow her to credit and when the little Soeur de Charite found a few minutes for visiting her patient's wound, her bright face was pale with horror and her eyes red with weeping.

'Our good Archbishop!' she sobbed, when she allowed herself to speak, and to give way to a burst of tears. 'Ah, the martyr! Ah, the good pastor! The miserable—But no—my poor people, they knew not what they did!'

And as Louis, completely awakened, questioned her, she told how the good Archbishop Affre had begun that Sunday of strife and bloodshed by offering his intercessions at the altar for the unhappy people, and then offering his own life. 'The good shepherd giveth his life for the sheep,' were his words, as he went forth to stand between the hostile parties, and endeavour to check their fury against one another. She herself had seen him, followed by a few priests, and preceded by a brave and faithful ouvrier, who insisted on carrying before him a green branch, as an emblem of his peaceful mission. She described how, at the sight of his violet robes, and the white cross on his breast, the brave boy gardes mobiles came crowding round him, all black with powder, begging for his blessing, some reminding him that he had confirmed them, while others cried, 'Your blessing on our muskets, and we shall be invincible,' while some of the women asked him to carry the bandages and lint which they wished to send to the wounded.

On he went, comforting the wounded, absolving the dying, and exhorting the living, and at more than one scene of conflict the combatants paused, and yielded to his persuasions; but at the barricade at the Faubourg St. Antoine, while he was signing to the mob to give him a moment to speak, a ball struck him, and followed by the weeping and horror-struck insurgents, he was borne into the curate's house, severely wounded, while the populace laid down their weapons, to sign a declaration that they knew not who had fired the fatal shot.

'No, no, it was none of our people!' repeated the little nun. 'Not one of them, poor lost creatures as too many are, would have committed the act—so sacrilegious, so ungrateful! Ah! you must not believe them wicked. It is misery that drove them to rise. Hold! I met a young man—alas! I knew him well when he was a child—I said to him, 'Ah! my son, you are on the bad train.' 'Bread, mother—it is bread we must have,' he answered. 'Why, would you speak to one who has not eaten for twenty-four hours?' I told him he knew the way to our kitchen. 'No, mother,' he said, 'I shall not eat; I shall get myself killed.''

Many a lamentable detail of this description did she narrate, as she busied herself with the wound; and Louis listened, as he had listened to nothing else that day, and nearly emptied his travelling purse for the sufferers. Isabel and Virginia waylaid her on the stairs to admire and ask questions, but she firmly, though politely, put them aside, unable to waste any time away from her children—her poor wounded!

On Monday forenoon tranquillity was restored, the rabble had been crushed, and the organized force was triumphant. Still the state of siege continued, and no one was allowed free egress or ingress, but the Captain pronounced this all nonsense, and resolutely set out for a walk, taking the passports with him, and promising Lady Conway to arrange for her departure.

By-and-by he came in, subdued and affected by the procession which he had encountered—the dying Archbishop borne home to his palace on a litter, carried by workmen and soldiers, while the troops, who lined the streets, paid him their military salutes, and the people crowded to their doors and windows—one voice of weeping and mourning running along Paris—as the good prelate lay before their eyes, pale, suffering, peaceful, and ever and anon lifting his feeble hand for a last blessing to the flock for whom he had devoted himself.

The Captain was so much impressed that, as he said, he could not get over it, and stayed for some time talking over the scene with the young ladies, before starting up, as if wondering at his own emotion, he declared that he must go and see what they would do next.

Presently afterwards, Fitzjocelyn came down stairs. His aunt was judiciously lying down in her own apartment to recruit her nerves after her agitation, and had called Virginia to read to her, and Isabel was writing her journal, alone, in the sitting-room. Lady Conway would have been gratified at her eager reception of him, but, as he seemed very languid, and indisposed for conversation, she continued her occupation, while he rested in an arm-chair.

Presently he said, 'Is it possible that you could have left that bracelet at Miss Longman's?'

'Pray do not think about it,' exclaimed Isabel; 'I am ashamed of my childishness! Perhaps, but for that delay, you would not have been hurt,' and her eyes filled with tears, as her fingers encircled the place where the bracelet should have been.

'Perhaps, but for that delay, we might both have been shot,' said Louis. 'No, indeed; I could not wonder at your prizing it so much.'

'I little thought that would be the end of it,' said Isabel. 'I am glad you know its history, so that I may have some excuse;' and she tried to smile, but she blushed deeply as she dried her eyes.

'Excuse? more than excuse!' said Louis, remembering his fears that it would be thrown away upon her. 'I know—'

'He has told you!' cried Isabel, starting with bashful eagerness.

'He has told me what I understand now,' said Louis, coming near in a glow of grateful delight. 'Oh, I am so glad you appreciate him. Thank you.'

'You are inferring too much,' said Isabel, turning away in confusion.

'Don't you mean it!' exclaimed Louis. 'I thought—'

'We must not mistake each other,' said Isabel, recovering her self-possession. 'Nothing amounting to what you mean ever passed, except a few words the last evening, and I may have dwelt on them more than I ought,' faltered she, with averted head.

'Not more than he has done, I feel certain,' said Louis; 'I see it all! Dear old Jem! There's no such fellow in existence.' But here perceiving that he was going too far, he added, almost timidly, 'I beg your pardon.'

'You have no occasion,' she said, smiling in the midst of her blushes. 'I feared I had said what I ought not. I little expected such kind sympathy.'

She hastily left him, and Lady Conway soon after found him so full of bright, half-veiled satisfaction, that she held herself in readiness for a confession from one or both every minute, and, now that the panic was over, gave great credit to the Red Republicans for having served her so effectually, and forgave the young people for having been so provoking in their coolness in the time of danger, since it proved how well they were suited to each other. She greatly enjoyed the universally-implied conviction with regard to the handsome young pair. Nor did they struggle against it; neither of them made any secret of their admiration for the conduct of the other, and the scrupulous appellations of Miss Conway and Lord Fitzjocelyn were discarded for more cousinly titles.

The young hero fell somewhat in his aunt's favour when he was missing at the traveller's early breakfast, although Delaford reported him much better and gone out. 'What if he should be late for the train?—what if he should be taken up by the police?' Virginia scolded her sister for not being equally restless, and had almost hunted the Captain into going in search of him; when at last, ten minutes before the moment of departure, in he came, white, lame, and breathless, but his eyes dancing with glee, and his lips archly grave, as he dropped something into Isabel's lap.

'Her bracelet!' exclaimed Virginia, as Isabel looked up with swimming eyes, unable to speak. 'Where did you find it?'

'In the carriage, in the heart of the barricade at the Porte St. Denis.'

'It is too much!' cried Isabel, recovering her utterance, and rising with her hands locked together in her emotion. 'You make me repent my having lamented for it!'

'I had an old respect for Clara's clasp.'

'I never saw a prettier attention,' said his aunt.

'It is only a pity that you cannot fasten it on for her.'

'That could only be done by the right hand,' muttered Louis, under his breath, enjoying her blush.

'You have not told us how you got it!' said Virginia.

'It struck me that there was a chance, and I had promised to lose none. I found the soldiers in the act of pulling down the barricade. What an astonishing construction it is! I spoke to the officer, who was very civil, and caused me to depose that I had hired the carriage, and belonged to the young lady. I believe my sling had a great effect; for they set up a shout of acclamation when the bracelet appeared, lying on the cushion as quietly as if it were in its own drawer.'

'The value will be greater than ever *now*, Isabel,' said Lady Conway. 'You will never lose it again!'

Isabel did not gainsay her.

The Captain shrugged his shoulders, and looked sagacious at his patient's preparation for the journey before him.

Louis gravely looked into his face as he took leave of him, and said, 'You are wrong.'

The Captain raised his eyebrows incredulously. As they left the city, the bells of all the churches were tolling for the martyred Archbishop. And not for him alone was there mourning and lamentation through the city: death and agony were everywhere; in some of the streets, each house was a hospital, and many a groan and cry of mortal pain was uttered through that fair summer-day. Louis, in a low voice, reminded Isabel that, on this same day, the English primate was consecrating the abbey newly restored for a missionary college; and his eyes glistened as he dwelt with thanksgiving upon the contrast, and thought of the 'peace within our walls, and plenteousness within our palaces.'

He lay back in his corner of the carriage, too much tired to talk; though, by-and-by, he began to smile over his own musings, or to make some lazily ludicrous remark to amuse Virginia. His aunt caressed her wounded hero, and promoted his intercourse with Isabel, to his exquisite amusement, in his passive, debonnaire condition, especially as Isabel was perfectly insensible to all these manuoevres.

There she sat, gazing out of window, musing first on the meeting with the live Sir Roland, secondly on the amends to be made in the 'Chapel in the valley.' The Cloten of the piece must not even be a Vidame nothing distantly connected with a V; even though this prototype was comporting himself much more like the nonchalant, fantastic Viscount, than like her resolute, high-minded Knight at the Porte St. Denis.

CHAPTER XXI
THE HERO OF THE BARRICADES

The page slew the boar,
The peer had the gloire.
          Quentin Durward.

Great uneasiness was excited at Dynevor Terrace by the tidings of the insurrection at Paris. After extracting all possible alarm from her third-hand newspaper, Mrs. Frost put on her bonnet to set off on a quest for a sight of the last day's Times. James had offered to go, but she was too restless to remain at home; and when he had demonstrated that the rumour must be exaggerated, and that there was no need for alarm, he let her depart, and as soon as she was out of sight, caught up the paper to recur to the terrible reports of the first day's warfare. He paced about the little parlour, reviling himself for not having joined the party, to infuse a little common sense; Fitzjocelyn, no more fit to take care of himself than a baby, probably running into the fray from mere rash indifference! Isabel exposed to every peril and terror! Why had he refused to join them? The answer was maddening. He hated himself, as he found his love for his cousin melting under the influence of jealousy, and of indignation that his own vehement passion must be sacrificed to the tardy, uncertain love which seemed almost an insult to such charms.

'What needs dwelling on it?' he muttered; 'doubtless they are engaged by this time! I shall surely do something desperate if they come here, under my very eye. Would that I could go to the Antipodes, ere I forfeit Louis's love! But my grandmother, Clara! Was ever man so miserably circumstanced?'

A hand was on the door; and he strove to compose his face lest he should shock his grandmother.

It was not Mrs. Frost.

'Louis! for Heaven's sake, where are they!'

'In the House Beautiful.'

James breathed—'And you! what makes you so pale? What have you done to your arm?'

'A little affair of the barricades. I have been watering the French Republic with my blood.'

'Rushing into the thickest of the row, of course.'

'Only escorting Miss Conway through an assault of the Garde Nationale said Louis, in a tone as if he had been saying 'walking up the High Street.' How could he help teasing, when he could make such amends?

James began to pace up and down again, muttering something about madness and frenzy.

'It was not voluntary,' said Louis. 'When the carriage was confiscated for the service of the nation, what could we do?—I can tell you, Jem,' he added, fervently, 'what a gallant being she is! It was the glorious perfection of gentle, lofty feminine courage, walking through the raging multitude—through shots, through dreadful sights, like Una through the forest, in Christian maidenly fearlessness.'

James had flung himself into a chair, hiding his face, and steadying his whole person, by resting his elbow on his knee and his brow on his hand, as he put a strong force on himself that he might hear Louis out without betraying himself. Louis paused in ardent contemplation of the image he had called up, and poor James gruffly whispered, 'Go on: you were happy.'

'Very happy, in knowing what cause I have to rejoice for you.'

James gave a great start, and trembled visibly.

'I did not tell you,' pursued Louis, 'that the single moment when she lost her firmness, was when she thought she had lost a certain ivory clasp.'

James could endure no more: 'Louis,' he said, 'you must try me no longer. What do you mean?'

Louis affectionately put his hand on his shoulder: 'I mean, dear Jem, that I understand it now; and it is a noble heart that you have won, and that can value you as you deserve.'

James wrung his hand, and looked bewildered, inquiring, and happy; but his quivering lips could form no words.

'It was a time to reveal the depths of the heart,' said Louis. 'A few words and the loss of the bracelet betrayed much: and afterwards, as far as a lady could, she confessed that something which passed between you the last evening—'

'Louis!' cried James, 'I could not help it! I had been striving against it all along; but if you could imagine how I was tried! You never would come to plead your own cause, and I thought to work for you, but my words are too near the surface. I cut myself short. I have bitterly reproached myself ever since, but I did not know the harm I had done you. Can you forgive me? Can you—No, it is vain to ask; you never can be happy.'

'My dear Jem, you go on at such a pace, there is no answering you. There is no forgiveness in the case. Further acquaintance had already convinced me that she was lovely and perfect, but that 'she is na mine ain lassie.' Yes, she caught my imagination; and you and my father would have it that I was in love, and I supposed you knew best: but when I was let alone to a rational consideration, I found that to me she is rather the embodied Isabel of romance, a beauteous vision, than the—the—in short, that there is another who has all that I am wanting in. No, no, dear Jem; it was you who made the generous sacrifice. Have no scruples about me; I am content with the part of Una's Lion, only thankful that Sans-Loy and Sans-Foy had not quite demolished him before he had seen her restored to the Red Cross Knight.'

It was too much for James; he hid his face in his hands, and burst into tears. Such joy dawning on him, without having either offended or injured his cousin, produced a revulsion of feeling which he could not control, and hearing the street-door opened, he ran out of the room, just before his grandmother came hurrying in, on the wings of the intelligence heard below.

'Yes! I knew my own boy would come to me!' she cried. 'Even Miss Conway has not begun to keep him from me yet.'

'Nor ever will, Aunt Kitty. There are obstacles in the way. You must be granny, and mother, and sister and wife, and all my womankind, a little longer, if you please.' And he sat down fondly at her feet, on a footstool which had been his childish perch.

'Not distressed, you insensible boy?'

'Very happy about Isabel,' said he, turning to look at her with eyes dancing with merry mystification.

'A foolish girl not to like my Louis! I thought better of her; but I suppose my Lady has taught her to aim higher!'

'So she does,' said Louis, earnestly.

'Ungrateful girl! Why, Charlotte tells me you led her straight over the barricades, with cannon firing on you all the time!'

'But not Cupid.'

'Then, it is true! and you have really hurt yourself! And so pale! My poor boy—what is it? I must nurse you.'

'I had so little blood left, that a gnat of tolerable appetite could have made an end of me on Sunday, without more ado. But, instead of that, I had a good little Sister of Charity; and wasn't that alone worth getting a bullet through one's arm?'

Aunt Catharine was shuddering thankfully through the narration, when James came down, his brow unclouded, but his manner still agitated, as if a burthen had been taken away, and he hardly knew how to realize his freedom from the weight.

Mrs. Frost could not part with her boy, and Jane Beckett evidently had a spite against 'they French bandages;' so that Louis only talked of going home enough to get himself flattered and coaxed into remaining at No. 5, as their patient.

The two young men went in the afternoon to inquire after the Conway party, when they found that her ladyship was lying down, but Isabel, who had been summoned from a wholesale conflagration of all the MS. relating to the fantastic Viscount, brought down Miss King, apparently to converse for her; for she did little except blush, and seemed unable to look at either of the friends.

As they took leave, Louisa came into the room with a message that mamma hoped to see Mr. Frost Dynevor to-morrow, and trusted that he had made no engagements for the holidays.

James murmured something inaudible, and ran down stairs, snarling at Louis as he turned to the Miss Faithfulls' door, and telling him he wanted to obtain a little more petting and commiseration.

'I could not waste such an opportunity of looking interesting!' said Louis, laughing, as he tapped at the door.

Delaford marshalled out the poor tutor with a sense of triumph. 'His hopes, at least, were destroyed!' thought the butler; and he proceeded to regale Marianne with the romance of the Barricades,—how he had himself offered to be Miss Conway's escort, but Lord Fitzjocelyn had declared that not a living soul but himself should be the young lady's champion; and, seeing the young nobleman so bent on it, Mr. Delaford knew that the force of true affection was not to be stayed, no more than the current of the limpid stream, and had yielded the point; and, though, perhaps, his experience might have spared her the contaminating propinquity of the low rabble, yet, considering the circumstances, he did not regret his absence, since he was required for my lady's protection, and, no doubt, two fond hearts had been made happy. Then, in the midnight alarm, when the young nobleman had been disabled, Delaford had been the grand champion:—he had roused the establishment; he had calmed every one's fears; he had suggested arming all the waiters, and fortifying the windows; he had been the only undaunted representative of the British Lion, when the environs swarmed with deadly foes, with pikes and muskets flashing in the darkness.

Fanshawe had been much too busy with her ladyship's nerves, and too ignorant of French, to gather enough for his refutation, had she wished for it; and, in fact, she had regarded him as the only safeguard of the party, devoutly believing all his reports, and now she was equally willing to magnify her own adventures. What a hero Delaford was all over the terrace and its vicinity! People looked out to see the defender of the British name; and Charlotte Arnold mended stockings, and wondered whether her cruelty had made him so desperately courageous.

She could almost have been sorry that the various arrivals kept the domestic establishments of both houses so fully occupied! Poor Tom! she had been a long time without hearing of him! and a hero was turning up on her hands!

The world was not tranquil above-stairs. The removal of the one great obstacle to James's attachment had only made a thousand others visible; and he relapsed into ill-suppressed irritability, to the disappointment of Louis, who did not perceive the cause. At night, however, when Mrs. Frost had gone up, after receiving a promise, meant sincerely, however it might be kept, that 'poor Louis' should not be kept up late, James began with a groan:

'Now that you are here to attend to my grandmother, I am going to answer this advertisement for a curate near the Land's End.'

'Heyday!'

'It is beyond human endurance to see her daily and not to speak! I should run wild! It would be using Lady Conway shamefully.'

'And some one else. What should hinder you from speaking?'

'You talk as if every one was heir to a peerage.'

'I know what I am saying. I do not see the way to your marriage just yet, but it would be mere trifling with her feelings, after what has passed already, not to give her the option of engaging herself.'

'I'm sure I don't know what I said! I was out of myself. I was ashamed to remember that I had betrayed myself, and dared not guess what construction she put on it.'

'Such a construction as could only come from her own heart!'

After some raptures, James added, attempting to be cool, 'You candidly think I have gone so far, that I am bound in honour to make explanation.'

'I am sure it would make her very unhappy if you went off in magnanimous silence to the Land's End; and remaining as the boy's tutor, without confession, would be a mere delusion and treachery towards my aunt.'

'That woman!'

'She is not her mother.'

'Who knows how far she will think herself bound to obedience? With that sort of relationship, nobody knows what to be at.'

'I don't think Isabel wishes to make her duty to Lady Conway more stringent than necessary. They live in utterly different spheres; and, at least, you can be no worse off than you are already.'

'I may be exposing her to annoyance. Women have ten million ways of persecuting each other.'

'Had you seen Isabel's eye when she looked on the wild crowd, you would know how little she would heed worse persecution than my poor aunt could practise. It will soon be my turn to say you don't deserve her.'

James was arguing against his own impulse, and his scruples only desired to be talked down; Louis's generous and inconsiderate ardour prevailed, and, after interminable discussion, it was agreed that, after some communication with the young lady herself, an interview should be sought with Lady Conway, for which James was already bristling, prepared to resent scorn with scorn.

In the morning, he was savage with shamefacedness, could not endure any spectator, and fairly hunted his cousin home to Ormersfield, where Louis prowled about in suspense—gave contradictory orders to Frampton, talked as if he was asleep, made Frampton conclude that he had left his heart behind him, and was ever roaming towards the Northwold turnpike.

At about four o'clock, a black figure was seen posting along the centre of the road, and, heated, panting, and glowing, James came up—made a decided and vehement nod with his head, but did not speak till they had turned into the park, when he threw himself flat on the grass under an old thorn, and Louis followed his example, while Farmer Morris's respectable cows stared at the invasion of their privacy.

'Tout va bien?' asked Louis.

'As well as a man in my position can expect! She is the most noble of created beings, Louis!'

'And what is her mother?'

'Don't call her mother! You shall hear. I could not stay at home! I went to the Faithfulls' room: I found Miss Mercy waiting for her, to join in a walk to some poor person. I went with them. I checked her when she was going into the cottage. We have been walking round Brackley's fields—'

'And poor Miss Mercy?'

'Never remembered her till this moment!'

'She will forgive! And her ladyship?'

'That's the worst of it. She was nearly as bad as you could have been!—so intensely civil and amiable, that I began to think her all on my side. I really could be taken in to suppose she felt for us!'

'I have no doubt she did. My good aunt is very sincerely loth to hurt people's feelings.'

'She talked of her duty! She sympathized! It was not till I was out of the house that I saw it was all by way of letting me down easy-trapping me into binding myself on honour not to correspond.'

'Not correspond!' cried Louis, in consternation. 'Are you not engaged?'

'As far as understanding each other goes. But who knows what may be her machinations, or Isabel's sense of obedience?'

'Does she forbid it?'

'No. She went to speak to Isabel. I fancy she found it unwise to test her power too far; so she came down and palavered me,—assured me that I was personally all that heart could wish—she loved her dear child the better for valuing solid merit. Faugh! how could I stand such gammon? But I must perceive that she was peculiarly circumstanced with regard to Isabel's family, she must not seem to sanction an engagement till I could offer a home suited to her expectations. She said something of my Uncle Oliver; but I disposed of that. However, I dare say it made her less willing to throw me overboard! Anyway, she smoothed me and nattered me, till I ended by agreeing that she has no choice but to remove instanter from the Terrace, and forbid me her abode! And, as I said, she wormed a promise from me not to correspond.'

'You have no great loss there. Depend upon it that Isabel would neither brave her openly by receiving your letters, nor submit to do anything underhand.'

'Nor would I ask her!—but it is intolerable to have been tricked into complacent consent.'

'I am glad your belle-mere knows how to manage you.'

'I told you she was only less unbearable than yourself. You have it from the same stock.'

'The better for your future peace. I honour her. If she had let the Welsh dragon show his teeth in style, he would only have had to make unpleasant apologies when the good time comes.'

'When!' sighed James.

'If Isabel be the woman I take her for, she will be easily content.'

'She is sick of parade; she has tried how little it can do for a mind like hers: she desires nothing but a home like our own—but what prospect have I of any such thing? Even if the loss of my fellowship were compensated, how could I marry and let Clara be a governess? Clara must be my first consideration. But, I say, we ought to be going home.'

'I thought I was at home.'

'My grandmother and Jane won't be pacified till they see you. They think you are not fit to be in a house by yourself. They both fell on me for having let you go. You must come back, or my grandmother will think you gone off in despair, as you ought to be, and I shall never dare to speak to her.'

'At your service,' said the duteous Fitzjocelyn. 'I'll leave word at the lodge.'

'By-the-bye, are you up to walking?'

'Candidly, now I think of it, I doubt whether I am. Come, and let us order the carriage.'

'No—no;—I can't stand waiting—I'll go home and get over the first with granny—you come after. Yes; that's right.'

So the hunted Louis waited, contentedly, while James marched back, chary of his precious secret, and unwilling to reveal it even to her, and yet wanting her sympathy.

The disclosure was a greater shock than he had expected from her keen and playful interest in matters of love and matrimony. It was a revival of the mournful past, and she shed tears as she besought him not to be imprudent, to remember his poor father, and not rush into a hasty marriage. He and his sister had been used to poverty, but it was different with Miss Conway.

He bitterly replied, that Lady Conway would take care they were not imprudent; and that instant the granny's heart melted at the thought of his uncertain prospect, and at hearing of the struggles and sufferings that he had undergone. They had not talked half an hour, before she had taken home Isabel Conway to her heart as a daughter, and flown in the face of all her wisdom, but assuring him that she well knew that riches had little to do with happiness, auguring an excellent living, and, with great sagacity, promising to settle the Terrace on his wife, and repeating, in perfect good faith, all the wonderful probabilities which her husband had seen in it forty years ago.

When Louis arrived, he found her alone, and divided between pride in her grandson's conquest, and some anxiety on his own account, which took the form of asking him what he meant by saying that Isabel aimed higher than himself.

'Did she not?' said Louis; and with a sort of compunction for a playful allusion to the sacred calling, he turned it off with, 'Why, what do you think of Roland ap Dynasvawr ap Roland ap Gruffydd ap Rhys ap Morgan ap Llywellwyn ap Roderic ap Caradoc ap Arthur ap Uther ap Pendragon?' running this off with calm, slow, impressive deliberation.

'Certify me, Louis dear, before I can quite rejoice, that this fun is not put on.'

'Did you think me an arrant dissembler? No, indeed: before I guessed how it was with them, I had found out—Oh! Aunt Kitty, shall I ever get Mary to believe in me, after the ridiculous way in which I have behaved to her?'

'Is this what you really mean?'

'Indeed it is. The very presence of Isabel could not keep me from recurring to her; and at home, not a room, not a scene, but is replete with recollections of all that she was to me last year! And that I should only understand it when half the world is between us! How mad I was! How shall I ever persuade her to forget my past folly? Past! Nay, folly and inconsistency are blended in all I do, and now they have lost me the only person who could help me to conquer them! And now she is beyond my reach, and I shall never be worthy of her.'

He was much agitated. The sight of James's success, and the return to his solitary home, had stirred up his feelings very strongly; and he needed his aunt's fond soothing and sympathy—but it was not difficult to comfort and cheer him. His disposition was formed more for affection than passion, and his attachment to Mary was of a calmer nature than his fiery cousin would have allowed to be love. It took a good deal of working-up to make it outwardly affect his spirits or demeanour, in general, it served only as an ingredient in the pensiveness that pervaded all his moods, even his most arrant nonsense.

The building of castles for James, and the narration of the pleasing delusion in which he had brought home his aunt, were sufficient to enliven him. He was to go the next morning to call upon Lady Conway, and see whether he could persuade her into any concessions: James was very anxious that Isabel and his grandmother should meet, and was beginning to propose that Louis should arrange an interview for them in Miss Faithfull's room, before the departure, which was fixed for Monday.

'I intend to call upon Lady Conway,' said Mrs. Frost, with dignity that made him feel as if he had been proposing something contraband.

Louis went first, and was highly entertained by the air of apology and condolence with which his aunt received him. She told him how excessively concerned she was, and how guilty she felt towards him—a score on which, he assured her, she had no need to reproach herself. She had heard enough from Isabel to lead to so much admiration of his generosity, that he was obliged to put a stop to it, without being skilful enough to render sincerity amiable, but she seemed satisfied, eagerly assured him of her approval, and declared that she fully understood him.

Had she explained, he would have thought her understanding went too far. She entirely forgave him. After all, he was her own sister's son, and Isabel only a step-daughter; and though she had done her duty by putting Isabel in the way of the connexion, she secretly commended his prudence in withstanding beauty, and repairing the dilapidated estate with Peruvian gold. She sounded him, as a very wise man, on the chances of Oliver Dynevor doing something for his nephew, but did not receive much encouragement; though he prophesied that James was certain to get on, and uttered a rhapsody that nearly destroyed his new reputation for judgment. Lady Conway gave him an affectionate invitation to visit her whenever he could, and summoned the young ladies to wish him good-bye. The mute, blushing gratitude of Isabel's look was beautiful beyond description; and Virginia's countenance was exceedingly arch and keen, though she was supposed to know nothing of the state of affairs.

Lady Conway was alone when Mrs. Frost was seen approaching the house. The lady at once prepared to be affably gracious to her apologies and deprecations of displeasure; but she was quite disconcerted by the dignified manner of her entrance;—tall, noble-looking, in all the simple majesty of age, and of a high though gentle spirit, Lady Conway was surprised into absolute respect, and had to rally her ideas before, with a slight laugh, she could say, 'I see you are come to condole with me on the folly of our two young people.'

'I think too highly of them to call it folly,' said the heiress of the Dynevors.

'Why, in one way, to be sure,' hesitated Lady Conway, 'we cannot call it folly to be sensible of each other's merits; and if—if Mr. Dynevor have any expectations—I think your son is unmarried?'

'He is;' but she added, smiling, 'you will not expect me to allow that my youngest child is old enough to warrant any calculations on that score.'

'It is very unfortunate; I pity them from my heart. An engagement of this kind is a wretched beginning for life.'

'Oh, do not say so!' cried the old lady, 'it may often be the greatest blessing, the best incentive to both parties.'

Lady Conway was too much surprised to make a direct answer, but she continued, 'If my brother could exert his interest—and I know that he has so high an opinion of dear Mr. Dynevor—and you have so much influence. That dear, generous Fitzjocelyn, too—'

As soon as Mrs. Frost understood whom Lady Conway designated as her brother, she drew herself up, and said, coldly, that Lord Ormersfield had no church patronage, and no interest that he could exert on behalf of her grandson.

Again, 'it was most unlucky;' and Lady Conway proceeded to say that she was the more bound to act in opposition to her own feelings, because Mr. Mansell was resolved against bequeathing Beauchastel to any of his cousinhood who might marry a clergyman; disliking that the place should fall to a man who ought not to reside. It was a most unfortunate scruple; but in order to avoid offending him, and losing any chance, the engagement must remain a secret.

Mrs. Frost replied, that Mr. Mansell was perfectly right; and seemed in nowise discomfited or conscious that there was any condescension on her ladyship's part in winking at an attachment between Miss Conway and a Dynevor of Cheveleigh. She made neither complaint nor apology; there was nothing for Lady Conway to be gracious about; and when the request was made to see Miss Conway, her superiority was so fully established that there was no demur, and the favour seemed to be on her side.

The noble old matron had long been a subject of almost timid veneration to the maiden, and she obeyed the summons with more bashful awe than she had ever felt before; and with much fear lest the two elders might have been combining to make an appeal to her to give up her betrothal, for James's sake.

As she entered, the old lady came to meet her, held out both arms, and drew her into her bosom, with the fond words, 'My dear child!'

Isabel rested in her embrace, as if she had found her own mother again.

'My dear child,' again said Mrs. Frost, 'I am glad you like my Jem, for he has always been a good boy to his granny.'

The homeliness of the words made them particularly endearing, and Isabel ventured to put her arm round the slender waist.

'Yes, darling,' continued the grandmother; 'you will make him good and happy, and you must teach him to be patient, for I am afraid you will both want a great deal of patience and submission.'

'He will teach me,' whispered Isabel.

Lady Conway was fairly crying.

'I am glad to know that he has you to look to, when his old grandmother is gone.'

'Oh, don't say —'

'I shall make way for you some day,' said Mrs. Frost, caressing her. 'You are leaving us, my dear. It is quite right, and we will not murmur; but would not your mamma spare you to us for one evening? Could you not come and drink tea with us, that we may know each other a little better?'

The stepmother's affectionate assent, and even emotion, were a great surprise to Isabel; and James began to imagine that nothing was beyond Mrs. Frost's power.

Louis saved James the trouble of driving him away by going to dine with Mr. Calcott, and the evening was happy, even beyond anticipation; the grandmother all affection, James all restless bliss, Isabel serene amid her blushes; and yet the conversation would not thrive, till Mrs. Frost took them out walking, and, when in the loneliest lane, conceived a wish to inquire the price of poultry at the nearest farm, and sent the others to walk on. Long did she talk of the crops, discourse of the French and Bohemian enormities, and smilingly contradict reports that the young lord was to marry the young lady, before the lovers reappeared, without the most distant idea where they had been.

After that, they could not leave off talking; they took granny into their counsels, and she heard Isabel confess how the day-dream of her life had been to live among the 'very good.' She smiled with humble self-conviction of falling far beneath the standard, as she discovered that the enthusiastic girl had found all her aspirations for 'goodness' realized by Dynevor Terrace; and regarding it as peace, joy, and honour, to be linked with it. The newly-found happiness, and the effort to be worthy of it, were to bear her through all uncongenial scenes; she had such a secret of joy that she should never repine again.

'Ah! Isabel, and what am I to do?' said James.

'You ask?' she said, smiling. 'You, who have Northwold for your home, and live in the atmosphere I only breathe now and then?'

'Your presence is my atmosphere of life.'

'Mrs. Frost, tell him he must not talk so wrongly, so extravagantly, I mean.'

'It may be wrong; it is not extravagant. It falls only too far short of my feeling! What will the Terrace be without you?'

'It will not be without my thoughts. How often I shall think I see the broad road, and the wide field, and the mountain-ash berries, that were reddening when we came; and the canary in the window! How little my first glance at the houses took in what they would be to me!'

And then they had to settle the haunts she was to revisit at Beauchastel. An invitation thither was the ostensible cause of the rapid break-up from the House Beautiful; but the truth was not so veiled but that there were many surmises among the uninitiated. Jane had caught something from my young Lord's demeanour which certified her, and made her so exceedingly proud and grand, that, though she was too honourable to breathe a word of her discovery, she walked with her kind old head three inches higher; and, as a great favour, showed Charlotte a piece of poor dear Master Henry's bridecake, kept for luck, and a little roll of treasured real Brussels lace, that she had saved to adorn her cap whenever Mr. James should marry.

Charlotte was not absolutely as attentive as she might have been to such interesting curiosities. She had one eye towards the window all the time; she wanted to be certified how deeply she had wounded the hero of the barricade, and she had absolutely not seen him since his return! The little damsel missed homage!

'You are not heeding me!' exclaimed Jane at last.

'Yes; I beg your pardon, ma'am—'

'Charlotte, take care. Mind me, one thing at a time,' said Jane, oracularly. 'Not one eye here, the other there!'

'I'm sure I don't know what you mean, Mrs. Beckett.'

'Come, don't colour up, and say you don't know nothing! Why did you water your lemon plant three times over, but that you wanted to be looking out of window? Why did you never top nor tail the gooseberries for the pudding, but sent them up fit to choke my poor missus? If Master Jem hadn't—Bless me! what was I going to say?—but we should soon have heard of it! No, no, Charlotte; I've been a mother to you ever since you came here, a little starveling thing, and I'll speak plain for your good. If you fancy that genteel butler in there, say so downright; but first sit down, and write away a letter to give up the other young man!'

Charlotte's cheeks were in a flame, and something vehement at the end of her tongue, when, with a gentle knock, and 'By your favour, ladies,' in walked Mr. Delaford.

Jane was very civil, but very stiff at first, till he thawed her by great praise of Lord Fitzjocelyn, the mere prelude to his own magnificent exploits.

Charlotte listened like a very Desdemona. He was very pathetic, and all that was not self-exaltation was aimed at her. Nothing could have been more welcome than the bullets to penetrate his heart, and he turned up his eyes in a feeling manner.

Charlotte's heart was exceedingly touched, and she had tears in her eyes when she moved forward in the attitude of the porcelain shepherdess in the parlour, to return a little volume of selections of tender poetry, bound in crimson silk, that he had lent to her some time since. 'Would she not honour him by accepting a trifling gift?'

She blushed, she accepted; and with needle-like pen, in characters fine as hair, upon a scroll garlanded with forget-me-nots, and borne in mid air by two portly doves, was Charlotte Arnold's name inscribed by the hero of the barricades.

Oh, vanity! vanity! how many garbs dost thou wear!

Delaford went away, satisfied that he had produced an impression such as he could improve if they should ever be thrown together again.

The Lady of Eschalott remained anything but satisfied. She was touchy and fretful, found everything a grievance, left cobwebs in the corners, and finally went into hysterics because the cat jumped at the canary-bird's cage.

CHAPTER XXII
BURGOMASTERS AND GREAT ONE-EYERS

> When full upon his ardent soul
> The champion feels the influence roll,
> He swims the lake, he leaps the wall,
> Heeds not the depth, nor plumbs the fall.
> Unshielded, mailless, on he goes,
> Singly against a host of foes!
> > Harold the Dauntless.

'Jem! Jem! have you heard?'

'What should I hear?'

'Mr. Lester is going to retire at Christmas!'

'Does that account for your irrational excitement?'

'And it has not occurred to you that the grammar-school would be the making of you! Endowment, 150 pounds—thirty, forty boys at 10 pounds per annum, 400 pounds at least. That is 550 pounds—say 600 pounds for certain; and it would be doubled under a scholar and a gentleman—1200 pounds a year! And you might throw it open to boarders; set up the houses in the Terrace, and let them at—say 40 pounds? Nine houses, nine times forty—'

'Well done, Fitzjocelyn! At this rate one need not go out to Peru.'

'Exactly so; you would be doubling the value of your own property as a secondary consideration, and doing incalculable good—'

'As if there were any more chance of my getting the school than of the rest of it!'

'So you really had not thought of standing?'

'I would, most gladly, if there were the least hope of success. I can't afford to miss any chance; but it is mere folly to talk of it. One-half of the trustees detest my principles; the others would think themselves insulted by a young man in deacon's orders offering himself.'

'It is evident that you are the only man on whom they can combine who can save the school, and do any good to all those boys—mind you, the important middle class, whom I would do anything to train in sound principles.'

'So far, it is in my favour that I am one of the few University men educated here.'

'You are your grandmother's grandson—that is everything! and you have more experience of teaching than most men twice your age.'

James made a face at his experience; but little stimulus was needed to make him attempt to avail himself of so fair an opening, coming so much sooner than he could have dared to expect. It was now September, and the two months of waiting and separation seemed already like so many years. By the time Mrs. Frost came in from her walk, she found the two young gentlemen devising a circular, and composing applications for testimonials.

After the first start of surprise, and telling James he ought to go to school himself, Mrs. Frost was easily persuaded to enter heartily into the project; but she insisted on the first measure being to consult Mr. Calcott. He was the head of the old sound and respectable party—the chairman of everything, both in county and borough—and had the casting vote among the eight trustees of King Edward's School, who, by old custom, nominated each other from the landholders within the town. She strongly deprecated attempting anything without first ascertaining his views; and, as the young men had lashed themselves into great ardour, the three walked off at once to lay the proposal before the Squire.

But Mr. Calcott was not at home. He had set off yesterday, with Miss Calcott and Miss Caroline, for a tour in Wales, and would not return for a week or ten days.

To the imaginations of Lord Fitzjocelyn and Mr. Frost, this was fatal delay. Besides, he would be sure to linger!—He would not come home for a month—nay, six weeks at least!—What candidates might not start—what pledges might not be given in the meantime!

James, vehement and disappointed, went home to spend the evening on the concoction of what his grandmother approved as 'a very proper letter,' to be despatched to meet the Squire at the post-office at Caernarvon, and resigned himself to grumble away the period of his absence, secretly relieved at the postponement of the evil day of the canvass, at which all the Pendragon blood was in a state of revolt.

But Louis, in his solitude at Ormersfield, had nothing to distract his thoughts, or prevent him from lapsing into one of his most single-eyed fits of impetuosity. He had come to regard James as the sole hope for Northwold school, and Northwold school as the sole hope for James; and had created an indefinite host of dangerous applicants, only to be forestalled by the most vigorous measures. Evening, night, and morning, did but increase the conviction, till he ordered his horse, and galloped to the Terrace as though the speed of his charger would decide the contest.

Eloquently and piteously did he protest against James's promise to take no steps until the Squire's opinion should be known. He convinced his cousin, talked over his aunt, and prevailed to have the letter re-written, and sent off to the post with the applications for testimonials.

Then the rough draft of the circular was revised and corrected, till it appeared so admirable to Louis, that he snatched it up, and ran away with it to read it to old Mr. Walby, who was one of the trustees, and very fond of his last year's patient. His promise, good easy man, was pretty sure to be the prize of the first applicant; but this did not render it less valuable to his young lordship, who came back all glorious with an eighth part of the victory, and highly delighted with the excellent apothecary's most judicious and gratifying sentiments,—namely, all his own eager rhetoric, to which the good man had cordially given his meek puzzle-headed assent. Thenceforth Mr. Walby was to 'think' all Fitzjocelyn's strongest recommendations of his cousin.

There was no use in holding back now. James was committed, and, besides, there was a vision looming in the distance of a scholar from a foreign University with less than half a creed. Thenceforth prompt measures were a mere duty to the rising generation; and Louis dragged his Coriolanus into the town, to call upon certain substantial tradesmen, who had voices among the eight.

Civility was great; but the portly grocer and gentlemanly bookseller had both learned prudence in many an election; neither would make any immediate reply—the one because he never did anything but what Mr. Calcott directed, and the other never pledged himself till all the candidates were in the field, and he had impartially printed all their addresses.

Richardson, the solicitor, and man-of-business to the Ormersfield estate, appeared so sure a card, that James declared that he was ashamed of the farce of calling on him, but they obtained no decided reply. Louis was proud that Richardson should display an independent conscience, and disdained his cousin's sneering comment, that he had forgotten that there were other clients in the county besides the Fitzjocelyns.

No power could drag Mr. Frost a step further. He would not hear of canvassing that 'very intelligent' Mr. Ramsbotham, of the Factory, who had been chosen at unawares by the trustees before his principles had developed themselves; far less on his nominee, the wealthy butcher, always more demonstratively of the same mind.

James declared, first, that he would have nothing to do with them; secondly, that he could not answer it to the Earl to let Louis ask a favour of them; thirdly, that he had rather fail than owe his election to them; fourthly, that it would be most improper usage of Mr. Calcott to curry favour with men who systematically opposed him; and, fifthly, that they could only vote for him on a misunderstanding of his intentions.

The eighth trustee was a dead letter,—an old gentleman long retired from business at his bank to a cottage at the Lakes, where he was written to, but without much hope of his taking the trouble even to reply. However, if the choice lay only between James and the representative of the new lights, there could be little reasonable fear.

Much fretting and fuming was expended on the non-arrival of a letter from Mr. Calcott; but on the appointed tenth day he came home, and the next morning James was at Ormersfield in an agony of disappointment. The Squire had sent him a note, kind in expression, regretting his inability to give his interest to one for whom he had always so much regard, and whose family he so highly respected, but that he had already promised his support to a Mr. Powell, the under-master of a large classical school, whom he thought calculated for the situation, both by experience and acquirements.

James had been making sure enough of the school to growl at his intended duties; but he had built so entirely on success, and formed so many projects, that the disappointment was extreme; it appeared a cruel injury in so old a friend to have overlooked him. He had been much vexed with his grandmother for regarding the veto as decisive; and he viewed all his hopes of happiness with Isabel as overthrown.

Louis partook and exaggerated his sentiments. They railed—the one fiercely, the other philosophically—against the Squire's domineering; they proved him narrow and prejudiced—afraid of youth, afraid of salutary reform, bent on prolonging the dull old system, and on bringing in a mere usher. They recollected a mauvais sujet from the said classical school; argued that it never turned out good scholars, nor good men; and that they should be conferring the greatest benefit on Northwold burghers yet unborn, by recalling the old Squire to a better mind, or by bringing in James Frost in spite of him.

Not without hopes of the first, though, as James told him, no one would have nourished them save himself, Louis set forth for Little Northwold, with the same valour which had made him the champion of the Marksedge poacher. He found the old gentleman good-natured and sympathizing, for he liked the warm friendship of 'the two boys,' and had not the most remote idea of their disputing his verdict.

'It is very unlucky that I was from home,' he said. 'I am afraid the disappointment will be the greater from its having gone so far.'

'May I ask whether you are absolutely pledged to Mr. Powell?'

'Why, yes. I may say so. Considering all things, it is best as it is. I should have been unwilling to vex my good old friend, Mrs. Frost; and yet,' smiling benignantly on his fretted auditor, 'I have to look out for the school first of all, you know.'

'Perhaps I shall not allow that Mr. Powell is the best look-out for the school, sir.'

'Eh? The best under the circumstances. Such a place as this wants experience and discipline more than scholarship. Powell is the very man, and has been waiting for it long; and young Frost could do much better for himself, if he will only have patience.'

'Then his age is all that is against him? The only inferiority to Mr. Powell?'

'Hm! yes, I may say so. Inferior? No, he is superior enough; it is a mere joke to compare them; but this is not a post for one of your young unmarried men.'

'If that be all,' cried Louis, 'the objection would be soon removed. It may be an inducement to hear that you would be making two people happy instead of one.'

'Now, don't tell me so!' almost angrily exclaimed the Squire. 'Jem Frost marry! He has no business to think of it these ten years! He ought to be minding his grandmother and sister. To marry on that school would be serving poor Mrs. Frost exactly as his poor absurd father did before him, and she is too old to have all that over again. I thought he was of a different sort of stamp.'

'My aunt gives her full consent.'

'I've no doubt of it! just like her! But he ought to be ashamed to ask her, at her age, when she should have every comfort he could give her. Pray, who is the lady? There was some nonsense afloat about Miss Conway; but I never believed him so foolish!'

'It is perfectly true, but I must beg you not to mention it; I ought not to have been betrayed into mentioning it.'

'You need not caution me. It is not news I should be forward to spread. What does your father say to it?'

'The engagement took place since he left England.'

'I should think so!' Then pausing, he added, with condescending good-nature, 'Well, Fitzjocelyn, I seem to you a terrible old flint-stone, but I can't help that. There are considerations besides true love, you know; and for these young people, they can't have pined out their hearts yet, as, by your own showing, they have not been engaged three months. If it were Sydney himself, I should tell him that love is all the better for keeping—if it is good for anything; and where there is such a disparity, it ought, above all, to be tested by waiting. So tell Master Jem, with my best wishes, to take care of his grandmother. I shall think myself doing him a kindness in keeping him out of the school, if it is to hinder him from marrying at four-and-twenty, and a girl brought up as she has been!'

'And, Mr. Calcott,' said Louis, rising, 'you will excuse my viewing my cousin's engagement as an additional motive for doing my utmost to promote his success in obtaining a situation, for which I consider him as eminently fitted. Good morning, sir.'

'Good morning, my Lord.'

Lord Fitzjocelyn departed so grave, so courteous, so dignified, so resolute, so comically like his father, that the old Squire threw himself back in his chair and laughed heartily. The magnificent challenge of war to the knife, was no more to him than the adjuration he had heard last year in the justice-room; and he no more expected these two lads to make any effectual opposition than he did to see them repeal the game-laws.

The Viscount meanwhile rode off thoroughly roused to indignation. The good sense of sixty naturally fell hard and cold on the ears of twenty-two, and it was one of the moments when counsel inflamed instead of checking him. Never angry on his own account, he could be exceedingly wrathful for others; and the unlucky word, disparity, drove him especially wild. In mere charity, he thought it right to withhold this insult to the Pendragons from his cousin's ears; but this very reserve seemed to bind him to resent it in James's stead; and he was far more blindly impetuous than if, as usual, he had seen James so vehement that he was obliged to try to curb and restrain him.

He would not hear of giving in! When the Ramsbotham candidate appeared, and James scrupled to divide the contrary interest, Louis laid the given at once for the Reverend James Roland Frost Dynevor; the bookseller followed as soon as he saw how the land lay; and Ramsbotham and Co. swelled the majority as soon as they saw that their friend had no chance.

Poor Mr. Powell went home to his drudgery with his wrinkles deeper than ever; and his wife sighed as she resigned her last hope of sending her son to the University.

Mr. Calcott had, for the first time in his life, been over-ridden by an unscrupulous use of his neighbour's rank; and of the youthfulness that inspired hopes of fixing a claim on an untried, inexperienced man.

The old Squire was severely hurt and mortified; but he was very magnanimous—generously wished James joy, and congratulated Mrs. Frost with all his heart. He was less cordial with Louis; but the worst he said of him was, that he was but a lad, his father was out of the way, and he wished he might not find that he had got himself into a scrape. He could not think why a man of old Ormersfield's age should go figuring round Cape Horn, instead of staying to keep his own son in order.

Sydney was absent; but the rest of the family and their friends were less forbearing than the person chiefly concerned. They talked furiously, and made a strong exertion of forgiveness in order not to cut Fitzjocelyn. Sir Gilbert Brewster vowed that it would serve him right to be turned out of the troop, and that he must keep a sharp look out lest he should sow disaffection among the Yeomanry. Making friends with Ramsbotham! never taking out a gun! The country was gone to the dogs when such as he was to be a peer!

whole blame of the split upon Mr. Calcott; while, as to poor Mr. Powell, no words were compassionate enough for his dull, slouching, ungentlemanly air; and he was pronounced to be an old writing-master, fit for nothing but to mend pens.

But Mr. Walby's was still their sole promise. The grocer followed the Squire; the bookseller was liberal, and had invited the Ramsbotham candidate to dinner. On this alarming symptom, Fitzjocelyn fell upon Richardson, and talked, and talked, and talked, till the solicitor could either bear it no longer, or feared for the Ormersfield agency, and his vote was carried off as a captive.

This triumph alarmed Mrs. Frost and James, who knew how scrupulously the Earl abstained from seeking anything like a favour at Northwold; and they tried to impress this on Louis, but he was exalted far above even understanding the remonstrance. It was all their disinterestedness; he had no notion of that guarded pride which would incur no obligation. No, no; if Jem would be beholden to no one, he would accept all as personal kindness to himself. Expect a return! he returned good-will—of course he would do any one a kindness. Claims, involving himself! he would take care of that; and off he went laughing.

He came in the next day, announcing a still grander and more formidable encounter. He had met Mr. Ramsbotham himself, and secured his promise that, in case he failed in carrying his own man, he and the butcher would support Mr. Frost.

The fact was, that Lord Fitzjocelyn's advocacy of the poacher, his free address, his sympathy for 'the masses,' and his careless words, had inspired expectations of his liberal views; Mr. Ramsbotham was not sorry to establish a claim, and was likewise gratified by the frank engaging manners, which increased the pleasure of being solicited by a nobleman—a distinction of which he thought more than did all the opposite party.

To put James beyond the perils of the casting vote was next the point. Without divulging his tactics, Louis flew off one morning by the train, made a sudden descent on the recluse banker at Ambleside, barbarously used his gift of the ceaseless tongue, till the poor old man was nearly distracted, touched his wife's tender heart with good old Mrs. Frost and the two lovers, and made her promise to bring him comfortably and quietly down to stay at Ormersfield and give his vote.

And so, when the election finally came on, Mr. Calcott found himself left with only his faithful grocer to support his protege. Three votes were